Infidelity For
First-Time Fathers

Also by Mark Barrowcliffe

Girlfriend 44

Infidelity For First-Time Fathers

by Mark Barrowcliffe

Headline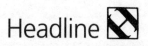

First published in 2001
by HEADLINE BOOK PUBLISHING

10 9 8 7 6 5 4 3 2 1

ISBN 0 7472 7103 8

Typeset by Avon Dataset Ltd, Bidford-on-Avon, Warks

Printed and bound in Great Britain by
Clays Ltd, St Ives plc

HEADLINE BOOK PUBLISHING
A division of Hodder Headline
338 Euston Road
London NW1 3BH

www.headline.co.uk
www.hodderheadline.com

To Wendy and Reg Bell –
for keeping me warm at night.

'It was one of the deadliest and heaviest feelings of my life to feel that I was no longer a boy – from that moment I began to grow old in my own esteem – and in my esteem age is not estimable'
– Lord Byron, *Detached Thoughts*, 15 October 1821

'To find a friend one must close one eye. To keep him – two'
– Norman Douglas, *Almanac*, 1941

In this novel I have referred to a number of historical facts. Following the time-honoured practice of all the best academics they are entirely made up.

1

Perfect Day

The day I learned I was to be a father was one of the happiest of my life.

It was mid-September, 82 degrees, and Londoners were wishing the summer dead. The sunlight and holidays were gone but a skulking heat remained, ignoring the darker nights, the pressing clouds and the first Hallowe'en lanterns in the shops, like a boyfriend refusing to register the 'I'll call you' look in his lover's eyes.

So the city sweltered unseasonably in traffic jam and tube bottleneck, sandwich shop queue and meeting room, everyone hot, everyone rushed, while I – floating like a sprig of coriander on this human stew – lay naked in the fan draught, immune to the bubbling calefaction of the streets, on Cat my girlfriend's bed.

I was old enough to welcome the news of my impending parenthood, God knows I was old enough. Thirty-five, the top of the loop, taking the long look at the horizon before the inevitable tailspin towards three score and ten.

It was an ideal time for me to welcome children into my life, particularly since, in Cat, I had a woman I wanted in a way I hadn't really known before.

We already had several children, in my mind. Sad – or as we used to call it, romantic – as it is after so brief a relationship, I had pictured us lounging by a river bank looking into each other's eyes while the kids, the products of our perfect passion, gambolled nearby.

The children would be expensively dressed in old-fashioned clothes, the way that posh children are, like something out of *The Sound of Music* (not the Hitler Youth, clearly). We'd tear our gaze away from each other, watching while they played with a hoop and stick, or maybe a model sailing yacht. Obviously that's the fantasy, in reality it would be a Gameboy or something, but I try to resist yielding to marketing in my dreams.

And when the wine was poured, and as the children slept, weary from their games, we would discuss art and books, and amaze each other with our insights.

'Hmm,' she would say, 'I'd never thought of that . . .' Well, you can always dream.

Then I would lean back, with Cat hanging over me, her hair tickling my face as I noticed how age was making her even more beautiful and wondered how I could want her more with every second.

'Look,' she'd say, hand bending fine as a willow to the river, which would be free from punts and the class of university student that rhymes with them, 'swans – they pair once and forever.'

'Like us,' I'd say, 'like us,' and I'd surrender myself to sunlight and kisses.

By coincidence this fantasy was playing in my mind as she rose in glory like the dawn to go to the lavatory. At that stage of our relationship every parting bore a pain. I had a physical need for her, an animal ache. Like the rain-frozen walker wants a warm bed, like the child-blasted parent wants sleep, I wanted her – body, mind and soul.

Tell her, I thought. Tell her how you feel. Lay yourself open to love. Before you go thinking me soft, I should record that I don't often think this sort of stuff and have all sorts of normal fantasies about scoring winning goals, lottery bonanzas, cars, the lot. Also,

I've been arrested twice (OK, once it was mistaken identity and once it was for disturbing the peace with a banjo, but nevertheless I *was* arrested), and I used to box for the Southern Counties. I'm also man enough to admit that last point was a lie. So I'm not soft, all right?

There were things holding me back from expressing my inner feelings about Cat. We'd only been seeing each other for a few months and it seemed dreadfully premature to whip out the 'L' word. I'm not like Lee Henderson, my oldest friend and new business partner, who says expressions of love should enter at about six months – which in his book of sexual manners neatly coincides with his first request for sex up the wrong 'un. 'Love and buggery must enter together,' he'd said, like a home economics mistress explaining that many a mickle makes a muckle, 'you can't have one without the other.'

'You can,' I'd said. 'I have.'

'Yes, but it isn't so much fun,' he'd said, examining the back of his hand for the tell-tale wrinkles he'd just read about in a paranoia-inducing magazine he'd found at a supermarket checkout. 'It's the ideal combination of the pornographic and the romantic – the whole range of human needs.'

A wistful, faraway look had come over him, like a seventy-year-old footballer examining the shirt he'd worn when he'd lifted the cup.

I'm not like Henderson, though. It's not a cynical thing for me. I can't trot out words in return for bizarre sexual favours. I wanted to say I loved her because I loved her and I was ready for the next stage – nights by the fire, the school run in the morning, taking the kids to Cubs and asking them if the bloke who runs it ever makes them do anything 'funny'. Really, I'd wanted this for years. The fact that I loved her so soon, so ridiculously soon, and that I knew it was ridiculous to say so but was going to say so anyway, would show the depth of my feeling.

Not that the sexual thing wasn't part of what I felt for her. That day we'd been shagging on and off since we'd woken at 11, and the night before that we'd been shagging until we went to sleep at dawn. What Henderson terms my 'pork sword' was vaguely stirring to life again, like a sleepy child forcing itself awake at the party because it's convinced it's going to miss something.

If we did it again I feared that Social Services might place a care order on my knob. But I still really wanted to try. She had a sexual magnetism strong enough to rip the rivets out of your door.

Other than the extreme youth of our relationship making me feel reticent about declarations of love, there was also the extreme youth of Cat to consider. She was only twenty-four and, though she acted older, she looked younger. While it was a mild concern, and slightly embarrassing, to get those 'you sick old bastard, I wish I was in your shoes' looks from blokes in the street, I know you'll believe me when I say that the fact she appeared barely old enough to order a beer in an American bar in no way made her less attractive to me. I know it's disgusting to hear an old bloke perving over a young woman like this, but that's what old blokes do. The skittles and the dominoes are only a front. Bowls was only invented to give us an excuse to be in a public park without arousing the suspicions of the authorities.

Back to the bed. As I lay there, inspecting the woodchip on her ceiling, head against the thin partition wall through which I could practically hear the plants photosynthesising in her flatmate's bedroom, I was revving myself for the big one, the 'I love you'. I had an idea that if she looked shocked or overwhelmed, I'd just say, 'Isle of Ewe this weekend? You and me, lovely scenery, B&B – I'm paying.'

She had been a long time in the loo, and I was afraid that if she was much longer I'd lose the impetus. The next thing I remember she had come back into the room and was looking at me lying on her bed.

Then the silent film of my memory acquires a sound track and I hear words. They weren't mine.

'I'm up the duff.'

I recall thinking this was strange because Cat had never

spoken so bluntly, nor in such a distant, metallic voice before. Nor without moving her lips.

Then I realised what had changed in her absence. I appeared to have answered my mobile phone and be speaking to someone – someone who was identified by six letters on the phone's display. ANDREA.

'You're going to be a daddy,' said my fiancée.

2

Equally Cursed
And Blessed

'Well,' I said, sliding my gaze to the left of the sofa where Andrea
was sitting among a pile of health education leaflets and pawing
at Dr Miriam Stoppard's *Conception, Pregnancy and Birth*, 'there's
a film by Ang Lee we could nip out and see in Ealing. Either that
or it's Wim Wenders' "challenging even for his mum" picture
Wings of Desire at the NFT.'

I'd been getting into art films as a way of adding meaning to
my life, which is what they do, according to the experts. I think
they have a point. There's nothing quite like four hours of really
top-class boredom for making you feel superior to your fellow
humans. I remember when I saw *He Stands In The Desert
Counting The Seconds Of His Life, un film de* Jonas Mekas. Three
ice creams, two packets of popcorn and a farm-bake flapjack it
took me to wriggle and chomp my way through that. Came out
feeling like Saint Francis of Assisi.

'Or there's some Japanese Noh Theatre on at the South Bank,
if you fancy it,' I said. Andrea was reading a leaflet entitled *Goal
Setting in Pregnancy* and drawing up a list of 'gestation achieve-
ments' that she hoped to complete.

She drew breath. 'How about you bend me over the back of

the sofa and shag me while I watch Corrie, and then I'll suck your knob while you watch the football?' she said.

I gave a fragile little smile, like a diplomat presented with a plate of monkey brains at the emperor's birthday nosh up. It wasn't that I didn't fancy Andrea, far from it. It was just that, with Cat and everything, there were so many complications.

There was the guilt, for a kick-off. Not quite of the Lady Macbeth, 'Will these boxer shorts never be clean?' variety but not far off. I mean, I'm really not cut out for treachery. I'd never even thought of playing away before. When I say that, I'd obviously constantly indulged in the imagined infidelities necessary to any stable relationship but I'd never even got near to actually doing anything about it.

More pressing than the guilt, however, were the physical demands. It would have been bad enough addressing the carnal needs of a twenty-four-year-old girlfriend and a fiancée as I stared into the ravening maw of my thirty-sixth birthday at the best of times, without the effects of pregnancy on Andrea's sex drive. Where it had once been a normal gravelled drive of, say, twenty yards or so, with pregnancy hormones dancing through her veins it had become one of those magnificent drives you see leading up to the top stately homes in the country, with topiary and lines of trees next to it. You couldn't maintain a drive like that alone, and the way things were going I was seriously considering taking on staff to help. There was a retired old boy a couple of houses away who looked like he had time on his hands.

Having been out with each other for eight years, and as law-abiding citizens, Andrea and I had previously stuck firmly to the statutory requirement only to have sex when it was entirely unavoidable and then no more than three times a month. This sudden explosion of desire was killing me.

Then, of course, there was the threat of fellatio, never very appetising at the best of times. Andrea's chop work most reminded me of that of a ferret called Skippy I'd seen on a documentary about pest control in the Black Country.

I'd tried everything to get her to reduce the level of full-fanged vigour she applied to the practice, even drawing her attention to the chapter in *The Alrightness of Sex* on removing the chocolate from a Magnum without disturbing the ice cream, but to no avail.

'I enjoy doing it hard,' Andrea had said, 'it's meant to be about my pleasure, too, isn't it?'

She hadn't even got the hint when, during one particularly savage bout of mastication, I'd invoked the Geneva Convention and started shouting, 'Stewart Dagman, Lance Corporal, Number 8900902.'

I particularly tried to ensure she never got to see *Just 17* magazine. The last time she'd got hold of a teen mag we'd spent a week trying to find all sorts of spots and zones and discussing the needs of 'strong women', as opposed to the infinitely more pressing concerns of weak men. I'd taken out a subscription to *Cosmo* for her in a bid to keep her off the hard stuff.

'So Ang Lee it is then?' I said hopefully, as Andrea slid across the sofa like a python towards a mouse. I love Ang Lee – sounds like an art house director, actually does kung fu movies. The best of all possible worlds.

'No,' she said. 'Take a look at this.'

She held open her copy of Dr Miriam Stoppard's *Conception, Pregnancy and Birth*, tapping excitedly at a chapter heading. I felt my fur freeze as I read the title: 'A Sensual Pregnancy'. My skin stayed still but I felt every muscle within it straining for the door.

'Shall I read to you?' asked Andrea, her hot breath on my ear.

'Just paraphrase, if you would,' I said, 'for brevity's sake.'

'In brief,' she said, snuggling into me, 'and out of briefs,' she theatrically slid down her knickers, 'it says that my increased levels of hormones mean I will especially enjoy all aspects of sensuality, from intercourse to massage.'

'Great,' I said, involuntarily crossing my legs, my boxer shorts feeling like very skimpy protection.

Now massage, giving or receiving, has the same effect on me that watching kidney dialysis or injections has on others. There's something about it that makes me pay far too much attention to the circulatory system. All the blood goes from my head, my limbs tingle and I start to feel like I've been next to an electric heater for too long.

'You take the phone off the hook like it says in here, and I'll get the massage oil,' said Andrea.

'We haven't got any massage oil,' I said. I knew this for a fact because I'd surreptitiously binned the last lot in about June.

'Yes, we have! I bought some aromatherapy stuff today.'

'Smashing,' I said, going out into the hall and muttering about staining the sofa.

I went to the phone and removed the receiver. It occurred to me that I should have unplugged it at the wall but I thought that by following the book exactly I'd at least get some respite when its dislodged receiver alarm went off. Marvellous the technology nowadays. If you'd have told them twenty years ago you could one day get a feature like that for under a tenner they'd have laughed at you. Anyway, I digress.

I returned to the room to take my medicine, aware that following the dictates of La Stoppard and her like is what is expected of the decent father-to-be. This was despite the fact that Andrea had asked for this massage when I was already looking at a mention in dispatches for valour in the face of being asked to shag your permanent girlfriend more than once in an evening at the age of thirty-five.

I sat on the sofa, glumly manipulating the feet as prescribed in the book, an action which made me uncommonly aware of the blood coursing through my forearms. I was just about maintaining consciousness when the phone started its alarm and allowed me to go out and get some air.

I let it sound for a few seconds, cold technology restoring the senses that hot biology had scrambled.

I then returned to the task in hand, to maul the back and the shoulders. I even took care to lubricate the skin, oiling her up until I could see my face in her, as recommended by the good Stoppardo, when in fact I'd had a very early start and actually wanted to watch a documentary about Vikings. I also felt the stomach, where Andrea said she could feel the baby. I pointed out that it was no more than an inch long and we'd have as much chance of feeling it as we would her bile duct. She still said she could feel it, though.

As I've said, she'd already had me at it as soon as I'd got through the door that evening. I was feeling pretty much like a spent balloon and had been looking forward to sitting down for the rest of the evening massaging nothing more than a tube of Pringles and a couple of Budvars in front of the TV.

It was no good, though. Despite the phone going and my own partially successful attempts to stop her ravishing me on the living-room floor by nipping in a video to tape *Vikings, Right or Wrong?* I had to go through with it again.

Andrea had sensed my reluctance but had unfortunately found it more of a challenge than a turn off.

'Some men would welcome an offer like this,' she'd said, extending a coil around my chest, 'some men would fantasise about a woman like me.'

'After eight years you have to decide whether you want me to fantasise about you or shag you, you can't have both,' I said. You have to take a stand somewhere, you really do.

'Shag, please,' she said, remoting on the telly to reveal Ken Barlow in a right tizz about something.

I didn't really find it that unpleasant. I was enjoying it a bit, sort of, like you might enjoy an exercise class you didn't want to go to. You're jumping up and down, congratulating yourself for being virtuous, but one eye's always on the clock.

However, there is a line that a fellow of the right trouser draws in these things and that line stops way short of the fashionable implement of Beelzebub that is known as the scented candle. Now old Stoppard chops doesn't specifically recommend these, but neither does she warn against them, which to my mind is an oversight.

I remember precisely the words that alerted me to Andrea's intent. I was just wondering if we'd ever get the massage oil out of the carpet when she said, 'I'm going to get a scented candle,' and greased out from underneath me like a sausage from a drunk's hot dog.

Like any upright fellow trying to regain his composure after giving of his very best in a good half of the positions that *Dr Dre's Guide to Pleasuring the Lady Wife* video shows, I quailed like a dog before a riding crop.

Not only was I probably going to have to continue shagging her but I was going to have to do it in the smell of burning chewing gum. I blame Stoppard for Andrea's new commitment to experimentation. The idea had never entered her head before she'd read 'A Sensual Pregnancy'. The word 'sensual', by coincidence, is always linked to scented candles in my mind. I remember being at college and getting off with some hippyish girl who had taken me back to her flat and whipped one out.

As I lay naked with her, choking in the smell of melting Spangles, she'd produced a long stiff feather, 'from an eagle', she'd said. She'd gently stroked it all over my body, while softly intoning 'so sensual'. It induced a rebellion of the flesh halfway between an itch and a spasm which, because I wanted to shag her, I'd put up with until she reached the neck. That was when I'd had to leap off the bed and rub myself all over with a towel to get rid of the heebie-jeebies. I didn't see her again.

Why didn't I complain about the vile candle? Well, to be honest, I was scared to. In the couple of weeks since becoming pregnant Andrea had been very insistent about her wants. We'd been to the supermarket, for instance, and she'd insisted on buying forty-eight pots of yoghurt. When I'd suggested that perhaps three might be a more manageable number she'd pinned me against the cold meats and said she wanted forty-eight and was having forty-eight.

The following morning, however, the sight of yoghurt had made her feel sick and she'd run from the room and thrown up when I was halfway through a Fruits of the Forest. She'd made me promise to take the yoghurts away and destroy them. Throwing away, apparently, wasn't good enough. Then there was the fact that she'd taken a liking to slicing up and frying chamois leathers – this when only three months gone. It re-minded me of some of the worst excesses of Hannibal Lecterdom so if scented candles were what she wanted, scented candles she could have.

Wondering how many more sensual batterings I'd have to take until the baby arrived and allowed us all to leave candles to their correct job of lighting during power cuts, and feathers solely to the job of keeping birds airborne, stiffened my resolve to reduce my number of sexual partners to my preferred number – one.

Later that evening, as I sat breathing through my mouth, I watched Hayes battle it out with Chelsea in a televised pre-season friendly I'd taped a month before. My mind wandered as Andrea applied the molars to my tenderest part and some brickie rounded an expensive French World Cup winner to slot Hayes's fourth.

No one would understand what had made me take up with Cat in the first place. I certainly hadn't a clue, so how could I expect them to?

I suppose one useful area of exploration might be the night classes. There is an iron rule in life: man at nightschool has no girlfriend. There is another one: show me someone who's in a lot of clubs and I'll show you someone with no friends.

Before I met Cat I'd attended Spanish on a Thursday night, badminton on Monday and Wednesday, football training on Tuesdays, and played football on a Sunday. On Fridays, if I was free from work, I'd attend to football club or badminton club business (I'm secretary of both), and on Saturday I'd generally watch telly. But I had both a girlfriend, a fiancée even, and friends. On paper.

So what was wrong? In a word, children.

My friends had started to disappear into families a few years before. Well, not to disappear exactly but to be there in a different way.

Suddenly the invitations that had said 'House Party, 8 till police intervention. Bring Bottles and basic first aid' dried up and new ones started to arrive saying: 'Benjamin is one, help us celebrate. Noon till afternoon nap (2.35 p.m. – please help us by leaving quietly before then).

Mark Barrowcliffe

One of these invitations, ostensibly from my mate Reg, came directly from his wife whose name escapes me. When I'd been to the party he'd served me orange juice and introduced me to some child-joggling bloke in dungarees as 'a friend of the family'.

'I'm not a friend of the family,' I'd said, 'I'm *your* friend. Remember university? The mad weekends away . . . coming off that motorbike together . . . the bet that you couldn't get my girlfriend to shag you – and you treating me to an Indian with the proceeds of your win?'

He'd just bitten his nails and said how he wasn't worried his kid hadn't started walking yet but he was going to the doctor's on Monday just to make sure. His wife had then intimated it was time for people to start leaving. I wondered if he'd bet me that I couldn't shag her. It didn't seem likely and, besides, he'd probably find Indian food 'obvious' or something nowadays.

Once it had been as natural as masturbation for us to see each other every weekend. Now, though, the most I'd meet up with my mates was about once every four weeks, never in a group as they couldn't all get baby sitters on the same night, and, while I was far too old to stay out all hours, I wouldn't have minded staying out *some* hours. Instead excuses about being 'up very early' and 'incredibly exhausting days' would be muttered as they finished their Spritzers and disappeared for the nine o'clock train.

I remember meeting up for a drink with Dave 'Mad Bomber' Harris, he who once hired a piper to play while he changed his duvet cover (well, it's a once-in-a-lifetime event, he'd said) and who'd had such a fear of the Hoover that he'd called it 'Metal Bird, Him Make Noise'.

I'd planned to go to a pub but he'd said, as he tucked a copy of *Period Living* under his arm, that he had a headache. I'd said, quoting his own time-honoured advice to those with hangovers or illness, that he should 'drink through the pain barrier'. He'd rolled his eyes and suggested we should go to a Starbucks because he thought a really good coffee might sort him out. A few years before I'd managed to convince him that pasta grew on trees. His idea of a really good coffee was any that he didn't have to get off his hungover arse to make himself but there he was, valuing 'a lovely Colombian Blue Bean' and probably making his own pasta for all I knew.

And take the skiing holiday. Every year for well over a decade we'd been on a cheap skiing holiday with the lads. And every year for the last five years there had been fewer and fewer people coming. Now it was only me and Henderson. What happened? Well, here is the list of the skiers of '89.

Dave 'Mad Bomber' Harris – sane and with child. Doesn't want to come. Refuses to give excuse, just doesn't want to come.

Peter 'Bites Your Balls' Fairchild – monastery. Caught God when there was a lot of it about one Christmas.

Phil Arbuthwaite – dead. Fucking dead. Not of anything spectacular either, just went to sleep and never woke up. Heart problem apparently. Begs question: who next?

Mark Gemmil – Institute of Further Blah, Sarasota. Wife, open-necked shirt, moustache. Circular card every Christmas using words like 'fall' for 'autumn'. Will never see again.

Andy Hill – no one ever sure whose mate he was. Over-friendly in the way that makes you feel bad about disliking him. May have to consider inviting owing to lack of numbers. Bound to come, depressingly.

John 'Laughing Boy' Adams – always a nervy individual, currently living in halfway house in Plymouth after mistaking police station for alien landing craft one day. Too sensitive for world, therefore condemned to live at raw edge of existence with drug addicts and the insane. Would go and visit him but had to get restraining order to stop him bothering me two years ago. Now cannot come within half a mile of me.

Pete Winterson – far too successful and in advertising. Enviable lifestyle too depressing. Always says he wants to come out and then never can at last minute. Now makes me feel dull. Expect to see again when career takes dive. Hope it's soon.

The Three Daves – the inseparable Smith, Struthers and Peterson, they of the legendary Shepherd's Bush flatshare. The noise of their constant parties made their downstairs neighbour, a kindly, elderly gent called Mr Schmidt, commit suicide.

Received year's supply of Matzos from the West London Board of Jewish Deputies when it turned out he'd been a Nazi war criminal. What Mossad had been unable to achieve in fifty years of espionage, the Daves had managed in eighteen months of playing New Order at no-compromise volume. Like they said, to hear him banging on the ceiling to get them to turn it down, they'd have had to turn it down. Sadly the Daves now no longer on speaking terms after argument about company cars went sour.

This gradual erosion of my mates wouldn't have bothered me so much had I the bosom of a good woman to turn to. Which I did. On paper. I say 'on paper' again to indicate that things were not as they seemed, not to indicate that I have bosoms on paper as, unlike Henderson, I deplore pornography. To be fair, he pointed out to me the last time we met that he hates it too, sometimes. 'When?' I'd asked him.

'Normally that second just after it's all over,' he'd replied. He'd said that the moment he'd made damp the Kleenex he could somehow hear the girl in the magazine's voice and he'd imagine her getting up and putting on cheap gold jewellery and one of those thin leather coats of the sort that makes him shiver – the sort worn by women who stand perished at bus stops in the rain.

'God giveth with one hand and taketh away with the other,' I'd reminded him.

Personally I blame some of the difficulty Henderson has had with his wife, the Iron Julie, on his liking for jazz mags. He'd once complained that the presence of a real woman limited his imagination.

I wouldn't have minded the presence of a real woman, though. I'd been going out with Andrea for eight years, living with her for four, and engaged for two. Our wedding was set for the September – nearly a year away. Andrea and I loved each other, we were mad about each other, I had her picture on my desk, she had mine on hers, I sent her flowers, she bought me whisky, I told her I couldn't live without her, she said she thought of me every day – although could she just put me on hold for a second because she had an important call coming through? In fact, we did everything couples are meant to do short of actually seeing each other.

I worked hard and did sport or Spanish; she just worked hard – days, evenings, weekends. I think we managed, on average, about three hours a week together. I don't know how it got that way, it just did.

So I'd been praying for a kid for ages, partly as a fresh focus for my relationship with her, a way to force us to reassess our priorities and make time for each other again. I could, I know, just have said 'Why don't we reassess our priorities and make time for each other?' but sometimes the simplest ways out are the hardest to find. It's just embarrassing to talk like that, isn't it? Much better to swallow your reservations, get engaged and cross your fingers. It wasn't like we didn't love each other.

There was, of course, more to my desire for children than just as an expensive form of psychotherapy for me and Andrea. They would also give me renewed access to my friends. I admit there was something of the 'if you can't beat them, join them' attitude in me. If I had kids I'd have something to talk to my mates about, I could go on family picnics without feeling like the ghost at the feast – plus I could give up going to all those sports clubs, or at least go less. I'd be a member of the kiddie club, I wouldn't need another.

There were all the soft reasons too. I like kids. I could just see myself, after the week or so of sleepless nights, putting the baby to bed and settling down for a lovely evening of togetherness with Andrea discussing infant jaundice and other conditions. I actually thought I'd make a good dad. I'm the ideal father – I'm fun, I'm a laugh, I love wasting money on crap, I have a drinks cabinet with no lock on it and I'm very forgetful. What more could a child want?

Then I met Cat and my world turned upside down. I could not resist her, and God knows I tried. Like any honest cheat, I had never, ever intended anything to happen between me and her. The decent adulterer, the moral deceiver, fights each step of the way, opposing with every inch of his will the very thing he wants most in the world.

And that is what I did. But it was as if I'd grown another sense that rendered the others monochrome by comparison. Yes, I got black and white touch and smell. Don't ask me how but I did. I couldn't shut it down, I couldn't not look.

But just as powerful now was the pull of Andrea and the baby. I'm not the kind of person who goes around casually getting engaged to people, as is the fashion today. I love Andrea and when I said I'd marry her it was because I wanted to be with her forever. OK, if she continued to work as hard as she normally did 'forever' would amount to about fifteen minutes in her company, but I did love her. She was my girl, my number one, as you'd expect since we'd been going out with each other for nearly a decade. OK, Cat was my number one too, in a different way, but equal first is still first. Can you love too much? asks the poet. I don't know but you can certainly love too many, replies the management consultant.

I was very much aware, too, that the Andrea I'd been cheating on wasn't the Andrea who had emerged since the pregnancy. I had the feeling I was discovering someone else, someone I liked more than the person I'd been engaged to. It occurred to me that I was seeing a side of Andrea I'd never seen before, and I had the strange feeling that I didn't really know her.

When I say I didn't know her, I mean, I could quite easily go on to *Mr and Mrs* with her and do OK. I'd be able to tell you that she likes the Oralia Gold brand of toothpaste and gets angry with me when I buy the supermarket own brand stuff which, I point out, is almost identical apart from its ingredients. I could tell you that she suffered a fit of conscience about the age of twenty-two, which meant she embarked on a career in the charities when business or the media might have been more suited to her temperament (there's little point being a high flyer in an underground car park).

I could tell you, again, that she's obsessive about work, that you'll never find a more dotted 'i' or more crossed 't' than one she's looked at; that this – if anything – has been the biggest point of argument between us. I'm interested in her work but not in living each day, blow by blow: 'And then, while I was unwrapping the Club biscuit – an orange, I think. No, one of the plain ones – Sheila came in carrying the green file. Well, you'll recall me telling you all about *that* particular file two years ago . . .'

I could tell you that if we share anything it's a sense of humour, which she loses when she's over-concerned by work and which I lose when I hear her being over-concerned, but I honestly don't know because, you see, with the pregnancy, she changed. Not wholly, but significantly.

For instance, on the Friday morning before she found out she was pregnant, she'd come into the kitchen with work very much on her mind. I was up early as I was going to a breakfast meeting with Henderson and was just enjoying reading about a dull nil-nil draw between two teams I had never heard of in hockey – a game I don't care about – when she slammed on the kettle and began to blow. If you contrast this with the Tuesday morning after she'd become pregnant, you'll see what I mean.

Friday (Before Pregnancy).

'Come on, come on, come on!' She was talking to the kettle which wasn't boiling quickly enough. 'Dag.'

'Yes,' I said, noting in the paper that Kidderminster Golems had given Northwich Sea Beasts a right thrashing. I didn't seem to be able to identify what sport they were competing in, but the victory sounded very exciting. They'd won four rubbers to three.

'Can I talk to you about a problem?'

'Of course,' I said, shivering inwardly.

The problem was that Daphne at work was muscling in on Andrea's fundraising project, and had been schmoozing up to one of her chief donators. The problem was, well, she didn't mind this so much, but with the whole Yemen thing about to explode and with the donator's acknowledged sensitivity to MATTERS LIKE THAT, she was afraid Daphne might blow the whole thing for both of them. That's what the problem was. Partly. What did I think she should do?

Before counselling, of course, this would have caused a real row between us. I'd have said I needed to relax before I went to work in the morning, she'd have said I didn't take her seriously, I'd have said I didn't take myself seriously so why should I bother with anyone else, and the next thing you knew we'd be rolling around the kitchen under WWF rules.

Counselling had changed things, though. We'd sat in a bald, functional room with someone called Robert. I'd asked him if I could call him Mr Smith, as I'm uncomfortable with instant familiarity, but he'd insisted that I call him Robert. Informality, it seemed, was the form.

'Your problem, Stewart,' he'd said, 'is that when Andrea asks for advice you interpret it as a request for a practical solution.'

'You mean, when she asks for advice I interpret it as her wanting advice?'

'Yes.'

'That's wrong?'

'It's not always a good idea,' he'd said with a beardy smile.

Back on that Friday morning before the pregnancy announcement I was putting this insight to good effect.

Andrea was telling me that the problem also was that Daphne was on exactly the same level as Andrea, and their boss Jane was away on maternity, to return or be replaced Christ knows when so there was no one Andrea could turn to. *Furthermore* the problem was that if Daphne got this donator, she couldn't tell me who in case I told someone, on board one of her projects then the donator might withdraw from the fantastically important work unblocking or stopping up something in the Yemen.

'That's terrible,' I said. 'How does it make you feel?' The counselling had been great. I'd realised on week ten that was the sort of thing you were meant to say. Why they can't tell you that as soon as you walk through the door, I don't know. I think by letting you work it out for yourself they just get more cash out of you. It really was as simple as that. I was fairly sure the sports reviews I was reading were for Kabbadi – the Indian British Bulldog-type game – but I couldn't be sure. It could have been Beach Volleyball or 10m Air Pistol shooting. Anyway West

Dudley Ghouls had given Smethwick Rubberneckers a right sorting.

Andrea acknowledged my contribution with a nod and continued. *To boot* the problem was that if that happened (what? I wondered), Daphne would have a higher net worth of contributions to the charity than Andrea, and might take Jane's place if she didn't come back from maternity leave.

And eke the problem was, if Jane did come back, then the whole nightmare of last year would begin again and, though Jane was an obsessive workaholic and control freak, would she now have the energy to give to the project, what with the baby problem and everything?

'Yes, I see,' I said, pretending to give ear.

The problem was, *per se*, if Jane didn't come back and Daphne took over, Andrea had no problem working under her, but Daphne really didn't have the experience and, technically, Andrea – though there for a slightly shorter time – was better qualified to do the job. Christ, there were times when she wanted to jack it all in and become an organic farmer! She'd got the brochures, God knows.

Of course, you had to stir this lot in with the problem that – *Christmas crackers!* – Daphne's boyfriend had just left her, which was a terrible shame, though he was a bastard, and Andrea felt sorry for her. She'd seen this happen before and – *'You are straining the patience of this court.' 'I will conclude shortly, m'lud.'* – the problem was Daphne would make a mess of it. All this, of course, was only the beginning of the problem.

I was halfway through my third 'awful, how do you cope?' – as prescribed by counsellor – when she kissed me over the paper, tornadoed through the door and was gone. Two minutes later she'd returned. She'd done her normal trick of walking up to the tube with her coffee cup still in her hand and wasn't going to throw away a third in a fortnight.

Now the Tuesday after the pregnancy announcement had been rather different, rather more, I might say, like when we had first met.

Unusually I'd woken first at 8, approximately thirty minutes after Andrea normally gets into the office. I'd been a bit reluctant to wake her – waking Andrea when she's late is a bit like going up to a bees' nest, screaming, 'Bees! Time to get up, pollen to be collected, honey to be made!' and giving it a bloody good shake. However, the penalty for leaving her sleeping was to share angst and guilt until dead, so like a boy on a bet going to pull the ear of a sleeping pit bull, I tugged her shoulder at arm's length.

She stirred and sat up, clearly still asleep. Then she lay down again and started to snore. Now from an early age I knew very well the danger of returning to lighted fireworks, as my dad had always made me throw things at them to see if they'd go off while he hid behind the old coal bunker. However, I had no choice. The longer Andrea slept in, the more stressed she would be when she woke. In the end I decided to stand in the doorway and shout 'Andrea!' so I could make a hasty exit should we start to re-enact that last scene in *Carrie* when all the furniture goes flying about. All that happened, though, was that she woke, looked at the clock and said, 'Arseholes, I'm late.' Then she grinned and performed an advanced snuggling manoeuvre beneath the duvet.

Intrigued, I went to her bedside and shook her. 'Andrea, you've got to get up for work.'

'Sod work, I'm calling in sick.'

'You've got morning sickness?'

'I'm sick of getting up in the morning, if that's what you mean. Tell them I'm sick. Morning sick. Ring. Go.' She was clearly still half asleep.

'This is a bit soon for a hormonally directed change in personality,' I said. Not that I was displeased with this.

What separates people I naturally get on with (as opposed to employ) and those I don't is this very attitude. Almost anyone I've ever liked, with the exception of Andrea, is the kind of person that can answer (b) to the below question.

Q: There is a temporary fuel shortage in Britain. Do you:

(a) leave for work two hours early in order to fight your way in by public transport;

(b) ring the boss and say you're stranded at home. Omit to

mention that you have a full tank of petrol in your car and that you normally go in by bike anyway.

'It's not hormonal. It's me. This is the excuse I've been looking for. Go. Ring.'

She said this in short bursts, semi-conscious. It reminded me of the way that messages from the fleet are normally read out in films. 'Wolf Pack sighted, Scapa Flow. Over. England Expects. Over. Fetch me cup tea. Over. Make it milky. Message Ends.'

I could feel the warmth coming off her and very much wanted to get back into bed. Having just come off the heavy drinking extravaganza that was the Environmental Disaster Oil Company golf weekend (actually been at Cat's), I was very tired myself. Andrea has a special smell to her when she was in bed that to me was like nasally administered Horlicks. She emanated a feeling at once comfortable and delicious – like a hot water bottle on a cold night. One sniff and I started yawning immediately.

I remembered it that night on the sofa as Andrea continued to chew my cud. I looked over to where she'd left the GP advice leaflets and *Conception, Pregnancy and Birth.*

This is what I should want, I thought, this is my dream come true. I wished I could just put things on a list, prioritise, order, like I would have done at work, not just sit recalling the smell of Andrea's sleep and Cat's perfume, of safety and excitement.

This pain needs to stop, I thought, as I willed myself into a sullen and resentful orgasm.

'This baby's going to be the best thing that ever happened to us,' said Andrea, looking up at me.

'I hope you won't be encouraging the child to talk with its mouth full like that,' I said.

One thing was certain – I was going to have to make a decision sooner rather than later.

3

Always Look On The Bright Side Of Life

Just confront her, I thought, face her down, let her know it's your life and you do as you like with it.

Already slightly late for work, I was flat to my hedge, shoulders pressing into the wet foliage, ears pinned back like a stalking cat. I waited for her to move. But she wasn't moving. She would move, I knew, but never, ever, when you expected it.

You can't predict her, you can't second guess her, she has powers, senses, abilities, whose form you cannot begin to comprehend. You might as well try to hide from God. I straightened up. I'd face it like a man.

Mrs Batt, the lollipop lady who worked at the school facing my home, had always irritated me but in the week since Andrea had announced her pregnancy – a week in which I'd had the misfortune to be working from home – she'd been driving me mad.

Every time I looked out of the window, agonising over my future, Cat vs Andrea and the Baby, she would be there at the bottom of the drive like a luminous green conscience patrolling the borders of my mind with a sign that read: 'Stop, Children!'

The problem with Mrs Batt had started about a year before.

Normally I have little truck with the natives of Hillingdon where I live. I'd prefer the anonymity of central London, given a choice, but since you can buy a detached four-bedroom house with private drive (like mine) in Hillingdon for the price of a cardboard box on the Embankment, Hillingdon it is – suburb of people carriers and security lighting, at least in our posh bit. If this sounds a little harsh, I'd just like to record that a house two doors down from mine has no number. It's simply called 'The Nook'. You'll see why I prefer to keep my eyes to the floor when passing the neighbours in B&Q on a Sunday.

But when I'd been setting up the new business I'd skived off from my job with the Biggest Company on Earth for a week or so to draw up a business plan at home. One day, on my way to the shops for a packet of Cartesian Duos ('The biscuit that thinks it's a cake!'), I'd accidentally said hello to the lollipop lady. Ever since then, whenever I see her I never know whether she expects me to talk to her or not. I mean, can I just nod as I go past? If I nod will she pointedly say hello? If I say hello, will she just nod? How many times should I nod to every one time I'm expected to talk? If I don't talk to her, what's the point in saying hello? And so on and so on. It's the sheer uselessness of it all that drains me. Neither of us is ever going to say anything that is remotely interesting to the other. Why do we bother? Also, if I do talk to her, she always says the same thing.

'Good morning, Mr Dag.'

'Good morning, Mrs Batt.'

'Still here, you see.' She'd wave her lollipop.

'You'll be here for a long time, Mrs Batt.' I'd know what this was leading to but wouldn't be able to think of anything else to say.

'Yes, not going back in the loony bin just yet,' she'd laugh.

'They call them psychiatric wards nowadays, Mrs Batt.' I try to maintain PC standards whenever possible.

'No, this was definitely a loony bin. Clunk!' She'd mime turning a key in a lock and dropping it into a drain.

Mrs Batt was convinced that modern children experience far too little old-fashioned brutality in their lives and her lollipop did not sleep in her hands as she smote the tardy road crossers. My normal strategy was to start my run from the bottom of the drive just as she started to belabour some child's ears.

That morning my fear of being late for the first course my new business was running – I'm in management training – meant I had to front the embarrassment. I buried my head in a letter and passed her in a kind of brisk slouch. My movements weren't as limber as they might have been, Andrea's appetites having raged all the way through *Channel 9000 Pre-Season Action*, past an episode of *The Sopranos* and well into *Late Night Art Guff*.

'Good morning, Mr *Dad*!' sang out Mrs Batt in tones suitable for marshalling packs of hounds. 'Aren't you a lucky man?' Did I say she'd never say anything interesting? That was interesting to me – like it's interesting to find a rat in your duvet. The crowd of mothers at the school gate all turned to look at me, a wave of approval breaking across the street. Andrea had obviously told her the news. Andrea had no problem talking to Mrs Batt.

'Yes, Mrs Batt, yes,' I said, shrinking deep inside my creeping fur. Her expectations swept over me like an Atlantic roller over a first-time surfer, bowling me along head over heels. These are meant to be the good things in life, I thought, the little smiles of approval from half-strangers, the congratulations from work-mates. But I was a fraudster and success for the fraudster is never complete – the drugs cheat runner, the fake war hero, me ... our successes taste of toupee glue. Which I imagine is something like fish paste but probably isn't.

The irony was that if you'd come up to me six months before, when I didn't even know Cat existed, and shown me that scene with Mrs Batt, I'd have been delighted. I'd wanted kids for ages. I wanted kids now. I just didn't want ... I don't know what I didn't want. Complications.

As I stood sardined on the tube, thrust up against a small over-aftershaved man and attempting to keep my balance by pressing my nose into the glass of the door every time the train started or stopped, I considered what Mrs Batt might do to me if she found out I'd been two-timing Andrea. I knew nothing about her point of view really, but I didn't have her down for a liberal. All I could hope, I concluded, was that she would go for battery rather than insertion when it came to use of the lollipop.

At Hammersmith an Eastern European-looking woman squeezed her way on next to me and began to nose-yodel for money. A thicket of Japanese tourists stood rapt. I expect they thought they'd entered some sort of endurance game show.

I turned my neck away from the woman's uproarious snout in an effort to preserve my hearing. My eyes fell on an advertisement for some car-hire firm or something.

'Take the easy way out,' it read. Now in my situation, particularly given the proximity of a nose-yodeller, I could well have taken that as an exhortation to suicide.

However, I saw it differently. The easy way for me was to get rid of Cat. Then I'd be an honest, decent, one-woman-and-that-woman's-your-mother father. The other way, well, that was hard indeed.

Just outside Hammersmith station the train came to a stop. The nose-yodelling ceased briefly and we stood like latterday slaves in the darkness of the hold, listening to the creaking of the tube like a ship breathing in the swell.

Morally, I thought, there was only one course of action open to me. I would do the decent thing: shag Cat a couple more times at most and then let her go. I owed it to all concerned to make a clean break.

'Because I love you I must leave you,' I said, rehearsing the line. It sounded good. Well, not good, believable. Brave. The brave bit worried me. Bravery sounds good on paper until you realise that you wouldn't have to be brave unless there was first a serious threat to your health and well-being; therefore being brave puts you in the firing line. That's why cowards like me prefer to avoid it.

'Because I love you I must leave you,' I said again, unfortunately out loud. The over-aftershaved man, who had maintained the impassivity of a Buckingham Palace guard throughout the nose-yodelling, looked at me as if I had gone mad.

In these dark places, he seemed to say with his gargoyle's eyes at once cold and lecherous, love is an aberration. Though a style of mittel-European singing that folk have considered wearing for nearly five hundred years isn't, presumably, I thought.

The driver's voice came over the Tannoy.

'I'm sorry, ladies and gentlemen, we have a passenger on the line at Gloucester Road. We're going nowhere for the foreseeable future.'

A groan went through the train, affording slightly more space as everyone's ribs contracted.

Somewhere down the carriage someone began to whistle the tune to 'Always Look On the Bright Side of Life'. I thought of Cat. She's my bright side, I mused, as the nose-yodeller took up the tune.

Last time I'd seen her we'd been in her room. It was incredibly messy, with piles of magazines, records, bills, bags and books strewn over the floor.

'At least it's as messy as it can get,' she'd said. 'If it was any less messy there would always be the uneasy feeling that it might get worse. Like this, you know where you stand.' She'd been getting ready for work, doing her minimal make up in the mirror, dressed only in her jeans. Every movement she made seemed to draw me closer to her. It sounds like a cliche but she made me feel young again, like the responsibilities of the world counted for nothing when I could watch her putting on her mascara like that. Nothing, I'd thought, nothing is as important or as alive as this (see sections on old bloke perving above and below. Throughout, really).

'Or you don't,' I'd said, picking my way carefully away from the bed. 'Have you ever thought of just throwing it all away?'

'It'd only just fill up again,' she said, picking a record off the floor and putting it on to a turntable. I thought people had finished with vinyl years ago.

'Nature abhors a vacuum, eh?'

'And I abhor a vacuum cleaner,' she'd said, putting on a track by some new dance act – the sort that sounds like a washing machine with a pebble in it.

'Do you like this?' she'd asked, jigging her head from side to side. I wondered if she was still at the age where she'd force herself to like music just because it was trendy. I certainly was. I mean, it wasn't like I didn't want to make the switch from Radio 1 with its cutting edge, up-to-the-minute happenin' toons to Radio 2 with its music. It was just that I didn't see myself quite as a Radio 2 listener.

'Like is wholly too simple a word to cover the full range of my responses,' I'd said as the singing began. It sounded like a rather short-tempered Jamaican repairman was having a bit of difficulty with the above machine.

'Would "dislike" convey those very responses?' she'd said. In fact it was all I could do to listen to that music when out and in some sort of discotheque or other young coves' gathering spot. Before work and with a mild morning head was unthinkable. Apart from when I was with her when it became somehow funny and endearing.

'It would come closer.'

'Would "all sounds the same, they can't write a bloody tune and you can't understand a word they're saying, things used to be different in my day" be getting warmer?'

I took on a look of surprise. 'That's uncanny, how did you guess? Unless, of course . . . yes, I get it, it *does* all sound the same and things *did* used to be different in my day.'

She laughed then and drove her head into my shoulder, like a much prettier version of Basil Brush.

'You old bastard!'

'I feel old.'

'Actually,' she'd said, putting a paw up to my face, 'you really do. Yuk, it's like lizard's flesh, that's disgusting.'

'Thanks,' I'd said.

'Only joking. It's well known women find older men very attractive.'

'You're just saying that.' She had a picture of some boy band, all six packs and bandannas, on the wall. She'd assured me it was ironic but I had my doubts.

'Well, yes, I am, but think how much it shows I like you that I'm willing to lie for you in that way. I have a great respect for the truth. It costs me a lot to bolster your ego through deceit.'

I laughed. She'd had some difficulty, I thought, with the word 'like'. The 'l' had been fine, there had just been a short pause before the 'ike'. As if, I thought, she might have been thinking about slipping in an 'ove'.

'Give us a kiss,' I said, pulling her down on to the duvet I'd bought her. She'd only had a single duvet when I'd met her, which had made staying the night a bit of a trial. It was bad enough constantly having to make up business meetings in Glasgow and Edinburgh without waking up feeling like you'd spent a night on the tiles on Sauchiehall Street. The bed was very small, but with the large duvet it became cosy rather than an experiment in exactly what level of backpain is achieved when one half of a human is allowed to be warm, the other placed in a howling draught. Could I leave her with just that duvet to remember me by? I consoled myself with the thought that, even if it all went wrong, I'd have the basis of a really belting Country and Western tune there. '36 Togs But No You'. Nashville would go wild for it.

'I had a dream about you,' I said, hugging her. Now I realise this is the corniest possible line, beloved of medallioned chest-wig sporters with stubby fingers and winter tans the world over, but it was also true. She'd been juggling piglets with a banana hoop while Henderson, who was really a dog, looked on dressed as a dog. Yes, he was a dog dressed as a dog – the same kind of dog that he actually was for a triple disguise. I'm sorry. There is no bigger failure of manners than relating one's dreams. It's like a verbal fart.

'Was it an erotic one?' said Cat, leaning away from me and looking incredibly sexy.

'No,' I said, 'not as such. More pornographic really. I think the eroticism might arrive when I get to know you better. For the moment I think I regard you largely as an object. On an unconscious level, of course. My higher brain values you and respects you as a fascinating, multi-dimensional human being.'

'Yes,' she said, clipping on her bra. 'I've been trying to reduce you to a sex object, but I'm afraid it's not working.'

'Too fat?' I said. I'd noticed I was three pounds over the *Men's Health* ideal for my size. And that was with restraining the drinking. In my mind, though, I was as fat as my appetites wanted me to be, somewhere between Yokozuna and the Goodyear blimp.

'I'm not sure,' she said. 'I can never make up my mind whether you're one of those blokes who looks better with a bit of weight on.'

'Gladiator type?' I said, ruffling very much as I'd seen that bloke in *Gladiator* do just before shouting 'Unleash Hell!' to his assembled legions. That film had done my head in. I'd been settling down for some historically accurate swashbuckling when he comes out with that line. Anyone who's ever so much as read the listings for the Discovery Channel knows the Romans had no concept of Hell. But there he is, old Maximus Australianus, rattling down the line of troops like a good 'un. I'd rather proudly whispered this to Andrea, and she had proudly whispered, 'Just enjoy it, can't you?' back through bared fangs.

Then some speccy bloke from behind me had pointed out that the film is set in the second century of Roman rule when Christianity (I quote) was 'an oppressed but seductive force. It would have been entirely plausible for a Roman leader flirting with the new religion to let out his true feelings in the stress of battle.' I spent the rest of the film desperately looking for a Volkswagen driving across the back of the Colosseum in order to retrieve the situation.

'You're probably better off fat,' said Cat. I noted she didn't disagree when I'd used the word. I'm not that much of a porker. More like an ex-footballer three months into running the pub, you know. Athletic but with a manly swell above the belt. Fairly athletic, anyway. 'It's kind of a general, unspecific ugliness, isn't it, fat?' she continued. 'You just look at them and go, "Ooh, fat, don't want to speak to you," and quickly look away, without bothering to see if they might be really ugly in other ways too. If you lose a couple of pounds I might realise what a genuine minger I've got on my hands.' She stroked my hair and looked into my eyes, smiling.

'I'd never thought of that,' I said. 'I'd always seen fat and ugly as interdependent, sides of the same coin, but now I see that they can exist simultaneously but independently in the same human being. Thank you, you've broadened my mind.'

'Absolutely,' she said. 'It's like this kid at college who used to have a crush on me. He was about 20 stone and had all these self-esteem issues. As I pointed out, he didn't just want to pin his self-loathing on his weight, he had a whole host of other shortcomings. He'd have been bloody ugly at half that weight.'

'When did you point this out?'

'Oh, he was stalking me in a rather elephantine way.' She waved her hand. 'They persuaded me to come in on his therapy sessions. They were afraid the tree outside my window wasn't strong enough and he might do himself an injury.' She wiped a bit of sleep from the corner of my eye. I'd have found that irritating if anyone else had done it, but with her it seemed as intimate as a kiss.

'Wasn't that a bit dangerous?'

'It was by the time we'd weakened the top branches with a saw.'

'I meant, going to the therapy.'

'It was interesting. It was part of a liberal psychoanalytic programme they had there. What was it called?' She put her finger to her lips in an exaggerated thinking pose. '*Victims Have Responsibilities Too*, that was it.'

'You are joking?'

'I wish I was. They said if you had the right not to be stalked you also had a responsibility to your potential assailant. I got thrown off, though. They said I didn't deserve a stalker if I wasn't going to take it seriously.'

'It's a serious issue, stalking,' I said, 'you could have been killed.'

'No,' she said, 'not when they're that fat. You can have fun with it. You run up to them and shout, "Chase me!" We used to do a sweep on how long he'd last. When you're that overweight, do you know, you burn off masses more energy than a normal person. One of the Physics lads we knew calculated that if you could harness the energy of all the time he spent "thinking" about me at night he'd have enough power to run his own bedside lamp.'

'You knew someone who did Physics? But you're a girl, what topsy-turvy world is this? Do ships sail on the land, does the cow milk the man, do women go to war?' I said. We'd had a science student who'd spoken to a woman once and it had made the local press – even when it turned out it was only his mother.

'They threw him off the course and he had to change to psychology,' said Cat.

'I'm glad to see some standards remain,' I said. Psychology, of course, is the choice of boys who are gifted at science but who don't particularly like heavy rock. 'What happened to the stalker?'

'He fell out of the tree and died when one of the branches broke.' said Cat.

'Seriously, what happened to him?'

'He fell out of the tree and died when one of the branches broke.' She was twizzling my ear.

'Didn't you get into trouble?'

'No, I don't think the police bother calling in the finest forensic minds of a generation when a 280lb drunk man snaps a branch climbing a tree.'

'But you killed him!'

'No, we checked – it wasn't one of the branches we'd sawed. Ironic, really. Teach him to cross me, though.' She gave a little laugh which I found rather disturbing.

She reminded me of Andrea, in a way. I've always liked that sort of strong, independent woman, the sort that drives too quickly and can drink you under the table while retaining roughly the figure of a comic-book heroine and having no emotional needs whatsoever. Oh, there I go again. They don't exist, do they? It's just the old subconscious playing up. I really must get this id thing under control. Next time I'm going past

Kwik Fit I'm going to go in and get them to look at my Super Ego. It started making a strange noise when I was about seventeen and now I'm sure it's not working at all.

Cat was sitting up on the bed. She still hadn't put her top on and I was calculating the chances of a quick one before we set off for the day. See what I mean? The silencer on the exhaust system of my brain was definitely blown.

My counsellor used to point out that the reason I like strong independent women is because I don't want to have to do anything for them myself.

'Exactly,' I'd said.

'No, I meant it as a criticism,' he'd said, placing his hand on his beard in dismay.

'Oh,' I'd said.

I sat up beside Cat and we kissed again with a hunger. My lips always felt deliciously sore after I'd been with her, not because she had stubble but because of the ferocity of her kisses. We broke and I looked into her pale grey eyes.

'I love you,' I said, 'I want to be with you always.' The particular and the fussy will note that this is precisely the sort of thing the modern engaged gentleman should avoid saying to anyone other than his fiancée. I don't know why I said it but I did. It wasn't that it just slipped out, I'd planned to say it. I suppose that, in Cat's presence, nothing else seemed to matter. My love for her made me forget everything else, Andrea, my engagement, everything. I thought it would all just melt away and I would have that feeling you have when you look out of the window and see that the snow has gone and it seems hard to imagine that it was ever there. Well, I can see now that it wasn't the clearest possible way to think.

'I love you too,' she said. I noticed a tear had come into her eye and felt amazed that I'd stirred up such emotions in someone, 'but I have to go to the toilet.'

'Fly, my beauty, fly,' I said.

The pebble-in-a-washing-machine music stopped and I heard Cat's flatmate, the wheezing Chloe, pointedly putting on some Stravinsky. When I say heard, I mean the walls were thin enough for me to hear her opening the CD case. The violins of 'The Rite of Spring' sprang up at top vol, sounding very much like someone had removed the pebble from the washing machine and replaced it with a cat.

I was in a blissful state and random thoughts spun through the galaxies of my mind. Spring. Primavera. What a lovely Italian word. Only they would have the delicacy and artistry to name a season after a pizza. 'I want to stay with you forever.' Yep, I'd said it.

Even in the hell-heat of the tube train I shivered. I'd rather put that declaration of undying passion out of my mind since the news of Andrea's pregnancy. It made the simple 'I have a fiancée I haven't told you about who is pregnant' speech rather more complicated.

Little things about Cat came rushing back to me. The night we'd first met by that buffet in the hotel. 'You're a vegetarian, I note,' I'd said, hoping to impress her with my attention to detail. 'I eat fish, though I am a strict hypocrite,' she'd said, scooping up a roll mop herring. 'I don't smoke,' she'd said, and then got me to buy her a pack because she was drunk. Us going to the cinema together. Film had a soporific effect on her. She'd fall asleep on my arm but always seem to know what had happened when she came out. Her, delighted, telling me that I was decadent for taking taxis everywhere, something I only did with her for paranoid fear I'd be seen by someone I knew on the tube.

Henderson, of course, thought the whole thing was just a physical infatuation.

'How do you know, when you're no longer lovestruck, you'll be any better off with her than you were with Andrea? How can you compare a woman you've come to understand and cherish to a bit of attractive young skirt?' he'd asked me. I swear he was licking his lips towards the end of this sentence.

'Thanks for reminding me of my moral duty.'

'It's OK,' he'd said, glancing left and right, although he knew no one in the bar could overhear us. 'Is her body incredibly fit?'

'Yes,' I said.

'What are her tits like?'

'I'm not telling you. I'm a sophisticated businessman conducting a clandestine affair with a mature and complex young professional woman, not a fourth former banging the youth club bike.'

'Go on,' said Henderson, 'is she really dirty?' He reminded me of a schoolboy, really, sticking his front teeth over his bottom lip like a ten year old reading the *Cosmo* problem page.

'I thought you were playing the role of moral counsellor?'

'Well, I'm allowed a quiet perv on the side, aren't I?' said Henderson, with the wounded outrage of a time-serving businessman who hears the new accounts boys are going to start questioning expense claims.

'No,' I said.

In many ways Henderson was still an adolescent. But for some time there had been forebodings that he was making the flip into mid-life crisis. I thought God might have granted him, and me, a period of relative stability in between.

I suppose it was rather touching that he still expected me to reveal, and exaggerate, my bedroom secrets as we had done before I'd met Andrea.

He didn't seem to realise that, even when you're being unfaithful, sex in your thirties is a mature thing, like drinking wine. In the teens one might drink it (the wine) solely for the alcohol. In the twenties for the taste or perhaps even the cachet. In the thirties one takes in the whole drink, savouring not the taste, not the smell, not the texture alone, but the wine's whole personalité.

So with sex, it is the whole woman that the mature and rounded man makes love to. Her personality and her body are one, you cannot separate them. This said, I really can't go any further without mentioning Cat's tits, which were spectacular. Also – in a non-sexist way – I'd like to compare them to Andrea's as a way of showing how I relate to each of the women. Feminists will be glad I have resisted the overwhelming impulse to give them marks out of ten or English Tourist Board-style crowns.

Now Andrea's tits were like a couple of old mates that I

happened to run into now and again, always in the same old haunts, always with the feeling that today's togetherness was not quite at the level it had been years ago.

'Harry, Andy, how are you?' I'd say. 'Both in the pink, I hope.' I won't go into the reasons I ended up calling them Harry and Andy, it's unlikely to engender any sympathy for me. The names, however, are appropriate. These tits were like friends whose stories I knew by heart but still loved to hear. They were, in short, bosom pals. Sorry.

Cat's were very different. They were like the big kids at school, though, like many of the big kids, they weren't actually very big. They were like the cool bunch, the ones who made you feel so excited and so alive when you went on the rob with them up town, the ones who made every second in their company magical and dangerous, who told you that the home-done crosses tattooed on their arms meant 'borstal' and who later read maths at Cambridge. They were like Smithy who said you could shag his sister if you bought him a packet of fags, and who later turned out to be an only child. Alive, irreverent, cheeky, staying-out-late tits. Great tits.

As with the tits, so with the love. With Andrea it was a practical passion, a patient passion that waited until the dishes were done and the TV watched, the teeth cleaned and the duvet warm.

Or at least it had been until the pregnancy.

With Cat the passion was as impractical as art, taking no account of resources of time, money, or considerations of public decency.

The tube driver spoke. 'Latest from control, ladies and gentlemen. The delay will be . . .' He paused, presumably to build suspense. He reminded me of DJ Chris Tarrant teasing someone about a prize. 'You answered "Milosevic" for the £16,000 prize. Julie . . . Julie . . . Julie!'

'Interminable,' said the driver.

Interminable? So that was what all those English PhDs were doing for a living.

My own delay wasn't going to be interminable, I thought. If

I'd learned one thing from my trade as a management trainer it was that any decision is better than none. As soon as I could I'd talk it through with Henderson and, by the end of the day, I'd know what to do. For good or for bad.

4

The Magic Dragon

These thoughts were in my mind as I sat in the Movotel Wembley Park, wondering why Mrs Batt bugged me so much and trying not to eat my way through a plate of chocolate Liebnitz that had been set out for our delegates. I'm rather partial to biscuits in the same way I understand some inner-city sorts are partial to crack cocaine. I'd specifically asked the motel for Rich Tea, the methadone of the biscuit domain, but no, that was beyond them. There were the Liebnitz, Oat Spinozas and my favourites, Nietzsche Whirls (the biscuit with the God-shaped hole, slogan 'They're Super, Man!'). These are only ever sold in packs of twelve and never to minors in respect to their power-fully addictive waistband-busting qualities.

I decided that I wouldn't have another biscuit until Henderson got in. There was nothing in this situation I couldn't sort. Problem-solving was what my whole career had been about.

How many times had I been called in to sort out the problems of others, arriving in the boardroom with my sharkskin crop, my creases so sharp they leave vapour trails, my heft of the briefcase on to the desk that says 'Today, gentlemen, the bullshit stops'?

I looked down at my cuff, pure white, starched the way it's meant to be, a decisive, thrusting cuff set off by a winking black opal cufflink. Buttons are strictly for the backroom boys. Come on, I thought, summon the authority of the cuff. It's you, Stewart Dagman, corporate firefighter, simplifier of the complex, untangler of the web, he who is preceded by outriders crying, 'Still the donkey, quiet the mule, send the howling dog into the night, your saviour is among you and, like Christ the Tiger, takes all before him.'

It was just a matter of ordering my priorities. I'd draw up a flow chart and work things through. That way the solution would present itself and I'd be on to what I did best – action.

The thing about problem-solving isn't to pick where you start, it's just to start. I adopted my practised corporate sneer, the one that says 'the big boys are here', and arrogantly lifted my Mont Blanc – even mighty prophets have had difficulty in getting mountains to come to them, I shifted mine for £300 in a Bond Street stationery shop – not thinking, not mediating the stream of genius, like Mozart just listening to the voice of God.

I looked down to see what I had written. At first I thought it was just a little smudge on the bottom of the page. Then I made it out, in tiny letters in one corner, almost apologising for itself, the word 'help'.

It seems it's going to be a bigger challenge than we first thought, I said to myself.

The last time those words had gone through my mind had been when I'd worked on the Pan-Am rescue package. Don't look for them, they're not there now.

I examined the biscuit tray, hoping the delegates would turn up before I finished the lot. My new firm specialises in management training courses. I had just broken away from my previous job with the Biggest Company on Earth to set up on my own with Henderson. He was a bigwig in sales, me in firefighting and training, so the two things just seemed to fit together.

This course was our most successful to date. We'd managed to attract seven people to it – just about breaking even once the massive expenses of mailshots and room hire had been taken into account. I read through my folder. *Positive Mindsets for Managers: Smiling for Profit.* I allowed myself just one more Whirl. The nervousness about Cat and Andrea was mingling with anxiety over spelling mistakes in the literature, and the mad idea that no one was going to turn up, despite the fact they'd all paid the best part of a thousand quid to be there.

I didn't feel very positive at that moment so I ironed on a grin and practised saying hello in the approved management consult-ant manner. This requires a level of enthusiasm on a par with someone who has discovered a cancer cure, nuclear fission and ecstasy all at the same time.

'Hello! Hello! Hello!' I said with practised verve, reminding myself of a community policeman failing to relate to young people.

I looked at my watch: 9.30 a.m. Half an hour before the first delegate would arrive. I needed to find reserves of positivity quickly. I tried to get in the right frame of mind by envisaging something I felt very positive about. This, believe it or not, is one of the techniques we teach. It might seem obvious and a rip off but, remember, there are people out there who are shocked to discover in slimming magazines that cream cakes are fatten-ing. Don't knock the bleeding obvious, there's good money in it.

Unfortunately my positive visualisation brought forth only an image of Cat and, by association, Andrea and a baby. I gave up when I began to see Mrs Batt floating before me doing a series of samurai exercises with her lollipop and decided to concentrate solely on the words of the opening chapter of our course.

Efficiency through Enthusiasm, I thought, grinning.

'A close friend, looking happy and relaxed,' snorted Henderson, staggering laden through the door, all Hugo Boss, briefcase, folders and overhead projector slides, like an anima-tion in the style of Picasso, though not by the master himself. 'That just about puts the tin lid on my misery this morning.'

'M40?' I said, looking at my watch. 'I told you you should have stayed here.'

I'd had the presence of mind to stay in the hotel the night before. No, in fact, I hadn't. I'd stayed at home – hence the scrape with Mrs Batt. I had, however, told Cat I'd stayed at the hotel – and that the hotel was in Moseley near Birmingham. (I needed an excuse to get back to Andrea as I'd only told her I had a lunch meeting that Sunday – see the tangled web we weave.)

I'd had the presence of mind to convince myself totally and utterly that I'd stayed at the hotel and never admit that I hadn't, even to my closest friend. I was quite good at this and knew that if I left it a few weeks I'd be convinced I actually had been there that night. It's sickie psychology. You tell work you had food poisoning, you tell yourself you had food poisoning, you envisage the querulous kebab, the suspect seafood, you eat lightly at lunch the next day. Around five you tell people you are 'starting to feel better' you think. Maybe even take another morning off to 'visit the doctor'.

When the boss refers to your bout of food poisoning six weeks ago, you say, 'Yes terrible,' not 'What food poisoning?' thereby securing your ability to do it again. If I were a management consultant advising on taking unwarranted days off, and I suppose I am, I'd say this: 'Think Sick. Live the Lie.' It could almost be the motto on the Dagman family crest.

'Bollocks to the traffic,' said Henderson. This was unusually irreverent. He loves traffic, he loves everything about the modern car, to the point where he lists road rage as one of his hobbies on his CV.

'It's just Julie, she's driving me mad.' He sat down. He's a curious chap to look at. Mildly beautiful, as I think Andrea once described him, but also, I think, mildly ugly. He's gone very pale recently, for a start, which I blame on his overuse of anti-aging UV protection; there's a touch of the Hammer Horror bloodsucker about his chops. His GP warned him that unless he laid off the day cream he was going to end up with vitamin D deficiency and rickets. 'At least it's a disease of childhood, so that's a step in the right direction,' Henderson had pointed out.

There's also something lopsided about him. All right, he's

as lean as a rutting stag (his words) through hours in the gym, and he has a high-cheekboned noble look to him, the sort of face that you could well imagine ordering the peasants' huts to be torched sometime around the Norman Conquest. But his beak, which might cause an eaglet mistakenly to cry out 'Father!' should he poke it into its nest, is off centre. It's like the rest of his body is heading for the photocopier while his nose is heading for the fax. The weirdest thing about him, which you don't notice until you've known him for a bit, are his eyes. They're different colours, one blue, one brown – or as he prefers it hazel, after his speech at the One to None sales conference was interrupted by a rival shouting, 'He's scratching his brown eye!'

'Oh, no,' I said. To be honest I was a bit disappointed that Henderson was going to start listing his domestic woes before I could get on to mine. He's one of those people who is always on the top or on the bottom. Either having the best or the worst time of his life. Since his marital difficulties he's been having the worst. Henderson and his wife, the Iron Julie, have not been getting on for a while. To be fair he married her for the best possible reason – all his mates were getting hitched and he felt left out.

A few weeks ago he proposed a trial separation, just for them to get things clearer, whereupon she proposed a trial separation of his head from his shoulders and he decided to sandbag up in a bed and breakfast with immediate effect.

Now he put his head in his hands, revealing his bald patch. When I say bald patch, I don't mean in the conventional sense. From the front Henderson looked like a normal human being. It's only when you get the plan view of the head that you realise the extent of his shame. He hasn't gone bald in an honest, middle out, crop circle kind of way. Nor has he receded. It's just that, for a few years, a band of pinkest Spam has been extending across the middle of his scalp, leaving a tufted island at the front. Bending the sinew and stiffening the limb, or vice versa, Henderson has managed, by gel and by tonsure, to construct a causeway of hair to the mainland but when he leans down it's as if a rubescent tide wells over it. The artifice exposed, he appears, well, balder.

Not that he looks that old. Two years ago, at the age of about thirty-three, his looks had fled but he went chasing hard after them, pounding out days on treadmill and rowing machine. Even I have to admit, from certain angles he still looks pretty good. Mind you, given the level of effort, he should do.

Having said this, for some time he has been losing it. Not losing it like our old mate Craig Petershall who, after a period of sustained hair loss, turned his back on a valuable franchise of ten Hoover shops, saying things like, 'What's it for – money, possessions, all that? Surely there's more. What does it all mean?' He found out what it was for when he gave it all up to work on an organic collective farm in France. Last I heard he was back and in Dysons.

With Henderson it's just the little things. His appearance, for instance. He's always been a keen hound when it comes to clothes – never having quite escaped the influence of the New Romantics – at least in spirit if not the detail, ribbon head bands being frowned upon in all but the most liberal business circles.

On a couple of occasions recently, though, I've met him outside work and he's been wearing black football-style shorts, a Tommy Hilfiger tee shirt, baseball cap and white sockless trainers. In brief, looking like a car thief. It is only a short step, I fear, to the ear-ring and over-gold watch.

I've mentioned it to him, of course. 'Henderson,' I said, 'if you're going to dress like shit, at least dress like middle-class shit.' All he'd really have to do is get a pair of Chino-style shorts and some sort of corporate polo shirt to look like every other weekending manager.

I remember him once standing looking at his reflection in a shop window.

'What is happening to me?' he said. 'You get one thing taped to the floor and another springs up in its place. If it's not putting on weight, it's wrinkles on the forehead.' He looked at the back of his hand. For ages he's been convinced he's getting liver spots. 'Do you know, I actually found myself lusting after a car the other day because it looked safe? I can't believe I've taken my eye off the ball like this.'

He rushed straight off into a skateboarding shop to buy some baggy pants and a brightly coloured Hawaiian shirt which, while not quite constituting losing it for a man of thirty-five, hardly represents getting it back either.

'No chance of her taking you back then?' I said, on the Iron Julie theme.

'No, she's made it quite clear that if I come back she'll be getting her dad involved.'

'Why would you be afraid of him? He's only a South London scrap metal dealer.'

Henderson paused while the wisdom of crossing a man who had ready access to gangs of low-paid, heavily muscled men, crushing machines, acid baths and large horrid spiky hooks sank in. Come to think of it, the Iron Julie had made one or two references to the 'problem-solving' capacities of her dad's boys before.

'I see your problem,' I said. 'Is it divorce then?'

'With all the revolting financial ruin that implies,' he said. 'I'm going to be spending the next six months hiding my assets under the carpets so her lawyers can't grab the lot.'

'This really has broken your heart, hasn't it?'

'It's getting me down, Dag, I only wanted pause for thought.' Henderson looked genuinely miserable, a sight made more strange by the fact that, as a salesman, his normal expression is one of disingenuous happiness. He went to ruffle his hand through his hair but drew back. Years of experience have told him that gel will not stand a meddler.

'Perhaps it's all for the best,' I said. I was particularly pleased with that inspired piece of sympathy.

'I don't know,' said Henderson, 'it wasn't much of a marriage but at least it was there. You know, it gave me a base. I feel like I'm back to square one now – alone and balding in the howling wilderness of singlehood.'

'Have you thought of seeing someone about it? A counsellor

maybe, if you're feeling stressed. Remember, I sure as shit don't want to talk about it,' I said. Of course, I meant the reverse, that I was more than prepared to talk about it, but there are ways of saying these things between men.

He smiled. 'Out of the question,' he said, 'I'll just bottle the fucker up and let it out in a large eczema attack around Christmas. It's more cost-effective.'

This was true, I knew. We were both temporarily skint since starting our own business. Not skint like poor people are skint – we still ran cars (well, he did), had houses in the London suburbs (well, I did), and could afford to go out most nights of the week if we budgeted carefully. But the very fact we had to budget carefully meant we were skint in our terms, particularly when you took into account the overheads of establishing a business – mailings, meetings, etc.

If we didn't start making money very quickly indeed, and it didn't look like we would, I was pretty much depending on an inheritance my mother had told me I had coming. I couldn't guess who it was coming from, but she had been very reassuring. 'There's richer relatives in this family than you think,' she'd said. 'You'll have a very substantial amount of cash within six months, count on it. At least £30,000.' The money was going to be particularly welcome now Andrea was pregnant and would be going on to maternity pay before long.

So counselling was off the cards for the foreseeable future. When I'd had it, it had cost me £50 a session. Valium was a tenth the price and it actually worked.

Henderson checked his watch, poured himself some tea, and sat back with his feet on the coffee table.

'Mixed,' I said, replying to his unasked question about my weekend.

'Still seeing this Cat?'

'Yes.'

He gave an ambivalent nod of the head. Like most people his first instinct is to draw a great deal of consolation from his friends' failings, so he should have been pleased that my forthcoming marriage was under threat. However, he liked

Andrea and was uncomfortable with me betraying her. I almost regretted telling him about Cat.

'I'm thinking of ending it though,' I said. I hadn't in fact known that's what I'd been thinking. I thought I'd been staggering around with the clear sight and cool appraisal of Daffy Duck with a bucket stuck on his head.

'Oh, yes,' said Henderson. It wasn't an invitation to further comment. He was examining the sides of his eyes with what appeared to be a make-up compact mirror. 'Can you see any lines here?'

'Yes.' I couldn't really, but if you're going to ask questions like that what sort of answers do you expect?

'Thought not,' he said, snapping the compact shut. 'Well, if it's going to pot with her perhaps you wouldn't mind accompanying me sometime this week on a hellish trawl through London's nightspots in search of a replacement girlfriend? For me, that is.'

'I see you've not quite recovered from your grief yet.'

'Recovered or not,' said Henderson, reopening the mirror and pulling at his jowl to test for slackness, 'it's time to get going. Do you think I've still got it?'

He stood up and made a series of movements like his armpits had caught fire while he was trying to scrape chewing gum off his shoe. It was exactly how you see ravers dancing on the telly.

'The height of fashion, as I understand it,' I said. 'But before you go on to the dance floor . . .' I adopted the manner of a squadron leader telling a pilot that the medical report was iffy and it was a desk job or nothing from now on '. . . I think you should know you are going bald.'

'Oh, I hadn't noticed,' said Henderson in mock surprise. 'Don't you worry about me, son. Bald men make better lovers.'

'Well, they rather have to, don't they?' I said. 'They can hardly rely on their looks.'

'What do you rely on?' he said. The last time someone had worn a look of desperation like that they'd been defending the Alamo. But, like Davy Crockett, he wasn't going down without a fight. 'And at least I'm not turning into a silver fox.'

He knew I was slightly sensitive about the wisps of grey that had appeared at the sides of my head. Mind you, not as sensitive as he was. Having a friend with greying hair caused him a great deal of pain, I know. 'If you're going to look crap, why can't you have spots or something?' he'd once asked me.

'I'm too old for spots,' I'd said, at which point he'd put his fingers in his ears, stamped his feet and shouted, 'I'm not listening!'

Henderson ran his finger across his nostrils to check for nasal tufting.

'I've seen you in Boots,' he said, glancing me up and down like a fishwife would look at her down the road who gives herself airs but is no better than she should be, 'pacing back and forth like a teenager outside a brothel in front of the Grecian 2000. Bought any yet?'

'No,' I said, blanching at the analogy, 'and anyway, better grey hair than nay hair.'

Henderson smirked and started examining his gum line in his mirror.

'You don't need to go to a rave to find a woman,' I said. 'You've got plenty of time to find someone you like.'

'Plenty of time? Plenty of time?' He stretched his face back like a Maori warrior performing a particularly fierce *haka*. 'Look at me, man.' He opened his briefcase to reveal a melange of vitamin pills, creams and mystery tubes. 'I'm held together with spit and tissue paper. If this new anti-baldness pill comes out maybe I'll have another year or so, but beyond that . . .' He shook his head and snapped shut the case.

I knew what he meant. Part of me thought that one day they'd just come up and say, 'This time thing, getting older, it's just a joke. Actually everything stops right here and now and remains the same forever. Fancy you falling for the old mortality gag.'

'I think you should try more practical solutions than cramming yourself into the old baggy gear and throwing some shapes at the local dance emporium,' I advised.

'I have Plan B here,' said Henderson, producing a copy of

Floodlight, the London guide to nightschool courses, from his briefcase. 'I've signed up for one a night.'

'Nightschool is the classic solution,' I said, 'though this is something of an extreme case. I rather thought a holiday to the Philippines might be more the ticket.'

'Ha, ha,' said Henderson, although I could see him making a mental note of it. It wouldn't be long, I thought, before I saw him with a *Dream Brides of Manila* brochure.

'What course are you doing?'

'Creative writing.'

'I didn't think you were interested in that?'

'I'm not really but it's practical. There's tons of women there who all want to feel special, and the blokes are all self-important losers who think they've got something to say. I'll only stay until the Christmas parties, see what happens and then jack it in in January.'

'Just like everyone else then.'

'It'll be like shooting fish in a barrel.' He fired an imaginary rifle at the floor, saying 'Bang, bang!' like little boys do. 'Even if I am firing blanks.'

He was referring to his infertility, the inability to father children, which in no way should be confused with impotence – the inability to run it up the flagpole and see who salutes it. When he was younger he had actually boasted about being infertile, looking on it as a guarantee that he wouldn't get caught in the boredom of parenthood and monogamy. There had been a virility to his sterility and he'd thought he had the right to throw it about like Buffalo Bill in a steer-roping competition. Now, though, with friends settling down with families and children, he was in a bit of a last-days-of-Rome scenario, still sucking on the chocolate-coated dormice while the barbarians banged at the gate and his hair fell out. I was about his only remaining link to the childless world.

I don't know how we'd got from me wanting to discuss my dilemma with Andrea and Cat and him wanting to talk about Julie to taking the piss out of each other's physical decay, but we had.

Henderson must have read my thoughts because he shut up his compact and said, 'So it's all coming to a close with this Cat, is it?'

I sniffed.

'I don't like Cat,' he said.

'You don't like her, you don't approve of her relationship with me, you think we should finish – but this didn't stop you going out with her and me three times so you could try to get off with her friends.'

'Of course not,' said Henderson, mystified, 'there was a chance of a shag. What exactly is your point?'

'None really,' I said.

'I just think you should return to the bosom of your intended, your betrayed.'

'Well, the problem is that if I do return to her bosom, I'm not going to be the only one on it, am I?'

Henderson, already vampire pale, went as pale as a vampire who hears the peasantry rattling the wooden stakes and garlic outside his door.

'What do you mean? She's got another man?'

'Don't be ridiculous! I've been meaning to tell you – Andrea's pregnant.'

The shock was clearly too much for him. No real emotion stirred in his face, it was as if the feelings were too powerful for him to know how to respond. He had the searching look of an old blind Russian peasant woman hearing the unmistakable footfall on the snow of the son she had thought lost to war, then reaching forward and saying, 'Dmitri, Dmitri, is it really you?'

I noticed he was trembling.

'She never said anything,' he said weakly.

'She only found out last week.'

'I spoke to her on Wednesday, I called up to get you. You were at badminton. She said nothing at all.'

His eyes were glassy and he spoke in a faraway voice, as if in a trance. I thought at any minute he would start saying, 'Arthur wants to tell Constance he went without pain. The legacy is in the china dog.'

'Well, perhaps she was waiting for me to tell you.'

I hardly had the words out of my mouth before he fell forward into his hands.

'This is a disaster,' he said weakly. Anyone entering the room at that moment would have concluded he was talking into his trousers, a standard male comfort in times of stress. I have known men whose trousers have actually replied but since what they had to say was hardly polite, I shan't dwell on it here.

'It's certainly a surprise but I don't think disaster's quite the right word. She is thirty-three.'

'Not for her, for me,' said Henderson, even more weakly. 'It's the *Titanic*, the Wall Street Crash and women getting the vote rolled into one. It's a disaster.' He was fiddling with the compact again.

'How does it impact on you?' But he wasn't listening, had flipped into a world of his own.

'How could you do this to me?'

'What?'

'I've only just got used to the idea of you getting married. Now this! It's all too quick. Too quick.' He had that look you see on the patient in *ER* just before the nurse says, 'I think we're losing him, doctor.'

Henderson had warned me not to rush into anything with Andrea when we got engaged six months before. I'd pointed out that, since I'd been going out with her for the best part of a decade, I didn't think I was exactly rushing in.

'I think you mean congratulations,' I said, 'or how is the mother-to-be? She's very well and looking forward to it, thank you, Henderson.'

'Congratulations for leaving me all on my own?' he said. 'Congratulations for selling your own mate down the Swannee? Congratulations for deserting me in my hour of need – for choosing the nappy over the cocktail, the dummy over the disco? Congratulations for leaving me without even a girlfriend while you sail off into parenthood? You've got your Blighty wound and it's "I'm all right, Jack".'

'What's a Blighty wound?' I said, fearing that he was

genuinely receiving messages from the spirit world.

'In the First World War, if you got wounded you got to go back to England – Blighty. That's what's happened to you. The whole uncertainty, the searching for a life partner, everything, it's over. You've got a baby and can pack away your dancing shoes, you lucky bastard. It's me who's stuck hollow-eyed at the rave.'

I couldn't think why we were mentioning raves. We hadn't been to one for years.

'How pregnant is she anyway?'

'Fully,' I said.

'No, how long?'

'Three months. It's due in March.'

'But that's the skiing trip,' he said in mild outrage.

'I might have to miss that.'

'That's it,' he said, shrugging his shoulders, 'I'm left here alone. The last one at the party, miles from home, no cab number, forced to stay until the morning.' He looked despondently into the remains of the biscuit display. 'I should have stayed with Julie. At least I'd have had something to fill up my days.'

'Puff the Magic Dragon,' I said.

'What?'

'In the kids' song. He got stuck living in the land of Ona Lee while his mate little Jackie Paper grew up and moved in with a motorcycle mechanic called Sven.'

'Is that your idea of offering support?'

'It is actually, yes. I'm pointing out that your plight has already been turned into art.'

'Oh, yes, a great comfort. I was just mentioning that to this old bloke from Guernica the other day,' said Henderson. 'I should stick to gloating, if I were you.'

'OK,' I said, rubbing my hands together. 'You do realise your worries are only possible at this unique historical juncture? In a previous century you'd have been dead by your age.'

I deliberately said 'unique historical juncture', as I knew the words really annoyed him. I was always using them. It was a phrase I'd just got into my head. It meant nothing, of course, but sounded great. As a management consultant I couldn't understand why Henderson didn't love it.

This offering support was a sore point with me. Andrea always said I wasn't very good at it – like when she'd split her head open on the cupboard, I'd thought I was being sympathetic and she'd said I wasn't. Saying 'You want to watch yourself on those doors – try to bleed over the sink' was both tender and practical in my book. At least I saved her having to clean the floor off afterwards.

'No prospect of an abortion, I suppose?' said Henderson, as if he was asking me if she'd mind posting a letter for him if she was going out.

'No,' I said. I realised this hadn't even occurred to me. Andrea was a committed career woman while I was trying to establish a new business; it would have seemed logical. But logic had nothing to do with it. I'd wanted a kid for so long and she'd seemed so pleased to be pregnant it hadn't even crossed my mind, even though the circumstances in which this child was arriving weren't exactly what child psychologists would recommend as ideal. I realised that, were I adopting the child, Social Services would disbar me if all the facts were known.

Henderson broke a biscuit in half and ground it wastefully into the ashtray. It was the last of my favourites, the Whirls.

'So, this is what it's come to, is it?' he said, bridling like a racehorse finding he has a donkey for a stablemate. 'The Cherokee are sweeping down upon us, I've copped an arrow, and you're going to leave me?'

'Aren't you meant to say, "Go without me, save yourself, give this watch to my mother"?'

'Go without me, save yourself, give this watch to my mother.' He proffered his Casio G Shock. I've told him businessmen shouldn't wear things like that but he won't listen.

'OK.'

Henderson pursed his lips in irritation.

'Look on the bright side,' I said, 'you're free to do what you like. No one's going to stop you from coming in at three in the morning, you don't have to get up all weekend if you don't want to. It's the James Dean fantasy – you don't rot, you burn.'

Even as the words came out a warmth swept over me, like the feeling in a cat's purr. In future I could say I was unavailable for staying out till 3, that I was in with my child. I could go out with people who wanted to be in by 9.30 and could want to be in by 8 without thinking I was missing out on anything. Fan-bleeding-tantastic.

'Well, I'd rather rot if it's all the same to you,' said Henderson. 'Do you think I want to keep using all this?' He shook the briefcase full of potions and pills at me. 'I'm looking forward to meeting the love of my life and never seeing the inside of a gym again.'

The problem between Henderson and the Iron Julie was that she hadn't been the love of his life. He'd edged around this problem with her before she'd tried to edge around his jugular with the sharp end of a nail file. Considering how cushy he'd had it, large house in Ickenham, borough of Range Roving to the Tennis Club, it had been a very brave thing to do. However, if Henderson has a motto it's 'Bravery, Then Regret'.

He always agonises over decisions, but unfortunately only after he's taken them. Like when he was going through his 'feel the fear and do it anyway' stage, which mainly consisted of him wearing tee shirts with things like 'Bring it on!' and 'No Fear' written on them. He organised for us all to go sky diving. He was quite full of himself until we got up in the air. That's when I noticed the first sweat stains appear on his 'Mad For It!' bandanna and the look in his enterrored eyes. I've still got the video of the instructor stamping on his fingers to get him out of the plane.

I looked at Henderson now. He'd never seemed to miss smoking since he gave up two years before. Now, though, he was stubbing yet another biscuit into the ashtray. I took a couple before he could waste the lot.

'My problem is that I think I may have found the love of my life. Again,' I said.

Henderson wore the expression of a 22-stone matron hearing someone complaining that sometimes they just forget to eat. 'You're a bastard, do you know that?' he said. 'That's two loves of your life – one of those could have been for me.'

'But what am I going to do about Cat?'

'What am I going to do about Cat?' mouthed Henderson like a sergeant major mocking a new recruit of the slightly too sensitive type. 'How about *me*?' he said. 'What am *I* going to do for a mate, and a wife, and everything?' A Sartre Florentine gave its life to the pile of crumbs in the ashtray.

'How about me? I've only just got used to betraying Andrea. Have I got to get used to being loyal to her now?' I reminded myself of a burglar I'd seen on the TV who was complaining that the police were making it impossible for him to make a living. Unlike him I didn't expect sympathy.

'How about me? I leave my wife to fall back on a network of friends to find there is no network.' He pointed accusingly with the remains of the biscuit.

'How about me? I take refuge from a stale relationship in an affair only to find the relationship revitalises itself in a way I'd only dreamed about.'

'No, how about me?' said Henderson, leaning into me. If I'd lunged with my teeth I could have got the biscuit from out of his fingers. 'From where I'm sitting it seems the only thing you've got to complain about is an embarrassment of riches.'

He withdrew his hands, one of which was hovering as if about to adjust my tie.

'Look, Henderson,' I said, 'really, how about me? What am I going to do about Cat? This is an immediate problem. Yours we can resolve over a week or so. I need to know, now, what am I going to do?'

He sat back in his seat. 'Don't know,' he said, clearly labouring under the effort of thinking about someone other than himself. 'I thought you were going to finish with her and go back to having just the one fantastically brilliant woman to grow old with. Will you cope?'

'I'm not sure I want to finish with her.'

'Want's got nothing to do with it. You won't have time for Andrea, a baby, Cat and most importantly me. You're having enough difficulty fitting us all in as it is.'

He was right. I'd hardly seen him outside of work since I'd been going out with Cat – although, surprisingly, he hadn't complained. When I'd moved out of the flat I'd shared with him four years before to move in with Andrea he'd pointed out that I'd known him for nine years longer than I'd known her – in fact he'd calculated that I'd spent roughly 10,000 more hours in his company than in Andrea's and that I owed him more loyalty. I'd known what he meant, sort of.

Is the love you offer your friends necessarily more shallow than that you offer your partner? It's supposed to be, isn't it?

'It's immoral to go on and, more importantly, you'll be found out. How are you going to keep them apart?' He didn't wait for an answer. 'You're going to have to put the Cat out, mate.'

I couldn't argue. It had been difficult enough to keep Andrea and Cat's suspicions to a minimum, though my job – which involved working away at hotels and long-distance meetings with clients – and my social life – which involved being out almost every night I had free – were ideally suited to treachery. A baby, though, would make the whole thing out of the question. I was already having enough difficulty putting Cat off from coming to see me at home. Not that she kept asking to, she had never mentioned wanting to come out to Hillingdon. It's just that I had felt I had to keep coming up with excuses why she couldn't visit anyway, which all seemed rather fishy.

In a way I was glad to have the issue forced, like you might anticipate having a tooth pulled. You're not looking forward to the experience but you know you're going to feel better when it's over.

'I guess I am,' I said.

'There's no guess about it, old son.'

'Unless I leave Andrea for Cat.' I was insouciant, like the quiet villain in a drama about hostage-taking who, cleaning dirt from his nails, says, 'We could just kill them all.'

'And why would you do that?' said Henderson.

'I think I love her.'

'But don't you love Andrea?'

'Yes, but in a different way.'

'How different?'

'Well, you know, with Andrea it's a slow-burning, long-term thing. We've been through a lot of problems and got to the other side. I know everything about her. With Cat it's that head-over-heels new thing.'

'You mean a teenage crush?'

'Maybe,' I said. This was one of my anxieties, that I couldn't distinguish Cat the person from Cat the blip of excitement you get with all new relationships. 'But, you know, weirdly Andrea and I have grown apart since we got engaged – until the baby.'

'That tends to happen when you're shagging someone else,' said Henderson. 'You're not committed enough to your relationship. Just spend some more time with her, you've lost touch with her, get to know her better.'

'It seems to me I could do with getting to know her worse,' I said. 'We used to have a lot more time for each other when we first went out with each other.'

'All you've got with Cat is the rush of the new. In ten years' time when your kid's finishing junior school you'll wonder how you could ever have thought that way.'

'Of course,' I said, 'I have to consider whether I even want kids or not.' I didn't know why I was saying that, I knew I wanted them. It could have been me trying not to make Henderson feel too bad (OK, unlikely) or it could have been that I was trying to talk myself into leaving Andrea for Cat. Or maybe it was a residual part of me talking, the person I'd been before everyone I knew started saying 'Teletubbies is really rather good' and complaining about the space prams take up in hallways.

'What do you mean?'

'It's not all comfort and joy, is it? I mean, imagine the grisly day your daughter exchanges her pony for a pony-tailed boyfriend, all sinew and knuckles and breast-sized paws, the discordant music of their intimacies humping through your bedroom walls. Or the horror of a son who won't fulfil all your fantasies of academic and sporting genius and wants a life of his own.'

Henderson looked hurt that I wasn't swigging out of a bottle of champagne, wearing a party hat and shouting, 'I'm the luckiest man alive!'

'And what if the kid was just dull?' I said. 'Imagine if it just wasn't very exciting.'

'You might be lucky,' said Henderson, 'it might turn out more like Andrea than you.'

'Ha, ha. I'm serious. Say it was interested in hi-fi separates? Then what would I do?'

'It's a risk you have to take. What else are you going to do with your life?'

'Leave Andrea. Be free.'

The problem with the freedom to do whatever you want, of course, is that it's quite constraining. You have to do whatever you want. Nobody tells you what that is. Whereas school, work, babies . . . these cosy jails are all laid out for you, allowing you to concentrate on the real business of life. Whatever that is.

Henderson had taken out some dental floss and was furiously winding it around his fingers. I got the strange idea he was tying himself up in a way, to restrain himself from punching me.

'When you say these things, remember that I'm the one with a one-way ticket for a lonely old age,' he growled. 'Pension on a Thursday, three-bar fire, huddled against the cold, knock on the door, "Oh, it's the postman, wonder if it's a letter from a friend," he says as he opens another credit card invitation, the treasured photo album: "Oh, look, there's Dag. I wonder if he's dead? Never really saw him after the children." '

'Hmm.' I flinched under this tirade. 'What about having kids with one person when you love another?'

'The kids come first. There is an old-fashioned concept called duty, you know.'

This was a very strange speech coming from Henderson. Duty, to him, was usually something you avoided on large packs of cheap cigarettes going through customs.

'There're also old-fashioned ideas called bubonic plague and war, but we don't go resurrecting them,' I said.

'Perhaps we should,' said Henderson, 'it'd make the M40 run a bit freer. And,' he began to look quite excited, 'a good war'd get rid of a whole generation of young men, leaving a whole generation of young women with no alternative but to look for men old enough to be their father. Or, as they are known round our house, me.'

Henderson was always picking up my expressions, or me his, I don't know which.

There was a short silence.

'Look, mate,' he said, 'don't throw this away. Don't make the mistake I did with Julie. Go for it.'

I was touched by his sincerity.

'You need to support Andrea,' he said quietly, which is a way he hardly says anything.

'I don't know ...'

'What other choice is there?'

'Come clean with Andrea, tell her I've fallen in love with someone else, see what she says?'

'Honesty,' said Henderson, 'the last resort of the truly desperate. What do you think she would do?'

'I don't know but then the ball would be in her court, she'd effectively decide for me, or the answer would come while we were arguing.'

'Honesty plus cowardice, a dream combination. When the going gets tough, the wise renounce all responsibility. Congratulations! A personal best in terms of shallowness.'

'All right, call me Pontius,' I said, making a hand-washing motion to make things clear for Henderson (bible studies not being his strongest suit), 'but do you think it's a good idea?'

'I don't know.' He appeared lost in thought as he cracked the top of an energy drink he'd produced from his briefcase. 'I've tried things the easy way. I've used all my soft skills to try to make you realise your position. I've even tried appealing to your loyalty to the baby – God knows your loyalty to me doesn't seem to come into it. Now can I show you this?'

From the open briefcase he tossed across a printed spreadsheet. I immediately knew what it was – the cashflow vs expenditure chart we'd used to secure a bank loan.

'Would you look at month fourteen and tell me what you notice about it?'

I didn't have to look.

'It's when we start making money. If all goes well.'

'If all goes well,' said Henderson, as if reciting part of 'The Bells of St Clement's'. 'And if things go badly?'

'I do not know,' I said, like the Great Bell at Bow.

'Exactly. So with Julie gone, who is the sole source of income for you and me, the one possible font of future loans? Who holds the key to our success, should we find ourselves in a make-or-break situation?'

'Andrea?'

'Well, I don't think your Cat is going to exactly shell out for a four-grand database, is she?'

'No.'

'And who actually owns your house?'

He was right. We'd transferred the house solely into Andrea's name in case we went bankrupt. The same mistake had meant Henderson was now out on his ear enjoying bacon and eggs the traditional way every morning while Julie put their house on the market.

'I can't put money above love.'

'No need to put it anywhere,' said Henderson, 'it's already there. We've put everything into this. And it's not even certain it'd work with Cat.'

I knew what he meant. We'd fantasised in bars and gym leisure areas about no more bosses, no more appraisals, the ridiculous amount of money to be made by selling our particular brand of old rope direct rather than being employed to reel it out by our companies. It was a hell of a lot to give up for an outside bet on happiness with a new girlfriend.

Secure love and security vs insecure love and insecurity. Not much of a contest.

'Shun her,' said Henderson, 'like the boarder shuns the day boy.'

'Did they have boarders at your comprehensive, Henderson?'
I knew the answer to this. It was also my comprehensive.

'It's what we called the rats.' He looked serious. 'You're going
to have to sack her. The business can't afford for you to be in
love.'

'Looks like I'll have to then,' I said, almost physically swaying.
I'd have to be honest with her, of course. There had been so
many delicate lies that brutal honesty seemed the only antidote.
Get it over with.

'Yes, do it now, and make it easy on yourself. The other
options don't bear thinking about. I'm your best mate and I'm
not going to stand by and watch you throw it all away.'

He held out his mobile on which he'd called up Cat's number.
I wondered when she'd given him that. She'd only met him a
couple of times after all.

Luckily I was prevented from speaking to her when a delegate
entered the room, his suit in eighties grey, his face in cardiac red.
We both sprang up with the excitement of Tiggers about to
begin a chorus of, 'And we're the only ones!'

As I pumped the delegate's hand, I reflected for a second. I
thought I'd detected a tangible nuance of threat in Henderson's
voice.

5

Wheel Of Life

It was on a day suitable for beginnings that I decided to end it.

The heat had finally gone and the first sniff of bonfires could be caught on the autumn air. The sky was clear and blue, striped with the vapour trails of aeroplanes taking people away, it seemed to me, to fresh beginnings, the endless new.

I, however, was opting for the limited old – not that Andrea would have been very pleased to have been described that way.

I had a meeting with a company in Victoria at 10 to discuss how they could cut their staff turnover – on a par with that of the front-line regiments in the First World War. So for two hours I'd sat in front of some pleasant, attentive business folk on the sixth floor: presenting, making little jokes, laughing at little jokes, and feeling like leaping through the window, screaming, 'I die for love!'

At last, the pie charts were returned to the briefcase, the multimedia was stilled, the questions ended and I made my way out into the bright air. The city felt clean in the new-season cold but my sense of dread was only deepened by the brilliance of the day. I felt I was defeating the expectations of the weather, like I was the only impure thing on a pure morning.

I'd arranged to meet Cat next to the Houses of Parliament as she'd had a press conference there and it was near to Victoria. We were going to walk down Victoria Street and find a coffee bar.

I'd decided to tell her it all, because I thought I owed her that and because the facts of the case were grim enough to ensure a clean break. I liked her too much ever to see her again.

I walked up from my meeting past Buckingham Palace and across St James's Park. This isn't the quickest way but I was a bit early so I sat down, watching a rabble of unpleasant school-children throwing bread and other items at the ducks, trying not to listen to the swearing and the squabbling and the fact that someone was going to get battered, but rather to the voice of the trees, stirred to murmur by the east breeze. I say it was east, it was coming up the Mall towards the palace, whichever direction that is.

I sank into my overcoat. I remembered the last time I'd been out in a park on such a day – walking on Hampstead Heath with Andrea, the day we'd got engaged. We'd stood close, shivering at the madness of the swimmers in the bathing ponds and laughing at the men who slipped by us, off to slake their fleshly thirsts beneath rhododendron and spruce.

'Shall we go and have some heterosexual sex in the bushes?' Andrea had asked.

'No,' I'd answered, 'that isn't what they're for. The world is not yet so perverse that people have straight sex on Hampstead Heath. Some things must remain forever innocent and gay.'

'It's a bit cold for them, isn't it?' she'd said, brrrrrring into me.

'It's never too cold for sodomy.' I was sure that was one of Henderson's sayings.

Times like that one on the Heath were when I'd felt most at ease with Andrea, content just to be with her. We'd made our way up to Parliament Hill and looked out over the vastness of the city.

'Would you like to get married?' I'd said then.

'Yes,' she'd replied, gazing into my eyes, 'I'd love to.'

'To me?'

'Oh,' she'd said, frowning. 'Er, can I get back to you on that one?'

And then we'd run to the nearest jeweller's to look at rings – a bad idea in a borough with the expensive tastes of Hampstead. If we could only get back to that, I thought, we'd be fine.

I'd walked on Hampstead Heath with Cat too, of course. We actually did have sex in the bushes.

We wouldn't be doing that again. Cat had to go. For the business and for the baby. Let's say it the short way – for me. So that I might have the future I'd planned and so I wouldn't dreadfully upset someone I loved, I had to get rid of her. The contemplation of saying goodbye made me realise how badly I still wanted her. But, as my mum used to say, want has nothing to do with it. Upsetting Andrea on her own would have been bad enough. With a baby around the stakes were just too high.

It had only been a few months, for God's sake. Cat probably wouldn't even be that upset. I hadn't had that thought before and it lifted my spirits slightly. I might find it shattering but she might not even bother that much. That, more than anything, told me I was on the right course.

Looking back on the night I'd met her, I knew now it would have been easier if I'd just walked away.

It had been about a month before I gave up working for the Biggest Company on Earth. It was our annual bash to mark (rather belatedly) the beginning of the new financial year – don't say you don't celebrate it, I know you do. It was held at a hotel expensive enough to forestall the junior staff getting slaughtered once the free drink had run out.

When you first start work you look on these events as an ideal excuse to get pissed and to meet people. By the time you get to my age, though, all you want is an excuse not to get pissed and to be on your own. In this frame of mind, I went for a look round the hotel. It was one of these big new minimalist places, all the ambience of a multi-storey carpark with plenty of pay and display from the guests.

I'd noticed a party going on in another room and, since there was no one on the door, I'd gone in. It was a businessy thing and I thought it might give me a chance of picking up a few contacts for when Henderson and I started the new company.

Naturally, as I prowled the cold hams of the buffet for potential clients, I was also, as befits my age and station, perving. I always perv. As I've already recorded, most of the attached older man's time is spent perving over young women. The degree of perving increases in inverse proportion to his chances of actually having sex with them. I was perving a lot that evening.

In my case the perv isn't in an outright 'oooh, er, knickers, knackers, knockers!' sort of way, but in a quiet, over the newspaper or behind the sunglasses manner. Us old blokes are masters of the glance from ceiling to shoe that lingers a little too long on the buttocks, the eyes that dance over every surface of the room but manage a *pasadoble* on the breasts. It's not the hot-eyed glance of the sex pest, it's hardly noticeable, just a brief ripple in the fabric of existence. We hope.

Obviously I find this behaviour disgusting and would prefer not to do it, but unfortunately it is mandatory. I could – and do – perv in my sleep. If you do it for long enough, apply yourself, it becomes second nature. You're on autoperv, you do it without even knowing it. Just like when you're driving you suddenly come back to consciousness after ten miles of blank scenery unable to remember anything about the road, you awake from autoperving not knowing who you've been perving on, under, round or past. But sometimes an emergency will arise that will make you realise you're not quite as good at it as you thought. Cat was just such an emergency.

I was thinking of our financial situation as we launched the new company and praying to God that I could get my mum to be less elliptical about the inheritance I was due for when I heard a voice.

'Have I got something on my front?'

I came back to focus on the room, or rather on the chest of a young woman who was standing next to me, spooning some potato salad on to a plate.

'I'm sorry?'

'I was wondering if I'd spilled something or if you were just ogling my breasts?' I don't know whether it was the age difference between us, or if she suspected I could be someone important, but she didn't seem angry. It was more like a defiant cheek really. The last time I'd seen someone with a look on her face like that was in a film where a young girl on a horse had been telling a handsome farm hand her father would hear of his insolence. 'You're a haughty one, young lady,' he'd said, followed by some salty comment about how she wouldn't look so high and mighty if she joined him in the straw. I put that from my mind.

She looked incredibly young to me, about twenty, with her hair in a grown-out bob of mousy curls.

'Well, you haven't spilled anything,' I said, looking down her front, consciously this time, 'so, that only leaves us ogling the breasts, which I was unaware I was doing. Sorry. It can happen to the best of us. Er, look, can we start again? Stewart Dagman, Head of Management Training, the Biggest Company on Earth.' I extended my hand while pointedly looking up at the ceiling.

I felt her take it and I returned my eyes to the level. She was looking at my crotch with laser-like intensity. I felt my legs buckle inwards like a man hearing someone describe an accident with a zip fly.

'I'd say we were even,' I said.

'Just about.'

'Now can you stop looking at me like that?'

'Sorry. It's just difficult to remember there's a person attached to them sometimes.'

Even though her comments were very modern, there was an old-fashioned grace to her. She reminded me of a nineteenth-century lady teasing a friend about who the Count D'Arbeville had been seen with at the summer ball.

I didn't know what to make of her. It wasn't immediate sexual attraction; you don't in fact have to be sexually attracted to someone to idly perv them up, especially on autoperv. To continue the driving metaphor, you can be perving along behind a Ferrari, tune out for a while and come back perving at the back of an HGV. I knew that I wanted her to stay, though.

'I've told you who I am, now how about you?'

'I'm . . .'

'Would you mind folding your arms before you reply? To forestall accidental sexual harassment.'

She actually thought this was funny. Christ, I thought, I appear to be chatting her up. I hadn't actually chatted anyone up since I'd met Andrea. That had taken me three years from first meeting her to first snog. I hadn't even tried since then. I remembered my dad, during one of his many skint phases, getting his old motorbike out of the shed and the mixture of delight and amazement on his face when it started at the first time of asking. 'Try doing that with your Japanese crap,' he'd said, as if I had been singlehandedly responsible for the decline of the British motorcycle industry by buying a Yamaha FS1E moped. Then the fear had crossed his face as he realised that, after ten years cocooned in his tank-like Volvo, he was going to have to ride it. After a morning's tinkering he announced, with relief, that it would never pass an MOT and advertised it for sale in the paper. I felt very similar about my chatting up motor which, unbidden, was spluttering into life.

'I'll fold my arms if you assume the football wall position.'

'Certainly,' I said, hands in front of package like one of those thin English defenders you see cat's arsing his lips as the Brazilian number 10 tracks a malevolent furrow towards the dead ball. See, cat's arse, Cat's arse. The sexual thing's poking a subliminal leg through the curtains of a relatively innocent sentence. Nobody asked it to, nobody wanted it. But that's what was happening in our conversation. I was engaged to be married to a woman I loved. I didn't want to fancy anyone else, I was just flirting, being silly, that was all. In fact, I think I was just seeing how far I could push it before she told me to sod off. Or at least that's what I told myself.

She told me she was a journalist from InvestOrone – an internet business service – and that her name was Cat Grey. I said with a name like that she must have had a hard time at school. She said she'd only been called Cat, short for Catherine, after a teacher had made a joke about Grey, Cat in calling the register, and she quite liked it. It could have been worse, she said, had her family name been Litter.

I found myself laughing out of all proportion to the funniness of the joke. No one else would have found it funny, no one else would have thought that our postures – she with her arms folded, me protecting my valuables – were anything but childish and crude. That alone should have told me to run screaming from the building. I'd been with her ten seconds and already we had in-jokes. I suppose I should have been glad I stopped short of calling her Miss Fluffy Bunny.

And that was it. I don't remember any more until I heard myself say, 'It's very busy in here, would you like to go somewhere we can sit down?' There was no sexual intent in this, although I admit that I'd stood in buffets with others before including, I think, Andrea, and never felt the need for seclusion.

I don't really remember much after that until we moved on to the bar.

I'm sorry this is a large leap but memory is like a cheap builder: it starts in one place, buggers off for a while and then comes back at an inconvenient hour to start somewhere else. The wise person is just grateful it's doing anything like the job it's meant to and doesn't ask too many questions of it.

Of course I remember the lies I told her while we were still at the buffet – three to be precise.

I told her, most importantly, that I didn't have a girlfriend and I wasn't married. This was the creep's favourite lie – the lie of exactitude. A fiancée is neither a girlfriend nor a wife.

I also told her I was Head of Management Training for TBCOE worldwide. Well, I implied it. I said I was Head of Management Training and she said, 'Globally?' And I said, 'Lord of all I survey.'

Now this isn't exactly a lie, in fact it's inexactly a lie, I only surveyed South East England – and even then not the City of London, for which there's a special division.

'That's a tough job,' she'd said.

'Well, I relish a challenge,' I'd replied, with a bit of a swagger.

'I just challenge a relish,' said Cat, picking up some pickle from the buffet, 'this is never real chutney!'

I laughed like I'd laughed when I'd first seen Basil Fawlty saying, 'No, we didn't, you invaded Poland!'

Thirdly I told her that I was thirty-six. A lie of contrition. I was so mortified that I was trying to impress her – a tacit betrayal of Andrea – that I deliberately told her a lie to put her off me. I was only thirty-five. Three distinct lies in the first hour of a relationship. I suppose there's something to be said for this – along the lines of 'get them over and done with now, we can move on to vile truths later'.

We talked some more, about her job, which she was doing while she considered what she really wanted to do, and about our pasts. Niether of us mentioned a partner.

It turned out we'd both done English at university and that she thought Nabokov was a great author, and that literature mattered and its study was underfunded. I said that I too thought Nabokov was a great author but that if the children of Middle England wanted to learn fancy conversation I wished they would do it at their own expense rather than troubling the taxpayer or, as he is known round our house, me.

'Our house?' she said. 'Do you have flatmates?'

'No,' I said – well, your fiancée can hardly be said to be a flatmate – 'it's just an expression.'

She said her favourite book was *Ulysses* by James Joyce. I said *Ulysses* had been my favourite too. (When I'd been a student I'd thought it would impress people that I'd done reading's equivalent of running the marathon. Backwards. In a gorilla suit. I'd said I'd loved it for the amazing depth of the interplay between classical references and the modern, the mundane and the obscene, an interplay only possible in the collision of the English and Irish languages and in a society adapting to consumer culture.) Now, though, I said I thought it was a pile of old bunny that anyone with access to an encyclopaedia could have tossed off in a weekend, providing they got pissed enough.

I remember her laughing, against herself, and had the rather pathetic but still sexy feeling that I was introducing her to the wacky and exciting world of embittered cynicism. I'd told Henderson about this afterwards and he'd described it as 'an intellectual deflowering', which had made me feel faintly sick. Mind you, it was the first time I'd heard him use the word 'intellectual' outside of its normal negative sense, i.e. 'A very intellectual point of view, David, congratulations. Now back in the real world . . .'

She asked me what my favourite book was now. I said that, after considering Thomas Mann's *Magic Mountain*, the whole of Dostoevsky (you really can't take him in parts) and *The Prime of Miss Jean Brodie* by Muriel Spark, I'd plumped for James Herriot's *Vets Might Fly* – so much more challenging than *It Shouldn't Happen to a Vet* – on account of its symbolism and its comic dogs. *It Shouldn't Happen to a Vet* contains comic cats, which are a much inferior literary device.

She said she hadn't previously considered the use of the comic dog in literature and I asked her what they were teaching at college nowadays. All in all I hadn't talked such bollocks since I'd been at university. I was having a great time.

'So you've never been tempted to write yourself?' she said. Had I? Not many. My entire twenties had been spent on teeth-gnashing, angst-driven ink-slinging in a bid to convince myself that I had a soul. It had rather the opposite effect. I wasn't going to let her know that, though.

'At college I tried to do a play based on a Freudian sort of theme. You know, there was one big messy beast of a character representing the primitive sexual drives of the id.'

'What was he called?' said Cat.

'Id, I believe,' I said. 'There was one very realistic, down-to-earth one called Ego, and another . . .'

'This is already lacking tension,' said Cat.

'. . . uptight repressed one called Super Ego,' I continued.

'Was there one representing the number of people who'd be willing to sit through it, called Nought?'

'I believe he was called Less Than Nought,' I said, 'which is why I eventually decided to direct my creative talents towards management accountancy. I find I can really say something about myself there, especially in the debit columns.'

'Are you always like this?' she asked.

'Darling, one has to seize one's opportunities,' I said, camply, 'this degree of flippancy is only possible at this unique historical juncture. Previous generations actually had something to worry about.'

'Haven't we?'

'You know, you're right,' I said. 'Oh, my God, I think they're about to run out of white.'

'Extinction, environmental disaster, the death of British sit com?'

'Not in my social set, I'm afraid. Although I did used to worry about the latter before I got cable. With UK Gold, life has no cares.' I flapped my wrist. I don't know why I get a fit of the gays every time I find a woman attractive, but I do. Maybe I'm subconsciously trying to sneak in under their radar.

Andrea, of course, had never allowed me to get away with this stuff, even at college, before we'd gone out with each other. I remember walking down Edinburgh's Royal Mile with her one day and saying, 'If meaning only emerges in context, and context is forever widening every time we speak, does the concept of "meaning" mean anything?' She'd run off in the direction of Princes Street screaming, 'Help!'

Even though there was part of me that found Cat's enthusiasm for life and books and thought rather naive, I fear to say it did remind me of a more intelligent version of myself at her age. It was exciting to meet someone who wasn't world weary, I thought world wearily.

Cat and I talked about where she lived – Stoke Newington, out towards the weeping waste of the east; what she did in her spare time – going out drinking and nothing else, like any self-respecting young woman; who her friends were and what they did – one of them seemed to be a lesbian who was spending a year crewing on a yacht with the idea, I supposed, that all the nice girls love a sailor. Not once did she mention the words 'we' or 'Danny' or 'Mike' or whoever to refer to some thick-legged and hairy young lover. For some reason I'd imagined her boyfriend as a prematurely bald type with freckles and swimming medals in his room, the way I always imagine wife beaters. And then the crunch, when I found out she was single.

I said I'd never been to Paris, which I know is unforgivable, and I had meant to go, but there had been so many other places to see. In fact Andrea had suggested going several times in the past few years but following recent football results I didn't want to give the French the chance to crow.

'You'd love it,' Cat said – she already had an idea of the sort of person I was, it seemed. 'Mind you, be careful when you go. I went during *prêt-à-porter* week this year and the whole place was heaving. If I hadn't been on a tour I wouldn't have got a hotel.'

'You went on a tour?' I couldn't exactly envisage Cat in with the grannies and the school kids.

'Well, not really,' she smiled and blushed, 'it was a weekend thing – romantic breaks for one.'

My eyebrows rose up my forehead, flipped down the back of my neck, wormed their way under my collar and had shot off down my trouser leg before I could say, 'May I register my surprise?'

'You went on your own, on a singles tour, to the city of lovers? That's very sad.'

'Yes, I know, but it seemed attractive at the time. It was an all-women thing, "for single women and those with a husband who's too big a pig to take them", or something like that.' She made a gesture with her hand like she was brushing away an irrelevance. 'I think the idea was to pair women without a partner with those who had one so the singles could see how terrible life with a man can be and the ones with men could see that life for the single woman wasn't all happy and free.'

'And where did the romance creep in – as in the "romantic break for one"?'

'Well, it didn't really, but "cynical breaks for one" wouldn't have been much of a marketing ploy.'

'So which camp were you in?'

'The single. I'd just left a boyfriend who was too big a pig to take me. I'd always wanted to go but he said that it'd be too traumatic after the last World Cup and European Championship and everything.' When she said 'single', I felt that tingle, from the back of the throat to the ankles, the same I get when I remember being with Andrea that ocean-wild evening after her first Ann Summers party.

'He wasn't being serious?' I tried to sound appalled, I really did, but I knew exactly what he meant. I could have taken open taunting, having the Tricolour rammed under my nose with the words 'Eat My Goal, *Anglais*', it was the air of quiet superiority I found most difficult to deal with. They were all at it, *hommes, femmes et enfants*, the whole lot of them, with a kind of icy hauteur I couldn't stomach: '*Le Football, c'est très simple.*'

'I don't know. He was quite young for his age and I don't think he wanted to go anywhere without his mates. I liked it anyway. I'd do it again.'

'You'll have to stay single or meet a pig.'

'I don't think either will be difficult,' she said, looking me up and down, 'have you got trotters?' Since we're mentioning animals' bodies, I remember when I was a kid butchers used to sell stuff called 'lights' – I now know these are the lungs. Back then I thought it was a word for all the insides – the kidneys, heart and stomach. It was in this childish sense that I felt my own lights leap, a visceral excitement, sharp and sudden, like when you go over a humpback bridge in a car.

I really have to go, I thought, and stayed.

I stayed while we debated, we agreed, we differed, we agreed to differ, we laughed and we teased. The teasing should have told me to stop but it didn't. In fact I moved from inactively betraying Andrea – doing nothing to remove myself from the situation – to actively betraying her, moving myself further in. I remember the words that did it.

'It's very noisy in here,' I said, 'would you like to go for a drink in one of the other bars?'

Now I know this is the second time I've mentioned this, but this is just how the memories are coming and, like when I go jogging, if I stop I'll never start again.

'Yeah,' said Cat, 'you can pay, though, since you're obscenely rich.'

God, she'd noticed I'd been going on about my conspicuous success – or rather the conspicuous success of the real Worldwide Head of Management Training for TBCOE (Carl Calvoretti, 32, android) that I'd rather bafflingly been pretending to have.

'Darling, I'll be paying for the rest of my life,' I said, like a drag queen who'd come to terms with suffering.

We left the room and headed for the mezzanine bar, past the, er, nothing, of the modernist interior and up to a harsh red leather sofa in the whitened space that was, rather imaginatively, called Bar Six. I was sure this had been the name of a chocolate biscuit years ago. My company party was winding down, with people filtering into the bar. I was afraid someone would spot me and come and talk to me but there were no stools in front of the sofa which would have allowed me to turn my back on the room. I didn't want anyone interrupting us, but also didn't want anyone seeing me with an attractive young woman who wasn't my fiancée, even if there was nothing in it to cause gossip. Even if it's entirely innocent people talk, largely because, I've concluded, it never is entirely innocent.

I'm sure I wasn't thinking this at the time, but leaving the party was just racking up our degree of separation from the rest of humanity. I suppose that unconsciously I was removing her from competition, or increasing intimacy, whatever you want to call it. If we liked each other enough at that stage it would progress to another bar, or perhaps I would insist on seeing her home, then coffee at her house, then bed. We would become progressively more isolated from the world around us until we physically shut it out under a duvet. Or at least, that was how I remembered these things had happened before.

And it's what seemed destined to happen then. I phoned Andrea from the loos. She was asleep so I left a message saying that I was with the MD and going on to his club (of the leather arm chair, crisply folded *FT* and the finest cigars Fidel can provide rather than the bangin' tune variety). I said if it dragged on too long I'd get a hotel in town and see her Saturday morning.

It's hard to believe now but I still had no intention of betraying Andrea at this point. I had every intention of not betraying her, in fact.

So why didn't I say, 'I've met this lovely young girl and we're just going to continue this very fascinating conversation, perhaps back at her house eventually? Don't worry, I am flirting with her and I do find her very attractive, oh, and I'm slipping into alcoholic autopilot mode, but I have sworn to myself that I will definitely jump into a cab should any wrongdoing loom.' At least if I had said that it would have made me realise that my chances of remaining faithful were on a par with those of an Elvis comeback. Hey, I'm not saying they were non-existent, after all.

Why didn't I turn to Cat and say, 'Just got to call the fiancée'? The defence requires a moment to reconsider its plea, Your Honour.

Now the observant observer will have noted that I was rather presuming in all of this that Cat was attracted to me – a man old enough to be her father.

Well, in fact, I was rather hoping the reverse: that she wasn't attracted to me at all and that I was just flattering myself. It would definitely have been a big relief if she'd said 'nice to have met you' and disappeared for a taxi. Uncertain of my own abilities to resist temptation, I was rather hoping that temptation was going to resist me. It wouldn't have been the first time.

Unfortunately she didn't seem willing to play ball. She asked me for a cigarette, in fact, saying she didn't normally smoke, only rarely, which made me think she must be nervous. I'd given up smoking years before, but thought, Sod it, and ordered a packet of fags from the bar.

For some reason we got to talking about our parents, which was another bad sign. I told her that my dad was a retired merchant seaman and that my mother claimed we were all descended from gypsies – despite my brother having traced the family back to watchmakers at the turn of the twentieth century. I think it's the family combination of dark hair and blue eyes that convinced my mother we must have been wandering moonblind over the shifting landscapes of European history for the last four hundred years, rather than getting good jobs and worrying what the neighbours would think.

'I never really knew my father,' she said.

'I'm sorry about that.'

'Don't be. It was quite a feat really considering how much he hung around our house when we were growing up.' She smiled cheekily. I recognised the polish of a well-worn joke, but I was glad she'd made it. It meant she was trying to impress me. What am I saying? I wasn't glad she'd made it at all. It terrified the bloody life out of me because it meant she was trying to impress me. This was the problem. One minute I was the proud upholder of the noble tradition of dirty old men trying to get into much younger girls' knickers, the next I reminded myself I was the kind of double-dealing serpent I normally despise.

'He wasn't what you'd call a hothousing parent then, your father?' I said.

Hothousing, I had read, is where parents emotionally cripple their children by forcing knowledge/sporting skills upon them from an early age. Eventually they grow up and go out into society where they fit in like a greenhouse orchid on the local football field.

'Hardly hothousing. More compost heap, chuck us out of the house and see what develops.' Cat puffed on the cigarette. From the stiff way she held it, I could see she wasn't used to smoking.

'Why didn't he take more of an interest?'

'He liked the pub. Used to say he was going down the road to see a man about a dog.' She looked at the floor, rolling her shoulders, almost physically grappling with emotion. 'Never came back with one, though.' She pursed her lips and gave a little shrug.

'That's terrible,' I said. 'What did your mum do about it?'

'Nothing unless she wanted a backhander. Anyway, she was all pills and vodka. That's growing up in the inner city for you. Do you know, I hadn't even seen a real cow until I went to university? Most of my friends from school are either in prison, pregnant or dead now.'

This shocked me.

'It's amazing you got to college from such a background,' I said. 'It's a massive achievement, to be where you are now. I mean, the way you speak and everything – I hope this isn't an insult – but it's so middle-class.' I guessed she must have had some sort of elocution lessons, although I could hardly believe anyone would bother with that in this day and age.

'I had to pay for it all myself,' she said. 'Oh, hold on. No. That was all from a play I heard on Radio 4 the other night. I am terribly sorry, I've misled you. I was brought up in the Surrey stockbroker belt and had every care lavished upon me. Oh, dear, yes, it's all coming back now. I had my first pony when I was six and I still write to my old nanny. Yes, the barn, the games room, checking the fences with Father in the snow.' She put her hand on my arm, as if she'd just remembered something so exciting she must tell me. 'And how could I have forgotten? The presents at Christmas, piles and piles around the tree, the open fire, the goose from our own farm, carol singing and midnight mass . . .'

'I get the point,' I said.

I sat still with pursed lips and arched brow, like Oliver Hardy trying to maintain his dignity, aloof from the custard pie fight.

'You should have seen your face!' She had a way of rocking when she laughed, like a mechanical sailor in a seaside funfair. 'Boom, boom!' She nudged her head into my chest, in that Basil Brush way. I recoiled, fearing that I'd put my arm around her.

'So your friends aren't pregnant, dead or drug addicts?'

'No, but a couple of them are bankers and that's worse,' she said, with mock seriousness. 'Did you honestly believe I was brought up in the inner city?'

'Well, it just chimed a bit with my own experience.'

'Oh, I'm sorry. I wouldn't have said it if I'd thought it was going to hurt you.'

'It's OK. It's just I did live in that sort of area and my dad was . . .'

'What? Oh, God, I've really torn it, haven't I?'

'No, no, you haven't. It's just he was killed by a loan shark.' I felt old, half-dead sadnesses stirring inside me.

'Oh, God, I've *really* put my foot in it!' She put her hand on my shoulder for comfort.

'Yes, it was on loan to Sea World Florida from the Baltimore Aquarium. He fell into its tank trying to retrieve his "I did the Grand Canyon Bungee Blitz" baseball cap.'

'You're not serious?'

Tears were rolling down my face. 'Of course not,' I said on a sob. 'He's actually still alive and collecting sea-faring memorabilia in Portsmouth. Boom, boom!' That, funnily enough, was the truth. The old half-dead sadness wasn't a real one, I'd experienced it in a film. I went to nudge my head into her chest but thought better of it. I did, however, notice her chest which looked, to put it bluntly, very nice. I averted my eyes before we started all that again. But on this subject, at what point are you meant, in the politically correct world, to look at a girl's tits? At what point are you allowed to consider her sexually? Before or after you have sex? I ask these questions in no tone of facetiousness, I genuinely want to know.

'But you were crying.' She hit me.

'Live the Lie,' I said. 'Feel the Sadness. Conjure the Gloom.' I was laughing and wiping away the tears. 'It's my motto. God, I'm a loss to sales.'

We looked into each other's eyes and I thought that I should, and shouldn't, kiss her.

Out of the corner of my eye I could see a couple of people from work who'd come up for a drink, both young men of about twenty-four, probably with tattoos and piercings beneath their suits – the latest examples of post-hippy tat designed to leave girls like Cat swooning. I hoped she hadn't got any body insertions, made a mental note to throw a fridge magnet at her chest if I ever saw her again and see if it stuck.

I wanted to kiss her, I didn't want to leave her to be chatted up by that couple of arseholes – well, actually, I'd spoken to one of them and he seemed all right but these were what we call in management circles contextually driven arseholes, i.e. in the wrong place at the wrong time and therefore arseholes, not arseholes *per se*.

On the other hand I wanted one of them to come and take her away from me, to get back to my fiancée and my life, to waken from this dream happy that nothing had happened.

Cat leaned forward, fixing my face with her eyes. I was reminded of a doctor examining the retina for whatever goes wrong with retinas. She seemed lit up by our laughter. I leaned forward too and parted my lips.

'I have to go,' I said.

She looked surprised. 'I'm up very early tomorrow.' Yes, thank God, the finishing tape. I'd made it to the end of the race against my own ego and libido.

'Sure,' she said.

'It's lovely to have met you.' We had clasped hands now.

'You too.'

'Can I see you again?' one of us said and I'm not interested in who. I think it could have been her, in fact I've convinced myself that it was, but I could have been living a lie about it, you know. Anyway, a steward's enquiry had been ordered in the me vs ego and libido handicap hurdle. And then, after the e-mail addresses and mobile numbers (I don't have a landline, this is all I need, I'd said) had been swapped, I did kiss her, but only on the cheek. I remember her perfume which I recognised as a cheap-ish brand one of the girls at work used. But Cat had made it something different. Then and after it seemed as if she'd taken that feeling you get when you first kiss someone properly and made it something you could catch on the air as she walked by.

I remember the warmth of her face and us sitting holding each other's hands, the curly mop of hair that made her seem like a good-looking female Harpo Marx, her steel-grey eyes, the swirling blur of background noise.

I want you, I thought. I want you like the sea wants a sacrifice of souls.

Now that's not the sort of thought that normally troubles my thinking tackle on the mezzanine floor of a business event, I can tell you.

In the grip of such a powerful emotion, I did the only thing I could.

'Goodbye,' I said, although it may as well have been 'beep beep', as I made like the roadrunner out of there. There was then a very embarrassing period while I stood by reception waiting for a cab.

The two boys from our firm came over and started chatting to her, which would have cost them both about £4,000 each in pay rises once I'd filled in the 'comments' section on their next course, had it not been for Cat. She kept glancing over at me. So often that I decided to wait for the cab outside.

The next thing I knew I was in a cab, halfway between elation and frustration. Then I was home, slipping into bed quietly so as not to disturb Andrea. The trouble is that I tend to slip like ocean liners slip down their launching slopes into the sea.

'Good night?' she said sleepily, her pale moon face and short dark spiky hair just visible on the pillow.

'Yeah, great fun.'

'And it's not over yet,' she said, kissing me hot and wet on the mouth.

And that, three months later, after I'd fallen deeply for Cat, was how I came to discover a very interesting fact. The pill is not a 100 per cent-effective form of contraception.

Of course, Cat and I had taken our time getting together properly. I remembered mentally handcuffing myself to the floor the night I'd first stayed over, listening to her breathe in bed and trying to tell if she was asleep. I remember the constant excuses for seeing each other – she had an uncle who was a finance director in a pharmaceutical company. He was always moaning about the state of his managers. Would I like to meet him? We could meet to discuss the best way to approach him, then meet so she could pass me over to him on the phone, then meet to discuss my meeting (not bad, actually), then meet so I could take her out for a meal to say thank you, then meet so she could return the compliment.

All the time I had been convincing myself of my purely innocent intentions, almost successfully.

When we had finally kissed . . .

My memories were interrupted by the realisation I'd arrived at the Houses of Parliament. I made my way past the mouth of Westminster tube, crossing through the bolus of tourists to the pier. I caught sight of Cat waiting on the opposite side of the road, the Big Ben side of the bridge, her long woolly coat about her on its first outing of the year, leaning over the rail and gazing out up the Thames towards Chelsea, Hammersmith, Oxford and the open sea, symbol – you're there before me – of the unknown.

There were roadworks all the way around Parliament Square and over Westminster Bridge, so I walked directly towards her across the car-free road. An idyllic shit day, I thought.

'Hi!' I said, in the breezy way of the truly miserable.

She turned to face me and I could see her face was swollen, like she'd been crying.

'What is happiness?' she said.

Normally I'd have said something like 'Isn't hello more normal?' but I could see by her face she wasn't in the mood for levity.

'That's a big question for lunchtime,' I said. She just looked at me.

'Tell me, what is happiness?'

'It's about other people. Meeting someone you feel you're really close to. Love really, that's what it's about.'

'I saw your friend Lee yesterday.'

'Where?'

'At work. He asked me to lunch.'

I immediately guessed that Henderson had adopted a belt and braces approach by filling her in on a few things early doors. I remembered the tone of threat in his voice when he'd told me to get rid of her. I couldn't quite believe he'd done it, but I knew him well enough to surmise that he might be capable of it with enough Red Bull inside him, in his 'I will forge a business empire in my image and nothing will stand in my way' mode, that the Iron Julie used to slap him for. But years in the playtime poker school had taught me not to make the mistake of leaping in early.

I wanted to apologise, I wanted to explain, but most of all I wanted to find out exactly what he'd told her before I said anything.

'What was he doing, asking you for lunch?'

'He's like you. He says it's about love too.'

'What?'

'Happiness.'

'There's not a lot else, is there, once you've got the food and shelter cracked?'

'And do you think you can feel that within weeks of meeting someone? Do you believe in love at first sight?'

Weirdly I thought of Andrea then. She'd said she was going for a scan that morning and, since I was working so hard at the new business, there was no need for me to come if I couldn't make time. I thought of her on her own now, looking at some readout or being felt by some stranger. I wanted to be with her. What if there was something wrong? She'd be finding out alone. For the first time my emotions, rather than my thoughts, told me I had a responsibility to this baby. I felt a metaphorical kick inside me.

'It takes about a minute,' I said. I'd meant to say 'Yes, I'm sure it happens all the time', but there's a metaphor for life there: you start by trying to quote the Beatles and end up quoting Take That. Both incorrectly. The London Eye on the opposite bank was turning, though you could barely see it move.

Next to us a group of Japanese schoolchildren formed a solemn line behind their teacher. They were about nine or ten and looked very sweet in their dark blue uniforms, a vast improvement on the motley English vulgarians I'd seen earlier.

Cat nodded towards them. 'And what about other sorts of love – the sort between parent and child, that sort of love? Do you never feel you're missing out on that?'

Her chin was trembling and I wanted to go immediately and

shoot Henderson. He wouldn't even allow me to do things my own way. No, instead this dear, lovely, amazing girl had to be shattered by a complete stranger. I wondered what unpleasantries he'd used, what terms he'd employed to shock her. I really wanted to nut him.

'I sometimes feel like that. You know, maybe one day. Yes, I think I'd like it,' I said.

'Do you think you'd make a good father?' Big Ben, uncowed by traffic, began to chime midday.

I had the sudden idea that she knew Andrea was pregnant and wanted to stay with me anyway. That she was going to try to talk me out of my responsibilities as a father. No, that would have been too complicated, I thought, even I don't deserve that, even I will be let off with anger and dismissal, never to see her again.

'I'd like to try.' Another ring from the huge bell.

Now she actually was crying. I'd made my position clear, even though the details were left unsaid – by me anyway. I was staying with Andrea. All that remained for me to do was to say it, as Henderson had said it, I supposed, but more kindly.

The banks of the Thames are used to bearing goodbyes, I thought, one more won't hurt. Millions of sailors setting off, the eagles of Rome, the crest of Elizabeth, the red tunics of soldiers ready for the spears of Africa or the fury of the Turks. Millions of people to whom duty was unquestionably more important than personal wishes. How many men had stood with their lovers as I stood with mine, ready to sacrifice everything for the cause? I imagined myself going with them, into a limitless, unbounded future, or into the guns, the wife and child at the dockside waving against the chimes of the Empire's clock.

Two fat, checked tourists, American like someone had paid them to represent all the old world's prejudices, strolled up and leaned across the rail to take in the view of the river.

'That way for France,' I heard one of them shout above the ringing. He was gesturing back over the road towards Greenwich, the opposite way from Chelsea and Hammersmith, though the right way for the open sea. France was that way, sort of. I had been imagining the soldiers travelling into an unknown that was located in the wrong direction. I always imagined the sea at the wrong end of the Thames. To me the east and Essex were too unglamorous to be the gateway to adventure; the spires and sunlight of Oxford would have made a more appropriate avenue for the dreams of travellers.

'I found out . . .' she said, the end of her sentence lost beneath the traffic and the bell. She looked so beautiful against the dark water and the pale sky.

'I'm sorry,' I said. 'I'm sorry.'

She drew closer to my ear. She thought I was saying I hadn't heard her properly. When is this bloody clock going to stop? I thought, my stomach tight with the fear of parting.

'I found out that . . .' she shouted as the twelfth and final bell sounded '. . . I found out I'm pregnant!'

The American tourists burst into applause and I looked towards the sea, though this time the right way.

I might have finished with infidelity, I thought, but it hadn't finished with me.

6

Today, Gentlemen, The Bullshit Stops

'Not like you to be menacing the plasterwork,' said Henderson, discovering me attempting to clarify my thinking by repeatedly driving my head into the wall of the toilets at the Movotel, Croydon. It had been nearly a month since Cat had announced her pregnancy and mysterious dents were appearing on the walls of lavatories in Movotels the circumference of the M25.

'Think of it as stress management,' I said, feeling my forehead for signs of a lump.

'Funny you should say that,' said Henderson, 'I have in my hand a piece of paper that represents a solution to all our problems.'

'The General Motors contract?' I said, wide-eyed. I knew he'd written to them, but this was a bit swift.

'Not quite.' He passed it over. It was a government health promotion document entitled *I'm Here Too – A Guide for Expectant Fathers*.

'What's this, Henderson?'

'Take a look inside.'

I did. It was a leaflet saying how traditional views of the role of the parents in child rearing can leave the father feeling excluded from the pregnancy, birth and upbringing. In short, it said, fathers have to fight to be recognised as valuable contributors to the whole process.

'So what?'

'Well, it seems to me you *can* have the best of both worlds. You were saying you wanted freedom to continue to do as you pleased – ergo to come with me on our annual ski-ing trip around the time of the child's birth, to stalk the ancient mansions of Hell in search of a companion for yours truly. Well, this is possible.'

'I don't follow?'

'Look,' he took the leaflet, 'even the committed, caring, conscientious father has a tough enough time getting into his kid's life. Think of the scope available to the feckless shit. If you play your cards right, Andrea and her mum will take the whole thing over, you'll never have to do a stroke. It'll be like it's never happened!' He beamed. 'This is gold, mate, gold!' He waved it in the air like my mum does when shouting, 'House! House!'

I could see what he meant. My own dad had given responsibility for almost our entire upbringing to my mother. Cut knee? Mother's department. Doing badly at school? Mother's department. Instructions on how to shave? Mother's department. Obviously he'd been kind in his way when we'd been kids – turning a blind eye when we nicked his fags, trying to discourage us from wasting time in higher education, keeping us out of pubs at an early age. Well, the last one's not quite true – he kept us out of *his* pub, where else we went he didn't really care.

'It's not quite as straightforward as that, I'm afraid,' I said.

'Why not?' A major reason, of course, was that there was no way Andrea was going to stay at home suckling while I, a chartered libertine, buggered about with my mates in some post-adolescent hinterland.

I knew this because when I'd commented that it really wasn't worth my cancelling the ski-ing trip – particularly as it was only a cheap one in Bulgaria – she'd come out with a sentence that I distinctly recall beginning with the words: 'If you think I'm . . .' and finishing with 'post-adolescent hinterland'.

'Well, to be honest,' I said to Henderson, who was washing his hands and regarding me sideways out of his one blue eye, 'I don't know how I feel about the whole thing.'

I hadn't quite worked myself up to telling him about the second baby. He'd regarded one baby as letting the side down; two would be the equivalent of signing up for the other team and netting four past 'the side' before you got to the half-time oranges.

'And I want to be certain before I make a decision,' I said.

'You mean, you still haven't offed her?' He made a chopping move with his hand. He'd been quite annoyed when I'd told him that I hadn't finished with Cat that day on the bridge and had been on at me ever since to do the decent thing.

Apparently I'd had no need to worry about his spilling the beans to her. He hadn't said a word about Andrea. He'd just been in the area where Cat worked and had sought her advice on buying some fashion pants.

'But you don't even like her,' I'd said.

'She's all right,' said Henderson, 'and anyway, as you well know, liking has nothing to do with it. In my situation I have to cultivate as many gatekeepers as possible.'

'What do you mean, gatekeepers?'

'Young women with other young women for friends. They hold the key to salvation.'

He had a point. He'd met the Iron Julie through a friend, a rather plain girl called Alex who had thought he was interested in her. She'd rather short-circuited when he'd started seeing Julie.

'No, I haven't offed her,' I said.

'I know,' said Henderson.

'How do you know?'

'I had a chat with her the other day.' He sounded too casual, like a burglar's lookout reassuring a policeman he was just taking the air.

'What were you doing chatting to her?'

'I just pressed the wrong button on my mobile, that's all. People do it all the time.'

I couldn't help noting that 'People do it all the time', to continue the police analogy, is precisely the variety of statement often followed by the words: 'You ain't got nothing on me, copper. Prove it or let me walk.'

'And how long did you chat for?' I said.

'Forty-five minutes or so. Don't get your knickers in a twist.'

I felt my boxer shorts spiralling about me. I don't know why but I felt jealous. It wasn't that I didn't trust Cat or Henderson, it was just that I knew him well enough to anticipate that he might have a go at stepping in should I step out. You couldn't blame him, it was just instinct. He'd seen that she fancied older men, he knew she might be free. If she finished with me he would be as compellingly drawn to her emotional distress as a shark to the flailing of a stricken fish. At thirty-five, single and balding, his appetite for love made a Great White look like a bit of a picky eater.

'What did you talk about?' I asked quietly.

'The weather, fashions, neutrino physics, ice hockey.'

'It was me, wasn't it?' I said.

'Er, yes.'

'What did you say?'

'I prepared the ground for you.'

'What do you mean by that?'

'I raised the idea that you might not be as committed to the relationship as she is.'

'What did she say to that?'

'Nothing.'

'What do you mean, nothing?'

'She just cried a lot.'

'This is great,' I said. 'Thanks.'

'Only a joke,' said Henderson. 'We talked about what a great bloke you are and what you might want for Christmas.'

I didn't believe him. She clearly hadn't told him she was pregnant, though.

'Well, it might be a joke,' I said, 'but what I am going to want for Christmas, if not this one then next, is a double set of toddler clothes. I suggest you get knitting.'

Henderson assumed a look of concern. The last time I'd seen him look like that was when he'd been gazing out of a third-floor window and had seen his new Range Rover getting towed away.

'Andrea's having twins?'

'If only life were that simple. Cat's pregnant.'

I still to this day don't know why I told him. I think because he was teasing me about the phone call with her and I just wanted to get him back. For such trifles do worlds burn. Trifles as in insignificant things rather than yummy jelly puddings, of course.

'Nahh,' said Henderson, like one of the girls in *Grease* telling Sandy she can't believe they stopped at kissing. 'Cat, who I have been talking to on the phone not an hour ago, is pregnant?'

'You said that call was last week?'

'I called her again today. It's the mobile, it goes off in my bag. *She* is pregnant?'

'Yes.'

'By you?'

'I hope so.'

'Well, that's it, I can pack it all in now,' said Henderson.

'What do you mean?'

'There's no point in going on, my travails are at an end.' He held up his hand. 'I have heard the bleeding lot. There is no more for me to know. The world holds no further surprises for me.'

'What was today's call about then? And why hasn't she mentioned to me that you called?'

'My telephone conversations with the girl are neither here nor there,' said Henderson, 'although on your present showing I think it might be safer if any future conversations you have with women in the fertile age bracket were conducted that way. You are right in the shit, mate.'

'I just don't like the idea of Cat facing this on her own, you know. I do really really care for her. It's not just the financial thing, it's the emotional stuff too. She's got nowhere to turn. I wish she was having an affair.'

'You wouldn't be jealous?' said Henderson, his nose twitching like a rabbit's in front of a carrot patch.

'Yes, but, you know, I'm a big boy. I could live with it. If they were the right sort of bloke.'

'What's the right sort of bloke?'

'I don't know.'

'How do you imagine him?'

'Older, quiet sort, you know.'

'What does he wear?' said Henderson.

'Baggy jumpers, old cords, sandals. Pipe man, probably.'

'Not what you'd call a bedroom dynamo?'

'I couldn't think about that,' I said. 'I'd want her to love him but, you know, in a companionable way.'

'So basically you want her to start having an affair with her dad?'

'Yes, really.' Henderson was right. I wanted her to be looked after but not too well. I still wanted her to find herself inexplicably drawn to the window at three in the morning, to leave her man dozing in their bed and peer out through the garden snow, cursing the moon for the wild thoughts of me that it stirred inside her. I wanted her to find love, but the sort that wives feel for their war-hero husbands who have suffered the cruellest wound.

'Although there is one alternative we might consider,' said Henderson, pinching at the flesh of his belly to check for tautness.

'You wouldn't mind if . . .' He inserted a finger into the waistline of his trousers. 'Shit!' he said. 'I should be able to put two fingers in there. I've put on weight.'

'What was the alternative?'

He removed the finger and spread his hands wide in the classic salesman's 'I hear your objections but why don't you buy the bugger anyway?' pose.

'It might work out quite neatly if . . .'

'Yes?'

'Well, if she's going to be free and everything, and you want a chance to see your kid grow up, who better to take over the reins than your old mate me?' He gave what I recognised as his attempt at a winsome smile, followed by a light flick with his wrists to mime riding a horse.

'Let me think about it,' I said. 'Yes, I've thought about it. Touch her and I'll kill you, you bastard. Go near her, think of her, speak her name, and you will receive my card, a visit from my second and your choice of weapons. I shall demand satisfaction in blood on the hoar-frost. When I breathe it is only that I might live to hold her again, when I eat it is only to sustain myself so I might once more be in her presence. It is only that I might see her face that I care if the sun rises. Go near her and I will cut you down like a common cur. Yes, I think that about covers it.'

'I hear what you're saying,' said Henderson in salesman mode, i.e. not hearing what I was saying, 'and I respect it,' also meaning the reverse, 'but think of the advantages of the situation. I want a partner and a kid. You've got two partners and two kids. You can only have one of each. However, you'd like the others to be well looked after. That's where I step in. Tatatata!' He opened his arms wide like a music hall comedian coming on stage. 'It's logical.'

'You don't even like her!'

'The detail can come later, but don't you see, this is an opportunity for both of us? If you weren't just thinking of yourself. You get to be near Cat and your child, I get membership of the kiddie club, Andrea's none the wiser. We could end up taking holidays together and everything. You might even get the chance to give her one on the side occasionally.'

'That's beautiful,' I said, 'as visions of Hell go. And anyway, doesn't Cat get a say in all this?'

'I'm not saying it's guaranteed. All I want is for you to say it's OK for me to give it a punt.'

'You are not giving my girlfriend anything, least of all a "punt",' I said. 'She doesn't fancy you anyway, she told me.'

'She's actually told you she doesn't fancy me?'

'Her exact words,' I lied.

'Wow,' he licked his lips, 'then she *does* fancy me.'

'You're missing something here,' I said. 'I used the word "doesn't", very similar sound to "does", entirely the opposite meaning.'

Henderson shook his head like an old pro boxer seeing the new kid go through some needlessly flashy moves in the opposite corner. 'When a girl tells a bloke she doesn't fancy his mate it means that she does. Why bring it up otherwise? She just wants to make the bloke feel safe. If she genuinely doesn't fancy someone else she wouldn't bother mentioning it at all, or else she'd say that she did.'

'Why would she say that she did if she didn't?'

'To make him jealous, and she'd only want him jealous if she had no intention of getting off with anyone else. If she did fancy his mate she'd be mad to say so, she wouldn't want her boyfriend jealous so she'd say that she didn't. Simple.'

What was Cat's expression for the bending of words or the straining of logic? Oh, yes. 'Warp Factor Ten!' I said, accompanying it by the twist of the hands and squeaking noise I'd seen her do while reeling as the perversity of Henderson's thinking swept over me.

What would I have said if he'd wanted to go out with Andrea and not Cat? I thought. 'Dream on, she finds you physically repulsive, she's told me so.' She had, actually, on a number of occasions. Her exact words were that he was 'beyond the pint limit'. What she meant was that the number of beers you'd need to sleep with him were actually more than you could drink. You'd collapse before your inhibitions did.

Would I have felt like killing him if he'd wanted to take Andrea on, though? Not really. Maybe because I felt so secure with her, the idea seemed ludicrous. I'd have said something like, 'Well, just look after her, will you?' I wouldn't even have had to say that. Andrea can look after herself. In fact, given her predilection for 'assertiveness' (see rabid violence, *ibid*), I'd have been more likely to have warned Henderson to look after himself. I'd have felt sad, very sad indeed, but I don't think I'd have been asking him to make his choice between swords or pistols. Which is weird because in lots of ways I'm as close to Andrea as anyone could be.

'Cat fancies me, therefore I should be allowed to make an approach,' argued Henderson.

I was forced to reflect on how the modern mind equates wanting with having, no matter what the moral impediment.

I knew he was half joking but I was mildly exasperated. Henderson's inability to take situations seriously sometimes gets on my nerves. It's like he hasn't changed since we were twenty.

I wearily waved a hand. 'This is immaterial,' I said, 'you're not having her. I am. I've decided she's the one I want.'

I didn't realise until I heard myself say it that I was speaking the truth. I might care for Andrea, I might love her, but I wasn't capable of feeling jealous about her in the same way as I did about Cat. I'd decided without thinking which, authorities from Elvis Presley to Barry White concur, is the best way of doing it. Christ knows, with thinking hadn't brought me much joy.

'You're going to go with Cat? Great,' said Henderson, bright as a bunny. 'Now Andrea I *do* get on with.'

'You're not having either of them,' I said.

'I can't believe your selfishness.'

'What?' I said. 'Despite all the evidence?'

'You'll never go through with it anyway. What'll happen is that you'll go with the classical solution – dither and dither until the shit hits the fan and everyone ends up unhappy. You don't even know if this girl wants you to stay with her.'

That was a very good point, I had to concede. I had kind of assumed that Cat would want me to stay around, she certainly hadn't told me to go. Our conversations about the future had all revolved around whether she wanted to keep the baby – she did – getting her a bigger place so she could look after the kid, what she was going to do about work, all the immediate stuff. We hadn't got on to the long view.

'If I love her like I think I do, then she's worth taking the risk for.'

'Easy to say when Andrea's not standing in front of you with her bollock-kicking boots on,' said Henderson. 'And what about her? How's she going to cope?'

'She's older and she's tougher,' I said. 'Her work's her priority, not our relationship.'

'I don't think she sees it that way,' said Henderson, shaking his head.

'How do you know, have you been talking to her too?'

'I've had the odd chat.'

'About?' I was a bit miffed by this. I didn't really talk to Andrea, what was he doing yakking on to her?

'She loves you. Not in any earth-shaking way, not in the way they write songs about or even poems on bog walls for that matter, but she loves you.'

'You've been talking to my fiancée about love?'

'And your girlfriend,' said Henderson. 'Someone has to look after your interests, you don't seem to want to.'

I shook my head with grim determination and felt the razored hair prickle at the back of my head.

'Well,' I said, 'then I at least owe Andrea the truth.' I remembered my boardroom catchphrase: 'Today, gentlemen, the bullshit stops.' OK, I'd never actually said it but I used to think it before I went into meetings in a bid to make myself feel important.

'Best of luck,' said Henderson. 'What time precisely do you intend to do this?'

'I don't know, this evening,' I said. 'Why?'

'I just thought I might have an ambulance standing by because if you break her heart she'll sure as shite break your head.'

'Never mind,' I said, 'I'll take what comes, emotional or physical. Sometimes, for your own good, you need a heart of stone.'

7

Today, Gentlemen, The Bullshit Begins Again

'I've knitted it in white, it saves the confusion with pink or blue.'

I heard Andrea's mum's voice from the front room as I returned that evening.

I was hanging up my jacket in the hallway when I saw, on the pine pew we'd rescued from a very expensive shop on the Wandsworth Bridge Road, one of those that employ mainly Kosovans, a copy of *Can Do, Will Do: Aggressive Mothering* by Barbra Blufour, along with the wedding magazines we'd scoured for florists and caterers.

Andrea had developed a mania for reading this sort of stuff since her pregnancy.

The presence of Andrea's mum and dad – all the way down from Ipswich – would make things difficult but I couldn't use that as an excuse to chicken out. At least it would give her someone to lean on, I thought.

I wished I'd been more prepared for her parents being there. Typically, they'd parked the car a way down the road instead of in the drive. Andrea's dad had a thing about 'clear access' and would never let us park our own car in their drive, 'just in case', so I presumed he thought that if he left his in ours I'd be worrying about it for their entire stay.

I attempted to steel myself for what lay ahead by looking into the hall mirror and pointing at myself. 'You are a selfish bastard!' I said, not as a criticism but as a reminder.

Drained of all compassion I entered the living room, envisaging myself as Charles Bronson going in to confront the people who did *that* to his family.

I opened the door to see Andrea's mum holding up a tiny cardigan skilfully embroidered with a small yellow duck on the right breast.

'Oh, it's lovely,' said Andrea, cooing up to the garment. 'Isn't it lovely, Dag?'

'It certainly is,' I said, regarding the beautifully knitted woollen shackle.

I could be honest to Andrea, maybe, I could look her in the eye and say, 'I'm not the man you thought I was,' but could I be honest to this poor innocent cardigan? Would Charles Bronson have shot that cardigan? Could I say, 'I see your fluffy wool, the sort that I love to hold against my face, I know you are warm and comforting, but I'm going to have to let you in on some rather unsavoury truths, cardigan, old mate. Up in Stoke Newington I have been seeing a very comfortable and very new chemise.'

Heart of stone, I reminded myself.

'And the bootees!' said Andrea. 'Look at the bootees!' The last time I'd seen excitement like that my sister had just *known* there was a pet reindeer inside the really big Christmas present.

I looked at the bootees. They were certainly very sweet, as portents of disaster go.

'Hello, Dag,' said her mum as I bent to kiss her – the traditional method of betrayal. I don't like this kissing thing very much. I mean, I don't kiss my own mother, why do I have to kiss anyone else's?

'Hello, Dag.' It was her dad, attending to the parakeet in its cage which they brought with them whenever they travelled. He was removing the cover which had, for some old-person's reason, 'Bird's Cover' written on it. Doubtless I'd stop finding it strange within ten years or so. He did this a lot. We once went on a picnic. All the Tupperware had things like 'Tupperware A (light comestible)' written on it, and each piece of cutlery 'P'. This, apparently, meant 'Picnic' to distinguish it from the ordinary cutlery. I didn't see the need to distinguish it, as it was always kept in a store in the garage, but there you go. And they say a spell in the Army does a man good.

'Hello,' I replied to her dad. I noticed the telly was showing *Who Wants to Be a Millionaire?* Andrea's family were highly traditional and never sat down together unless the TV was on.

Her mum frowned as I acknowledged her dad. It was the family custom to ignore Andrea's dad and I was clearly breaking with tradition.

'I've bought this too,' said Andrea's mum, brandishing a photo album with 'Welcome to Our World – Simply Beautiful' written in Letraset on the cover. She passed it over. She'd already filled part of it in with pictures of me and Andrea from when we first met, family gatherings I'd attended, days out we'd had. I wondered if she'd bothered to supply a marker pen so they could scrub me out when I dropped the bombshell.

It seemed I couldn't escape symbols of our togetherness. On top of the television was a newly placed picture of me and Andrea that her mum had forced us to have taken on a velvet couch in a 'proper studio' a few years before. From the look of the gilt frame (see, I said gilt – sounds like guilt, I could have said gold-plated, I really could) I'd say her mother had brought that down with her too. Some words my mum used to say whenever someone had done something particularly bad came into my head: 'Turn his face to the wall, Mother, his picture shall hang on black string.'

Andrea was clasping the bootees to her bosom wearing a look that leading ladies in amateur dramatic versions of *The Sound of Music* adopt when they're watching the kids begin the do-re-me-ing.

My hand rose to smooth my feathered brow. I reminded myself of the importance of being honest. I recalled the difficulty

I'd had for the past two or three months skulking off to 'meetings up north' that always seemed to mean I had to stay overnight, having to 'see some people in Europe' at the weekends, telling Cat it was still 'much easier' for me to come to hers than her to come to me (true, while I had a car), saying, 'Would you believe it? I had a massive water leak rendering my place entirely unvisitable until the insurance people have been in, the damage assessed, the wood dried out, everything paid for. Well, you know how long that can take!' It was a good job that she'd showed little inclination to visit Hillingdon.

When I'd been younger the idea of going out with two girls at the same time had been incredibly exciting. Now it was nearly killing me, the strain of remembering all the lies becoming unbearable. So much so that deep in my briefcase was my treachery calendar. It was a thing I'd got from an RSPCA shop. It had a picture of a kitten for every month and a space where you could record what had gone on each day, as long as you limited yourself to twenty-five words or less and completed this sentence in case of a tie break: 'Stewart Dagman deserves to be horsewhipped because . . .'

I'd drawn up a list of all the lies I'd told the various women, and split each day into two – where I'd told Cat I'd been and where I'd told Andrea. The psychologists would tell us that such a device is baying for trouble, should either woman discover it. They would note that perhaps I subconsciously wanted to be discovered. This, after all, is what they're paid to note. Just like when they're asked to provide a profile of the serial killer and he's always a loner, a white male, in a manual job, has difficult (to say the very least) relationships with women and a subscription to *Guns 'n' Ammo*. Rarely – if ever – is he a gregarious, retirement-age black broadcaster, a family man with a loving wife and a line in easy, relaxed wit. But what the psychologists would miss, in my case, is that I had hidden the calendar very well indeed in my briefcase and curled it up inside *Brrm! Brrm! Brrmm!*, a car magazine for the more discerning motorist I'd picked up on a genuine trip to the north.

I looked at Andrea. She seemed to be hovering feverishly

between the baby clothes and some wedding-chauffeur brochures. It occurred to me that, since the pregnancy, I didn't really know her.

The Andrea I'd known would have thrown up at half the stuff she was ordering for our wedding: the flouncy bridesmaids' costumes, the flowers, a horse-drawn carriage, for God's sake. What had happened to simplicity and style ideology, the formal, slightly severe 1920s look she'd originally chosen? Not that I was complaining. I like horses. A strange thought entered my head.

'I can't disappoint the horse.' After all he might have set his equine heart on that ride.

I put it from my mind and concentrated on exactly how I was going to tell her about Cat as I watched her mum hand over another garment. It was a small jumper in fine wool.

'And this was Andrea's,' she said, 'I kept it for her child.'

I held up the garment. It was a beautiful pale yellow, perhaps it had once been white, made from a delicate, soft wool. Holding it to my face conjured up exactly the feeling of security I got when I clambered in next to Andrea at night.

'It's lovely,' I said, 'really lovely.'

'You should remember to keep it so you can pass it on when you're in our position,' said Andrea's mum.

Now there's a thought, I thought.

I say it was Andrea's mum who was juggling the baby accoutrements, and it was, although at a squint it could have been her dad, there was so little difference between them nowadays. In their old age they seemed to be becoming the same person. Her mother had always been thin, sharp angles of elbow and knee poking through her checked skirts and frilly blouses, but with a ginger to her movements that, in a younger woman, might have suggested some considerable facility for the martial arts. There was a constant 'new broom' quality to her that wanted decks cleared, surfaces sparkled and plates washed, preferably just before you finished eating off them.

'Right,' she would say, as we lounged yearly in the soft Christmas light of the suburban living room, snapping us from a reverie of sherry, tangerines, glitter and TV repeats, 'I want action.' She'd then appoint each of us the task of clearing up some imperceptible mess or deciding the whole night's television watching at one go or going to fetch something from the petrol garage – the only place still open.

If Mrs Ellis wanted action, she was looking in the wrong place with Mr Ellis. He wasn't lazy, far from it, it's just that he was by nature a weigher and balancer of possibilities and probabilities. Andrea always said his motto was, 'We don't see opportunities, we see problems.' He never wanted to set out on a route before it had been proved beyond all reasonable doubt that it was the best possible one and, since no one is ever certain of that, he would never have set out on anything at all without his wife's size four up his backside.

As it was, there are National Trust walking trails which are troubled by fewer footprints than his arse. He has been kicked out on to many routes, often simultaneously, much against his better judgment. Being by nature a 'one thing at a time' man, someone who thinks not of the peaks until he has breasted the foothills, this has caused all manner of dithering. And if there's one thing Andrea's mum can't stand it's a ditherer.

I don't want to make out that Andrea's dad was in some sort of subservient position here, far from it. His general strategy, when confronted with some sort of 'plan' by his wife, was to raise objections to any course of action whatsoever. Cruise to Acapulco? Think of the cost. Redecorate the house? Are you sure the new wallpaper will look nicer than the old? New furniture? You call it old, I call it comfortable. Cup of tea? Have you any idea how many people are killed each year performing mundane household tasks?

Of course, he would give in on most of these things but, should anything go wrong, he would be ready to strike, as the wolf upon the fold. 'Of course, had it been left to me . . .' he would fang in, as it turned out that with the repayments on the sofa, cruise and wallpaper combined they were struggling to pay the gas bill, seriously threatening their ability to make a cup of tea at all, let alone die in the process. Of course, it hadn't been left to him, it had been left to both of them, but he never quite saw that.

It seemed to me, whenever I'd been round there, that the only thing the Ellises ever exchanged was anxiety.

Despite the differences between them they were melding into one person. Looking at them, it would be easy to say that he had been subsumed by her personality; certainly he was thinning down in old age although he said he'd been on a diet, and his former, plodding, thoughtful style had become more urgent. Like his wife, he now always had to be doing something, tidying, gardening, reading, as opposed to how I'd seen him before, smoking his small cigars and making a port last for an evening. He used to have the air of a man on the verge of uttering some great profundity, without, of course, ever uttering the profundity, sometimes without ever uttering anything. Now he did nothing but utter, the whole time, he seemed to talk about anything. The ruminative quality had left him and he too wanted action. Already that summer they had been on three weekends away and, remarkably, were planning a mini cruise – to Bilbao.

For her part, Mrs Ellis seemed to have mastered the art of sitting still occasionally, of just being. The last time we'd visited them I noticed that not one piece of DIY, that I could see, had been done since I had been to their house at Christmas – nearly seven months before. She had not made him do anything.

The Ellises had come to an understanding, despite their differences, but it had taken them so long. If Andrea and I could achieve this it would make having a child almost fun. We'd still have all the problems about fitting it in with our lifestyles but that might be an interesting change. It seemed so very hard though.

'What do you think it'll be, Dag, a boy or a girl?' Andrea's mum said now. Henderson had already made up his mind on this subject, of course. He'd entered a 'Lee Dagman' for the Get Rid! Soccer Skills school already, hoping he had a future England star on his hands. He had asked if we'd had a scan and Andrea had told him the hospital wouldn't reveal if it was a boy or a girl because some cultures have female children terminated.

'So because of the behaviour of a few idiots, we have to wait?' said Henderson.

'You have to respect other people's cultures,' said Andrea.

'Even if they're a load of bollocks?'

'Especially if they're a load of bollocks,' said Andrea. She certainly had this PC thing down to a tee.

Mr Ellis had begun to burble. 'Happy and healthy, that's all we want.' He was half in our conversation, half in one of his own. Once he had begun talking more he had realised a truth that strikes many men of his age – that, as they listen to no one, no one listens to them. He had embarked upon a defensive strategy of addressing a good portion of his comments to himself. Pride, however, made him go through the motions of saying things out loud.

'We'd like a girl, on balance, wouldn't we, Dag?' said Andrea.

I noticed she'd been nest building. The whole house was spotless and she'd shoved my 1930s, a little bit too knowing to be really modernist, Arnco bendy lamp half behind the curtains. I bet she'd have that down the bottom of the garden by the time the baby arrived. If, of course, I was still here myself.

'Yeah, a girl, or a boy, or anything really,' I said. I was thinking of Cat. I'd told her I had a weekend's residential so I couldn't see her.

'You said you'd like a girl,' said Andrea.

'A girl would be good,' I agreed.

'Why a girl?' said Andrea's dad on a note of concern.

'I'd love a girl,' said Andrea.

'Why a girl, though?' said her dad.

'Only six months and we'll know, I don't think we'll bother finding out before,' said Andrea, rubbing her tummy. She'd asked me to do that on a couple of occasions and I'd smiled and done it. I didn't want to, though. Say you felt an arm or something. I don't have to spell out the implications for your continuing sex life.

'Why a girl?' said her dad, with the measured patience of a man used to repeating himself.

'I don't know how I'll resist looking at the ultrasound,' chirruped Andrea.

'It's better if it's a surprise,' said her mum.

'Why not have a boy?' said Andrea's dad, his voice betraying no more irritation with repetition than does the speaking clock.

'Did you have any preference about what you wanted when I was born?'

'Just happy and healthy,' said her mum. 'Why do you particularly want a girl?'

'I feel it's . . .' said Andrea as I said, 'Well, it's . . .'

'After you,' we both said.

'Dag thinks there's a whole lot of rubbish you're expected to pass on to boys and he doesn't feel very comfortable with it.'

'What do you mean?' said her father. There was a long pause.

'What do you mean?' said her mother.

'Oh, you know, be the hardest in the infants, hit them before they hit you, this is the football team you have to support, lessons in not standing out or drawing attention to yourself among other boys, lessons in standing out and drawing attention to yourself with girls, why it's time to throw away your teddy bear and develop your interest in violent video games, never admit to liking anything complex too much . . . that sort of stuff.'

'Sounds like we should all hope it's a girl,' said Andrea's dad.

There was another long pause, during which I think he went into the kitchen and hanged himself. No, come to mention it, he didn't because I remember that at about 10.30 that night Andrea's mum made him go out to the petrol garage to get some film for her camera. 'Get it now and then we don't have to spend all tomorrow worrying about it,' she'd said. He didn't hang himself at all. In fact, I know what he did because I went in there to make tea ten minutes afterwards and found him organising us a string and twine drawer.

'Well,' said Andrea's mum with the amazed disgust of a woman whose scratchcard has failed to yield a prize, 'we should all hope it's a girl if that's what you're going to teach it.'

'It seems only fair to socialise it properly,' I said.

Andrea's mum laughed, though if Andrea had said that she would have affected disgust. Lots of people are irony bypass zones when it comes to their kids.

'Why do you have to be so unpleasant?' she would have said, instead.

However, while Andrea was incapable of watching the St Irrelevant's school choir going through 'Away in a Manger' without making vomiting noises when she watched it on the TV with her own mother, she could manage a fair few 'aahs', 'ooohs' and 'sweeeeets' when she watched it with mine. It was the same with me really. I cut her mum all sorts of slack I was unwilling to cut my own.

Andrea, of course, goaded her mother terribly. She didn't want to, she wanted the kind of close relationship mothers and daughters are meant to have, the sort that begins as close and just gets closer and closer until one day on some terrible ward, the mother surrenders her physical existence entirely but lives on as vibrantly as before inside the daughter's mind. It's a kind of birth in reverse.

The problem was they were a bit too similar. They were both intensely ambitious and hungry for success, but Andrea's mum didn't think her daughter was quite ambitious enough. She detected a niff of the father's trepidation within her daughter and concluded that it needed a fair dose of moral air freshener.

'So, when are you going to know about this Senegalese project?' Mrs Ellis would ask.

'I don't really want to talk about it, Mum,' would say Andrea, a surprise to me since the only subject that had been allowed in our home for the past eight weeks was Andrea's application for the Senegalese project.

'Well, maybe you *should* talk about it. You're not just going to breeze into the interview and make it up on the spot, I hope.'

At which point Andrea explodes and investigators find pieces of us all up to a mile and a half away.

Although they're working class like my own parents, they have attitudes that were shaped by the 1960s – not the horrible '60s of hippies and complaint, incense and tarot cards that scarred my mother's psychic landscape, but the bright early '60s of possibilities and new kitchen appliances. They are open to new experiences and ideas, willing to be educated and to educate, even, occasionally, to swearing in front of their children.

'Who's a pretty boy then?' said Andrea's dad to the parakeet. It ignored him.

I made a cup of tea and we sat with it in front of *Who Wants to Be a Millionaire?* 'I only watch this because I can't believe how stupid the contestants are,' said Mrs Ellis, who clearly loved the programme. We are our entertainment, though she didn't want to be seen as hers.

We watched for a few minutes before someone, twitching with greed, failed on the £250,000 question.

'There'll be a lot more of this for you in future,' said Andrea's dad, who had obviously finished arranging the twine to standards of military precision. I didn't know what he meant. A lot more money . . . a lot more what?

'You won't have time for TV, you'll be too busy with bottles and nappies,' said her mum. 'Are you going to decorate a room for it now, or are you going to wait to find out if it's a boy or a girl?'

'Are we sure we want it, really?' I said without thinking.

'There's nothing on the other side,' said Andrea's dad, and everyone for a change heard him.

Christ, I thought, I'd made a bit of a Freudian slip there. Had I really wanted Andrea to get rid of the baby? Amazingly I hadn't even considered it. Ten years before it would have been my first thought.

'Names,' said her mum, 'what names have you thought of?'

'Florence,' said Andrea.

Once again, the magnetic attachment of hand to brow. Not little Florence, not little floral Florence the flouncy bouncy toddler who loved bunny rabbits and who my id or my ego or something within me wanted thrown out with the clinical waste?

'Bit old-fashioned, isn't it?' said Andrea's mum. This from a woman who had looked down into a crib at a starry, spangle-eyed bundle of hope and said, 'I name thee Andrea.' Andrea! A name like wet toilet paper.

'Old-fashioned is the latest thing,' said Andrea.

'If it's a boy,' said her mother, 'I like Zak.'

Great idea, I thought, call it Zak. As soon as it realised what its name was it'd throw itself under a bus.

'Mother,' said Andrea, 'it will not be called Zak. We're not third-rate pop stars. If it's a boy it'll be called George.'

'Not Boy George,' said her dad, who clearly hadn't been listening. No one else seemed to hear him.

'We did get a list of our favourites off your father's web page,' said her mum.

'Internet,' he said.

She pulled a printout from her handbag. I wondered if there was a program you could get to stop people looking up sites they had no right to be in.

'Leon Alfonso, how about that?'

I bit into a Nietzsche Whirl – a special edition, the God-shaped hole wasn't its normal question mark but a cross. They did Stars of David and sickle moons as well.

'Or Hunter Lee. Pete and I like Hunter Lee, don't we, Pete?'

Andrea's dad nodded vigorously.

'Ooh, no,' said Andrea.

'Evan Joseph? Tyrell Jacantha?' said her mum, reading down the list.

'This wasn't an American internet site, was it?' asked Andrea.

'I don't know,' said her mum.

'I think Florence or George would be fine,' I said.

'And have it called Flo!' goggled her mother.

'I like Flo,' I said.

'Ooh, you *are* old-fashioned,' said Mrs Ellis. 'Why not give it an inventive name? You know, after someone you like or something. What's that band you're mad on? Spandau Ballet. You could call it Spandau.' I shouldn't have been surprised at this suggestion. Mrs Ellis was into amateur dramatics and there had always been a faint whiff of the greasepaint about her. When footballers and other lower-class people give their children names like Manhattan, she says, 'Well, I think it's nice and different,' as opposed to the rest of us who take the opportunity to look down on them in a very condescending way, even though we wouldn't mind their looks/ability/money.

Andrea had not been mad on Spandau Ballet since she was sixteen, but her mother had not grasped the idea that her tastes had progressed. Every Christmas we have to put up with a Spandau Ballet poster, or key ring, or mug. I don't know where she gets them from. Even Spandau Ballet probably don't have those things any more. Still, it's the thought that counts, isn't it? Well, yes, but surely only if it's the right kind of thought. As Andrea had pointed out.

'Or Ballet,' I said, referring to the child's name.

'That's quite classy, isn't it?' said her mum. 'Ballet Dagman. Spandau Dagman. It'd stand out.'

'People who have children called "Ballet" or "Chanel" are also the kind of people who call their dogs "Armani" or "Tyson" and have regular visits from Social Services,' said Andrea.

'I like Armani for a dog,' said Andrea's mum. The bird had been lucky to get away with 'Percy'.

The frightening thing was, she was being serious. I didn't bother pointing out that the aim of a name is to blend in, not to stand out. It's the person who should impress, not what they are called. Having an unusual name is the equivalent of wearing a wacky tie. The one time I have worn such a tie (psychedelic Father Christmases, purchased by secretary) I felt a terrible responsibility to live it down. It was as if I was trying to say, 'I might have a weird tie, but I'm OK really, I'm not an idiot or a junior doctor.' An unusual name does the same thing, you're always having to get round it before you can get on with being you.

'Who's a pretty boy then?' said Andrea's mum to the bird.

'Who's a pretty boy then?' said the bird.

'What makes you think it'd be called Dagman?' said Andrea, wresting her mother's attention back from the bird. She wouldn't take my name when we got married, which I'd agreed with, though clearly this idea was feminism run riot. 'It wouldn't automatically take Dag's name.'

There was an uneasy silence, like that following a fart at a funeral.

'What else would it be called?' said her dad.

The silence deepened to one normally associated with moments of great national mourning.

'What else would it be called?' I said.

The silence deepened further to the kind of silence that exists for the split second before the guns start firing.

'What else would it be called?' her mother fired back.

'Ellis,' said Andrea. 'Our name.'

'No, no, no, no, no,' said her dad, like a foreman watching his favourite apprentice bolt something on the wrong way.

'Why not?' said Andrea. 'Ellis is a nicer name than Dagman.'

'Nice has nothing to do with it,' said her mother, firmly. 'It's just the way things have to be.'

'Why?' said Andrea.

'I don't make the rules,' said her mother, as if telling her she wasn't going out dressed like that.

This was very similar to my argument with her about the lounge. I'd said it was called a lounge, she'd said it was called a sitting room.

'Well, things are just what you call them, there's nothing that makes this more of a lounge than a sitting room. If everyone calls it a crocodile, it's a crocodile,' I'd argued.

'No, it isn't,' said her mum, 'it's meant to be called a sitting room.'

'By who?'

'God,' said her mum, 'the source of all authority.'

So there you have it, God says sitting room. If you want to know any of his other opinions, ask Audrey Ellis.

'How do you feel about this, Dag?' she said.

'Best wait and see.' There was no easy sentence to cover my true emotions so I hit the platitude button.

'Wait and see what? If it comes out with a name tag on the back of its duffel coat?' said Andrea's dad. This made me laugh, at which Andrea and her mother scowled. I got the feeling they didn't want him treated like a human being, in case he got used to it and started taking liberties. 'We'll see how we feel at the time,' I said.

'No, the baby needs to know now,' said Andrea's mum, 'it's got to be certain of its identity. They can hear you in the womb, you know.'

For the third time my hand rose to straighten the runkled fur of my brow. I hoped it wasn't going to hear me announce my treachery to its mother.

Who Wants to Be a Millionaire? had finished and the news was on. It had been a slack day for pain in the world and the news crews had clearly been scrabbling about for unpleasantness to entertain us. There was something about how being brought up in one-parent families affects children's health.

'Can we turn this off? It's depressing me,' said Andrea. 'I can't even think about that with the baby inside me.' She felt her tummy. 'Feel, Mum, I think it's moving!'

'Not at this stage, dear,' said her mum, beaming indulgently.

'Quite,' I said, flipping over to *Family Fortunes*. We watched in respectful silence as the bovine Joneses took on the asinine Smiths. For all that I didn't like them, you could see there was a bond of togetherness in each family. It showed on their faces. They genuinely loved each other, hoped each other's hopes, dreamed each other's dreams, lived the ebb and flow of modern life together, felt elated when each other's scratchcards yielded cash, deflated when they didn't. It was a bit scary really.

'You'll be able to enter for this soon,' said Andrea's dad. Neither of the women paid him any attention, although I had had enough.

'Andrea,' I said, 'can I have a word in private?' Now or never, I thought. I'd already got the number of Henderson's B&B in my pocket, should I need a place to stay.

A scene came into my mind. It was our wedding day. Andrea was patting the horse in front of my carriage. In my pocket I could feel the dead weight of a large calibre revolver.

I was stepping forward, putting the revolver to the horse's head.

'I'm just going to show Mum the wedding dress pictures, can we do it after that?'

I was about to say 'No, we'd better do it now' when her dad interrupted me.

'Actually, this might be a good time,' he said. 'I need a few words on my own with you, Dag.'

He turned to the women. 'Can you give us an hour? This might take a while. Man to man talk.'

I didn't like the sound of that.

'As long as you like,' said Mrs Ellis, with no curiosity. I think she'd given up thinking he could have anything *that* meaningful to say years before. As it happened, she was wrong.

8

Finishing It

'Cup of tea?' I asked Andrea's dad as he casually wedged a chair back under the door handle to prevent it from opening.

He gestured at the half-full mug he had on the table. I'd finished mine so I put the kettle on for myself and took the chance to inspect the biscuit tin. Empty. I had looked that morning and been sure I had a few Berkeley Rocknuts left, but no sooner had I turned my back than they were gone. I was starving.

'So, a man to man chat,' I said. 'Sounds ominous.' The man to man chat is normally the sort where an older man who thinks he knows it all tries to point out to a younger man who thinks he knows it all that he doesn't know it all. I didn't relish a 'benefit of my wisdom upon becoming a father' scenario like out of some schmaltzy film.

'It is ominous.' He was very serious. 'Andrea,' he said in a slightly louder than usual voice. 'Andrea.'

'She won't hear you with the telly on,' I said.

'That's what I was testing.'

I stopped stirring the tea bags in the pot and gave him my attention, still aware of a dull biscuit craving in the pit of my stomach.

Mr Ellis sniffed and drummed his fingers on the table. Fish fingers, I thought. I hadn't had those in years. Filet o' Fish.

'I'm going to tell you something now that you must tell no one. If it ever gets out, I'll kill you.' It flashed into my mind, I don't know why, that I have never liked Filet o' Fish since I ate three once when drunk, and I felt guilty for drifting off the subject in hand. Not that I yet knew what the subject was, other than him threatening to kill me. Even that brought me back to McDonald's. I'm from Portsmouth – a navy town. Visiting fast food establishments in my youth after the pubs had shut was what could be described as 'character forming' – particularly when the marines were in town.

'Can you keep a secret?'

This is a bit of a stupid question, to my mind. If you're the sort that likes spreading juicy gossip you're most unlikely to say 'no'.

I should have told him not to trust me. I keep secrets like old ladies keep pewter – strictly for display. I can see now why people often entrust their most carefully guarded thoughts not to those closest to them but to strangers. The information that could burn a loved one may only singe a stranger. This is the role of the counsellor, or the shrink, sometimes even the priest. I wasn't a stranger to Andrea's dad, but I was the nearest person far enough away from him to make him feel comfortable talking about his feelings. I knew he didn't really like me, but in a complicated way. He didn't think I was a complete idiot or that I was nasty to his daughter, there was just something unpleasant about me that he couldn't put his finger on.

'It's about the baby. I may not live to see it born,' he said, and pursed his lips as if he'd already said too much and was straining to keep anything more revealing in. I breathed out, suddenly feeling very guilty for the scant attention I'd been paying him.

He seemed sadly out of place in the kitchen, as if the aluminium of the cooker, the bareness of the walls, the wired glass of the cupboards had all been designed to offend him, as if Andrea and I had said, 'Look at these fine modern units, your units of floral pattern and your life mean nothing.' I knew that he would say we should have our own choice in design, but the fact that he'd told me such a personal thing in an environment I knew he hated and didn't understand made the rejection seem all the more emphatic. The kitchen seemed suddenly in want of a cream plate with a picture of a fern on it, to make him comfortable. At least there was the incongruous pine table we were sitting at, I thought. I should never have let Andrea talk me into that.

'Oh, dear,' I said, which was one of the things the counsellor always recommended me to say, but in this case was genuinely heartfelt.

'It looks like I have a very bad illness, the worst sort.' I didn't say anything, just kept looking at him. He looked back.

'Cancer?' I offered, after a while.

'No. Well, yes. Of a sort.'

He obviously wasn't going to be very forthcoming in this department and I didn't want to go for the twenty questions 'Guess my Nemesis' game so I just resorted to staring into space or, more precisely, at the clock. Nine o'clock.

'Andrea doesn't know and neither does her mother. If it's what they think it is then my chances aren't good at all.' He put his hand to his head. 'It's quite a strain.' I could see him struggling with his fear.

I have on my desk in my office a very handy stress manager. It's a small sign saying: WE ARE ALL GOING TO DIE. The idea that whatever you say and do ultimately counts for nothing is very calming to me. Somehow, though, it didn't seem much of a relief if you actually *were* going to die. I'm comfortable with ideas, it's reality I don't like.

I nodded as Mr Ellis bent his head into his hands. I remember thinking, bizarrely, that his posture wouldn't be doing his state of mind any good and he should sit up straight. These errant thoughts don't mean I felt no sympathy for him, far from it, they just mean that I had inappropriate thoughts, which I often did. The one thing I remember from when my very first girlfriend – a vegetarian – split up from me, her face livid as a slapped arse as we stood mute outside McDonald's, was 'I wonder if those chips she's eating were fried in animal fat.' There we go, McDonald's again.

But I felt for Andrea's dad, even though I didn't know him, even though she didn't know him really. It can't be easy to confront the certainty of death in a cold kitchen with a relation who's little more than an idea to you.

'But you have a chance?' I said.

'Yes,' he said. 'There is a treatment, but it's so long and so painful and the chances of success aren't good, I don't know if I can face it. I have to, though, for Andrea's sake and for Audrey's.'

'You haven't started treatment yet?'

'I'm sixty-five, there's a waiting list.' I recalled that the recommended treatment in the NHS for anyone over the age of sixty is the words, 'Well, you've had a good innings.'

'Why don't you go private?'

'I'd have to sell the house to pay for it and then there's no guarantee it would work.'

'Sell it then.'

'I'm not leaving Audrey in some hovel. And I want something to pass on.' He sadly nodded his head towards me. 'Look,' he said, 'it's what killed my dad. I know what it is, and . . . I'm afraid of the consequences.' This admission of fear was obviously a very difficult thing for him, he couldn't even look at me, just waggled at the table, which was slightly uneven.

I'd never seen him like this before. I'd only done the three times a year handshake with him, the careful conversation about sport – he liked golf, so we could talk about that, even if I did feel it was an extension of my working life. But the heart-to-heart thing was different. It curiously reminded me of having sex for the first time. You'd talked about it and mythologised it for so long beforehand but when it happened it was still nothing like you expected.

Reality defeats all imagining. I couldn't advise him here. There is no course for personal effectiveness for the terminally ill, for maximising your potential when you have no potential. Nowadays, I thought, of course McDonald's do a full blown vegetarian option, including Indian meals. I couldn't believe I was thinking that.

'I'm sorry,' I said. Inadequate, but true.

Andrea's granddad, I knew, had died of some sort of bowel cancer. For the first time the reality hit me and I looked at this sad, scared, maybe dying man – pale and bald and wanting help but knowing none could come.

'This thing's knackered,' he said.

'Sorry?'

'Your table's been chucked together by a cowboy. It's not even, look.' He rattled it from side to side to demonstrate the uneven legs.

'It's original French, eighteenth-century,' I said.

'It's original knackered.'

Don't say 'like me', I thought, just don't say 'like me'. I didn't want him sounding like a bad BBC drama. It's not that bad BBC dramas don't pick up on the way people speak, it's that they do and it's depressing to think that people are capable of saying such trite things.

'You'll need to have those legs out and glue some support in there. How much did this piece of old tat cost?'

'Oh, £200.' It had cost £850.

'You were robbed. You can get something just like this at B&Q for about £75.'

'You were,' I was going to say dying, 'talking about your illness?'

'Yes,' he said, still rattling at the underside of the table. 'It says on the internet one in twenty remission after five years. Not much of a chance.'

'No, but it *is* a chance. I don't see how they can put a figure on these things anyway. It might only be five per cent, but if you're in that five per cent then it's one hundred per cent for you and you'd be mad not to try.'

'Got the bugger,' said Andrea's dad, pulling out a thick wodge of newspaper that had obviously been stopping one of the legs from rattling. 'There you are. French eighteenth-century *Daily Star*. You want to take that bugger back.'

I had always assumed that Andrea's dad had been whipped into doing constant DIY by his wife, but here he was doing it under his own steam. Perhaps that's what a lifetime of training does. Or perhaps he enjoyed it but also pretended not to enjoy it.

He tossed the newspaper on to the table. 'I suppose I haven't taken enough risks in my life,' he said. 'Not like you.'

'I haven't taken any risks,' I said. I had a funny feeling I wasn't going to be breaking that proud record that evening either. Walking out of the kitchen, heavy with the news of her father's illness, to admit my treachery to Andrea wasn't something I really relished. I didn't know how I could ever come clean with her, given her dad's condition. In the game of trumps, Cat vs Andrea, they had been neck and neck. Andrea had whipped out a dying father, though, and it didn't look like Cat had any sort of reply.

Really it should have made no difference, but it did.

'The business, that's a risk, walking out on a steady job.'

'I could always walk back into one.'

He nodded. 'Things are different nowadays, I suppose.'

'They are.' I had a powerful need to say something to comfort him.

'You'll be OK,' I said, placing my hand on his shoulder to reassure him.

He looked at my hand as if it were that of death itself.

'Please, no,' he said.

'I'm sorry,' I said, removing the offending member.

'No, don't be. It's just it's difficult enough to talk about these things at the best of times without that.'

'Yes,' I said. It seemed that he was having enough of a problem dealing with feely without going for touchy as well.

'Is there anything you want me to do? When are you going to let the family know?' I said the F word. I'd never really seen myself as part of a family before, even though technically I was. I realised that whatever I thought, whatever fantasy of freedom I had had, was irrelevant. I'd been part of Andrea's life for years, sharing the good times and the bad. The fact that I hadn't married her was irrelevant, I was hers for better or worse. Love was irrelevant, there was something more – what I owed her after eight years. Duty, I suppose. She needed me, Cat needed me, but Cat's claim was not as strong, I wasn't embroiled in her life in the same way. I'd look after Cat as best I could financially and I'd still love her but I knew, looking at the grey face of Mr Ellis, that I had deeper responsibilities to Andrea.

'I don't want them to know until they absolutely have to, it's more than Audrey could bear,' he said.

I remembered Andrea's mother's face when we'd last been up to their house. She'd been quieted, not listening to him but letting him speak. The mini cruise to Bilbao, the lack of push towards home improvement, the weekends away. She knew. You don't live with someone for forty years and not know things like that, even if you've never allowed them a word in edgeways in that time. Mind you, what did I know about how they were when we weren't there? People present themselves differently when they've got guests. She might have been the model of attentiveness at all other times.

'Not wanting to be morbid, Mr Ellis, but is there anything you'd like to put straight before you die?'

For a minute I think he thought I was talking about the table, asking him if he'd mind finishing a bit of DIY before a one way trip in the Boat of Millions of Years (copyright ancient Egypt and encyclopaedia CD ROM which I had been browsing on my lap top).

'Like what?'

'Is there anything you'd like to say to anyone or get off your chest?'

'I've written letters,' he said.

I wondered what they'd say, whether they'd be like all those notes that Henderson's dad used to leave about the place. He'd spent years ignoring his family and doing what he wanted. In his old age he had the cheek to be surprised that no one loved him. 'Nose bleed yesterday, four hours. Think my number's up this time. No one cares. So lonely,' the notes would say. I remember the acute embarrassment of having Henderson hold them up to ridicule in front of me.

'All he would have had to say was sorry rather than leaving stupid notes,' said Henderson. In fact that's not true, but it would have been a start.

In many ways Mr Ellis had been the model father. Other than never speaking to his wife or daughter – an oversight anyone could make – he had very little to reproach himself for.

'You're . . .' I was going to say he'd been a good father, but I thought it best left unsaid. That kind of openness is for another generation of men, probably the one after mine.

'Just look after them, you know. They're my girls.' Tears appeared in his eyes and he bent beneath the table with the wodge of paper to try to stuff it back in between the leg and the thing next to it.

'Don't worry,' I said. 'Don't worry about that.'

There was no way out. At some point in your life God says to you, 'Thought you were a selfish bastard? Well, try this.' I had failed the test. Something in me wasn't quite selfish enough. I thought I should have felt glad, but a truly selfless person wouldn't have experienced the levels of disquiet that were burning inside me. I was going to do what was right, or less wrong, but I found that no consolation whatsoever.

I was going to have to sacrifice Cat.

9

Lesbian Action

Funnily enough Cat wasn't able to see me for the week after Andrea's dad had announced his illness. She was off covering a conference in Frankfurt.

'Why Frankfurt?' I'd asked.

'For the conference, or is that some sort of wider, philosophical question?'

I could see what she meant. When people have cracked the 'What is the meaning of life?' problem they'll move up to the big one: 'Why Frankfurt?' Once we know the answer to that I'm sure we'll have an insight into the whole human condition.

I was a bit relieved. It enabled me to take my time over telling her. Of course there was the problem that she'd want to tell Andrea just what a bastard I'd been but it was a risk I'd have to take. I did think of telling her that Andrea already knew, but I decided only to lie further if I really had to and only for the noblest of reasons – i.e. to save my skin.

Actually I'd come to know Cat as very kind hearted. Once I filled her in on the doomed Mr Ellis I doubted she'd want to upset Andrea any further. She wouldn't blame her for all this, she'd blame me. However, there was the nagging doubt that

Cat wouldn't just say 'go and never darken my duvet again'. What if she wanted me to stay? Well, like General Patton, I'd have to blow up that bridge when I came to it.

She certainly seemed to have changed her attitude to the pregnancy since the tears on Westminster Bridge. Then she wasn't sure she wanted the baby – after all she'd only known me a few months. An abortion, though, was not on the cards. She'd found out she was pregnant at about four months when she'd been to the doctor because she'd missed several periods. She said it had never occurred to her that she could be pregnant because she was on the pill. That gave her eight weeks, more or less, if she wanted to terminate her pregnancy, but she didn't know if she could go through with it, particularly, as it turned out, because she'd already had one, when she was sixteen.

'What happened?' I'd asked.

'It was just one of those things, you know those parties you have when you're that age where everyone just gets off with everyone.'

No, I didn't, although I'd spent most of my adolescence trying to get invited to one.

'It was just a quickie – the first time I'd done it. I didn't think you could get pregnant the first time.'

'Did it upset you?'

'Not as much as having the baby would have. It'd be eight by now. Can you see me with an eight year old?' She gestured at the cardboard walls of her flat. Then she looked straight into my face. 'Do you think I should have an abortion?' she asked.

'I think it's a decision entirely for you,' I'd said. One of the advantages of being the kind of PC new man I am is that you can mask cowardice or indecision behind concern for the woman's right to choose. I was concerned for her, of course, but I was buggered if I knew what I wanted her to do.

I thought she'd answered her own question, though, as she'd stopped smoking and drinking.

That week also saw me decorate the spare bedroom, ready for our new arrival in Hillingdon.

*　*　*

I'd originally tried to resist taking on yet another addition to our family, but Henderson had talked me into it.

'You know I'm staying at a B&B at the moment, at the firm's expense? At *your* expense to put it in language you understand,' he'd said like an adolescent stressing the sheer logic of being allowed to borrow the family car.

'Yes,' I said, like the adolescent's father who had worked long and hard to be able to afford that very car.

'Well, it's costing £120 a night.'

'This B&B hasn't got the word "Ritz" displayed outside it and five little stars glinting in the doorway, has it?' I'd said. I couldn't see at the time where this was leading.

'It's not a hovel,' said Henderson, 'but neither is it luxury. You don't get the Ritz for £120 a night.'

'Hmm.' To me B&B meant £17 a night, en suite lice and don't worry about the damp, it's there for character.

'I think it's an unnecessary expense,' said Henderson.

'We are in complete accord, my dear fellow.'

'I think I should move into your spare room.'

'We are in complete disaccord, my dear fellow.' I knew Andrea wouldn't want Henderson clumping about the place when we had a baby on the way.

'Look at the advantages,' he said.

'OK.' I paused. 'No, there aren't any.'

'It would save money and, if the shit hits the fan between you and Andrea, you'll have someone there to argue your corner.' Having Henderson argue my corner would be like being defended on a murder charge by Norman Wisdom.

'No,' I repeated, 'and weren't we discussing my problems?'

'Oh, go on,' said Henderson. 'Please.' He had a look on his face like kids' storytellers do when they say, 'And then, children, the puppy died.'

While I can be quite obdurate against reasoned argument, there's something about straightforward grovelling that is guaranteed to undermine the citadel of the Dagman resolve.

Also, at the back of my mind, just over the mental patio but before the mental fishpond, I saw the weed of an idea sprout. As far as I knew he'd had no contact with Cat for a while, but I hadn't forgotten the amount of slaver he'd spilt when he'd suggested hooking up with Cat. If I moved him into my house I'd be able to keep an eye on him.

'Oh, all right then, I'll ask Andrea.'

'Good-oh,' said Henderson. 'I'll shift my stuff round on Saturday.'

'I haven't asked her yet.'

'I phoned her today,' said Henderson.

It seemed that more and more I was being sidelined from making any important decisions in my own life. Under normal conditions, like any self-respecting man, this would have filled me with a great deal of satisfaction and enabled me to concentrate on the serious business of enjoying myself. These, however, were far from normal conditions.

'I'll drop all my stuff from the hotel off on Saturday and get my feet under the table properly early next week,' he said.

Feet under the table? I thought. I wasn't too sure I liked the sound of that.

On the Saturday morning he duly arrived but, as he stepped out of his Range Rover Autobiography (that's what it's called, check if you don't believe me), I noticed a large unidentified mass crammed into the passenger seat beside him.

'Hello,' said Henderson. 'Here we are, how the www are you, Dag?' He has been doing his best to incorporate internet language into his conversation recently, a good ten years after everyone else. I was still reeling from his use of 'I'm off for an http, or as we call it in the trade, "a forward slash",' to delegates a week before on his way to the loo. I was glad the ribald possibilities of 'logging on' hadn't yet occurred to him. Henderson said this 'everyday use of internet language' made us look like we knew what we were talking about although I argued it made us look like demented acid casualties.

'I'm fine,' I said, as the mass in the passenger seat opened the door and stepped out on to the gravel.

'Ah,' said Henderson, 'Dag, meet Dave the Lesbian.'

I looked over at the expanse of white blazer, the voluminous black trousers, the motorway of white belt, the McEnroe of frizzy hair, the life-boat moccasins. Dave the Lesbian was what in the world of professional Rugby League is referred to as 'a big lad', and in the world of anything else 'a physical freak'.

'Charmed,' said Dave, extending a hand of the sort more normally seen on foes of Godzilla.

'Charmed,' I said back. Picking up on linguistic traits is the sort of thing we consultants recommend if you want to get on with people. In practice it irritates the hell out of everyone, but here I found myself doing it instinctively. The Lesbian's hand-shake was light and easy – I'd been expecting a builder's crush. It occurred to me that he might actually *be* a Lesbian, but I put the thought out of my head as politically undesirable. Andrea had taught me enough for me to know that on meeting a 6'8", 260lb slab of female muscle sporting a wispy moustache and a five o'clock shadow the caring male merely attends to the finer cadences of her conversation.

I was sure Dave couldn't be female, though I am not one to stereotype.

I stood in a slightly forward position, on the balls of my feet, my hand held up to face level with palm towards Henderson and the Lesbian. My posture, if not my voice, said, 'Why is he here?'

'Dave's helping me out for a few days,' said Henderson. 'I had some trouble getting my stuff out of Julie's and there was quite a scene with a couple of her lads. The Lesbian helped me deal with the problem and he's going to be staying on for a bit in case they come back for afters.'

'Hang on a minute,' I said, 'as I understand it, not only are you moving into my home but you are bringing with you a minder, paid for by our business no doubt, in case your wife attempts to send round thugs to my pregnant fiancée's home in order to give you the beating you so richly deserve. Not only that but you are willing to use words like "coming back for afters", like some pantomime cockney.'

'Don't dramatise things,' said Henderson. 'Dave's a deterrent, they won't try anything with him here. Anyway, Julie doesn't know where I am.'

'How do you know each other?' I said.

'Ironically we met through Julie,' said Henderson. 'I work out now at the Lesbian's gym.'

'Are you a gangster?' I asked him, suddenly and ridiculously emboldened by the feel of my own gravel beneath my feet, an Englishman's home his castle and all that.

'No.' The Lesbian smiled.

'Thank God for that.'

'Don't need a gang,' he said.

'What?'

'Only joking. I run a gym, that's all. Protection work is strictly freelance. I'm helping out H here because I like him.' His voice sounded unusually educated for a professional thug. It had some sort of middle-European twang to it that I couldn't place.

H? Maybe Henderson was a gangster.

My suspicions on that front weren't assuaged by the sight of him pulling a shotgun from the back of his Autobiography. I recognised it as the one he'd bought when he'd developed a brief mania for clay pigeon shooting back in the late '90s.

'What's that?'

'Double insurance,' said Henderson.

'From that I take it you can foresee a situation where you would be discharging firearms on my property?'

'Only in an emergency,' said Henderson with a wink.

'Oh, that's all right then.'

'I won't load it and I'll keep it out of the way.

'Do,' I said.

Henderson had taken the shotgun upstairs and placed it under his bed and was on his fourth load of stuff – why he wanted to bring his German Car Giant Summer Meeting Most Fluky Putt prize with him I didn't know – when Andrea appeared.

The morning sickness behind her, the zeal for work diminished, she was up and about on Saturday morning doing household tasks. I have to say pregnancy suited her. Her hair was shiny, her skin glowed, she appeared in the pink of health. She was in an extraordinarily good mood too, even when Henderson baited her about her washing up gloves.

'It's good you're in the gloves, Andrea, I approve of that,' he said, 'but I just don't get one thing.'

'What?' she said, flicking some suds at me.

'As a woman, what are you doing out of the kitchen?'

'Other than being the sole source of income for this household?' She was bouncing up and down slightly on her toes, like a fencer waiting to time her lunge.

'Yes.'

'Gestating a baby really,' the bouncing was getting faster, 'I find they grow better in the open air.'

'Oh, that's OK then,' said Henderson.

'Anyway what are you doing here? You won't find a life partner in our drive.'

'He's standing right there,' said Henderson, in mock offence.

'Are you sure you're only moving in short-term?' asked Andrea.

'Sure,' he said.

'Why don't I believe you?' She was still bouncing but she had taken her tea towel off her shoulder and was holding an end in each hand, cracking it tight. Knowing Andrea well, I recognised the portents of growing sexual tension. I was going to say mounting sexual tension but mounting is past the tension and into the fulfilment phase. Clearly tea towel cracking is low on the list of indicators of arousal – human behavioural specialists tend to draw attention to pupil dilation, body posture and the words 'Fancy a shag?' as signs of attraction before mentioning strange behaviour with Royal Wedding commemorative kitchenware.

However, I knew Andrea well and, as I watched the Duchess of York's face contorting in her hands, I had a sneaking suspicion that with Henderson and the Lesbian out of the way it would be back to the treadmill of the connubial bed for me. Cat and I had been at it like billio, as my mum used to say, Andrea had been cracking the whip (literally on one occasion), and I had about had enough. It wasn't a matter of sexual performance so much as physical. I'd torn a muscle in my abdomen and my pectorals felt like they had after that one time I'd joined Henderson at the gym. In short, I felt like I was falling to bits.

Still, I thought, stiff upper lip. Although it wasn't the stiffness of my lip I was worried about. I always reminded myself that men of my age fought and died in the last war, what right had I to complain about anything? Then the thought struck me that, in fact, men of my age were exempt from service on grounds of age in the last war. That was a sobering thought.

'Once he gets his feet under the table I have a suspicion they'll be there for a long time,' said Andrea, narrowing her eyes theatrically.

'You have a nagging doubt, my doubting nag?' I said, peering into a black bag of Henderson's that seemed to contain mainly monogrammed socks.

'Yes, I have, you bugger!' She ran after me, flicking me with the tea towel. 'And you didn't do the washing up last night.' She was chasing me round Henderson's car, flicking away at my arse.

'I meant to, and we all know it's the thought that counts,' I said, making a very fast turn by pivoting around Henderson's wing mirror.

'Between the intention and the act falls a shadow,' she said, cracking me again. That had been on a programme about modern poets we'd watched the night before.

'Between the meal and the washing up falls a documentary,' I said, turning and growling at her. She gave a shriek and ran the other way and we started the chase again in reverse, until finally I grabbed her from behind with my arms round her belly, taking care not to be too rough because of the baby. Then I felt it move.

'Oh my God!' said Andrea. 'It just kicked!'

'I know,' I said, 'I felt it too.'

'That's the first time. We felt it together!' said Andrea, turning to kiss me.

'How romantic,' said Henderson. 'Now could I get to my boot?'

I found myself staring with a fixed smile. Our every intimacy felt like a betrayal of Cat. This has got to stop, I thought.

There had been many intimacies around that point. I remember us lying on the sofa together one night after work.

'Ooh, I'll tell you what I saw today,' Andrea said.

I tensed, expecting some new piece of information she'd picked up from someone's desk to make her think they were after her job/lacked the necessary ambition. I still hadn't got used to the idea she had a new set of priorities, or at least seemed to. She'd even had a new business card printed with 'Andrea Dagman' on it. Her job title was 'Mother and Head of Fundraising', with a little photo of her on it. I hoped it was a joke.

'What?' In a swift movement she pulled up her tee shirt and down her bra.

'This!'

Now Andrea's tits have always been one of her best features. Not big, but shapely and beautifully pale. I've already noted that they're like old friends. Well, this was like meeting an old friend who had rather fallen in with the wrong sort. I could tell they were the same breasts – they were in the same place, that was a clue – but a terrible transformation seemed to have come over them, equivalent to what happens to scientists in silent films when they fall behind the desk and emerge with hairy paws.

I'm aware that this is an incredibly sexist thing to say but, you know, it's what I thought, sorry. I don't know what the non-sexist way is of saying that someone seemed to have replaced her normal breasts with the kind of thing you imagine middle-aged women in the Soviet Union had to put up with when proper breasts weren't available unless you queued for days. The kind of whitened, shapeless things that might be the result of standing too near the cooker when boiling cabbage soup, perhaps, or wringing out laundry by hand. When the expression 'I haven't laughed so much since my auntie caught her tit in the mangle' was coined, this was the very sort of tit I had imagined.

Mark Barrowcliffe

When I discover how to say that in PC language I will but my only guide to that sort of stuff is Andrea, and I can hardly ask her, can I?

'Look at that then.' She gestured at her nipple, which was noticeably darker and was taking on the appearance of the top of the sort of mushroom commonly offered to children in forests by old women with pointy hats and broomsticks. It had some sort of nodules on it. She pressed one.

'See.'

'What are they?'

'Montgomery's tubercles.'

'Are they dangerous?'

'They're meant to be there.'

'They're very nice,' I said, seeing if they looked bigger through a squint.

'And look – look at this.' She traced her finger down a thin blue line on the breast, rather like a vein. In fact, I think it was a vein.

'Christ almighty, woman, put it away,' I said.

'These aren't tits any more,' said Andrea, 'they're udders! Moo!' And she poked a veiny mound into my face. I recoiled but she wasn't having any of it. She pounced on top of me, pinning me on my back.

'What's the matter with you? Afraid of natural femininity? Only happy with woman as idealised image, rather than reality? Well, you're not getting away until you suck this tit.' She pressed the veined dug into my face.

'Of course I'm afraid of natural femininity. Can't we wait until they look all ivory and smooth again?'

'No, we cannot. Now suck and say, "I am a grown man, I appreciate woman in all her diversity, I celebrate her variform physicality." ' She was laughing, particularly when she rolled out 'variform', but I was in danger of suffocating.

'But I don't appreciate woman in all her diversity. In fact, I'm very picky,' I said, my voice breast-suppressed.

I couldn't throw her off because I was afraid for the baby.

'Say you appreciate woman!' She pressed down harder on my face.

It was say it or suffocate. 'I appreciate woman in all her diversity.'

'I celebrate her variform physicality.'

'I celebrate her variform physicality.'

'Now suck.'

I gave a quick suck. The nipple felt curiously bumpy in my mouth. Not too bad, actually.

'Thank you. Women 1, men 0,' she said, rolling off and laughing. 'And if you think you're getting away without shagging me this evening, you've got another think coming.' I blanched, trying to find it funny. The tits had been bad enough, what horrors had sprouted in other locations?

I'd read in *Steady Now, You're A Dad* that all sorts of unmentionable darkenings and engorgings took place. I know I should have been prepared for all those but I have to say I wasn't really. You spend your whole life developing one image of what you fancy in a woman and then in the space of nine months you're meant to change it completely. I tried, I tried.

And so the week went. The Lesbian slept on the sofa, Andrea refused to accept that I'd pulled a muscle in my stomach and took me to a physiotherapist who helpfully suggested some less punishing positions, despite the fact I'd been mouthing 'ban sex' at him from the minute we got there. She knew she was pushing me quite hard. I found that out when we stopped at the end of the drive to talk to Mrs Batt.

We'd borrowed Henderson's car. Mrs Batt narrowed her eyes at us as if to say, 'I thought you'd put all that driving behind you since the company car went?' She had a natural antipathy towards motorists. I noticed her luminous coat had a logo on it: Standard Cars. Christ, I thought, is there nothing people won't stoop to sponsor? What next? Sponsored cats, dogs, birds and squirrels? Sponsored diseases of childhood? Measles that spell 'McDonald's'?

'Who are those gentlemen I see staying at your house?' asked Mrs Batt.

'They're doing secret work, Mrs Batt.' Like most people

Andrea enjoyed mildly goading the mentally ill.

'What sort of secret work?'

'If she told you it wouldn't be secret, would it?' I said.

Mrs Batt nodded, as if she'd been let in on some universal truth. She tapped the side of her nose and leaned into our car, rather too close to my face.

'Don't worry, I'll get it out of you,' she said.

'You won't,' said Andrea, tapping me between the legs, 'he hasn't got any left.'

This rather chilled the neck fur as it was the very phrase I'd used to Henderson the morning after I'd first slept with Cat. He'd noted that I was wearing the same shirt as I'd been in the day before. One of my insurance policies against getting off with Cat had been to leave the travel iron, boxers and fresh shirt out of my briefcase, even though I'd always kept them in there ever since a nasty incident with a Cornetto on my way to an area board meeting one day.

'Where have you been?' he'd said, blue eye gleaming.

'Shut up,' I'd said, hoiking out a Cream Wittgenstein from the biscuit barrel.

'I'll get it out of you,' he'd said.

'No, you won't, there's none left.' Now Andrea had used exactly the same words I'd used to Henderson. Had I picked them up off her, her off me, she off Henderson? I was amazed at how these things went around, popping up like little gremlins to remind me of my own deceit. It was only because I couldn't resist the joke that Henderson had found out, and here was my fiancée, cracking it at Mrs Batt.

I'd arranged to meet Cat on Saturday at the cafe in the crypt of St Martin's-in-the-Fields – about as far away as it is possible to get from a field in England – reasoning that, as a church, it was one of the few places you could go in mid-November free from Christmas decorations. I'd originally wanted to go to her house, but she'd wanted to go shopping in Soho so we would meet in town.

Psychologists would doubtless observe that I'd chosen to finish our relationship in a place associated with endings and death – but then that is the kind of thing they are paid to note. Not that I can criticise, as a fellow member of the money-for-old-rope brigade.

I arrived at the crypt in a high degree of discomfort. Beasts often reveal clues to the weather in their behaviour so I'd known it wasn't going to be a dry day when I'd looked out of my window that morning and noticed the local animals filing two by two into a large wooden boat at the bottom of my drive. My umbrella had protected my top half but my trousers – I'd bought 'cargo pants' to try to look trendy (Andrea said something about 'bulk cargo' to play on my weight paranoia) – were soaked from the knee down. My temperature was all wrong too. The problem with cities in the rain and cold is that the temperature keeps varying – hot in the tube, cold on the street, hot in the shops. It's what my mum would call 'mithering weather', the sort that's always bothering you, frustrating you, like a fractious child, taking the joy from whatever you're doing. Not that there was much joy in what I was about to do.

Cat was late and I sat hot and steaming over my cold and flat cappuccino, looking about the crypt, the golden light of the food bar warming the dark, people going into the brass rubbing centre. Maybe I'd do one after I'd laid it on the line to Cat, to cheer myself up. No, I wasn't that desperate. Brass rubbing is no solace in life. If rubbing a tombstone is your idea of fun, you might as well be beneath one, is my view.

I thought back to my first kiss with Cat.

It was our fifth meeting and she'd agreed to introduce one of her friends to Henderson, newly de-Julied and looking for love. I welcomed this move as it showed Cat and I were just going to be friends, our platonic relationship cemented in position by the company of others. If Henderson and Cat's friend thought we were just friends, if the whole world thought that, perhaps it would become too difficult to make it any other way.

The evening had been a great success for us because it was very amusing, although Henderson and Cat's friend Sarah had hardly got on. The problem was that he had just discovered energy drinks, which he thought helped him preserve a youthful attitude, although to me his attitude seemed nearer to Hitler's of the Nuremberg rally period.

Sarah, I had been reassured by Cat, was a solid gold 100 per cent low-to-no standards slapper.

This was specifically what I'd requested, as I could think of no other sort of young woman who would go for Henderson. Sarah, however, was thin and mousy and wore what looked suspiciously like a hand-knitted jumper.

'That's a slapper?' I'd whispered to Cat as we went into the restaurant.

'I thought you were joking? No one calls women slappers any more.'

'Oh, they definitely do,' I said, 'I hear it all the time.'

'She's very nice,' whispered Cat as Henderson finished some story to Sarah with the words: 'Right slapper!'

Sarah, who was a rather fey researcher at the Houses of Parliament, had womanfully tried to find points of mutual interest by discussing film. She'd just been to see some French art house thing about the skilful seduction of a young man who comes to be a teacher in a provincial town by a bloke who teaches tuba in the local band. *Le Horn* or something, it was called.

'I find the sight of two men kissing very sexy, don't you?' she said.

'I suppose I could do,' said Henderson, looking like he'd just scrubbed his teeth with pile cream.

Sarah had started visibly detuning during one of Henderson's stories about his ex, the first of many he was to tell that evening.

'It was just after I'd discovered Showbiz Vim,' he said. This was an energy drink with enough caffeine in it to run the Deathstar. 'I don't know, Sarah, if you've ever had that feeling the moment is not enough . . . that you need something more real, more raw?'

She supped glumly on her mineral water – still because she said she found the bubbles hurt her tongue. Henderson took the slight movement of her head for a nod.

'And you can't really get there. So I'm prowling the party, looking for action, argument. You know, Sarah, life.' He'd made a movement like a karate chop with his hand. To her credit, only her ears, eyebrows and hairline retreated in fear, the rest stayed put.

'And we start talking as you do. I'm having a few drinks, a lot of the old Showbiz Vim, and I really hit form, start motor-mouthing it about how we could blow the whole business world apart, reorganise it from top to bottom, teach the big boys how to make some real money. Bill Gates'd have to listen.' He'd obviously had a bit that night because he was practically buttonholing Sarah, who wore the kind of glazed expression that occurs when nine-tenths of the brain involuntarily begins trying to remember cab numbers.

'When this bloke, who's obviously some sort of bouncer, comes up and asks me to be quiet. I say, "It's not me who should be quiet, you fucker, it's the rest of you who should liven up. What is this place anyway – no decent food, no interesting people – and what is this terrible music? Call this a party?" And Julie comes up and says, "Look, just be quiet for five minutes, the kid's only seven. Give her a chance to blow out the candles on her cake." '

Sarah had been quietly appalled but she'd got her own back later.

'Do you remember,' I'd said later, sitting next to Cat on her bed, laughing, 'when she convinced him that there was a new mix between House and Garage coming out called Shed?'

'I think the high point of the evening was when she said, "They say dogs can see the wind." ' Cat aped Sarah's rather faraway manner of speaking. 'And he said, "Well, keep 'em away from my arse, love, or else they'll be blinded." '

'Did he actually ask her if she was willing to undergo IVF?'

'He said, hypothetically.'

'He didn't give her any sort of leaflet then?'

'I think some sort of pamphlet did change hands. Just one of the ones on "what you should know" rather than "preparing for your treatment".'

Cat laughed quietly and then stopped.

'Are we going to stop talking about Henderson?' she'd said, looking into my eyes.

'Why?'

'Because if you do, you can kiss me.'

And though we'd been in such a rush that her tooth had gone into my lip, it had felt amazing for the first time to touch her, to hold her, to step over the line.

And that was it, we'd spent the night going at it like they were about to take it away from us, which they might have been, and I'd staggered into work at 9 the next morning, literally drained.

'I thought that was never going to happen,' Cat had said.

'Yeah,' was all I could muster as I fled for the security of the 73 bus.

'Hi,' said Cat now. She'd come up to my table in the crypt without my noticing her.

'Gosh, I was just thinking about you.'

'That's good to know.'

She kissed me and went to order a coffee. Again I remembered that skydiving experience. I had accused Henderson of being reluctant, but I had hardly said 'Stand aside and see how a man braves the leap' myself. My problem was that I was going completely outside my experience. I simply couldn't see myself hurtling towards the earth though I knew that was what was going to happen. I felt like that when I looked at Cat. Exactly like that. I couldn't envisage saying what I had to say but I knew I was going to say it – to take a run at it and do it before thought could intrude.

I looked at my watch. 2 p.m. By five past I knew I would have changed my life utterly. I still hadn't touched the cappuccino.

I recalled all the conversations we'd had in the month since she'd told me she was pregnant; how she'd sat in that box of a flat of hers and said, 'I don't know, maybe it's not such a bad thing after all, maybe it was meant to happen. It's weird but I'm quite happy about it. I think I'm even into the idea.'

I'd felt like I was skulking in the shadow of her innocence, a corrupt thing waiting to poison her life.

I'd asked her what support she wanted from me and she'd said whatever I could give. She knew the business was only just taking off and I was very busy so she didn't want me there every second, just when I could. We'd see how it went before deciding to move in together or not.

Why do you have to be so fucking reasonable? I thought.

She hadn't told her parents about the pregnancy, or about me. She said they'd worry too much about her, particularly with me being so much older. 'I'll only tell them when it gets really noticeable,' she said. 'That way they'll have less time to worry before it's born.'

'You always think of other people, don't you?' I'd said.

'I'll use that in my next job interview. Any faults? Yes, I always think of other people too much.'

'Although my standards are so high I can be a little testy with those who don't live up to them . . .' I'd heard that one rather too often in interviews, so often that I longed for someone to say, 'I am a habitual thief', or 'Some people do find my serial groping difficult to deal with'. I swear I'd give them the job.

'Some people say I'm too tidy,' she'd said, tickling me under the ribs.

'We know those people as hamsters,' I'd replied, leaning back on the pile of magazines and unopened bills that she transferred daily between her bed and the floor.

I saw her silhouette against the light of the crypt coffee bar. She was getting a little bump. Here we go, I thought. No way back now.

10

Tales From The Crypt

'My mum's actually surprisingly pleased about it,' said Cat, returning with the coffee.

'Do your parents know how old you are?'

'They know how old I am, Dag.'

'I mean, how old I am?' I said. I could hear my voice cracking. I remembered an episode of *The Sopranos* I'd seen where some young punk was staring into the pistol and telling mob boss Tony Soprano that he knew nothing about it. (I can't remember what *it* was.) I sounded about that calm.

'I just said thirty-something.' She smiled. 'Anyway, my dad's only forty-four, you should have a lot in common.'

'Ha ha,' I said.

'He is only forty-four,' she said. 'He likes all those bands you like, The Smiths and all that.'

'Yeah, all right.'

'And he was into punk when he was younger.'

'Your dad was a punk?' This was a massive blow. To me dads weren't punks, they were teds or jazz fans or something. 'You'll be telling me that some dads grew up with the Inspiral Carpets next,' I said.

'Who are the Inspiral Carpets?'

I put my fingers in my ears like Andrea does. 'Not listening!' I said.

'Who are they?'

'They were a formative dance/indie crossover band,' I said. 'In the early nineties.'

'I was just out of junior school so you must have been – my age now, give or take! Gosh, imagine if we'd met then.'

'Please,' I said, 'no more, I beg you.'

She narrowed her eyes. 'So all your Spirally Carpets fans are going to be a minimum of thirty by now,' she said.

'You can't have a kid at thirty, not in our generation,' I said, 'you're still a baby yourself.'

'I'm only twenty-four,' said Cat, 'and please don't ever use the words "our generation" again. We're from entirely different generations.'

'Oh, yes.'

I thought it was time for a change of tack.

'What do you think they'll say when they find out how old I am?'

'I don't know. Come and see, if you like. You won't be able to meet my dad, though, he's working in South Africa at the moment.' She smiled and held my hand. I withdrew mine, though I wanted to keep it there.

'Well, yes. Look, there's a bit of a complication in all this.'

'You've got to work?' said Cat. 'I knew you might.'

'No, not exactly. Well, I do have to work.' Christ, that really is an unnecessary level of detail, Dagman. It's like breaking the news of the dropping of the atom bomb by starting with a description of what the aircrew had for lunch.

Cat's face fell. 'You've had second thoughts about me having the baby?'

She said this rather loudly, attracting the attention of a kindly-looking old lady at the next table.

'No,' I whispered. To be fair I'd been so shocked by the whole thing I hadn't got much beyond first thoughts. 'It's just there are some complications in my life you should know about.'

Complications. I imagined a picture of Andrea and a baby. Underneath it would be written 'Complications'. I didn't want to think of them that way.

'Henderson's hinted about this,' said Cat, 'he said you were having second thoughts.'

'Did he?' I said. 'When?'

'A while ago, it doesn't matter. Do you or don't you want to support me through having this baby?' Cat spoke loudly again, though neutrally. There wasn't any anger in her voice, it was almost like she was a dinner lady asking a dithering schoolboy to choose – semolina or Spotted Dick. Though, as with a dinner lady, backing away from the decision was not an option.

'I do want to.'

'But you can't?'

The old lady at the next table was looking directly at us, more kindly if anything.

'I can.'

'But you don't want to?'

If you'll shut up for a second, I thought, I can put you out of your misery.

The old lady stood up and walked towards the door.

'I do want to.'

'So what's the problem?'

I choked. Even the second after I'd told her wasn't as difficult as the second before. I thought all sorts of weird things – angels dancing on a pin head, the far horizons, villages burning under pirate attack. A more insightful chap than I would have taken a good look at his thought processes and said, 'Brain, old bloke, you're avoiding the issue here.' I just gargled in a semi-hallucinogenic state.

The old lady had returned. She put a leaflet on the table between us, briefly shaking her hands over it like a conjurer magicking away a watch from a handkerchief. She clearly wanted to say something but didn't.

Abortion – The Truth, said the leaflet.

Cat shot her a look like Coco, a particularly venomous spaniel who used to live at the top of our road, used to shoot Kitchener, a tabby who favoured the tree above his front garden.

'It's so hard to say,' I said.

'I don't think it is,' said Cat, fiddling with her napkin and ignoring the woman at her side.

'If you need to talk to anyone about this . . .' said the old lady.

'We don't,' said Cat.

'It's a huge step you're taking . . .'

'I'm sorry,' said Cat, 'but the defence of deeply held principles is no excuse for rudeness. Kindly be off.'

I was reminded, bizarrely, of Henderson.

'Please think about it,' said the old lady. 'Read the leaflet.'

'Read my lips. Sod off,' said Cat. I'd never seen her angry before. I felt grateful to the old woman. I had the feeling that if she hadn't been there all that emotion would be coming in my direction. 'I can't stand Christians,' said Cat under her breath. It made me regret my choice of venue for our meeting.

The old lady looked very hurt. She stood up but before she left, said, 'I'll pray for you.'

'Don't,' said Cat.

'I will.'

'I don't want you to.'

'I don't think you have any choice in the matter,' I said.

'I'll get someone who's better qualified than me to speak to you,' said the old lady.

'Don't!' said Cat.

If it had been difficult to tell her before, it was becoming impossible now.

'Shall we go?' said Cat.

'We have to pay,' I said.

'No, we don't, we paid at the bar.'

'Oh, yes.'

We left the crypt and made our way out into the rain, umbrellaing up as soon as we were out of the narrow exit. Coming from our right and the main church was the old woman, heartsinkingly with a young man in a combat jacket smothered in badges.

'Jesus Army!' said Cat. She looked absolutely distraught.

These, I knew, were the people you joined if you were too much of a twat to get into the Young Christians. You'll appreciate the level of social dysfunction we're operating at here.

'Hi,' said the Army man, 'I hear you need to talk.' He put his hand on Cat's arm.

'Let go of me,' she said. He didn't.

'I don't know what's going on here, but this lady says you're considering an abortion and . . .'

'Piss off!' said Cat, hitting him on the shoulder.

'Ow!' said the Jesus Army bloke, looking very angry. 'That hurt!'

I don't know what sort of army the Jesus Army is, but I can't see a member of the Paratroop Regiment or French Foreign Legion responding that way when pushed slightly by a pregnant woman.

'Try turning the other cheek,' I suggested.

'Please . . .' said the old woman, taking Cat lightly by the arm.

She gave a shout, as if in pain, and clutched at her abdomen. It was then I noticed how pale she had become.

'Oh my God!' she said. 'I think I'm losing it. Oh my God. Get me to hospital. Dag, call a cab.'

I couldn't believe it. 'I hope you're fucking pleased with yourselves?' I said to the Messiah molesters. 'We had no intention of getting rid of it.'

'Cab!' shouted the old lady. 'Cab!' Her eyes were wild with distress. I felt mildly sorry for her. In her way she'd only been trying to help. Later I would recall the time my mum had bought my dad a yellow sweater for Christmas. She'd got it from Marks so she could take it back if he didn't like it. He said he did like it but would have preferred it in blue. My sister and I had only been trying to help when we boil-washed it using fountain pen ink instead of soap. At the time, though, I was too angry to think of that, and too sorry for Cat.

'Cab! Cab!' I shouted into the gloom of the Charing Cross Road.

But it was raining and none came for what seemed like forever. Eventually we saw an orange light emerging out of the downpour. Cat couldn't stand, she was just leaning into me, weakly.

'St Thomas's is nearest,' said the old lady.

'*Will you go away?*' I said.

'There's no blood coming out,' said the Jesus Army bloke, bending over and staring into Cat's crotch. He obviously liked physical evidence of suffering – probably why he hadn't become a Buddhist, not enough violence and pain.

We got into the cab and told the driver to get to the nearest casualty department. As it swung around Trafalgar Square I looked back at the old lady, rigid with shame and fear on the pavement.

The Jesus Army bloke was trying to show her a leaflet, smiling and telling her she'd go to hell, probably.

I didn't know how I was going to help Cat cope with this terrible thing that had happened to her. She'd only just got used to the idea of having the baby and now it was gone.

'Make that Soho,' said Cat, to the cabbie, 'we'll be all right.'

She was smiling slightly. 'You're OK?' I said. 'You're not having a miscarriage?'

'She wasn't going to go any other way,' said Cat flatly. All my fear about telling her about Andrea left me in the swell of relief.

'You're amazing,' I said, 'I can't believe that.'

She shrugged. 'Those people need to know that not everything's straightforward. Sometimes you do bad things even when you want to do good. Anyway, what were you going to say to me?'

I looked at her: damp, pale, beautiful.

'I'm engaged to someone else and she's pregnant too.'

'In that case, I'm going to have to entirely fuck up your life,' said Cat, drawing me into a kiss.

11

Sour Somethings

Like others before me, sex had brought me to Soho.

I realised as the cab slid through the rain-slickened streets, past the models' parlours, the private shops, the signs advertising non-stop continuous nudity, that something, God, Fate, whichever privatised company is running the universe at the moment, was showing me the real reason for the mess I was in.

Why had I come to Cat? For sex? No, I'd say because she filled a hole in my life. But what if she'd been eighty, just as interesting, just as much fun? Would we still be emotionally entangled like that? No.

I hadn't thought when I told her about Andrea that I'd have to pay the cab, to buy a drink, to find a restaurant. I don't know what I'd expected – her to rush off into the night or something, or us to be magically transported to some secluded spot where we could discuss it like adults, or perhaps I thought it would be over in a flash. But mundanity attends even the affairs of the heart. I've often thought of the balcony speech from *Romeo and Juliet* and wondered if either of them had a nasty boil that was bothering them, or if she'd been bursting for the loo when she heard 'What light at yonder window breaks?' It certainly adds a different meaning to 'That I might touch that cheek'.

So I hadn't realised that Cat would decide to stop the cab the second after I'd told her, that I'd have to borrow £10 off her to pay the fare until I could get to a cash point, I hadn't realised I'd drop the change, that we'd have to find a relatively deserted restaurant so we could talk, how few relatively deserted restaurants there are in Soho, that we'd have to pretend not to be having the worst time of our lives and order food, that the food would come and show us why the restaurant was relatively deserted, that the waiter would say no, they didn't take credit cards, it said so clearly on the door. None of that.

These are the details I recall, this stuttering engagement with the raw mechanics of life while the rain fell and I broke her heart.

The cab had stopped.

'I'm not joking.'

'Yes, and your father was killed by a loan shark.'

'£3.80, please.'

I realised that I hadn't got any money in my wallet.

'Have you got some cash for the cab?'

'I think so.' She reached into her bag.

'Really, Cat, honestly, I'm not joking.' I said this with some heat in my voice, not because I was irritated but to make her believe me. 'I'm engaged to be married to another woman and she's pregnant too. I've been seeing her for eight years. Her name's Andrea.'

We hadn't got out of the cab due to the rain. The cabbie leaned back through his partition with a blank face and out-stretched hand. Cat put a tenner into it.

'I don't believe you. Prove it.'

'Would you like a receipt?'

'No, fine,' I said.

'Get one, I can claim it,' said Cat, her eyes fixed on me. I could still see she didn't believe me.

'Yes, then, we'll have a receipt.'

'How much shall I make it for?'

'The whole ten.' I just wanted to be out of there.

'Dag, the fare's only £3.80. You've got a fiancée?'

'Look,' I said, taking Andrea's business card out of my wallet, 'that's her. Five then. I never meant it to be like this.' The words sounded wooden on my lips, like in an imported soap. I wanted to give it more emotion but I reminded myself of one of those 'normal' people they get to advertise DIY superstores and the like. I was frozen before the strangeness of the situation and the most natural thing for me to do was to sound unnatural. It wasn't like I'd ever rehearsed this sort of thing out loud before.

The cabbie scribbled out the receipt and handed me the change with an expulsion of breath that indicated he didn't like ditherers. I dropped the change on to the floor and we had to hunt for it.

We stepped from the cab into the sheeting rain.

'Plonker,' I thought I heard as the cab drove away.

Cat held the business card up to the light of a cafe. 'This is your sister. It's a joke, isn't it?'

She stood soaking in the rain, hair plastered to her head, the picture of vulnerability. I wanted to help her and to make her happy again. I've often wondered why finishing with a woman is so difficult. I think it's because, from the time I was a small boy, I've been brought up to believe that I should be kind to girls, look after them.

'Yes, it's a joke.' I had an overwhelming urge to say the words, but I didn't.

Men butcher seal cubs. Worse, probably, they butcher children and grandparents and just about anyone really to get what they want. I needed a touch of that spirit, the efficacious brutality of my gender. I found it in three little words.

'I'm so sorry.' I took the card out of her fingers and put it back in my wallet.

We were already attracting glances from beneath umbrellas and from the sides of hooded tops. This isn't as hard as it might appear in Soho. True, no one will bat an eyelash if you walk past naked, covered in custard and screaming, 'I'm Randolfo, the human kazoo,' but genuine misery always draws a crowd, whatever the weather.

It was obvious that something was going on between us. No couple stands gawping at each other like that, while being soaked by the kind of rain that causes people to use the word 'ante' to refer to anything that happened before it, without a compelling reason.

'This isn't a joke, then?'

'No.'

Cat shook her head.

'I have to get out of this rain.' She hadn't taken her eyes off me since we'd stepped from the cab. Neither of us moved.

'Where were you planning on going?'

'To Bar Italia.' She gestured at the shabby but chic coffee house across the street. 'This is like a dream, Dag. Say it again, let me get things straight.'

Water was running down my neck and my jacket was soaked.

'I have a fiancée. She's pregnant. I've been deceiving you. You were my bit on the side.' The last part sounded the most brutal, but I somehow felt I still had to shock the belief into her.

'How many other lies have you told me?'

'Four,' I said confidently. There was my job, the fact that I was thirty-six, the fact that my house was flooded, and the fact that I didn't have a fiancée. That excludes all the lies I'd told her about where I was and what I was doing, but that was just one big lie really. Mind you, I thought, I'd better put it in, under a group heading. 'Well, actually nearer five.'

'I'm having difficulty taking this in.'

I wanted to get out of the rain so I nipped under the awning of a cafe. Cat followed.

'Look,' I said, 'we need to discuss this, shall we go some-where?'

'This is true, isn't it?' Her eyes were filling up. So, I could feel, were mine.

'Yes. I'd meant to tell you earlier but then you got pregnant and I didn't know what to do.'

'Are you eating?' A tight little gay with apron and menu was smiling at us.

'No, we're just deciding.'

'I'm afraid this area is for customers only.'

'Do we want to eat here?' I asked.

Cat shook her head, in disbelief rather than for answer.

'Then you'll have to move, I'm afraid,' said the waiter.

'Come on,' I said, and took her by the arm back out into the filthy night.

'What's her name?'

'Andrea.'

'Does she know about me?'

'No. Look, the rain's too heavy, shall we go inside somewhere?'

She shook herself free and walked on. I caught up with her. 'Cat, can we just do this in a civilised manner?'

'Do what? An act of barbarism?'

'Whatever it is we're doing.'

I could see tears on her face.

'What are we doing?'

'Talking about a dreadful situation.'

'If that's what we're doing, then yes.'

Oh, God, I thought, I hope this is enough to make her finish with me. I didn't think I'd have the strength actually to tell her to go myself.

It took us another quarter of an hour in which to find a restaurant deserted enough for us. It was like romance in reverse; we wanted to be alone, not to exchange sweet nothings but sour somethings. There was nothing to say as we traipsed the streets. I just avoided looking at her, she stared at me. Each place, though, was either too packed or too expensive. It wasn't like I wouldn't have paid for a posh place, just to be out of the rain, but there seemed something weird about finishing in an ambience of riches. Shabbiness seemed our only option.

We found it in an Italian somewhere off Dean Street, I think.

The waiters were nice enough and sympathetic to our soaking state but all I really wanted was to be alone with her in a cubicle, free of the combination of wet from our walk and heat from the restaurant. I was dying for the loo but I thought I'd just get things settled before I went.

Cat tried to smile as we were handed the menus. I think the waiter could see that we were a bit upset because he skedaddled pretty quickly.

'I'm sitting here with a total stranger,' said Cat. I couldn't tell if she was crying or if it was the rain. Her voice was more exasperated than hurt. 'What has been going on?'

And I told her, as much as I could: Andrea, Henderson, Andrea's parents, her dad's illness, everything. All I can really remember is that I must have gone into a quite unnecessary level of detail because she stopped me by saying, 'I don't need to know about the lollipop lady.

'So what happens now?' she said.

'I don't know. What do you think?'

'I think I was a bit on the side you banged up, a final fling that went wrong. I think I'm on my own.'

'I'm mad about you. I love you.'

'Do you love her?'

'Yes.'

Cat's lips gave a little tremble.

'Are you ready to order?' asked the waiter. He looked at our faces. 'A few minutes, maybe.' And he shot off like that peasant does when he comes round the corner to discover the occultists summoning demons in the film of *The Devil Rides Out*. I think that's the film anyway. It's not important. You get the idea.

'I'm going to keep the babies, you know.'

'Babies?' I said with an admirable degree of calm – roughly equivalent to that of someone falling down a mineshaft.

'It's twins, a boy and a girl. I was going to tell you and then that woman came up.'

In my self-absorption I'd completely forgotten she'd been for a scan. It should have been the first thing I'd asked her.

'So there's two of them?'

'That's what twins means. You can treat them as a single unit for the purposes of guilt, if you like.'

She didn't seem madly upset, just like an angry but controlled woman arguing with an assistant over taking something back to a shop.

I was at a loss for what to say next. The only thing that kept coming into my head was that line from counselling.

'How does this make you feel?'

Now I have been led to believe that these words are the ideal thing for blowing into the nostrils of the hoof-stamping female. However, to continue the horse metaphor, they only served to make Cat rear up in a very alarming way.

'How do you think it fucking well makes me feel?' she hissed. Her mood had gone from that of a woman returning something to a shop to that of a woman returning it through the plate-glass window.

Behind her the waiter, who had started his run for our table with pad poised, curtailed it and returned to the kitchen.

'Well, very bad, I should guess.'

'That would be correct,' she said.

There was a silence. I really was humming for a wazz and needed to make my break to the loos at the soonest possible juncture.

'What do you intend to do?' she said.

This was rather a tricky one. Like most men, once you leave the sphere of mechanics, work, DIY and sport, I rely rather firmly on women to make the important decisions in life.

I rather envy my great-grandfather's generation who used to come home and hand their pay packets over to their wives without opening them. They'd get pocket money back, of course, but in anything else they were blissfully removed from the decision-making process. Their wives even bought their clothes for them.

Thanks to the advances of the women's movement in the 1960s, however, we're all equal now and have to stand naked and quivering before the mammoth array of choices millennial capitalism can present us with. We didn't ask for it, we didn't want it, but our opinion counts. So we're sent out shopping for clothes and we're supposed to have opinions on what kind of trousers we want when really we don't want trousers at all. We haven't wanted them since our teens when they were all we wanted, them and cars.

Despite our razor-creased suits, our crisply laundered shirts, our individual but unshowy ties, we don't want any clothes, really, we just have to have them for warmth and for convention's sake. We'd be happier with an all-purpose garment we could wear wherever. I've often thought a housecoat would be the ideal thing. We don't get that luxury until our nineties when we don't give a shit and wander to the pub in our pyjamas and slippers.

But until then we can't say 'it's your mother's department', or 'the wife handles that', we're expected to have opinions on life and to act on them – unless we try really hard. And I have tried hard.

Like when I'd proposed to Andrea. I mean, it was me who proposed but it was Henderson who told me she thought it was about time I popped the question. And when we'd moved to Hillingdon – that was Andrea's choice. And setting up the new business – Andrea had said Henderson and I should strike out on our own. And having the kid(s) – that was out of my hands too.

With Cat, I didn't know what I really wanted. To stay with her? Maybe. To stay with Andrea? Perhaps. That the whole thing had never happened? No, strangely, not that.

'I'll do whatever you want me to,' I said, a conventional but effective return of serve.

'No, I want you to tell me,' said Cat, finding the baseline with complete ease and leaving me flatfooted somewhere near the Robinson's Barley Water dispenser.

All I could do was tell her the truth. Things were that bad.

'I love you both and, even if I have a choice, even if you still want me after all this, I can't decide. I just don't know.' My feet were dancing beneath the table with urinal desire. It seemed insensitive to call for a break, though.

Cat sat physically steaming from the damp. She said nothing. Behind her the waiter had noticed the lull in proceedings and decided to strike. He ushered forward a small boy of about nine.

'My dad wants to know what you want to eat.' He was at least trying to fake the Italian accent.

I looked at Cat. She looked dreadful: hollow-eyed, wet-haired, shirt still drying on her body. And she was twenty-four and good-looking to begin with. I wondered what I looked like.

I felt so sorry for her. I went to take her hand in mine but she withdrew it. 'Don't,' she murmured.

'Spaghetti bolognese do you?' asked the child, who had dropped the am-dram Italian accent.

I nodded.

'And house white?'

I nodded again and he shot back to his father.

'I really need to go to the loo,' I said.

'Then go,' said Cat.

I nipped out for the sweetest relief a human can know, all the time wondering if I was doing the right thing.

I returned to the table.

'I don't want to be with someone who doesn't know if they want to be with me,' said Cat quietly.

I steeled myself. I'd known that if she told me to go then I'd get the immediate feeling I'd done the wrong thing and want her back. Rejection is a powerful aphrodisiac. I reminded myself that the best thing for everyone was a decision, one way or the other.

'Does that mean it's the end for us?' The words didn't really have any meaning. I just couldn't stand the silence.

'I'd say so, wouldn't you?'

I couldn't really reply, although part of me was relieved.

'What will you do?' I asked.

'Have the babies. Bring them up. Love them.'

'What will you do for money?'

'Get it off you.'

'Yes, of course.'

'Don't say it like you're being generous. It's my right.'

'I know.'

This raised the rather sticky question of how I was going to explain to Andrea that a good slice of my income would disappear every month. It wasn't that I didn't want to pay Cat the money, I did.

'Will I see the kids?'

'I can't say. No, I don't think so. It's too confusing for them to have a father half in and half out of their lives.'

'What will you call them?'

'I think you've missed your window for sentimentality,' she said. I hadn't seen her like this before which, even a psychologist might note, was hardly surprising given that most people try to avoid situations of soul-rending sadness on a day-to-day basis. She seemed to get stronger through being upset. The wonder-why kid was gone and there was a cold certainty about her.

We sat for a while longer. The food was taking ages. We couldn't complain but if ever you were going to get chained to a table by slow service that was a bad time for it.

'What's she like, this fiancée of yours?'

'Nice.' The word came out like a slap in the face.

'I'm glad of that. Be specific. Tell me exactly.'

'I can't.'

'Why not? You've told me enough lies, don't you owe me some truths?'

'*Bon appetit!*' said the child, who had appeared at the side of our table with the food. He made a low bow, which I guess he thought was funny, and retreated at a speed to suggest he'd dropped a hand grenade on to the table. I noticed the waiter was opening our wine by the serving hatch, out of the embarrassment-exclusion zone.

'What's she like?'

'She's . . .' I was going to say 'a bit like you really'. Why, I don't know, as it was completely untrue, but the brain plays weird tricks under pressure.

'She works for a charity.'

'Which one?'

'International Rescue.'

'And?'

'She's not really the type to do that. She just fell into it after university. She'd intended to go into the media but was having a worthy fit at the time.'

'And?'

'She's very focused on her work. We don't get much time for each other.'

'You're talking about yourself again.'

'I'm telling you about our relationship. For the purposes of this conversation that's the only way she exists. She has no meaningful life outside it to you and me at this point.' I heard myself getting angry. In a way a row would have made things easier.

'She's funny and she's kind in her way. Very self-centred when it comes to work.'

I felt I had to balance every positive with a negative. Like anything nice I said was an insult to Cat. 'We get on, you know, we get on.'

'Clearly.'

What would I say? That pregnancy seemed to have reclaimed her from the demons of ambition, that it seemed to have made her again the girl I'd first met all those years ago, that I loved the way she smelled, that I felt I had to look after her, that you don't just throw all that time together down the drain, even if you want to. What else would I say? That I really, really wasn't sure and that, because I wasn't sure, it seemed easier to stay where I was.

'So what made you be unfaithful to her? What made you use me?'

'I didn't use you, Cat, I fell for you. I wanted you, and I still want you more than I have ever done anyone.'

'Apart from Andrea?'

'More than Andrea, but things aren't that simple.' I did really want her more than I wanted Andrea at that point, but I knew that were I having the same conversation with Andrea, I would want *her* more.

'What's not so simple?'

'This now. I've been honest with you and things will never be the same again, will they? You can't feel the same way about me after this.'

'Don't push this back on to me.'

'And ties. She's financially involved with the business. Her father's dying. She's got nowhere to go if she doesn't have me.'

'And I have?'

'I know,' I said, 'I know. I'm so sorry it had to end like this.'

'It seems you had made a decision before you came here.'

'I wasn't aware that I had.'

'So if I told you I forgive you and I want us to be together?'

'Then I'd come with you.' The child placed the wine on the table like a dog trying to steal a chop from under the cook's nose.

'No, you wouldn't.'

'I would.'

'You don't sound like you would. Everything about you says you want to go back to her. And anyway, I don't forgive you. This is the lowest blow I've ever been dealt.'

I remembered a saying of Henderson's whenever I'd complained about my relationship with Andrea: 'That's what lovers are for, to make the good times bad and the bad times worse.' He'd been joking, sort of, but I could see what he meant. How many arguments had I had at cinemas, theatres, restaurants, with how many girls before I met Andrea? How clumsily had I offered support or sympathy or whatever, and only made things worse? How often had I stood arguing with someone thinking, If you were one of my mates this wouldn't be happening, why didn't I stick to them? Apart from with Cat. I'd never had a row with her. Mind you, it had only been five months.

'I'm sorry,' I said. I wanted to say something about the greatest love causing the greatest hurt but the words wouldn't come, perhaps because I wasn't in a 1980s New Romantic band.

'Didn't you realise this sort of thing could happen when you started seeing me?' she said.

If she meant that they'd both get pregnant, then definitely not, I thought.

'I didn't think. I didn't think anything.'

'You just followed your dick.'

'It really wasn't like that, Cat. I couldn't resist you.'

'Don't make this my fault,' she said. 'All I've done is fall for a man old enough to be my father.' On certain inner-city estates, I supposed, there were steel-willed souls who waited until ten years old to have their first kid. 'I should have known you'd have baggage.'

'Not this much though, eh?'

I wished I hadn't said that. There was something of the 'gosh, what a lovable chump I am' in my voice, which wasn't what I was feeling at all.

I could see Cat weighing things up in her head, wriggling slightly on the seat, physically wrestling with the futures in front of her. Anyone else would have been crushed, I thought. Not her. She was already moving on.

'I think I should go.'

Her wine and spaghetti were untouched. So were mine. She stood and put on her soaking coat.

'Cat,' I said, 'I really do love you.'

'Fuck yourself,' she said. 'You'll be hearing from the Child Support Agency.'

She went back out into the rain, slamming the door as she went. I had no urge to chase her, I felt entirely defeated. From the kitchens I heard a whoop of, 'Oh, yeah!' At least I was providing entertainment for the chef, even if he wasn't providing any for me. I sat drinking the wine, not thinking anything, just seeing scraps of possibilities circulating in my head – me with twins and Cat, me with Andrea, me under a truck.

The mobile rang.

'Hello,' said Andrea, 'you're late.'

'Am I?' I said. I looked at the time. It was four o'clock. The light was dying outside.

'Will you be home soon?'

'Yeah, I'm just doing a bit of Christmas shopping.'

'It's not the twenty-fourth already, is it?'

I laughed.

Cat didn't know that I always did my Christmas shopping on Christmas Eve, locking myself into Selfridges until I had presents for everyone. She'd never know.

'I'll come back now.'

'OK. I thought we could just stay in and watch telly tonight.'

'You, me and Henderson?'

'He's going out, aren't you?'

'I am!' I heard a voice say in the background.

I really wanted to be going with him. I could have done with a skinful that evening.

'See you about seven then,' she said.

'Yeah.'

'Love you.'

'You too.'

I put the phone down and called for the bill. It was then I discovered they didn't take credit cards.

When I'd first gone out with Cat I hadn't thought it would end like this. If I'd imagined it at all I'd thought of me sinking into the sea while she wept on the lifeboat, of being parted by war or famine or murder, of her trembling kiss still on my lips as I went to the gallows – not her running soaked for a tube while I accompanied an angry waiter to a cash point in the rain to pay for wine I hadn't liked and food I hadn't eaten.

It was only when I came to put the cash card back in my wallet that I realised Cat didn't quite intend to relegate herself to a monthly deduction from my current account. Andrea's business card was missing. It seemed Cat had been busy while I'd been away from my seat.

12

Letter Bomb

I didn't hear anything from Cat for a month, during which time I began to suspect Henderson was deliberately trying to drive me mad.

It wasn't just that when he asked if he could show me what he'd bought Andrea for Christmas it was the DVD of *Fatal Attraction*. It bore a sticker on the box: 'With three extra minutes of bunny boiling!' and included a version of the ending where the cheating husband actually cops it with the steak knife.

It wasn't just that he seemed to have evolved an uncanny ability to be in every room of the house simultaneously. Wherever I wanted to go, whatever I wanted to do, he or his residue was there. If I wanted access to the bathroom sink in the morning, for instance, I could forget it. The routine went something like this. I know because Henderson has a horrible habit of leaving the door open when he ablutes.

Lavatory. Shower. Drench floor of bathroom. Dry, though not the floor. Discard towel. Shave while whistling the tune from *The Great Escape*. Then exfoliate, then mud mask. Then wash off, then some sort of face bath that shot water around the face – and the rest of the bathroom. Hydrotherapy, said Henderson.

'It works,' Andrea had said, 'the floor looks years younger.'

Then the sunblock, then the moisturiser, retinol, then the mighty rattle of pills – chromium, selenium, Q10, ginseng, fish oil, starflower oil, B complex – teeth clean, floss, Regaine to encourage hair on the head, clippers to discourage it on ears and nose. Glue hair back with extra strong gel.

Then a couple of minor fettling adjustments to the steam-pinkened plums before, at last, put on underpants.

If I wanted a meal, he'd be in the kitchen watching the Lesbian (who was now sleeping in Henderson's Range Rover in the drive, though I suspected Andrea let him sleep in the house if ever I was away) cook and then washing up in a way that left stains on the cutlery, or if I wanted a cup of tea he'd have used the last bag.

I took my revenge as best I could by putting Henderson on to the Golden Years mailing list in order to depress him. I'd get a pair of those special spiky garden-aerating clip-ons for free for that.

It wasn't just his advice that was driving me mad either. 'Spirits are very aging,' he'd say as I attempted to relax with a post-work whisky.

'I don't care,' I said. 'Having a stable relationship, I don't have to worry about that sort of thing.'

No, it was two other things that really bothered me. One was that I was fairly sure he was still meeting Cat occasionally. He did his best to take all the meetings in town, for instance, and some nights he didn't come home until the early hours. One night he didn't come home at all.

'Where did you get to last night?' I asked him as we ate dinner the next evening.

'Out and about,' said Henderson.

'Where, exactly?'

'You're not my keeper, are you?'

'Yes,' I said, gesturing to the room, 'I am.'

'I'm still not telling you, keeper.'

'He's allowed a private life, Dag,' said Andrea.

'He's not allowed my fucking private life,' I said under my breath.

This would have been bad enough. But in the really annoying way he has of never being pinned down on anything, what really drove me mad was that as soon as I'd finished with Cat he seemed to change his mind as to the wisdom of the idea.

'I mean, you did seem to love her,' he was saying as the Lesbian drove us to a winebar in Kew. It occurred to me that this was a diversionary tactic, or that he was trying to get me to deny loving her so that he could steam in. I wasn't going to do that. I did love her, it was just that life hadn't let us be together. Andrea needed me more, plain and simple, and it wasn't about what I wanted, unfashionable as that way of thinking may be.

'Every time you mention her you have a certain shimmer about you,' said the Lesbian, 'like Marlene Dietrich describing her first male lead and saying, "Now *he* was a real man!" '

I'd been a bit reluctant to allow the Lesbian in on my secret but Henderson had assured me he was as discreet as the grave. In fact he'd assured me he was as discreet as the grave after he'd gone ahead and told him, so it hardly mattered if he was as discreet as a former royal nanny – he knew.

'Well, it's all a bit late now.'

'Nah,' said Henderson, 'she'll come round if you work on her. Buy her a box of chocolates. Women are suckers for that.'

What was he driving at? I wondered. I would have bet my life and my happiness that . . . oh, hang on, I'd already bet my life and happiness on something else, it'd have to be my bottom dollar then. I'd have bet my bottom dollar that he'd been trying to snake his way in with Cat. What was he up to, trying to get me to approach her again? Did he want an irrevocable split? To really, really sour things? I couldn't think of anything more designed to enrage Cat than turning up with a box of chocolates, saying, 'Sorry about the baby and the fiancée and everything. Here, have a rum truffle and forget about it.'

'Well, I don't want her to come round. The great thing about what's happened is that at least now there's a measure of certainty about the whole thing. And if women are so easy to get round you buy Julie a box of chocolates,' I said.

Henderson cowered, like a child on a freezing playing field seeing the leaden ball descend towards him and hearing the hairy-arsed games teacher scream, 'Head it, you poof!'

'So you're still convinced you want to give up the carefree life?' said Henderson. 'There won't be any coming down the winebar for a quick afternoon snifter once you've got the baby.'

He can't have shagged her, I thought. If he had he wouldn't be on this tack.

'As convinced as I've been for about the last ten years of hollowness and emptiness,' I said. 'You've changed your tune, what about duty and looking after Andrea?'

'I don't think I'd given the proper weight and consideration to my own needs at that point. I simply cannot be the last one to achieve a settled family life,' said Henderson.

'What do you mean?' I said. 'You simply cannot? You simply *are*, mate, get used to it.'

The Lesbian gave a large shrug, with something of the effect of a solar eclipse.

'Right,' said Henderson. 'Dave, turn the car around, sod the drink.' He rolled his shoulders like a gangster boss who has been pushed that little bit too far.

'Desperate times call for desperate measures. We're going to Wind in the Willows country,' he said.

I wondered if Wind in the Willows was cockney rhyming slang for something, but couldn't think of much to rhyme with willows. Pillows, billows, Rezillos? No, the latter were a long-forgotten punk band. There wasn't even cockney rhyming slang for Sex Pistols, so the Rezillos wouldn't get a look in.

'Just because I won't be coming for a drink in four months' time doesn't mean I don't want one now,' I said.

'Hard luck,' said Henderson, as the car sped towards the M4.

'Can I just check, Henderson,' I said, 'you're not planning on having me killed, are you?'

I saw his head tip to one side, like he was considering it.

'Not at the moment.'

'So where are we going?'

'You'll see,' he said. Flipping open his phone, he dialled.

'Mrs Collins? Lee Henderson here. It's about that bit of business we discussed the other day. I'd like to collect now, if possible? Wonderful, we'll be with you inside an hour.'

We came off the M4 just after Slough, skirting its anytown light industrial perimeters before plunging into countryside and a vision of old England.

'Cookham,' said Henderson to the Lesbian.

'I used to work round here,' he said.

'What as?' I asked nervously. This being a timeless vision of rural England I naturally assumed that the youth were all bored senseless and off their heads on drugs. I could just imagine the Lesbian selling that sort of stuff.

There was a silence and we drove on.

'What as?' I repeated. 'Some sort of villain?'

'The worst sort,' said Henderson.

'What is the worst sort nowadays?' I said, feeling curiously innocent. When I'd last checked 'worst sort' had fallen somewhere between wife beater, child molester and rapist, but I wasn't sure if something had taken their place. People are so inventive nowadays.

'Leave it, will you?' said the Lesbian.

'How much did you make out here, stealing from the old, the sick and the vulnerable, Dave?' asked Henderson.

I could almost feel the heat of the Lesbian's beamer from behind his McEnroe hairstyle.

'About four grand a week,' he said in tones normally used by penitent schoolchildren when asked if they thought what they had done was very clever.

'What did you do?' I asked, wondering what dark villainy yielded that kind of money in a rural community.

We were pulling past a pond with a view of a wide common. I remember a church in the background but I might be wrong.

'Dave was . . .'

The Lesbian put his hand to his face. 'Don't mention this when we get out, Henderson,' he said.

'Don't worry, I don't want lynching. People can be touchy

about that sort of thing round here.'

'Dave was . . .' even in the car he had to glance to left and right, as if someone might have attached themselves to the wing mirror and be listening '. . . a plumber.'

I used a word I wouldn't normally use on someone of the Lesbian's size. I hadn't realised the depth of social outcast Henderson had brought into my home.

We drove on in silence to a house at the side of the Thames, a large modernish farmish place with a garden which, past a couple of sheds and some swings and slides, led down to a mooring at the river.

'This must have cost a bob or two,' said Henderson.

'I'll wait in the car,' said the Lesbian. I wondered if he'd pillaged this neighbourhood in his previous 'trade'. It would have been more acceptable if he'd been a burglar. At least a burglar doesn't charge you VAT, or get halfway through the job then tell you he's going to have to nick twice as much as he originally thought.

The door was answered by a smart-looking woman in blouse and Liberty scarf, struggling to restrain two bloodhounds who were having a right good bay.

'Lee,' she said, extending her chin. I took this to mean that she would have extended her hand, had it been free.

'Mrs Collins,' said Henderson, bowing slightly, 'my colleague Stewart Dagman.'

'*Enchantée*,' said Mrs Collins. She pulled both dogs up by their collars as if about to throw them bouncer-style through the door but instead made a kind of weird flip with her wrists that impelled both animals into an inner room. She closed the door on them and looked at Henderson fondly. 'I knew you'd be back,' she said, 'Lee Junior is waiting for you out the back.'

'Lee Junior?' I said. The thought that Henderson had bought a secret son, I have to confess, had never occurred to me. This woman looked his type, though.

'That's right, Lee Junior,' said Henderson as Mrs Collins led us through the house, which was surprisingly messy given the neatness of its owner.

Riding tack, fishing gear, dog leads and all manner of outdoor kit was stacked in uneven piles throughout the hall.

'Excuse the mess,' said Mrs Collins, 'we've just . . . oh, sod it, it's always like this.'

We laughed and, as I recognised a well-worn joke, I remembered Cat and our first meeting. I wondered how she was, whether she'd grown big like Andrea, or if it was still barely noticeable on her.

'He's in here,' said Mrs Collins, leading us to a shed.

She opened the door and I could hear some rustling from within.

Christ, I thought, what's he come to, an illegal baby farm?

'Lee Junior!' called Mrs Collins. 'Your father's here to see you.'

She bent down over a cardboard box. I could see someone had put an old duvet inside it, and that there were feeding bottles strewn about the floor, but I couldn't see what she was holding.

'Say hello to Daddy,' said Mrs Collins, turning to show us the huddled form, the folded flesh, of a bloodhound puppy.

'Hello, son,' said Henderson, shaking the puppy's paw.

'You've not entered him in any soccer schools yet, have you?' I asked.

'No, but I reckon he'll clean up at the running events on school sports day. Maths might be a problem, though. Still, we'll get by, won't we?'

The bloodhound looked quietly confident.

'Here, I got this for him, you can put it on him.'

He took a small collar from his pocket. On it was an identity tag. On one side was Henderson's mobile number and on the other just one word: 'Loyalty'.

'Is that his name or his motto?'

'It is his motto and his creed,' said Henderson, who had already taken on something of the dog's rather lofty look. 'Loyalty above all else, always. Here at last is a friend I can trust not to leave me in the lurch – a friend who will never, at least not after what the vet's going to do to him, run off to answer the call of a family. This is my son and my best friend, my mate, my drinking companion, source of laughs and capers, my confidant, my chum.' He shook the tiny creature gently by the jowls for illustration. The dog looked neutrally at him. If Henderson was up for a life of companionship, it seemed early doors that Lee Junior had his doubts.

So maybe he's not after Cat after all, I thought. I wouldn't have banked on it, though.

'Shall we go to the house and I'll give you the pedigree forms?' said Mrs Collins.

'Where are you going to keep this animal?' I said.

'It's OK, I've cleared it with Andrea.'

'And have you cleared it with me?'

'Can't remember.'

'We can take that as a no then.'

'I'm going to need something when you're gone,' he said.

'How about a life?' I said. 'Why not get one of those? We haven't got room in our house for a dog.'

'All right,' said Henderson, quite hurt, 'tell the puppy you're leaving it behind – go on.'

He held Lee Junior up to my face. The doleful eyes gazed back at me trustingly. I noticed the sneer on my face easing into a nice little grin. I chucked the beast behind the ear. Christ, I thought, I'd better never see Cat's kids, it would kill me.

'Buy the puppy,' I said.

We returned to our house (I mean my house, *my* house) straight away, but not before Henderson had stopped at a pet shop and bought all manner of pet accessories, including a dog guard for the Range Rover that looked more suitable for restraining Zoltan, Hound of Dracula than Lee Junior, Hound of Henderson. Mind you, I could talk. I'd already bought one of those overland pushchairs, the sort that look like army surplus, a backpack for child-carrying (papoose) and a whole new wardrobe for going out in, including modern trousers so I'd look OK for all the attention I'd be getting. This despite being skint. The great thing about having kids is that you get an excuse to use a bit of kit.

The situation with the business wasn't good but neither was it desperate. It would have been desperate had it not been for the inheritance which my mum had assured me would be arriving before Christmas. 'December the twenty-fourth at the latest,' she'd said through a fag on the telephone.

So I approached Christmas in relatively good spirits, or as good as we could afford under the circumstances. In truth I was getting a bit concerned about my drinking. It wasn't that I was throwing them down me in the day, just that I'd got up to two bottles of wine a night to myself. Even Henderson had told me to take it easy. I knew then that I should rope it in. In British business you're not considered to have a drink problem until you're actually dead from it and they refuse to cremate you in case you go up like a Christmas pudding and burn the place down. So I made a resolution to recommence my exercise regime, which had rather dropped off, and to concentrate on working my problems through in my head.

The arrival of the bloodhound had slightly assuaged my fears on the Henderson/Cat front. I reasoned that his purchase of a child substitute meant that he'd probably given up chasing Cat, who contained two real ones. The trouble was that I was bursting for someone to talk to and I had no one.

So I was in the kitchen with the Lesbian, who had promised to make us some sort of baklava – I'm no expert on puddings, something with custard or other pudding stuff in it anyway – when I did hear from, or of, Cat again.

I recall it very well because I was getting on with the Lesbian splendidly. I found his former life fascinating and he seemed to like describing it. In retrospect I shouldn't have kept sampling the cooking sherry, but there you are, it seemed to go particularly well with the sponge fingers the Lesbian had bought.

'Why are you acting as Henderson's chauffeur at the moment?' I said. 'And how much is he paying you?' It can't be very well paid, I thought, or at least hoped, given that I was the one paying it.

'You don't want to know,' he said.

I suppose that was some consolation for the dreadful mess

my private life was in – associating with a genuine gangster type who said things like 'you don't want to know', in a half menacing way. It made me feel I was a little bit dangerous, one to look out for, a man of the world.

'Do you have to say that sort of line a lot in your work?'

'What sort of line?'

'You don't want to know ... leave it aaaaht ... shaaat it!' I was a bit pissed, as you can see.

'You ask a lot of questions, don't you?' said the Lesbian, leaning forward.

'Sorry,' I said, eyeing his mighty paws.

'No, that's one thing I might say because it's the kind of thing people expect me to say.' He made to prod me in the chest. ' "You ask a lot of questions, don't you?" '

'I see,' I said, impressed and flattered, like the boy whose dad has just shown him the special karate chop with which he felled a platoon back in the Sudan. 'So do you often have to fight people in your line of work?' I asked, in what I took for a cool-operator kind of style but probably made me look like I'd got something in my eye.

'I've never been in a fight in my life,' said the Lesbian.

I found this mildly disappointing.

'Isn't that rather hard to avoid as a minder?'

'If you hit them hard enough in the first place it never gets as far as a fight,' said the Lesbian with a cheeky wink.

I felt strangely naive and embarrassed, though excited, like a thirteen year old who's chatting up a girl at a disco when she tells him she has done it before.

'Cor,' I said, which is not a word I've used since I *was* thirteen. 'Cor!'

'There's no need to look impressed,' said the Lesbian, which immediately made me assume the demeanour of a man who heard this sort of thing day in, day out, 'I'm just making the most of my natural abilities.'

I felt a little ashamed that, like most men, violence has always held a fascination for me. It's the ultimate way of taking your destiny into your own hands. The problem of course is that the recipients of violence have a nasty way of fighting back, a nasty way that considerably diminishes its appeal for me. But my dad always idolised violent people, without ever getting involved himself – although he would throw imaginary punches as he watched the cowboys brawl on telly. He was full of stories about how, when he'd been in the Navy, proper bullies had started on him but quickly backed down when he'd given them his 'famous chop'. He'd illustrated this with an exaggerated movement of the arm which normally caused him to overbalance slightly. Still, the combined effects of this bollocks, as well as school and youth club, had meant that I'd internalised it so much that it now was me. I find it acutely embarrassing and I try to stamp it down whenever it comes up, but given the chance to talk about beatings and hammerings and who took six bouncers, I jump at it. Not that I've ever done anything about it, of course. I find the reality sickening, I only like it as a fantasy.

'Is that your only talent then, hitting people? What else do you do?' I was a bit angry with the Lesbian for noticing that I'd been impressed, particularly after he'd been trying to impress me.

'No,' he said, 'I'm a good listener.'

'What makes you think that?'

'Well, the Boyle gang used to employ me as a torturer. I think I developed the skill there.'

'You are joking, aren't you?'

He looked at me. I was going to say he looked at me menacingly, but if someone of the Lesbian's dimensions looks at you it only can be menacing, really.

'Of course I'm joking,' he said, 'but I think I have a certain empathy with people. It makes me quite good at what I do. I used to be in the extortion caper for a while. Now people assume that the whole demanding money with menaces business is all about frightening people.' He made a threatening motion with his spoon. 'There's a lot more to it than that. If you just scared your clients too much you might end up driving them away, or out of business if you ask for too much money, or you might end up with them taking the mickey if you ask for too little. It takes a certain flair to go for the right approach. You need a certain . . .' his mighty mitts tickled the air, like a conjurer abracadabraing a rabbit out of a hat '. . . sensitivity.'

'You should become a counsellor,' I said, reflecting that it was a weird world when the only person I knew who said 'taking the mickey' instead of 'taking the piss' was a professional extortionist. 'You could do a service to your own trade: "Do you put the angst into gangster? Murder and mayhem getting you down? Talk to someone who really understands your problems." '

'Once I've made my pile I may well consider it,' he said, wiping sugar off his moustache where he'd been licking the cake mix. 'Take your situation. I'd love to help you with that.'

'What is my situation?'

'Fiancée pregnant, girlfriend pregnant, gone but not forgotten. You caught between the two. It's fascinating.'

'Shh,' I said. 'I would remind you that the only person currently dwelling in my house who does not know about my girlfriend is my fiancée.'

'Just shows what a tough and unpleasant situation you're in when you put it like that,' said the Lesbian.

I swallowed the remains of my third large sherry and looked about the kitchen for a less sickly tipple.

'It's done now, but do you see how I was torn?'

'Oh, yes,' said the Lesbian, 'commendably torn, though. Self-fulfilment versus duty. And you chose duty. Like Captain Oates. "I may be some time." Commendable.'

'Didn't Captain Oates die?' I asked.

'But he was remembered as a good man.'

'I don't want to be remembered as a good man, I'd rather be experienced as a living bastard,' I said.

'Your actions say you're a good man,' said the Lesbian.

'So you think I did the right thing?'

'Only you can decide that.'

'Please,' I said, 'don't go all Obi Wan Kenobi on me.'

'You could have decided that you couldn't make a woman happy if you weren't happy yourself, so you could have behaved selfishly. That would have been a caring selfishness. You could, on the other hand, have worried about how you were going to treat both with an equal degree of respect.' He stroked the 'tache. 'And in a way you did treat them both equally, you deceived your fiancée and you shat on your girlfriend. So you were even handed.'

I felt like I used to at school, just at the bit when the headmaster was saying something like, 'We're well aware of who committed this outrage and it would be better for that boy if he stood forward now.'

The Lesbian continued. 'The nicest way of saying it is that you chose to stay with the woman you thought needed you most but now you seem unhappy. You acted caringly but wrongly, leaving two out of three people in the triangle miserable. I presume the girl is unhappy?'

'I don't know.'

'I think she must be. Children on the way, no man about. Very young. She must be. How do you feel about living a lie with your fiancée?'

'Not good.' I glanced at the door, even though I knew Andrea was out.

'There is one course of action,' said the Lesbian, 'but it's the action of a great man, not simply a good one.'

'What?'

'Suicide,' he said, gently and seriously, like a teacher explaining to a couple of barrister parents that it would be better for all concerned if Johnny went into the remedial set.

I laughed. 'You're not going to get much repeat business as a counsellor if that's your idea of a viable suggestion.'

'I'm serious,' said the Lesbian. 'If you want to treat both women equally and you want a clear unequivocal way out, commit suicide. Then they both realise how badly the situation was hurting you, they both receive money, both children are brought up equally, both women experience the same loss. There's no chance you might have a moment of weakness and do more damage in the future, plus you have peace of mind, the satisfaction of knowing you're doing the right thing. And in me you've got the contacts to make it look like murder. A bungled burglary for instance – no questions on the insurance. It's hard to resist, I think you'll admit?'

'Thanks, but no thanks.'

The Lesbian was getting quite into it. He leaned forward, pointing the spoon.

'You come home, "oh, my, an intruder", a struggle, your head repeatedly driven against the wall.' He made a thumping motion with his hand. 'Smiles all round, another satisfied customer.'

'I don't want to die,' I said.

'You've started drinking like you want to die.'

I shrugged. 'I'm not killing myself.'

'Then kill your guilt,' said the Lesbian. 'Tell Andrea about this woman too. Then you'll at least be honestly unhappy.' I got the feeling that was what he'd been leading up to in a funny way.

'It would kill her,' I said.

'She'll find out anyway, these things have a habit of coming out. What are you going to do in eighteen years' time when Cat's kids turn up on the doorstep looking for you?'

'I'll cross that bridge when I come to it,' I said. 'Andrea doesn't have to know. I've been thinking about this and it'll be difficult but possible to explain away the CSA payments. Henderson's going to have to back me up in fiddling the accounts so she won't notice it.'

'Your friend plays his own game,' said the Lesbian.

'What do you mean by that?'

'Nothing more and nothing less.'

I heard the door go and Andrea greeting Lee Junior.

'Not a word,' I whispered.

'You should tell her,' he said. 'Believe me, you won't be able to keep it a secret forever.'

'Want a bet?' I said as Andrea slammed into the kitchen.

'Who's this Catherine Grey you've been having an affair with?' she said, brandishing a letter at me. She was quite red in the face, I couldn't tell if it was with anger or the weight of the child. Even though she was only six months gone she was already finding the extra load difficult to adapt to.

Although my heart rate leaped to levels normally associated

with humming birds who hear the price of nectar has gone up, I affected the innocent smile of the truly guilty.

'I'm sorry?' I said, though inwardly meaning it without the question mark.

'I got this letter today from a Catherine Grey you have been seeing behind my back. Explain yourself.'

It felt like a dream. Everything said I'd been sussed but something was missing. I put my finger on it. Andrea had not yet shoved my face into the blender and, although she looked hot and flushed, she wasn't crying or screaming, just quietly demanding.

'I'm having an affair, am I?' I said, trying to appear mildly bored, like a gentleman pointing out to his butler that he'd just dropped some cigar ash on to his trousers and that he could hardly be expected to reach down and brush it off himself, but with a feeling of inner calm equivalent to that very same gentleman should the butler decide to remove the ash with a blowlamp.

'Look.' Andrea slapped the letter down on the table.

The Lesbian crushed almonds and whistled the tune of 'There May Be Trouble Ahead'.

I spread the letter out on the table, avoiding picking it up and revealing the tremor in my hands.

'Dear Ms Ellis,' it began. Cat had Andrea's business card. Bunny boiling was afoot, I knew, and no rabbit in the land would sleep safely in his hutch until the menace had been laid to rest.

'I hope you won't mind my writing to you, but I met your partner Stewart Dagman and he said you might be able to help me out of a fix.

'I am a journalist working for the InvestOrone internet news service – the one-stop source for all your business information. We're doing a feature on how high-flying executives . . .' I knew Andrea would have liked that bit '. . . juggle childbirth and their careers. Your partner said you are expecting a baby and that you have an important executive role in a leading charity. I would love to meet you . . .' I started fiddling with the wodge of *Daily Star* that held the table together and that Andrea's dad had stuck back in '. . . to discuss this with a view to producing an article. I hope you can make time to see me.

Yours

Catherine Grey

Features writer

Investorone.com'

'Exciting, isn't it?' said Andrea.

'Electrifying,' I said, calming down to roughly the level I was at when I was fifteen and crashed my dad's car after 'borrowing' it one day.

'So where did you meet her, this secret woman of yours? This bit on the side.'

'I can't remember. Must have been some corporate do, you know, we're always handing out cards and chatting, could be anyone. I honestly don't remember her.' I put my finger to my mouth as if thinking deeply. 'That's a bit worrying, isn't it? Perhaps I'm going mad, perhaps I have been having an affair with her and I've forgotten all about it. It's possible, I suppose. Be sure and tell me if she's good-looking, I wouldn't want to think I'd been having an affair with a woofer.' I laughed and it sounded like my first CD had sounded when I compared it to vinyl – clean, contained, a perfect reproduction that encompassed the exact sound of a laugh but none of its soul.

'I'm quite flattered, though, that you think I've still got it in me. Life in the old dog yet, eh?' I said. 'Woof woofola, grrrrrrrr, grrrrrr, grrrrr!'

'Oh, no,' said the Lesbian.

'What?' said Andrea.

'I think I've over egged this pudding.'

I took the point and shut up.

'You really can't remember her at all?'

'No.'

'Oh, well, I've said I'll meet her after Christmas. I've never been interviewed before. It'll be interesting to have my life put in the spotlight like that.'

'Quite,' I said. I looked at the Lesbian, who was dusting

pistachios over the baklava or whatever it was.

'I was interviewed once for a programme on body building,' he said.

'Did you enjoy it?' asked Andrea.

'Yes,' said the Lesbian, 'although in a weird way I ended up finding out more than I revealed.'

His bushy brows dived towards me. I felt something prod my trousers. Andrea had left the door to the kitchen open and the dog had come in and attached his nose to my leg.

'This will be quite different, I expect,' I said. 'I think I feel like a walk.'

'Dinner'll be ready any minute,' said the Lesbian.

'What is it?' said Andrea.

'Crispy duck with plum sauce.'

'Do you like plum sauce?' said Andrea, sidling up to the Lesbian like a little girl to her big brother.

'Yes, I love it.'

'Bender!' said Andrea, playground style.

We'd only been living with Henderson for ten minutes – though it seemed much longer – and already Andrea had picked up one of his many euphemisms for what biologists term gentlemen's relish. I often thought he had so many words for the man spoor because his own plum sauce lacked the necessary zing.

'I'm just going to walk around the garden for five minutes to put an edge on my appetite,' I said, fingers itching for my mobile.

'You've never done that before in your life,' said Andrea.

'I want Lee Junior to go to the loo,' I said, unclamming the dog from my leg. I ruffled his fur and felt for his collar.

'See how my hair's thickening with the hormones?' said Andrea.

'Loyalty,' I said, examining the dog's tag.

'You should give H some,' said the Lesbian. I presumed he was talking to Andrea.

13

The Devil You Know

I really needed to call Cat, but I didn't want to draw attention to myself. So I let the dog's tag fall from my fingers and left the kitchen in a casual stroll, roughly the sort Linford Christie had used to win the 1992 Olympic 100 metres final.

I tried ringing Cat on every number I had for her but met with answering machines or no reply.

Her mobile message, which I presumed she wasn't using for work any more, said, 'This is Cat, please leave a message. If that's Stewart (she called me Stewart, not even my mum calls me that) then please don't. Ever.'

I was shocked by the iciness in her voice, though I know I had no right to be. Weirdly it made me warm to her. In the same way I don't like people who leave wacky answerphone messages, I'll always be drawn to someone who'll leave an unpleasant one. It shows they value feeling over social conventions, that their private life is more important to them than what colleagues may think.

I know that, in feeling warm towards her, I was missing an important point – that the spiky, feisty message was being spiky and feisty at me, but what can you do? Strange are the movements of the human heart.

I couldn't think what to say to the voicemail, 'please leave my fiancée alone' being the gist of it, although I think I eventually said something more civilised like 'we need to talk'.

Why she wanted to see Andrea I had no idea. If she was going to reveal all she could have done that by letter. She couldn't be going to attack Andrea, could she? My mind was racing, but strictly as a back marker. I really was without a clue.

Ironically Henderson, who I'd been thinking of as a rival for Cat's affections, even if I was strictly a rival in absentia, was now my only hope of contact with her.

I desperately wanted to avoid her meeting Andrea. If she spilled the beans then I'd be in the worst of all possible worlds. I'd have lost the woman I wanted to be with most, and I wouldn't even have done the right thing by Andrea, the woman I wanted second most. I'd have achieved the reverse of what I'd set out to, both women dreadfully upset, me with neither. I'd be down to the woman I wanted third most, a post for which there were mercifully no contenders.

Henderson came Range Roving up the drive towards me in a burst of Whitney Houston.

'Just checking the tape for my mum,' he said, for some reason winding down the window rather than stepping from the car.

'Henderson,' I said, as Whitney began a note, 'can I ask you – have you spoken to Cat recently?'

'Depends what you mean by recently,' said Henderson. 'Recently in geological terms ... recently in terms of ages of man?'

'In the past week.'

'Oh, that sort of recent. Yes.'

'Why?'

'Just making sure she's OK. I thought you'd be pleased.'

'Which is why you didn't bother mentioning it to me before this?'

'I didn't think you'd be that pleased,' said Henderson, 'and anyway, if you can't report good news, why report any news at all?'

'So she's said something about me to you, has she?'

'Nothing nice.'

'Has she said anything about intending to do me or Andrea harm?'

'She's been far too busy with pistol shooting lessons to mention anything like that.'

'I'm being serious, Henderson.'

'I've only talked to her on the phone, she hasn't brought it up, why?'

'She's written to Andrea asking to interview her for her website. They're going to meet.'

Henderson assumed the expression of someone suddenly remembering they've left their handbrake off and turning to see the car hurtling towards the fruit stall. He stared at my feet.

'I don't know why they're going to meet, or if it's sinister, or what,' I said.

'Cat's not the sort to do anything physically unpleasant,' said Henderson, 'although I wouldn't rule out some sort of revenge ploy.' He was still looking at my feet.

'What do you think she'll do?'

'Just tell Andrea about your affair, I suppose.'

'She could have done that in the letter.'

'Perhaps she wants to do it face to face. If she's that angry she might want to see that she's causing some grief,' he said. 'It'll have a much bigger impact on Andrea to see your mistress in front of her than it would to hear about it in a letter.'

I gulped. Previous experience with women had told me that it's impossible to guess what they're thinking. I'd brought this up with 'Mad Bomber' Harris over the *latte* the other day.

'I always find it's a good idea to ask them,' he'd said.

'I couldn't countenance such wild-eyed folly,' I'd replied.

No, I've always preferred the time-honoured male method of making sweeping assumptions despite the obvious facts. When you discover what they're thinking, of course, it all seems so obvious in retrospect. Like with Andrea on the anniversary of the day we first kissed each other. I had, naturally, assumed that she was joking when she said we should do something special to celebrate it, the diary already being blighted by too many festival days and anniversaries and occasions to remember as it is. No one in their right mind would want to increase the amount of times you have to traipse grudgingly to the shops to buy cards, chocolate eggs, pancake mix, presents. Where's it going to stop? Goat sacrifices at Beltane? Am I going to end up in the dog house because I don't bring a little eye of newt for the cauldron on Walpurgis Night?

When, however, a year after our tongues had bullied off for the first time, it became apparent I had made no plan, bought no card or sweetmeat, Andrea left the house and came back two days later with a suspiciously circular love bite such as might be inflicted by a Hoover hose.

My mistake had been to suppose that, like any right-thinking person, her aim was to avoid all fuss or sentimentality whenever possible, when in retrospect it seems obvious I could have taken her question, 'What treats have you planned for this anniversary, an occasion very dear to my soul?' as a major clue to her thoughts rather than projecting my own desires on to her. See how I've got the knack of the counselling thing?

'What am I going to do, Henderson?' I said. 'And why are you looking at my feet?'

'Just thinking how little I'd like to be in your shoes right now.'

I felt like I was going to explode. I'd done the decent thing, gone for the woman I thought needed me most, and God had rewarded me with the treatment he reserves for his most loyal disciples – further trials.

'There is, of course, Plan B,' said Henderson.

'What was Plan A?'

'You don't go chasing after the first decent-looking piece of skirt that comes your way in ten years.'

'Plan A's out then,' I said. 'Plan B is?'

'Diversionary tactic, mate. I get Cat to go out with me – at least until her blood cools.'

'We've already been through this one, Henderson.'

'Admittedly, but when you were at a slightly higher ebb than you are at the moment. I gauge that you are approaching the very ebb where dignity, self-respect, even jealousy will go out of the window as you attempt to salvage something from the wreckage of your emotional life.'

I knew what he meant but I still couldn't bear to think of him with Cat. It was hard enough to think of me doing without her; thinking of him doing with her was beyond the pale.

'I'd like you to talk to her, nothing more,' I said.

'I still think it'd be safer if I shagged her,' he said, nodding like a mother reassuring her son she's put a little something to keep him warm in his lunchbox. 'Better the devil you know,' he said. I almost glimpsed a hint of a horn poking out from underneath the hair thickener. I could tell he was on that half-serious ground he favours. If I got upset he'd claim he'd just been joking, but if I said OK, do it and godspeed you, black emperor, he'd be after her faster than a fat girl into a sailors' disco. Portsmouth upbringing showing there, I'm afraid.

'No, Henderson,' I said.

'Belt and braces approach, mate. Talk and shag. The professional's combination. For when you need to know the job's been done.' As I would have expected, he illustrated his words with a peck of the hand and a shake of the hips. I was reminded of having watched him dance to 'The Birdie Song'. When I say reminded, I mean my attempts to suppress the memory had temporarily failed.

'You keep your belt and braces on,' I said. I knew what 'shag' was code for. This wasn't any innocent drunken adventure he was talking about, no. He was using the word as shorthand for 'attempt to embark on fulfilling lifelong relationship', or some close and poisonous equivalent. In a way, I thought, it was logical for Henderson to start seeing Cat. She'd get support – emotional and financial – for the babies; he'd get the stability he was after. Logical like it would be logical for us not to wear clothes in the street on sunny days, even when greeting the in-laws. Logical like it would be logical for me, given my status as a small businessman and most of my views, to vote Conservative. Logical but impossible.

'And,' I had a thought, 'you can speak to her over the phone.'

'I'm hardly likely to get it out of her over the phone, am I?'

I could see what he meant. But there again, if he restricted his contact to the mobile he'd hardly be likely to put it into her either.

'What do you want me to talk about?' he said.

'Why she wants to meet Andrea.'

'Nothing else?'

'Well, if you could see your way to talking her out of it, I'd be mighty grateful.'

'Grateful to the tune of allowing me a pop at her?'

'No.'

'One tiny pop? A minuscule little feeler?' He put out his hand in an air tickle.

'Absolutely not.'

'I think you're asking a lot of me. The least you can do is let me lean close and say, "You know, I wish it had been me and not Dag who'd met you that night." '

He sphinctered his lips and narrowed his eyes. I'd last seen a look like that when I'd been on a corporate to some big rugby game. The club captain had asked me what I wanted to drink and I'd said 'any decent alcopop will do'. Apparently not the recommended tipple.

'Nay, nay and thrice nay,' I said.

'Can I just stare wistfully into space and say, "I don't think Dag realises what he's throwing away?" '

'Just ask the questions, will you?'

'Anything else?'

'Just make sure she's all right,' I said as the Lesbian called us in for dinner and Whitney finished her note.

14

Should Old Acquaintance Be Forgot

Henderson had arranged to meet Cat on New Year's Eve at lunchtime, something I was very much opposed to.

My reason for this was simple. Without the constraints of having to get up for work the next morning, and given the licence of what we romantically refer to as the festive period, he could have an easy twelve-hour crack at her without fear of time being blown. On the positive side, either of them might have arranged to go to a party in the evening. On the negative side, they might decide to go together.

Henderson certainly seemed to be planning for the long haul and was completely resistant to the idea that he should see in the New Year with me and Andrea.

'No,' he'd said, 'you'll want to be alone at that special time.'

'We're alone at unspecial times,' I said. 'Please, intrude.'

'I'll leave you two together,' said Henderson, like an aunt confirming she wasn't one to fuss.

'You haven't got something going on you haven't told us about, have you, H?' said Andrea.

She had a slight note of concern in her voice. Christ, I

thought, now *she* fancies him as well.

Henderson and Cat had arranged to meet in Stoke Newington which made for easy retirement to Cat's house. The early signs weren't good but I couldn't think of any other way out than to use him to find out what she was going to do.

Henderson kept saying things like 'she's not your property' and 'you can't expect to control her, you're out of her life'. However, I could control one thing.

'If you do go against my wishes and end up sleeping with her, Henderson,' I said, 'remember that her duvet is actually mine. I didn't give it to her, I just turned up with it. You are expressly forbidden from using my duvet.'

Henderson frowned. He has a great respect for property.

'A cold arse is a price worth paying for love,' he said with a wink.

'Oh, so now you love her?'

'Only joking,' said Henderson. 'She'll probably turn me down anyway.'

'She won't need to turn you down, Henderson, because you won't be turning yourself up. In . . . ascertain reason for contacting Andrea, perhaps advise against . . . then out. Nice and clinical.'

Obviously I knew that a large part of Henderson's alleged attraction to Cat was just him winding me up. But, as any half-decent physicist will tell you, there is very rarely smoke without fire. I knew that he would be very unlikely, malice aforethought, to get off with her, but with a couple of ales inside him, who knows?

So on 21 December I found myself in the offices of Johnston Ethical Investigations – company motto: 'Results, Cheap and Fast' – a firm of private investigators recommended by Dave the Lesbian.

Their office was situated in a little entry off Portobello, a squalid groyne of broken glass and chip paper resisting the tide of gentrification swirling around it. I'd like to report that the interior of the office was a charming jumble of papers rising in crazy stacks like a cartoonist's vision of Chicago or Manhattan.

Disconcertingly, however, the room I entered was bare accept for a throw away quality desk that hadn't been thrown away, a Calor gas heater – on full – and a variety of electronic equipment spilling out of boxes. This, to me, said they didn't do very much business.

Behind the desk was a blade-thin individual in a heavy coat. I wasn't surprised about the coat. He looked as though nothing short of arson would warm him up. On top of the unpleasant visual effect was the niff: Calor gas and excess disinfectant. Andy Sharma was his name – a private dick who smelled like a public john. I was very pleased with that one and knew that Cat would have enjoyed it too, had I been able to tell it to her.

This is despite the fact that it's a very unfair smear on his name. The place only smelled like a public toilet because of his attempts to get it clean but us hard-boiled detective client types haven't got time for political correctness. If it's fairness versus a half decent one liner, the one liner wins every time. I find this a very good rule by which to live one's life.

'Mr Dogman,' said Sharma, 'we've been expecting you.'

I was pleased he half remembered my name from the phone call I'd made to him but there again, I'd remember all my clients' names if I only had one. Anyway, this was my first and maybe last ever visit to a private eye, so I thought I'd milk it for all it was worth.

'My buddy Dave Agonopilou' – I gave the Lesbian's real tag – 'sent me your way. Thing is, I gotta tell you straight, I'm in a squeeze. My floozy's threatening to blow it on my old girl. I just gotta get the low down, pop.'

Sharma looked at me as if I'd gone mad, which I had.

'I'm sorry,' he said, genuinely apologetic, 'we only speak English or Hindi here.'

I felt a wave of embarrassment coming up from my boots. Talking like something out of a B-movie had seemed a hoot of an idea on the way up the stairs. I think my problem was that I'd seen the 'tec flick *Lady Don't Fall Backwards* on cable a few days before. That's the way the jam spreads, kid.

'What, in a major world language, is the problem?' said Sharma.

I'd actually thought he'd hit me with the mechanic's 'it's gonna cost ya' when I told him what it was I wanted – that is, live transmission of Henderson's conversation with Cat. I wanted to be listening in a van outside. There were two reasons for this. I wanted to hear direct what Cat had to say and I wanted to be able to call the Iron Julie with details of Henderson's whereabouts, should he look close to putting out a feeler, or any sensitive member, in her direction.

Sharma surprised me.

'Easy,' he said, 'and cheap. We can use this.'

He produced a pen linked by a thin wire to a briefcase.

'A unidirectional microphone complete with radio transmitter power pack,' he said. 'I just go into the restaurant, order my meal, point this at them, and you – sitting outside – get to hear the lot.'

'Does it work?' I asked.

'Come to the window, kid,' said Sharma. This was more like it, I'd been called 'kid' by a private eye. No one else I knew could say that. He turned on an amplifier which had a large aerial on top of it.

'See the broad on the street?' I think he'd been slightly seduced by the idea of being able to talk like a real private eye. Either that or he was taking the piss. He was pointing at a market trader.

'Yeah.'

He aimed the pen at the woman.

'Twofrapan . . . twofrapan,' said the trader.

'It's rather indistinct, isn't it?'

'That's how she speaks,' said the detective, focusing in on another woman who said she wanted the fruit at the front. He then widened the field to take in someone else who said it was a disgrace, although I didn't hear what. I must say I was impressed with the clarity of the reception.

'You said it was going to be cheap?'

'Twenty pounds an hour,' said Sharma.

'On New Year's Eve, that's not bad,' I said.

'Aahhh,' said Sharma, 'that'll be double time.'

'Aren't you a Hindu?' I said. 'It's not your New Year, is it?'

'We're all global citizens now, Mr Dogman,' said Sharma, 'especially at forty notes an hour.'

So it came to pass that I found myself sitting wearing headphones in a van outside the swankiest hovel in Stoke Newington, a French restaurant and takeaway combined called L'Escargot To Go. Sharma had said he'd have to go into the restaurant later than Henderson and Cat because he had to make sure he got a seat near them.

We waited, looking out through the one-way glass down the street. Henderson was the first to arrive, hopping out of a cab. I nearly got out of the van and stopped it there. Everyone has key pulling garb, a set of clothes they normally get lucky in. It's not necessarily what you look best in, it's not necessarily your most expensive stuff. The only thing that defines pulling garb is that you pull in it. And Henderson had been known to pull in his £1,000 bespoke Anthony Clare single-breaster – a suit whose arse had never touched office chair or Mondeo upholstery fabric – even the £300 optional extra stuff. When I say pull, I don't mean actually pull. Henderson had been quite faithful to the Iron Julie – he'd certainly never gone further than a quick snog after a works do. No, it wasn't that he'd actually done anything, but he'd had the chance which, in the grand scheme, is the important thing. Pulling garb gets you to the line, puts your hands on the rope and lets you feel the tension. Whether you give it a tug or not is up to you.

He was wearing the suit with an open-necked shirt and his Rex Baron bespoke brogues. He looked as good as a bald man can. Worryingly, I noted as he passed the van that he'd left off the hair thickening spray he'd been using recently. This could have been because the Lesbian had pointed out that he was knocking a fair few quid off the value of his Range Rover by darkening the head rests, or it could have been that he didn't want to risk staining the pillow, should he get lucky. That too was annoying.

Henderson looked to left and right, checked himself in the restaurant's window, Gold Spotted and entered.

After five minutes Cat came along, and I nearly got out of the van again, but for a different reason. She looked like something out of Dickens. You could see she was pregnant from the bulge at the front of her coat but the rest of her body, from her arms to her legs to her face (that's in random order, she's not a contortionist), seemed to have got thinner. Her hair lay lank about her shoulders, like she couldn't be bothered to brush it; her coat seemed ragged.

It did occur to me that I was projecting this vision of her, unable to think that she would do OK without me. I mean, a perfectly good coat doesn't go ragged in the space of a couple of months, does it? Maybe my brain was seeing what it wanted to, refusing to acknowledge that she might be doing well without me. Still, she looked sad and alone as she made her way up the street, hunched against the cold. She reminded me most of the poster for *Les Miserables*, the whey-faced child struggling against a harsh world.

You should have thought about this when you were having your way with her, said a voice in my head. From down the street I thought I saw a flash of luminous yellow. Ridiculous! Lollipop ladies don't work on New Year's Eve.

I pointed them both out to Sharma, and with £40 of my money – I'd forgotten he'd want expenses – he made his way into the restaurant.

I put on the headphones and waited in the jumper my mum had bought me for Christmas.

Andrea and I had been to see my mum and dad at Christmas. As I've already noted, nothing I say, and I mean nothing, fails to upset my mother. I had done it that time by not coming straight out and saying that I didn't like the jumper she had bought me. This was largely because I had liked it, though she had seen a look about me that suggested I didn't and she wondered why I had to pretend and go about in a jumper I didn't like when she could easily take it back.

After a bit of to-ing and fro-ing, during which I'd been goaded into saying 'For Christ's sake, it's a jumper, a token, does it really matter if I like it or not?' she'd burst into tears saying 'You don't think I'm strong enough to take rejection'. In the end I gave in and told her that I hated the jumper and why didn't she bother asking me the type of design I like before buying such a stupid thing.

I said I'd take it back myself because I couldn't even trust her to do that. She'd stopped crying, pleased that I'd given her credit for the mental strength to take my disapproval. I hadn't actually taken it back. I'd just have to remember not to wear it whenever I saw her. I could pretend I'd exchanged it for the complimentary car coat I'd got from the Ungoliant Pharma Co's Meet The Pros Golf Challenge.

The headphones crackled.

'You know,' said Henderson's voice, 'sometimes I think Dag didn't realise just what he'd got in you.' He gave a low chuckle, which sounded about as attractive as that of a Scooby Do villain at the point where he thinks he's winning.

Still, I felt myself stiffen.

'I want you,' said Henderson, 'that's all I can say, plain and simple. Be mah baby tonight!'

He then, bizarrely, started to whistle his favourite tune – the theme from *The Great Escape*.

My hand went to the door of the van.

'Let me be a husband to you and a father to your child. Dag really doesn't think of you any more. He's a bad apple. A rotter.'

I was through the door and in front of the restaurant, head phones pinging off my ears. I should have known better. The one thing I'd learned from my adolescence is that if you think it's difficult to walk away from a lover without pain, you should try a hi-fi. I peered over the half-curtains like a neighbourhood watchman observing the goings on next door. Henderson was sitting alone at the table. I stood there puzzled for a second, rubbing my ears. He turned to the window and we made eye contact.

'What?' he mouthed at me.

From the back of the room I saw Cat coming. She had been in the loo and Henderson had just been arsing about for reasons best known to himself. Before she could see me I dived back into the van and secured the doors.

I was glad Henderson had seen me. It'd give him pause for thought.

I put the headphones back on.

'It's good of you to meet me,' I heard Cat say. Henderson was some salesman, he'd actually convinced her she'd asked to see him.

'No problem,' he said. I couldn't tell if the microphone was no longer focused on him or if he had that faraway tone to his voice.

'Sorry about the loo,' said Cat, 'I'm having to go all the time at the moment. It's the baby.'

'No problem,' said Henderson mechanically.

'Would you like to order a drink?' came the waiter's voice.

'No problem,' said Henderson. He'd obviously been a little stunned to see me and was busy composing himself. Then he found his voice.

'How are you feeling about this whole Dag thing?'

'Much better,' said Cat. I didn't like the sound of that. Of course I did like the sound of it in theory, just in practice I wanted her still to love me. My moral side was disappointed to hear that she wasn't having the time of her life but, let's face it, I have a moral side like Manchester United have a pub quiz team. It's not the main focus of my existence.

'Any particular reason?' said Henderson.

'Probably because I couldn't have felt much worse.'

Henderson gave a brief professional snort, almost of the sort he chucks out day after day as a token of appreciation of the non-funny funnies of his clients. There was something else, though. He sounded nervous, although he had no right to be. Nervous is what you get when you're trying to get off with someone. When you're trying to dig something out of them you want detached and assured.

'Was it really bad?' said Henderson, sounding the reverse

of detached – terraced, practically.

'No, not really,' said Cat, 'I was fine. Nothing that a couple of suicide attempts couldn't sort out.' I felt a nausea rising inside me.

'You're joking?' said Henderson.

'No,' said Cat, 'only the one serious bid, actually.'

'Oh, shit,' I said to no one.

'Did it affect the baby?' said Henderson. I could hear a slight tremor in his voice.

'I doubt it,' said Cat. 'I tried to bore myself to death by going into an internet cafe at two in the morning and asking the guys what was so good about Tomb Raider.'

'What saved you?' said Henderson. I heard a squeak. He was doing that easy charm move where he smiles indulgently and leans back in the chair.

'They realised I was a girl and lost interest,' said Cat. 'They didn't notice for the first couple of hours, what with me being only a C cup.'

'Lucky that,' said Henderson, with another squeak that probably indicated a lean forward for a sly flick of the eyes at her tits. 'Seriously, though, how have you been?'

'Pretty bad.'

'In what way?' said Henderson. This line of questioning was straight out of our 'Be Liked – It Pays' course.

'The obvious way really,' said Cat. 'One minute I'm a single girl in a decent career. All I say is, "I'm not sure if this is for me," and, just my luck, my Fairy Godmother's listening. Wish granted. You're no longer a career girl, you're a single mother. I was sitting there navel gazing and suddenly my navel started coming out to meet my face.'

'It doesn't actually go towards your face, does it?' said Henderson with a faint hint of distaste.

'I was exaggerating for the purposes of an interesting thing to say,' said Cat.

'There is no greater consideration one can pay,' said Henderson. He was camping it up slightly. He reminded me of someone I knew.

'You sound like Dag,' said Cat.

'I do a good impression actually,' said Henderson. I couldn't work out if he'd twigged he was being taped or not. More than likely he was trying subliminally to imply that he could do a fairly good impression of me beneath the hot duvet of passion.

'How is he?' said Cat.

'He's Dag,' said Henderson. 'Look at that bloody great van blocking the view from the front of the restaurant.'

'It doesn't bother me,' said Cat.

'It wouldn't,' said Henderson.

'Is he happy?' Cat sounded suddenly serious. Don't be such a doormat, girl, I thought. I didn't like the idea of her not fighting back. I wanted her to keep her dignity in all this, for God's sake.

'So so,' said Henderson.

'That's a pity,' said Cat. 'I was hoping he was as miserable as sin.'

'You could always make him as miserable as sin,' said Henderson. Steady, I thought, we don't want *that* much dignity.

'Tell his fiancée, you mean?'

'That'd do it.'

'Hmmm,' said Cat.

I felt like a military commander who'd sent in his crack troops to oust some terrorists only to hear, 'Oh, look, you've wired that bomb all wrong, here let me show you how it's done,' coming over the radio. I was hot beneath my headphones.

'I'm considering it,' she said, 'but that would be pure revenge.'

'Can be very cathartic.'

'What are you doing?' I said into space. I couldn't work out Henderson's motivation here. Unless he'd guessed I was listening and was just trying to wind me up. Surely he was above that?

'The thing is,' said Cat, 'I do love him. Sad as it is, I want him to be happy.' I looked at my shoes. Sometimes, as an eavesdropper, it's better to hear bad about yourself than good. I felt a creep of guilt crawl across my body.

'Aren't you at all in touch with your negative side?' said Henderson. 'There has to be a yin yang thing here you know. Too much yin can lead to not enough yang and then where are we?'

'Oh I know,' said Cat. That's the level of the woman's generosity, going along with such rubbish.

'He says you've contacted his fiancée,' said Henderson.

'Thank you, at last,' I said, again to no one.

'Yes,' said Cat.

'Are you ready to order?' said the waiter.

'We are,' said Henderson, completely losing the thread.

They ordered, Henderson taking the lobster. He's never quite got the hang of the idea that women aren't impressed by your ordering the most expensive thing on the menu, probably because of the Iron Julie and most of her mates who will actually look down on you if you don't order the most expensive thing on the menu.

'Will you have champagne?' said Henderson.

'I'd better not, the babies.'

'They'll be fine,' said Henderson. 'I never got a hangover until I was nearly twenty-four. They're got years before they need to worry about that.'

'Go on then,' said Cat, 'but just a couple of bottles, no more.'

'That's my girl.'

'No, Henderson,' I said, 'that's *my* girl.'

'Yes,' resumed Cat, 'I have contacted Andrea. Has he asked you to find out why?'

'Say no,' I said. I didn't want her thinking she'd got me worried, if that was her aim.

'Yes,' said Henderson, 'he's very worried about it, if that was your aim.'

There was a silence, during which I reminded myself how much communication is non-verbal.

The champagne was brought and poured.

'Let's just say I'm curious,' said Cat. She said it with a slight edge to her voice that could have been taken for hostility. I reminded myself she could just be hamming it up for Henderson.

'As an adjective or a noun?' he said, that slightly posh lilt to his voice that indicates he's trying to be clever.

'When is it a noun?' said Cat.

'As in curiosity killed the cat?' said Henderson.

'How about as in "curious killed the cat"?' said Cat.

'What would it be there?'

'Grammatically incorrect,' she said.

'Am I right in thinking curious is only a noun when it's a completely different word, say "table"?' said Henderson.

'You are.'

'Thought so,' he said. '*Chin chin.*' I heard the chink of glasses and the tinkle of laughter. I don't like tinkles of laughter in circumstances like these, they can all too easily turn into the tinkle of bonking, if you see what I mean.

'So why are you seeing Andrea?' said Henderson. That's good, I thought, very good, butter her up get her relaxed, killer question. You have done well, my pupil.

Cat didn't say anything, though I could imagine her inclining her head and looking down to one side the way she did when she was lost in thought. I remembered the grace of her movements, like a real cat.

'So . . .'

'You don't need to repeat the question, I'm just thinking.'

'Sorry,' said Henderson.

I imagined Cat drumming her hand on the table, and struggling for the words, like she had in laughter the night I met her, like she had in tears the night we parted. Look, if you can't have a sentimental fit on your own in the back of a Transit listening to your best mate chat up the love of your life, where can you?

'I think I'm really seeing her for the sake of the babies.'

'What do you mean by that?' said Henderson. There he went again.

'It's just I'd like to be able to tell them about their dad

properly, everything. I want to be able to tell them what their dad's fiancée was like, what his friends thought of him, everything. There's a bit of me that wants to know him more fully now he's gone than I did even when he was here. I just want to find out how I could have been so wrong about someone, really.'

'That's exactly how I've felt whenever I've been stalking people,' said Henderson. 'Thank God there are laws to curb the excesses of my behaviour now.'

They both laughed but it wasn't funny. There in the detective's van, huddled behind the one-way glass and listening into the headphones, the terrible truth dawned on me. I was being stalked.

Then I had a brainwave. I pulled out my mobile and quickly text messaged Henderson.

'Will She Tell A?' I wrote.

I heard his phone buzz and then him excusing himself to Cat as he picked up the message.

'Business?' she said.

'Certainly not pleasure,' said Henderson. Then he said flatly, 'Do you intend to tell Andrea?'

'I intend to make up my mind when I see her.'

This wasn't what I'd been hoping for. A 'yes' and I'd have to bite the bullet and tell Andrea anyway, a 'no' and all would be sweet benison, get on with enjoying the rewards of duty rather than passion. This middle way was neither flesh nor fowl as Terence Trent D'Arby once commented, shortly before disappearing from view.

'Actually,' said Cat, 'I'm sorry about this but could I just go to the loo again?'

'Oh, go on,' said Henderson, 'just this once more, mind. I'll answer this call while I wait.'

I gazed out of the back of the van in contemplation. Henderson was suddenly outside. He was making a phone call and pressing his face childishly against the back window. As soon as he got through he walked away from the van, pretending to moon at me. A couple of minutes later he returned to the restaurant.

'Sorry about that,' he said, 'urgent message. More champagne?'

There was more glugging and a couple of gulps.

Then Henderson said, 'It is a shame about all this, though. Dag's got a lot of layers to him. It's hard to lose a love like that, especially when it could so easily grow through the children. I think he loved you. It's . . .' he appeared to be searching for the right words '. . . a shame. It's like you and he got it right but the world got it wrong. I think he'd still be with you if he could.'

Henderson was speaking the truth but so much was keeping me with Andrea. Her parents, the years we'd spent together, and now even the fact that I'd already upset Cat. At least I wouldn't upset anyone else if I just stayed as I was.

'Wrong time, wrong place,' said Cat.

'Tell me about it,' said Henderson.

'This sort of thing's happened to you?'

'Well, happens to everyone, doesn't it?' he said wearily. 'No matter how much you care for someone and they for you, things don't always work out.'

Now this statement of Henderson's might sound obvious and trite, and indeed was obvious and trite, but compared to most of what I'd heard him come out with in the last twenty odd years it was the Gettysburg Address, the Sermon on the Mount, 'I think therefore I am', and 'Nice to see you; to see you nice', rolled into one.

Furthermore it was a very clever intimation that he'd always carried a torch for Cat.

'What went wrong between you and Julie then?' That was something I'd never gone into too deeply with him, reasoning that he wouldn't want to dwell on it and would want the mental space to pull himself together.

'I don't know really,' said Henderson, 'I wanted kids, she didn't – that was a big difficulty. And I didn't love her. That's OK if you're getting other things you want but if you don't have love, you don't have kids and eventually you don't even have sex, where does that leave you?'

'So you wouldn't have her back?' said Cat.

'Oh, like a shot,' said Henderson, 'she kept the rose beds lovely.'

Cat gave a sad little laugh.

'Nah,' said Henderson, 'there's the right one out there for me, I know, I'll just have to wait.'

'You bastard,' I said to my shoes.

'You wouldn't have Dag back?' he said. There was a pause.

'I don't know. Half of me feels like trying to get him back, half of me feels like getting my revenge and half of me feels like walking away.'

'That's three halves to your feelings,' said Henderson.

'Yes, and they're not the half of them.'

'Of course,' said Henderson, 'if you really want to annoy him you should go for the shagging his best mate option. It's the classic.'

'That would be you, right?'

'Do you know, I believe it is,' said Henderson, as if the thought had only just occurred to him. 'But, like any gentleman, I'm naturally willing to do anything to help a lady in distress.' There was a low bow in his voice as he metaphorically twirled his cavalier's hat.

'You'd have to make sure I really enjoyed it,' said Cat. 'More than I ever did with him, just to really piss him off.' I thumped the side of the van, hurting my hand.

'I don't see any problem there,' said Henderson in the kind of voice you imagine Michelangelo might adopt, trying to reassure someone he could decorate their spare bedroom. 'What sort of thing had you in mind?' He took a particularly vigorous suck on what I assumed was a piece of lobster.

'Really, though, what do you think I should do?' said Cat.

'Oh, we weren't being serious?'

'No.'

'Of course we weren't. See Andrea and then see what you think. If you feel like telling her, tell her; if you don't, don't. It's a decision only you can make. But if you really love

Mark Barrowcliffe

someone then sometimes the best thing you can do is leave them alone.'

This was a side of Henderson I'd never seen before. This wasn't the Showbiz Vim kid, the pumper of handshakes, the striker of golf balls. It wasn't the advice I'd wanted him to give but it could have been a lot worse.

'I know he cares for you an awful lot but he's made his decision and maybe you should accept it. Or, if it makes you feel better, blow the lid on it. He's acted very selfishly, so why shouldn't you? Whatever happens you've got friends to stand by you. Anytime you need to talk you can call me.'

There was another pause as drinks were drunk and food chomped, I presumed.

'You're not quite the lad that you seem, are you?' she said.

Henderson gave a little sniff. 'It's just Dag's influence. It always takes me half an hour to get out of that boysie thing whenever I meet someone who's connected with him.' I bridled under the headphones. It was Henderson who always started the boysie banter. I'd have been happy to talk about serious things but it was him who always piled in with golf, cars or politics, or his version of politics, which normally went along the 'give me the rope, I'll hand 'em myself' tack.

'Is he so immature?'

'Not him, us. He's probably like me when he's on his own, it's just that we've known each other so long . . . you know, all that competitive banter, all the mad stories . . . it's what we do. Saves us speaking to each other, I suppose.'

There was another pause. Henderson ordered more champagne. He must have been nervous because he was clearly guzzling it at an incredible rate.

'It is quite funny though, sometimes,' said Cat. I could hear a smile in her voice.

'You're right,' said Henderson. 'Quite right. That's enough poetry and despair, tell me about you.' He resumed his bullish mode. 'I don't know anything about you, really. Where do you come from and what do you do? Start at the beginning.

What do your parents do for a living?'

'I never knew my father.'

'I'm sorry.'

'Don't be, it was a miracle considering how much he used to hang around our house when we were growing up.'

With a lurch I recognised the polish of the well-worn joke once more. That's what she said to me when we first met, I thought.

'My father was a vicious drunk, plain and simple,' said Cat.

I literally felt the ground move beneath me as she began the set up for her 'oh, no, now I remember he was in fact the kindest man nature has ever known' routine.

The more observant will have noticed that I said that I 'literally' felt the ground move beneath my feet. All too often in the modern idiom the word is used in a sloppy way to mean almost the reverse of its established sense. I am not a man given to such laxity. So let me say that what I wish I'd meant was that I practically, virtually, almost, felt the ground move beneath my feet. That's certainly what I thought at the time, that the blow of hearing Cat go into what I presumed was a mating song had shivered m'timbers and shaken m'rigging. I had assumed that I'd experienced what the French call a *coup d'force*, and we a body blow, a knock, so I quickly put my full concentration back into what was going on in the headphones. Cat had finished her joke and Henderson was laughing, telling her she should have come to his creative writing class, had he not been thrown out for his insistence that limericks were a valid art form. She was chuckling away like she hadn't had so much fun in ages, which I guess she probably hadn't.

'It's the rigidity and sheer discipline of the limerick I love,' said Henderson, camping it up in a mock-posh voice.

'You do sound like Dag!' shrieked Cat.

'We're at a unique historical juncture where such observations are possible. Previous generations had no time for such guff,' he said. Cat howled again. He did sound like me. It's a weird feeling to hear yourself reduced to a mannerism, an accent, to hear yourself as others hear you.

'The poet sets himself – and us, very much us – a problem, a statement yes, but also a question,' said Henderson. ' "Up in the old Khyber Pass . . ." '

Here we go, I thought.

' "Where the donkeys do munch on dope grass," well, the listener – and this is very much a living, vocal form . . .'

I admit that, when discussing football chants once, I had described them as 'a vibrant oral heritage', but I'd never said 'living vocal form'.

Henderson continued, '. . . the listener naturally asks what, what in the old Khyber Pass, what effect could cannabis consumption have on the equine constitution? There is tension here, tension but inevitability, all within the wonderfully rich English bawdy tradition.'

He definitely was doing me. He continued, ' "They don't smoke a joint, they say there's no point, when if they want they can sniff Dobbin's arse!" ' I heard Cat asking, in mild amusement, if it was one of his.

I wondered if this was really worth the investment of £40 an hour.

I was listening to Henderson congratulating himself on the limerick when I realised that I had indeed literally felt the ground move beneath my feet – or, to split hairs, my feet move above the ground. I glanced up momentarily to note that I seemed to be rising into the air. I scrambled to the partition of the van and looked through the one-way glass out to the windscreen to see the back of a tow-truck and the legend 'Hackney Council – working to keep London moving'. They were certainly doing a reasonable job on me.

'There goes that van that was irritating you,' said Cat.

'Yeah, I rang up and got it towed,' said Henderson. 'I can't stand illegal parking, can you? So what's the inside of your flat like?' I heard him say as the signal faded and the van moved out of range.

Two hours it took the detective to find the pound after I called him. By the time we got back to the restaurant it was answerphones-a-go-go and nothing to do but return to the ancestral pile and await Henderson's return. I had a feeling I might be waiting some time.

15

Crucial
Conundrum

I got back to the house at about 8 o'clock, weary from my exertions at the pound.

I don't know why but something had possessed me to take public transport home rather than getting a cab. I think it was probably the state of the minicabs in Stoke Newington, most of which would struggle to meet the safety requirements of a Viet Cong booby trap.

It took me a good couple of hours to return, creaking down to Liverpool Street on the overground, then squiggling along the Metropolitan line for an age, my only diversion a copy of *Corriera della Sera* I found and attempted to read.

I entered the house to hear music from the front room, Whitney or Celine or one of those. Andrea was catching Henderson's taste, obviously.

I stood for a second without turning on the light, just looking at the hall in shadow. It reminded me of a nativity scene in a glass box I'd seen one December outside a church in Italy. You put in a few coins and the wise men filed in, the donkeys ate and a light came out of the baby Jesus's crib. It was raining and no one had put any money in. The house had that feel to it of something lying dormant. Switch on the light, I thought, and it all starts again under its own steam. No further input necessary from me.

You've made your choice, you have no right to these feelings, I told myself.

I took off my coat and approached the living-room door. I thought of Andrea, realised that she might not have heard me come in, with the music on and everything. Since I was past the stage where I routinely liked to frighten the life out of people for amusement, I clicked on the light and called her name.

'Hello!' I heard from the other side of the door. I opened it and went in.

Henderson was lying flat on his back holding a champagne flute to his forehead. Andrea was sitting on the floor with the Scrabble board between them.

'Well,' I said, containing my surprise, nay, delight, 'this is a scene of domestic bliss.'

'Infidelity!' shouted Andrea. 'I set the trap and you walked right in, didn't you? Triple word score! You're hammered, Henderson.' She added seven letters to what I presumed was one of Henderson's contributions – the word 'ide'. Bullshit, not Scrabble, was his talent.

Cat must have gone home alone, I thought. Excellent. Then I realised that, while it could simply be taken as an indication that she didn't fancy Henderson, it could also be taken as an indication she was not over me and still hell-bent on meeting Andrea. It also meant she might be on her way to attend a fancy dress party where she'd meet some tattooed and pierced young buck with a great future in the city. I'd be glad if that happened, of course, on paper. And we all know about on paper.

'I've had too much to drink,' said Henderson. But not so much that he'd forgotten to remove the £5,000 Anthony Clare single-breaster, I noted. He wasn't wearing anything more than boxer shorts and a vest. The vest, I knew, was a 1970s retro thing, highly fashionable, highly ironic, still awful.

In nineteen fifty-something Cary Grant had destroyed the vest industry by removing his shirt to reveal a bare chest. I will simply record that Henderson looked unlikely to spark a revival in its fortunes.

'Perhaps you'd like to go upstairs for a kip, otherwise you won't be in a fit state to see in the New Year,' I said, pointedly. I wanted a chance to grill him properly about Cat.

'I need to finish the game,' said Henderson. He was really quite drunk. I hadn't seen him like this ever since he'd realised exactly how many calories your average pint contains. We'd worked out that on our twenty-something drinking habits one hour in the gym bought about fifteen minutes in the pub, before you chucked in the dry roasteds and cheese and onions. In the interest of Henderson's six pack he'd curtailed his drinking massively. That was really when the Showbiz Vim had stepped in.

'Don't worry,' I said, 'I can finish it for you.' I looked at the board. 'It's going to be difficult, though, there can't be that many more two-letter words left.'

'I've let him use some twice,' said Andrea. She had as well. There were two 'on's on the board.

'Id,' said Henderson looking up from the floor into my eyes, 'is a Freudian term for a bit of the old wahey! Remember that and you won't go far wrong, my son! And Ibo. They're tribes-men.'

'Tribes people,' said Andrea, correcting him without looking up from the tiles.

'The ones I met were blokes,' said Henderson.

'Where's the Lesbian tonight?' I asked.

'He's got the night off. Apparently it's impossible to get anyone to beat anyone up professionally on New Year's Eve, they're all out getting pissed,' said Andrea, 'hence Henderson is safe.'

'That's touching in a strange way, isn't it?' I said.

'I don't know why he bothers with that Lesbian,' said Andrea, brows arching as she conjured up another fiendishly long word, 'Julie's never going to have him battered, she's got more style. She'll do him through the courts.'

'What for?' I said.

'She'll think of something,' said Andrea, burrowing her eyes into her Scrabble letters.

The glass Henderson had been trying to balance on his head fell off on to the carpet.

'Do you need help getting to bed?' I said.

'Not half,' said Henderson, pronouncing the 'h' carefully, like a chauffeur in front of a grand lady.

I helped him up the stairs into the bedroom, with the ease with which one might squeeze an elephant into a fitting room.

'I hope you didn't get like this when you were with that young girl?'

'She's lovely,' said Henderson, rather worryingly.

'Did she say what she was going to do about Andrea?'

Henderson sat up, suddenly haughty. 'She will do as she pleases,' he said, like a High Court judge saying, 'And exactly who are these "Beatles"?'

'So you didn't find out?'

'I tried, Dag, I tried. It was so hard, though. I could only think of you in that van and of winding you up. Sorry.' He started to laugh.

'Yeah, right,' I said.

Henderson collapsed on to his head, whistled the first few bars of *The Great Escape* and fell to snoring loudly.

I was about to head downstairs when my attention was caught by a letter wedged face down under the lamp on his bedside table. No one actually writes letters any more, this being the age of e-mail, so I was curious to find out what it was.

It was in a blank, unsealed envelope, written in the kind of scrawl that I understand is favoured by doctors and the wider community of extortionists throughout the country. I picked it up. I didn't recognise the handwriting, but there again I don't really recognise my own.

'She Suspects,' it read. 'Danger on Way. Both beware.'

I would have guessed immediately it was of criminal provenance from the poor use of capital letters and the lamentable lack of any formalities. What tipped it for me, however, was the signature.

'A fucking friend', it said. No man of stamp ever signs himself in such a way. There was no envelope so no way of knowing where it had come from, or even if Henderson had written it himself.

Oh, dear, I thought, it looks as though the Lesbian might be needed after all.

Strangely this didn't frighten me that much. After all, it was Henderson who was in Julie's firing line – I was fairly sure the 'she' was her. I'd always got on with Julie, largely by agreeing with everything she said and admiring her 'beautifully tasteful' tropical-style master bedroom with en suite foot spa. Danger on Way. No, Andrea was right. It could only mean financial danger.

I looked down at Henderson snoring on the bed and suddenly felt immensely protective towards him. He'd been my mate longer than anyone, really. We'd been through thick and thin together, really, mostly thick – this was my first bit of thin. I knew him better than I knew anyone in the world.

He was filthy-minded, money-centred, childish and weak, but I did love him in that manly way you see in 1950s Hollywood cowboy films (not millennial cowboy bars). Could I begrudge him happiness with a woman I loved but couldn't have? Could I put my own discomfort above his narrow chance of familial bliss? Of course I could. I wanted Cat as far away from my life as possible, a clean break. I didn't want to live with my guilty secrets so close, and I didn't want to see her with another man, no matter how close a friend.

'I love you and I want you to marry me,' said Henderson, asleep.

'Sorry, darling, I'm spoken for,' I said.

'He will never know, I have curtains to cover us. They are rich and velvet.'

'He does know,' I said, 'and it will be curtains for you if you cover her.'

'Don't marry him,' said Henderson, 'my entire vehicle is at your disposal.'

It occurred to me to tape him saying all this. Ever since the nineteen-ninety-god-knows-what skiing trip where I'd fallen victim to the hand in the bucket of water while asleep so you wet the bed gag, I'd been looking for revenge.

That had really annoyed me. For one I hate that sort of pants-on-the-head sense of humour, and for two I hadn't liked wetting the bed. It was terribly annoying being accused of having no sense of humour when I wouldn't have found it funny if it had happened to someone else. Still, you pays your money and you takes your choice.

Tape recording, however, wouldn't really have sufficed. I guessed my best revenge was growing out of that sort of behaviour and showing I was a superior human being. Still, it was very tempting to pull Henderson's boxers up the crack of his bum.

'She's not going to marry me,' I said, 'she never was.'

'I knew the Range Rover would do it,' said Henderson. 'Four-wheel drive works every time.'

'I'll leave you to your drivel,' I said.

'Eats hills like these,' said Henderson.

I went back down to Andrea.

'Is he asleep?' she said.

'Yes, hopefully, until he needs feeding in a couple of hours,' I said. 'Do you know what he got up to tonight?'

'Seeing some client, I think,' said Andrea. She was looking back down at her Scrabble pieces. 'Would you play? I've got a great word I want to put down.'

'A client on New Year's Eve, that's a bit weird,' I said. I'd forgotten that Henderson's cover story was also my cover story, in a manner of speaking.

'I'm not really bothered, Dag,' said Andrea. There was an edge to her voice that boded a bit ill.

'I see,' I said. 'What does bother you?'

'The fact I'm six months pregnant, feeling mildly down, can't have a drink on New Year's Eve and there's the normal shit on the telly.'

'That would do it,' I said. I leaned over towards her and put my hand on her knee. I wanted everything to be all right for her. I wanted everything to be all right for everyone. Mind you, when there's a car crash there's no one who so sincerely hopes everyone's all right as the bloke whose fault it was.

'Kiss me,' I said.

'Not tonight, Dag,' said Andrea, 'I'm not in the mood.'

'You've changed your tune,' I said as she laid down 'justice'.

16

Camera Obscura

January went by in a spin. The business was taking in a reasonable amount of money, with the courses doing well, but it was spending it at an incredible rate too: marketing, hotels, booking rooms, organising catering. The problem with a trade like ours is that when you're making money you're really making it – £1,000 a delegate is pure profit once you've broken even. It's just that not breaking even tends to be rather expensive.

Still, the end was in sight. We reckoned that by the end of February we'd be turning a profit, if we could stave off the creditors for that long. My mum, though, was adamant that my inheritance was still coming through. Better still, the ski-ing trip was on. Brilliantly, fantastically, two of the three Daves had got divorced and been forced to start going around with each other again. With Andy 'no one likes him' Hill, Henderson, and maybe, if Andrea had the baby more than a couple of weeks before we went, me, we had a caucus. Even if I didn't go we were back on for future years. Life looked grand again.

There was, of course, the problem of the interview with Cat. It was set, ominously, for the lunchtime of Valentine's Day which, I have discovered, is on 14 February.

I tried talking Andrea out of it but nothing seemed to work.

'Wind her up, don't turn up there,' I said, 'it'd be a laugh.'

'In what way?' said Andrea, inspecting one of three Valentines.

'Don't know,' I said, inspecting none of none. A few years ago I'd been moaning on about the number of commercially driven anniversaries we have to put up with nowadays. Andrea had decided that, since I was so pure of spirit, I wouldn't be wanting anything for birthdays, Valentine's or Christmas any more.

I'd tried phoning Cat solidly for about two weeks. I got through to her flat quite easily but only managed to speak to the perpetually ill Chloe who told me that Cat had moved out, she was glad she had gone and not to bother her any more. No, she didn't know where she'd gone but wherever it was she hoped Cat got noisy neighbours.

If Cat had ever liked Chloe I'd have thought she was covering up for her, but a combination of our bonking, Chloe's chest complaint and walls with all the sound insulation of lingerie had been a recipe for constant arguments.

I bunged Sharma a few quid to check anyway. 'No sign. Two hundred quid, please,' he'd said.

I tried her work, but was told she was working from home and, yes, she had moved recently. When I'd said I wanted to write to her and could I have her address, I was told to write via the company. When I'd said I very urgently needed to contact her and couldn't really wait for a letter to be passed on the crisp young voice had asked me if I was a stalker. 'Yes, actually,' I'd said and put down the phone.

I e-mailed her again and again, but there is only so much you can say when someone's the love of your life and you just want them to stay away. 'Sorry about everything' is the best I came up with.

This aside I had managed to put the meeting out of my mind. It could have been because Henderson was fretting so much about the 'death threat' he'd received, in other words the letter I'd seen in his room. He'd taken it to be fingerprinted by the police, but luckily (I'd picked it up, remember) they'd said they were very busy and that, owing to cuts, they had to prioritise the seriousness of crimes. If he wanted quick service, the sergeant had said, he should come back when he was dead.

'I just might!' said Henderson, recounting the story.

As a goodwill gesture, and for Henderson's safety, we'd allowed the Lesbian into the second spare room provided he started paying rent or Henderson started paying him less.

Oddly Andrea didn't seem to mind all this. I think she enjoyed the Lesbian's company and found Henderson's paranoia about Julie something of a hoot. Apart from that my only achievement in six weeks had been to train Lee Junior to sit on command by rewarding him with sniffs of my leg.

I still hadn't entirely rid myself of suspicion on the Henderson/Cat front. For a start, despite having the Lesbian move in, Henderson was spending less and less time at home.

'He has to,' said the Lesbian.

'Why didn't you have to before?' I said.

'Upgrading of emergency code since the letter,' said Henderson, as if briefing the Desert Storm boys. 'If I stay in the same place I become too easy a target.'

'You're not Fidel fucking Castro!'

'Fidel Castro's quite sexy,' said Andrea.

'Oooh, you cat!' said Henderson with a 'sailing close to the wind, aren't I?' wink at me.

'You know I don't mean it,' said Andrea, pinching his bum.

'Come, let me smash your blockade, capitalist pig,' said Henderson, sidling up to Andrea while showing a greater knowledge of Americo-Cuban politics than I had hitherto suspected.

So I was in a fatalistic mood the morning of the meeting, like a father watching his teenage daughter head off with a bespotted tough, his best hope that the boy had clean fingernails.

I waved Andrea off in Henderson's Range Rover, which he'd allowed her to borrow since the pregnancy, and sank into despair – unrelieved by the sight of Mrs Batt patrolling back and forth like Heimdal, guardian of the Rainbow Bridge to Valhalla.

Not that I had quite used every weapon at my disposal. I'd realised that if I couldn't stop the meeting I could at least find out what was said in it. To this end I'd got back on the blower – sorry, phone – to Sharma and engaged his services once more.

I'd agreed with him that it was probably best if I stayed out of the picture, given the fact we couldn't really afford too many more pound-release fees and that having me involuntarily burst on to the scene might have direr consequences than it had with Henderson.

The meeting was going to be in the Windows restaurant above the Hilton overlooking Hyde Park. This was a place that held particular resonance for me as I'd taken Cat there when I was trying to impress her, and Andrea on her birthday. I'd had a good time with both, which is roughly the winning entry in the 'sum up in under ten words why S. Dagman's life came off the rails' competition.

I'd delved into Andrea's internet diary which she kept on the work server and found out when they were meeting. This felt deceitful but, I reasoned, small beer compared to the levels of deceit I had attained so far.

For once I was actually teaching an evening course at the Movotel in Moseley, Birmingham, as opposed to just saying I was. I'd hired a car and set off for the North at around 2 in the afternoon. The course began at 8 and I wanted to make absolutely sure I'd have a good margin of time to burn on the sanity-sapping M6 interchange. The lunch was fixed for 1 p.m. and scheduled to last an hour. The private eye was going to bike up the tape. I thought that, given the motorbike's advantage in the traffic, we might arrive at about the same time.

The traffic was worse than I'd expected, however, and I didn't get to the hotel until around 5. An hour later the tape was in my hand and I was heading towards the video recorder in the room I'd booked. I obviously hadn't bothered calling Andrea as I wanted to be fully up to speed with the meeting before plunging in. I'd also taken the precaution of having one or two stiffeners lined up to help prepare me for the inevitable panging my brain would be taking.

I put the tape into the recorder and pressed play. The camera panned the view from the top of the Hilton, though with little resolution.

The image on the screen was just a swirl of lights, which is a shame because the Windows bar has commanding views, particularly at night, when the city seems to burn in amber lights as you, high above it, fiddle – though normally with some complicated seafood arrangement rather than the Nerolean violin.

By day the streets seem serene, the chaos of Hyde Park Corner muted by distance and great sheets of glass. From that height the lines of cars below seem to pulse to a silent rhythm as they round the Victory statue and flicker up towards Marble Arch. There is no hint of the mad jostle for the racing line that is experienced at ground level.

In Hyde Park the rollerbladers glide, or stagger like fawns, people promenade by the Serpentine and, swallowing your bisque, you can't tell if the tiny blob looking at the ducks is a tramp or a trader. The world without sound is a world without struggle. Everything seems from a Lowry painting, stick people on a wide plain.

The next frame showed Andrea, heavily pregnant, coming in and sitting down at a table. She spoke briefly to the waiter, saying she wanted a still mineral water. I was amazed by the quality of the recording and wondered why we'd never tried this sort of thing in business before. Knowing the exact size of people's training budgets, or even what they thought of you, could be an enormous advantage. Mind you, three years in jail for industrial espionage could be a major disadvantage.

Andrea took out a palm top. I knew she'd have made notes for the meeting on this. She never goes into anything unprepared. The advantage of the palm top is that when you flick through your notes before a meeting you look like an organised professional checking your incredibly busy diary, not like a child scampering through its last-minute revision before a spelling test.

It had been a while since I had just looked at Andrea, taken her in. I saw her almost every day in passing but rarely sat back and considered her in detail. Even on the video I was struck by how big she'd become. It was strange that as an image her pregnancy seemed more real than it did when I saw her in the flesh. She looked less like herself, flattened and fattened by the camera, and more like a painting of a pregnant woman than the person I lived with.

I realised that up until then I'd seen the pregnancy, both the pregnancies, as something that was happening to me – not to Andrea and, perhaps more importantly, not even to the children. I'd been so caught up in myself that I'd kind of thought I'd sort the situation with the two women out and then everything would be OK. I'd forgotten that I was one of the most unimportant people in the whole process. I wasn't giving birth, I wasn't being born.

Considering the birth I felt like I do when I watch the *Countdown* conundrum, knowing that there is a way to make sense of it but for the life of me unable to see it. One thing was obvious – the solemn reality of childbirth had passed me by.

I don't think this is so unusual, though. Friends I'd spoken to, male friends I mean, had told me that the whole thing seems completely unreal, virtually until the child starts speaking. You go through tests, you attend ante-natal classes, you learn to help the mother regulate her breathing, you sympathise, you carry heavy objects. But you're trying to bond with a child you can't feel and can't see. Try as you might it's not going to be as real to a man as it is to the mother. It's only when you can hear it fart that you'll really start to think you might have something in common.

There was a kerfuffling noise from the video and Cat came in. I was going to say that I got that top of the rollercoaster feeling, but in fact it was more the intense and insistent nausea of the bottom of the rollercoaster, having been through the loop the loop, barrel roll and the longest vertical drop in Europe.

I heard her before I saw her. 'Andrea?'

'Yes?' Andrea turned.

'Cat Grey, how are you?' From the tone of Cat's voice I could tell things were as bad as they could be. She wasn't going to attack Andrea, she wasn't going to have a screaming fit. She was going to sympathise with her.

'I'm very well. Gosh, you didn't tell me you were pregnant too.'

Cat sat down. I could see by the heavy way she dealt with the chair that she must have put on quite a bit of weight since I'd last seen her, although because the detective hadn't filmed her approach I didn't get the same look at her I'd had at Andrea.

'That's the main reason I'm interested in doing this article,' said Cat, which in one way was the absolute truth.

The women went through the ordering bit and Cat took down various details of Andrea's life and career. This seemed to go on interminably; Cat really did appear to be interviewing her for an article on childcare and the busy executive mother.

I finished the beer I was drinking and ordered a bottle of wine from room service. I was beginning to feel quite confident about the whole thing as the women discussed whether it was easier for working mothers today and if the children suffered.

I was waiting for the wine when Cat said, 'So is your partner supportive of you as a career woman and mother?'

'Oh, totally,' said Andrea.

'You have a solid relationship then?'

'Oh, yes. I love him very much and he loves me. Aren't you going to write that down?'

I looked at my watch. It wouldn't be long before I'd have to go downstairs and start greeting delegates, so I hit fast forward to see if blows were going to be exchanged, tears burst into, etc. Besides, I was incredibly keen to find out what each woman had revealed to the other. If I wound on to the end of the tape I'd immediately know if the old bag had been let out of the Cat and if both my relationships were at an end. Normally I fight like the devil to avoid hearing the ends of films and the scores of videoed football matches. I don't even feel my Christmas presents. This short cut, though, was too irresistible. The last time I'd felt remotely like that was when I'd discovered Brodie's notes at my

A levels and realised that I wasn't going to have to finish *Jude the Obscure* after all.

The room service bloke came in and theatrically opened the very cheap wine, while I pressed fast forward. I signed for the wine and handed over a tip, something I regretted doing as I only had 20p in my pocket and it seemed something of an insult.

I pressed play. It was about halfway through the spool and I couldn't resist taking a look to see how things stood. The two women were still seated and no obvious strangulation had occurred, which was a good sign.

'I love him so much, I really do,' said Cat. Something had changed about her. She moved her hand to her eyes. I realised she'd been crying.

'I can see that,' said Andrea, extending a sympathetic paw.

I felt a swell of pride. I don't say it's right, I don't say it's clever, but this girl loved me and for a second I forgot all the bullshit and just felt good.

Andrea continued, 'But you're still humping this mate of his?'

Suddenly I remembered a large part of the bullshit and no longer felt so tickety boo. I know I mentioned earlier that I'd thought all meaning was dependent on context, but it would need a pretty wide context before what Andrea was saying sounded OK. I pressed pause. Henderson was, as I watched, setting up the multimedia in a downstairs conference room. He'd be alone. I could nip in, strangle him with the overhead projector wire and be off before anyone was any wiser. I pressed play again.

'I haven't actually done anything with him, but I am thinking about it,' said Cat. 'I'm not sure why. I think it's a comfort thing. He's been so nice and kind, and you know how you get when you're pregnant?'

'Oh, I know,' said Andrea.

'I think it would devalue a lot of what I had with him, though.'

'It'll double its value if he finds out,' said Andrea, raising a finger in a 'have-you-run-that-through-your-thinking-gear?' sort of way. 'Believe me, a man never values something more than when he loses it, except when his best mate gains it. You must shag the friend, whatever else happens. In the name of the living God, shag the friend.' She had an intensity to her voice, mildly patronising if anything, like an IT person telling you your computer would work a whole heap better if you plugged it in.

'Just for revenge?' said Cat.

'And for your own self-respect,' said Andrea. 'But don't leave it there. As far as I can see it this bloke is a bastard and you're well shot of him. The first thing you need to do about it is tell his wife. I'd want to know if I was her. Spare no details. Send photos, love letters, anything as proof. Then ring him up and tell him what you've done with his best friend. After that all you have to do is put all the information on an internet site linked to his business and make sure you e-mail the MDs of all his key contacts. That should teach the bastard a lesson. If anyone did anything like that to me I'd have his balls, no question.'

She was clearly grasping Cat's hand quite firmly. I went to take a swig of the wine and then noticed I hadn't filled the glass. I rectified the error immediately.

'Oh, I don't know,' said Cat. 'I don't think his mate has any real intentions towards me.'

'Listen,' said Andrea, 'you're twenty-four years old and pretty – *all* men have intentions towards you if they think they can get away with it, short of a few career flight attendants and hairdressers. Look at the evidence. A few days after this repugnant rat finishes with you his friend phones you up asking if you "just want to talk about it" and takes you out – to an expensive restaurant, am I right?'

'It didn't have any prices on the menu, if that's what you mean.'

'Exactly. He also buys you a small gift "just to cheer you up".'

'It was a cheap teddy bear,' said Cat, dawning realisation in her voice.

'Right. And has he been round since?'

'Yes. We've just talked . . . you know, been out for meals.' So she'd been out to a restaurant with the bastard *before* I'd slapped the surveillance on her.

'Stayed up until the early hours?' said Andrea.

I could see Cat nodding. Andrea went on, 'And he's incredibly understanding, is he?'

'Yes.'

'I don't want to sound like your mother, dear, but there's nothing so understanding as a stiff dick. Men would pretend to understand anything in return for a bonk. The first few times.' Andrea patted her mouth with the napkin. 'I expect he has a few subtle digs at this bloke of yours.'

'Yes, he's a bit hard on . . .' she nearly said my name and my heart leaped '. . . Terry, I suppose.'

This made me bridle a bit. I didn't feel like being called Terry, even as a subterfuge. I'd have thought my *nom d'amour* would have been something more solid and sexy. Harrison, that would do, or maybe Marlon.

'Has he suggested a friendly weekend away yet?' said Andrea. Henderson, I knew, was planning a trip to the Lake District, 'to get his head together', he'd said.

'The Lake District,' nodded Cat.

'He is just so definitely up for it,' said Andrea. 'Shag the bastard. That way everybody's happy, or rather miserable. It'll be a great consolation.'

So Henderson had been after Cat but it didn't sound like anything had happened yet. I felt jealous, not in the 'I'm just a jealous guy' sense of jealous but in the 'Lord thy God is a jealous God' sense of jealous – lightning bolts, plagues and a blight on thy first born-style jealous. So jealous I could have lain naked on a snooker table and no one would have seen me, or gone to a fancy dress party as the Grinch without having to invest in make up. Man, I was green.

'I'm taking it nothing has really happened yet?' said Andrea.

I instinctively leaped into the bed and hid beneath the duvet.

'Nothing *much*.' I heard Cat's voice muffling through the quilt. 'Although he is very attractive. There again, a lot of people are attractive when you're in our state.'

I buried my head under the pillow for a few moments, trying to get my thoughts together.

Henderson had been trying to get off with Cat, the mother of my children. OK, I wasn't going to see her any more but that didn't mean he could go steaming in – and steam he would if Henderson's verbal enthusiasm for sex translated itself into his performance between the sheets.

I blanched at the image. My Cat with that bespammed gym freak. Actually, it occurred to me, he had a better body than I did. God, she might even enjoy it more.

'So you think I should just burn all my bridges?' said Cat.

'If you blow the lid off the whole thing then one way or another it'll work out. Either you'll end up with him or you won't. And if you don't then you didn't have anything worth while anyway. You have to make sure the love you have is like . . .' Andrea looked about, searching for a word '. . . steel!' She brought her hand down heavily on the table, causing Cat to start a bit.

Steel. That was what Andrea and I had. Something hard and enduring, not to be dented by the odd affair. Her words were curiously comforting to me. Even if I had lost Cat I still had the affection and love of a formidable woman.

'God knows, you don't want to find out in a year's time that you don't love him. You don't want to make the same mistake I did.'

'What mistake did you make?' Cat and I asked simultaneously.

Andrea coughed politely into her napkin. 'I settled for second best.'

'What does that mean?'

'It means I spend my life at three-quarters happy, three-quarters fulfilled, every day a "what if?" on my mind. I'm living a half life, a smile on my face and an ache in my heart, losing myself in my work and pretending everything's fine. I wish I'd had more courage when I was your age, then I wouldn't be in the mess I am now.'

Andrea clasped at her chest, as if to rip off her top, bodice-style.

'You're not in a mess,' I said to the tape. 'Well, you are, but you're not meant to know you are.'

'That's why the affair began, really,' she said.

I stopped the tape and tried to take in what I'd just heard. I'd been prepared for Andrea to be turned into a spitting ball of fur and teeth by news of my infidelity but I hadn't thought she'd say she didn't really care about me. I didn't know how to feel. I'd got my GCSE in feelings, all the basics, jealousy, kindness, love even, but this was a degree-level question.

I'd known it hadn't all been fantastic with Andrea before she got pregnant but I'd thought the relationship had suffered because she was so into her work – not that she was so into her work because the relationship was suffering.

I rewound the piece and played it again. I'd rarely seen her so animated. Normally when she talks about anything other than work she seems at a bit of a remove, mildly sarcastic, not fully engaged. I was beginning to see why.

This certainly begged the big question – if I was second best, who was first best?

I felt everything falling away. As I looked at the tiny gesticulating figure on the screen before me I had a growing and sickening feeling that I hadn't ever really known my fiancée. It's hard to sum up the shades and nuances of my emotions at that point but I think saying that I felt I'd been taken for a complete twat just about covers it.

The fact that Andrea was saying she didn't love me seemed to make my own infidelity worse instead of better. All the furtiveness, the lies, seemed more pathetic somehow. On this evidence she wouldn't have been bothered if I had told her. Strangely, I didn't feel angry. If anything I just wanted Andrea to love me again, for things to be as I had thought they were. I'd got used to the idea of me being in the wrong. Being wronged demanded the sort of philosophical adjustment normally asked of captured US pilots attempting to get their tongues around 'capitalist running pig-dog' for the first time in their lives.

Now I know this doesn't sit very well with my earlier declarations of jealousy, but I was feeling both things. I wanted Cat and I wanted Andrea. Or at least, I wanted Andrea to love me so I could go back to feeling uncomplicatedly jealous about Cat and not have to contend with any other emotions.

But in that tape pause I came to a realisation. I'd always known, at the back of my mind, that Andrea didn't love me. We'd thought we'd grown apart when really we'd never been together. For a couple of months maybe when we'd first gone out with each other, but beyond that short period we were with each other just because it was easy.

The baby had made us closer – it would, wouldn't it? – but when it came down to it Andrea and I were mates, nothing more. That spark, that feeling of cold clear mornings they call love, just wasn't there. There was something else maybe, something more like I had with Henderson. Well, that had always been the feeling of hot unclear nights, but you know what I mean: the mates thing. What I'd thought I had with him until I found out he was trying to shag my ex-girlfriend.

I was now uncertain whether to go on with the tape or to go back, not that either option looked particularly appealing. I wanted to find out, if I was second best, who was first best, which would have involved rewinding, but I also wanted to know whether Cat told Andrea about me, which would have involved fast forwarding. I realised that there were no short cuts available. If I wanted to get the full facts I was going to have to watch the whole thing. I pressed play.

'Did you ever feel that overwhelming love?' said Cat.

'I remember the first night we met,' said Andrea, shaking her head, 'we were no more than children.' Cat moved the napkin before her face. No matter how fascinated she was and how much she sympathised with Andrea, no sophisticated woman can hear a sentence like that without feeling slightly queasy. 'We were at college at the same time, though we didn't get it together till years later.'

I too remembered our first meeting. She'd been struck with me from afar and had sent me a Valentine she'd made herself. I'd been very impressed with it, as it seemed she'd done some research on my personality and come up with an entirely apt card. It contained a quotation from a book, I can't now remember which one, something about me walking in beauty like the night, which I used to do a lot of back then, but I can remember thinking it was thoroughly apt.

'I sent him a card and was amazed when he replied. We went out for a drink, we couldn't afford to eat out in those days, and on to Mojo's dancing afterwards. I don't know if you've ever had it but there was a real electricity between us, like we wanted to touch each other but daredn't because we thought we might combust. And when we did, well, it was like nothing else existed. The world just fell away.'

The sex, I recall, had been remarkably good, and worth all the crap electronic music I'd had to endure at the Mojo's. I remember I'd been desperate to make a move on her but, weirdly, despite the fact that she had gone with me to a nightclub and was giving me levels of eye contact normally reserved for professional opticians or interrogators, I wasn't sure enough to touch her, even though I was desperate to. It had been a Tuesday night and we were the only couple dancing with each other in the club – it wasn't considered that cool to dance in those days – everyone else lurking in the shadows in rain-coated isolation beneath the sounds of urban misery.

In the end she took the initiative, pressing her lips gently to mine and closing her eyes. I remember trying not to giggle because I thought she was going to start whistling. Then we'd kissed and she'd asked me if I always kissed with my eyes open, even though her own eyes had remained shut. I don't know how she did that, but it was certainly a sexy trick. I told her she'd have to hang around if she wanted to find out. I was pathetically pleased with that, as I thought I sounded like a rough and ready type from a soap opera.

The tape continued.

'I still remember our first kiss, on the dance floor. I felt my whole life changing at that moment. Everything before and everything afterwards seemed to revolve around that point.'

I knew how she felt. At that moment everything had seemed so bright. What had gone wrong?

'We were so happy at first. I couldn't believe he'd go out with me. He was the most handsome man I'd ever seen.' I sat up straight. This was news.

'You think that's going to last forever, don't you? That first windrush of love, absorbed in everything the other person's doing, when their breath in the night seems like some strange music.'

I breathed in and out. It didn't sound that musical. Perhaps it would do for some sort of rhythm section. I understood the rasp was a musical instrument of sorts. I could see Cat nodding on the film.

'Do you think he felt the same?' she said, sounding genuinely sympathetic.

'At first he did, but then . . .'

I hit pause. I didn't know if I was ready for this. She'd seemed so happy since the pregnancy, though, I just thought I owed her something. That was what had tipped it for me to stay with her – that and not wanting to dump her while her dad was dying.

I decided to order a brandy.

I rewound the tape a little bit and played on.

'At first he did, but then something happened. It was so dreadful.'

Dreadful was the right word. Despite the fact that I'd had in Andrea a girl who was clearly in love with me when she met me, I had never managed to take that love inside me and let it grow, with the result that she'd looked elsewhere. I had allowed a distance to develop that had grown and grown until we were both in a sham of a relationship. Surely it should have been enough to be loved by such an interesting, amazing girl as her? But it wasn't. She went on.

'He went away for a year on an exchange programme to San Francisco.'

I didn't remember that, and was sure I would have.

'He realised he was gay and got involved in the bath-house scene. We wrote for a while but when he got back he started going out with one of the brickies who was repairing the halls of residence.'

This too seemed to have slipped my mind.

'So that was the end of me and Mike. A year or so later I sent a Valentine's card to Dag, now my fiancé. My flatmate made me do it, more to get me out of the house than anything. And here I am, marrying him! It's funny, I didn't even fancy him when I sent it. I suppose it was an exorcism. I sent him the same poem as I sent Mike and went out for exactly the same evening I'd had when I first met him, Mojo's, everything.' She gave a little laugh. She wasn't crying, but she wasn't not crying either.

'Did it help?' said Cat.

'Not really. Maybe it wasn't an exorcism. More like a summoning. I'd kiss Dag, close my eyes and hope that when I opened them again it would be Mike in my arms. But it wasn't, it was just Dag. It still is. It always will be. No matter how hard I call him, Mike's not coming back. So that's the first affair I've been having – with someone who's not even there.'

First affair? There had been others? I'd clearly missed quite a lot earlier in the tape.

I was crying as I watched the telly, something I rarely do – largely because in my daily life I have very little cause to. I'm still not sure if they were tears of unhappiness. It was more confusion and frustration that I'd taken a series of decisions based on my appraisal of a situation and just got things wrong, read the signals incorrectly. I felt like the bloke in the final of the *Antiques Challenge Million Pound Giveaway* the other day. He'd been given a choice of two objects to take home and had picked a rather nice-looking vase, which he'd guessed, correctly, looked like it was worth a bob or two. Or £500 as it happened. As he'd said afterwards, Christopher Colombus's compass hadn't looked all that.

I was having to undergo a complete remapping of my emotional priorities. And yes, it does depress me that when I lose it I revert to management speak. It indicates that it's in my core, somewhere I'd prefer it not to be.

I'd prepared myself to be an understanding and self-sacrificing betrayer. I hadn't considered that I might be the one betrayed.

'That's hardly an affair,' said Cat.

'If half your heart's somewhere else then what is it?'

'And the others?' said Cat. Others? I thought, grasping my sock for comfort. I really should have watched this through at one go.

'Just men,' said Andrea.

'Oh, that's all right, then,' I said aloud, 'no other species.' I found myself laughing through my tears, hoping that the spin-the-bottle game my emotions were playing was going to come to rest on something definite soon.

'Nothing serious. Really. Well, one, but that's impossible.'

'And do you love Dag now?'

'I love him enough. As much as I need to.'

'What's enough?' said Cat and I together.

'Not passionately or anything but I am fond of him, we've been together a long time and I like to see him happy. If he went tomorrow I'd be upset but I'd get over it. I suppose the saddest thing is I'd be as happy with him as a friend as a lover.'

'Great,' I said, 'great! Why didn't you bother telling me this *before* getting pregnant? Before I fucked up my life for you?'

She continued.

'On his normal performance there's not a lot of difference anyway. He can occasionally raise his game but normally it's rather like having a St Bernard fall asleep on top of you, though with more slobber.'

I couldn't really see on the tape but I'd like to think Cat had a 'beg to differ' look on her face.

'The sex isn't,' she tried to conjure up the right word, 'electric then?'

Good conjuring, girl, I thought.

'No, more electrical in recent years.'

That wasn't my fault. The counsellor had suggested we try toys to liven up our sex lives. I'd come back with a Scalextric which had been great until Henderson broke it. Dodgy trans-former. Anyway, Andrea had got a lot more out of the visits to Charmagne's Secret Locker than I had.

'Why don't you go anywhere else?' said Cat.

'Oh, don't think I haven't been, love.' I pulled back my lips. I guess I must have resembled someone undergoing heavy acceleration, which I was in a way. Nought to nowhere in the blink of an eye. She was saying she'd had affairs. A shot of cold fury hit my brain. There were good reasons I'd gone off with someone else while she was implying she was motivated by, well, smut.

'But there were too many complications, and I'm too old for it now,' said Andrea, 'and since I've been pregnant I've been trying to make it work. It's not too bad, you know. We do have a laugh sometimes.'

I wondered what had made her blart all this out to someone she thought was one of my business contacts. Why had she never told me any of it? I decided I really did need to know exactly how they'd arrived at that point in the conversations so I rewound the tape to the beginning, took delivery of another bottle of wine and a brandy, and started again.

The tape began as before, obviously. The women went through an interview – Andrea's view on this and that, new paradigms of living (I thought I'd include that in a lecture once I found out what it meant), etc, etc. Then the formal interview ended, Cat asked Andrea if she thought she'd missed anything out and they settled into their food.

'How did you meet Dag?' asked Andrea.

'Oh, a business do. We got talking and he mentioned you. Said you're about to be married.'

'Yes.' I stopped the tape and rewound it. At first I thought it had slowed momentarily, but I'd been wrong. There was a definite note of uncertainty in Andrea's voice. 'Yeeees.'

'You don't sound very sure?' Cat had heard it too so it had to be real.

I felt like a very privileged archaeologist. By watching the end of the tape first I'd seen the ruins. Now I was going all the way back in time to see the cracks appear.

'Oh, no,' said Andrea, 'I'm sure, all right. I've ordered the cake.' She smiled brightly.

There was some miscellaneous munching.

'It's interesting, isn't it?' Andrea continued. 'In this article you're going to be making me out to be some sort of superwoman because I'm juggling success and a baby, but I think it's a lot more difficult to juggle lack of success and a baby. Look at you, you're just at the start of your career, how are you going to cope?'

'I'll get by.'

'Is your partner supportive?'

Cat actually looked happy at that point.

'Oh, Christ,' said Andrea, 'you're crying.'

Next time, I thought, I'll hire a detective with a better camera.

'I'm OK.' Cat had raised one hand to her eyes to shield the tears. 'I'm sorry, this isn't very professional.'

'Don't worry,' said Andrea, 'please, don't worry.'

I'd played out so many of these emotional scenes in restaurants in my life I wondered if there might be a market in opening a place with a No Feelings section, where you could guarantee you wouldn't be troubled by emotions, your own or anyone else's. Actually, I only wondered that later.

At the time the sight of Cat crying both moved and frightened me. I really wanted to know she was all right and she so clearly wasn't. In a way her anger would have been easier to cope with than her hurt. Also there was no way of knowing what might happen with hormones raging, emotions high and, oh, yes, right on her side.

I watched Andrea take her hand.

'What's the matter?'

'I haven't got a partner,' said Cat, 'not any more.'

'He left you?'

'He was never really with me. He's in another relationship.'

Oh, Christ, I thought, if Andrea doesn't click now she never will. Andrea didn't click.

'And he won't leave her?'

'He says it's up to me. If I ask him to then he will. But how can I ask him something that will break someone else's heart? And he should want to be with me, shouldn't he, if he's meant to be with me?'

Andrea drew in breath sharply. 'If he wanted to be with you

he'd make any sacrifice.' Now this was more like it!

'Perhaps he can't bring himself to hurt his wife and just needs me to do it for him.'

'Look,' said Andrea, 'you might not appreciate my saying this, but what a loser! I can't stand men like that. He's trying to make you take the decision so that if it all goes wrong it's not his fault. Mind you, it sounds a bit like my fiancé.'

If I hadn't already seen further into the tape I'd have thought, Good old Andrea, saying 'He's a lovable old so and so, my Dag'. As it was I knew she was really saying, 'He's a three-quarters lovable old so and so, my Dag', which rather took the shine off my feelings for her.

'He seemed very nice to me, when I met him.'

'Well, quite,' said Andrea. 'What does he do, your bloke?'

'He's in business, a sort of financial consultancy. He's been married nearly ten years.'

'Any kids already?'

'No.'

'How old is he?'

'Mid-thirties.'

'And going out with a girl your age? Christ, love, what were you thinking? Wait till you're as old as me before you get stuck with an old tosser. At your age you can have who you like. If I was you I'd be off like the butcher's dog.'

'I make it a rule never to go anywhere like a dog,' said Cat, laughing through her tears. I felt like I would be going somewhere like a dog, and very soon. That particular expression was one of Andrea's proudest pieces of wit. I could remember her saying it to me when we'd first met. And it's not like it's the kind of thing you hear every day. I'd obviously said it to Cat and now it was coming back from her to Andrea. I couldn't believe I'd even had the opportunity to say it to her, let alone that she'd remembered it, but there you go. I'd taken a little bit of my fiancée and given it to my girlfriend and now my fiancée was going to wonder where she'd got it from.

I hadn't decided that any of what I had learned would yet make me leave Andrea. I mean, where would I go? And one way of looking at it was that at least we were square – she'd strayed, I'd strayed, let's call it quits.

Andrea looked at Cat sideways.

'Is that a well-known saying?' Oh, Christ, I thought, here we go.

'It's from a film, I think,' said Cat.

'Which one?'

'*Carry On* something, I think.'

'No?' I could see what Andrea was thinking. All these years I thought I'd come up with a neat one-liner in the style of Noel Coward when in fact I've been quoting something in the style of Sid James.

'It's very weird,' said Andrea, 'it could almost make you believe in telepathy. I was just thinking of an ex-boyfriend of mine called Mike. That was one of *his* jokes. I wouldn't have had him down for a *Carry On* fan.'

I frowned. So I was getting recycled Mike jokes? OK, I had recycled them for Cat so I didn't have a leg to stand on, but it's one of life's ironies that when you haven't got a leg to stand on you usually end up kicking yourself. If you see what I mean. Something in me longed for a simpler world.

Cat smiled wearily. 'I'm sorry to be like this. I should go.'

'If you want to talk about it I've got all day,' said Andrea.

'No, you haven't!' I screamed at the TV. 'You're a workaholic. Isn't there filing to be done? Lives to be saved?'

'I would like to talk,' said Cat, 'because my problem is that despite what I know – that I should drop him, that he's treated me terribly – I love him. It's as simple as that. No one's ever made me feel like he does. There's a void inside me without him. I can't think of anyone else, I can't sleep. Have you ever had that?'

'I've had it but it passes,' said Andrea. 'Eventually you're just with them because you're with them and the alternatives are too difficult to cope with.'

Ah, the alternatives, I thought, those other men. If all this ends, I vowed, I was going to pick a woman with no alternatives at all. In fact they should put that in women's magazines: if you want to be more attractive to men make it clear you have very few options in life.

'What are the alternatives, for you?' This was typical of Cat. The conversation was meant to be about her but she had focused on Andrea.

'Other men,' said Andrea, simply.

'Other men!' I said, and then regretted not having swallowed my wine first.

'Have there been others?' said Cat.

'Have there been others?' I said.

'A couple.'

'A couple! As in bleeding two!' I said, drinking from the bottle.

'Are there still?'

'Are there still? A very good question,' I said.

'Not exactly. This changes things, doesn't it?' She patted her belly.

'What does not exactly mean?' I was hiding under the sheets and trying to drink at the same time, which compromised both actions.

'But I thought you were happy?'

'I am happy.'

'Though you've been having affairs?'

'I'm happy like that wall's white,' said Andrea. 'It was whiter when it was first painted, it's showing a few marks, but it's still recognisably white. I'm happy.'

'What were the others like?'

Say it wasn't a man, say it was a woman, I thought. That way there wouldn't be the same threat and there'd be scope for a beautiful and burgeoning perversity in our lives.

'Just men, you know. It's a long story. I've been trying to concentrate more on our relationship since the pregnancy, for the baby's sake. Dag seems happy enough now. I don't think he suspects. It'll probably all work out fine in the end.'

'That's what you think, my fine lady,' I said to the screen. Like most people, smugness is normally one of my favourite feelings. In this situation, however, it seemed a strangely shallow consolation.

[234]

The two women reeled through what I'd already seen, paid and made for the bar, at which point that modern Poirot Sharma turned off his camera. The detective later pointed out that I'd commissioned him to film their conversation in the restaurant. As soon as they went into the bar his job was over.

'Never spent any time in the Royal Canadian Mounted Police, then?' I said.

'If you want Mountie doggedness, try paying Mountie money.'

I stared through my sheet and tried to decide what to do.

'Take time for thought,' I told myself. For some reason I was pacing about the room covered with the bedsheet while swigging wine underneath it.

A voice came into my head. 'You've been betraying a girl who wasn't there.' It was true. It was an imaginary Andrea that I'd been wronging.

I picked up my mobile and called Cat's. I got the answer service again.

'Cat,' I said, 'I think I've made a big mistake. I really do need to talk to you. If you'll have me, I'd like you to marry me.'

All that remained for me to do was to go down to the seminar and let Henderson know where he stood.

17

The Power Of Positive Thinking

'So,' said Henderson, with all the enthusiasm of a TV evangelist banging a $5,000 whore, 'how are you, Kevin?'

'Absolutely wonderful,' said Kevin, Area Sales Dodophone, roughly with the enthusiasm of the whore. That is to say, looking OK on the surface but there was something dead about the eyes.

'That's right,' said Henderson. 'Absolutely wonderful!' He was halfway through his lecture on positive thinking for first timers. It's about how to get the most from people working for you. For £500 per delegate per day we convey the earth-shattering information that if you smile the world has been noted to smile with you.

'Arnold, how do you feel?' Arnold? Surely the first generation of Schwarzenegger fans can't be old enough to have a twenty-five-year-old kid, I thought.

'Mighty fine!' said Arnold in a class wag voice. Like most of the underpaid young in British industry he had the sartorial elegance of someone who had been forced to borrow his clothes after being caught in a storm.

'Oh, yeah!' said Henderson, prowling the floor. I nodded

along in the background, at once serious and appreciative, one of the faithful hearing the master's words.

Unusually for a lecture I had my mobile turned on, muted but on the vibration alert thing. I was dying for a response from Cat.

'OK,' said Henderson, 'that's the positive thinking side of team building. Now on to ...' He checked his watch and gestured towards the multimedia display. 'The Manager as Icon?????' came up. It was accompanied by a kitsch cartoon of a man on a podium with a blazing torch in his hand being worshipped by a collection of other office types. It was one of Henderson's favourite tricks to time his lecture so immaculately that things just floated up on the multimedia without him having to press anything. I have to say it was very impressive and showed an amazing management of the seminar.

'What do we think, ideally, should be the day-to-day social interaction of a manager with his staff?' I'd told Henderson about this 'his' thing. It would cost him nothing to say 'his or her'. He, however, had argued that as sexism is a fact of life in office culture, with men holding all the top jobs, he'd be insane not to target his talks at that group of people.

'For the good salesman sexism isn't a vice, it's an economic imperative,' he'd said.

At that moment his phone rang.

'Sorry about this,' he said to the audience. Unusual, I'd never known him leave his mobile on in a meeting before.

'Hello!' he said. 'Yes ... yes, I see. I can't talk about this now. Please. Give me one more chance. Don't go to him, I love you!'

The class fell into shoe-shuffling embarrassment. Henderson stared mutely at the phone. I guessed it was a trick. He's full of theatrics, one of the things that makes him such a popular presenter.

He swallowed hard and turned to me, white and shaking.

'She's my girlfriend, you bastard, you leave her alone!' he shouted. As happens in England when this sort of thing occurs, everyone instantly assumed fixed smiles, like judges at a village fête tasting the Vicar's wife's rancid home-made chutney.

'What are you talking about?' I said, and realised I was slurring. I'd had one too many stiffeners while I was watching the video.

'You know full well what I'm talking about. That girl's everything to me, she's all I've got in the world, and I'm not going to let you take her away.'

'She's having my baby, Henderson,' I said. The class gasped.

'And so is your fiancée! Isn't one enough for you?' The class gasped again.

'I'm leaving Andrea. She doesn't love me. I'm sorry but I intend to marry Cat if she'll have me.'

Henderson looked nonplussed. 'I'll kill you first,' he said. 'You might be my oldest friend but that only makes it worse.'

One delegate, a man in sports slacks and a coloured belt, started to get to his feet with 'let's calm down' gestures. It was a dress down evening and he looked dreadfully scruffy – like a scarecrow given life by an evil witch.

'You won't kill me,' I said, 'you'll learn to live with it. I told you to leave her alone in the first place. It's not my fault if you've fallen for her. What did she say on the phone? Tell me what she said?'

I'd lost my head. I was standing an inch away from him, shaking with rage.

'Now,' said Henderson, turning to the class, 'can anyone tell me what effect that outburst, had it been for real, would have had on the respect you have for us? Or if, for instance, Stewart here was actually drunk.'

The class burst into relieved laughter as Henderson pretended to strangle me.

I retook my seat and listened to him lecturing on the importance of maintaining the 'mystery margin' with your staff.

Later, after we had got the class to split into groups to discuss things – i.e. do our job for us – Henderson leaned back on his chair and whispered, 'You were just playing along there, weren't you?'

'Yes,' I said. 'Weren't you?'

'Oh, definitely.'

[239]

'So there was no mobile call?'

'Just an alarm call. Well timed, don't you think?'

'Very.'

'Are you leaving Andrea then?'

'No, no, no,' I said as if the very idea were preposterous. It was, really, wasn't it? What in the name of God was she going to do on her own? Heart of stone, I reminded myself. She didn't love me, though I couldn't believe it. And it sounded like she'd betrayed me. I'd only just got used to being the bastard in this situation and now I was going to be the bastardee.

My mobile buzzed. I almost tore it from my pocket. My mum's number appeared on the display. Although the call was unwelcome, it wasn't that unwelcome. The seminars had been picking up steam but we could really have done with that extra money from the promised inheritance. We'd gone ahead and had a load of leaflets printed up and decided to worry about paying for them later.

'Mum,' I said, 'how are you?' One of the benefits of having a mother who lives in a world of her own is that major upheavals in your personal life – i.e. splitting from partner – register no more on her emotional radar detector than bad things happening in the third world. It's not until you meet someone who does genuinely think that natural disasters in China are as bad as you failing to gain promotion that you realise how annoying that thinking is. I'm not saying it's wrong, I'm just saying it's annoying.

'Mum,' you say, 'I'm hitched to a woman who doesn't love me, while the woman I do love distrusts me bitterly and may be sleeping, nay, have an ongoing relationship with my best friend.'

'I know, love, but at least you're not one of those Ethiopian famine victims,' she says. Bob Geldof has a lot to answer for. If your concerns do penetrate then it's worse. You have to contend with her worrying as well as dealing with the problem facing you. This is why I stopped discussing anything emotional with my mother at about the age of 0.

'I'm well and I will be well until May when I will probably get a serious ear illness, if it bothers you,' she said, 'or maybe rear illness. Obviously I'm hoping for ear!' She laughed.

'The cards?' I said.

'More certain,' she said, 'I Ching.'

'I'm sorry you're going to be ill, Mum.' I knew you had to take all my mother's predicted illnesses very seriously. When she was actually dropping dead she'd no doubt be very angry if you fussed.

'There's the best news,' said my mum. 'It's definite: £32,456.87p, arriving Thursday.'

'Yes.' I punched the air. 'Can you tell me who it's from now?'

'I suppose so, though I don't want to tempt fate. It's your Uncle Tim.'

'Why didn't you tell me he was dead?' I said. I'd really liked Uncle Tim – he'd been an incredibly strong and positive supporter of most of my underage drinking with his bottles of home brew.

'Well, this is the hitch. He's not. Yet.'

'So how can I be inheriting money from him?'

'It is difficult,' said Mum, 'but you are. I've got all the details in the other room, they're still on the table.'

'I really don't understand?'

'Well, it's not easy but I'll try to explain. Have you got a while?'

'As long as you like for £32,456.87p,' I said, pinging out the p.

'Well,' said my mum, 'as I read it the Four of Cups represents wealth. Your Uncle Tim is the King of Swords.'

The phone seemed to go cold, numbing my brain.

'The Grim Reaper card represents change but also death. In the position it's in, next to your uncle's card, it means death.'

'You haven't based your promise of an inheritance just on the Tarot, have you, Mum?' I said, fearing the worst.

'Of course not, do you think I'm a fool?'

'No, I don't, so where's the real documentary evidence that I'm inheriting money from Uncle Tim?'

'On the computer printout, I got it sent straight over.'

'From a solicitor's?'

'Better, from a really good internet psychic. She gave me an exact figure for the money.'

The mobile, already cold, split with a loud crack and fell in several pieces on the floor. Then I froze too and did the same. I was swept up by a large woman with a brush and never heard from again.

'So here in the real world there's no reason whatsoever to expect that money to turn up?' I said, stiff-lipped.

'This might not be real to you but it's very real to me and I don't like it when you mock,' she said. I could hear the tears in her voice.

'Look, I'm sorry, Mum,' I said, 'I was just upset about the money.'

'Well, perhaps if you had a little more faith it might turn up,' she said, and slammed down the phone.

She left me feeling terrible. This is the mother's art. I felt bad for upsetting her when really it was she who had wronged me. No point moaning about it, though, that's the way it is the world over.

I really should have known, I supposed, but I just didn't think she'd be so stupid as to mislead me over something like that.

So things were worse than they'd seemed financially. If I was going to move in with Cat then I'd need to get some money from somewhere. The idea of taking another job would have to be considered. I wondered how Henderson would take that. Well, actually I didn't wonder, I knew he'd take it pretty badly but there wasn't a lot I could do about it.

There was another bleep on my phone. A text message. I picked it up.

'Call me – Cat.' My heart leaped.

'Anything I should know about?' said Henderson. His antennae were up, I noticed.

'I just need to use the rest room.'

'I've been hoping you would say that,' he said, fanning the air away from his face.

I got up, left the seminar room and flew down the corridor, past the prints of dogs playing cards, past the untouched

*Financial Times*es folded to a knife edge on the King Louis the however-many-there-were reproduction table, and into the loos, visions of famous reunions in my head – the family Von Trapp, the boys' ship coming home to Southampton after the long bloody years in the South Pacific, 'Say hello to your daddy, John,' hugs and kisses at railway stations, airports, other major transport terminals, Dr Zhivago glimpsing his life's love across the crowded tram – perhaps not, he dropped dead straight afterwards, didn't he? You see what I mean, though.

I locked myself in a cubicle and dialled, mentally noting how even the reunion had been changed by technology. You couldn't have done it in a toilet before, well not those of us who play with a straight bat, anyway. The spirit of romance has in no way benefited from the introduction of the mobile phone, I thought as I closed the loo lid/cocaine snorting area.

'Hello, Dag,' said a voice I hadn't heard in a long time.

'Hello, darling,' I said, 'how are you?'

'Well – no thanks to you.' This wasn't the metaphorical rushing through the buttercups to fling herself into my arms I had expected.

'All fine on the pregnancy front?'

'Yes,' she said.

I couldn't contain myself any longer.

'Please marry me! I got it wrong, I made a mistake. Please, what do you say?'

'I say you've got a hell of a cheek and that you're too late,' said Cat.

That wasn't 'Oh Brad, I'm so happy,' either.

'Too late?' I said, trying to keep any intonation out of my voice but managing surprise, concern and even a kind of shamed outrage anyway.

'I've decided to be with someone else, someone who's a lot nicer than you, though I know that doesn't cut it down too much.'

This didn't quite square with the 'I love him so much, I really do' of the video tape.

'Who?' I said.

'It doesn't really matter, does it?'

It matters if it's bleeding Henderson, I thought.

'No,' I said. I couldn't believe that the half day since she'd spoken to Andrea would change her mind this much.

'Please, Cat, I love you. I always have. I was staying with Andrea out of duty, her dad's incredibly ill. Please, I . . .' I didn't know what to say.

Neither did she apparently. There was silence on the line.

'You said all this when you dumped me,' she said quietly, 'what's changed since then?'

'I've been unfaithful to three people,' I said. I was going to explain how I'd betrayed myself, my own inner feelings, as well.

'There's someone else!' she shrieked.

I've since learned that it simply does not pay to get clever in these situations. Just say what you mean.

'No,' I said, 'I've been unfaithful to me. Most of all to me. I wanted you, I always wanted you, and I didn't have the guts to act on it.'

'How dare you attempt such a convoluted verbal conceit at a time like this?'

'Convoluted verbal conceit's pretty much a convoluted verbal conceit,' I said.

'I can be as convoluted as I like, mate, I'm the injured party. If you had any decency you'd be limiting yourself to monosyllabic grunts of apology and perhaps the odd penitent bray.' She gave a short snort, it could have been laughter, more likely derision.

'Sorry,' I grunted.

'That's better.' She did laugh, a bit. As she realised it her voice tailed off.

'I really need to see you, Cat.'

'Are you still with your wife?'

'She's my fiancée. Or rather she isn't. I'm going to tell her everything tomorrow night.'

'That should be nice for her,' said Cat. 'You should give me her number, maybe we could exchange notes on abandonment.'

'I thought you'd already done that,' I said. If I wasn't careful I was going to get into an argument with her, which was the last thing I wanted.

'And very instructive it was too.'

'In what way?'

'In an instructive way.'

'Did you like her?' I don't know why I bothered asking that.

'Yes, I did, I felt a lot of sympathy for her. Andrea seems a good woman.'

'She's a wonderful woman,' I said. What am I doing? I thought. I'm attempting to persuade someone to marry me by singing the praises of my current fiancée. On the classic reunion front this was like throwing your arms around the girl at the railway station and saying 'I've missed you so much, especially since this other girl I've been seeing is so much like you.' I tried to pull it back.

'I knew you'd like her. You see how much you and I have in common.'

She gave a sad little laugh. 'When are you going to tell her?'

'Tomorrow.'

'Why wait?'

'I'm on a course tonight, I can't do it by phone.'

'I suppose not,' said Cat. I could almost hear her thinking. 'So why the sudden change of mind?'

'The ashtray was full on the old one.'

She didn't laugh. 'I'm serious, Dag.' There was no kickstarting the old carefree chat we'd enjoyed before.

'I just realised I couldn't go on living a lie.' Particularly when Andrea was living one too, I thought. 'I want you. Only you.'

More silence.

'Can I see you?' I asked. 'Although I suppose there's no point if you're already with Henderson.'

'What makes you think it's Henderson?'

'Isn't it?'

'You have to make your own decisions, Dag, based on what's going on in your own life. If you don't love Andrea, show that you've got the courage to leave her.' That wasn't a 'no, it isn't Henderson'. Not a no at all.

'I am doing,' I insisted, 'tomorrow. Let me see you?'

'You finish with her and then we'll talk. I'll want proof you've finished with her, though.'

'What proof? A hair from her chinny chin chin?'

'I'll think about it,' she said. 'I know you've thought of doing this sort of thing before and not gone through with it.'

'How do you know that?'

'Lee told me. He said you were going to finish with her and then you found out her dad was going to die. I think you were just looking for an excuse to stay with her.'

'I probably was,' I said. 'It did seem like a big leap, but now it seems a bigger leap to stay where I am.'

'You can't leap to where you already are, Dag, I wish you'd pay more attention to what you say.'

'You can leap on the spot.'

'That would be a hop.'

'Only if it used one leg.'

'Hopping doesn't necessarily only involve one leg.'

'We're getting off the subject,' I said.

'We are.' I was sure I could hear her crying slightly.

'Look, I want to see you as soon as possible. Can I come over tomorrow night?'

She drew in breath. 'Yes. All right. It'll have to be late. Come over at twelve. You can sleep in Chloe's room, she's moved out.'

'I thought *you'd* moved out? She said so.'

'I stayed at my mum's for a bit. Chloe lied for me.'

'But she doesn't like you. Why would she lie for you?'

'She likes you less.'

'Keeping her up all night with my insistent sex drive, I suppose.'

'Your snoring. She said it sounds like a St Bernard with a heavy cold.'

That was the second time I'd heard myself compared to a St Bernard and I wasn't sure I liked it.

I didn't like the idea of sleeping in Chloe's room. It wouldn't seem natural. I realised I'd need longer than a couple of hours to get Cat round to the idea of us being together again, though.

'Maybe it'd be better to wait until Saturday,' I said. 'We'd have more time to talk.'

'You've arsed around enough, Dag. If you're not here tomorrow, don't bother coming at all.'

Without meaning to I'd showed hesitancy and uncertainty again. I couldn't believe myself sometimes. I tried to make amends.

'I can come over earlier if you like, I can easily make it by ten.' I was a bit old for the conversation till dawn idea.

'I'm seeing someone before then.'

'Who?'

'It's none of your business, but since you ask, Lee.' I inwardly wailed and gnashed my teeth.

'Do you love me?' I said.

'Yes,' she said, 'but I loved my dog Billy and I had him put down.'

'Midnight it is then,' I said, not wishing to dwell on my possible extermination, 'an appropriate time for a fairy tale to start.'

'It's also the witching hour,' said Cat.

18

No Way Back

It was 4.30 when I returned home the next day and a fully luminescent Mrs Batt, in the forest burning bright so to speak, barred the drive.

'Thinking of a few changes, Mr Dad?' she foghorned as I tried to slip past her to open the gate.

'Like what, Mrs Batt?' I shouted back, hoping she wasn't going to say 'finishing with Andrea', within earshot of the detention class children filing out of school. If that lot got a sniff of weakness I'd end up being given a name, probably seeing it sprayed on my gates.

There had already been some graffiti, mainly in talentless squiggles of children who gave themselves names like 'Gangsta' and 'Stripe'. I watched approvingly as Mrs Batt skilfully flailed at the one I suspected of being called 'Fats', chiefly because he was fat. I'd seen on the TV how they were starting programmes in schools aimed at people who bully such porkers. Naturally, when I'd turned on, I'd thought it was aimed at giving the bullies some more inventive ideas, in an aim to encourage the fat bastards to shed some pounds. But no. Apparently you can't say if someone's a fat bastard nowadays, even if they're incredibly fat. The whole country's going to the dogs.

Mrs Batt is one of the few who stand against this trend, lollipop swinging, head held high, a lone, if insane, warrior fighting against the barbarian hordes. She doesn't have to wait for the detention children but she prefers to in order to 'act against the trouble makers'. This is hard on those that have stayed for school play rehearsals, football practice or homework club but, as she says, indiscriminately applied violence never did her any harm. Give that woman an axe, I thought, and that school would know some discipline. Top of the GCSE league tables within a year.

'Oh, I know,' she said, 'I've been keeping an eye out.'

I nodded indulgently. Were it not for the terror she struck into the neighbourhood shites I'd have reported her to the psychiatric social workers years ago.

'Get everything you value out of there before the real trouble begins, that's my advice to you.'

'What are you talking about, Mrs Batt?' I said.

'Your secret's safe with me. I know your girlfriend's in the dark and I shan't say a word.'

I gave a shiver and got through the gate. Mrs Batt already freaked me out but this acquisition of psychic powers was taking things a bit far. She looked like a witch anyway. With a leap of the imagination that lollipop could quite easily become a broomstick.

'Thou shalt be king hereafter!' shouted Mrs Batt, or at least I thought she did, but when I looked around she was giving a backhander to a boy who appeared to have just offered her a sweet.

I'd scarcely got into the drive when Lee Junior attached himself to my trousers. He didn't do this in the leg-shagging paw clasp so beloved of canine traditionalists, just hoovered his nose to my leg and kept it stuck there. I didn't mind, in fact it was disturbingly pleasurable. Still, it slightly inhibited movement. As I made my way to the house I had the stiff-legged gait of a gunfighter ready for the draw.

The conversation with Cat was still echoing in my head. I

hadn't bothered saying anything about the surveillance. It would have seemed dishonest, but I didn't see why. Would it have been any more honest to have made a decision based on what I guessed the two women thought, rather than using the services of a professional in order to be certain?

Her pregnancy was progressing smoothly, I'd gathered, although she was very heavy and finding it difficult to get about. She was going to move in permanently with her mother in Kew in the next couple of weeks, as she was beginning to feel like she was in some 1950s social gloom documentary about single mothers in bedsits.

'When are they due now?' I'd asked.

'Twins are usually premature, so any time between now and March.'

Now was the end of February. I have to say, I've never liked the word 'now', it just seems too immediate for me. The French have the right idea with their word *'maintenant'*. Not nearly as abrupt and frightening, though meaning the same thing. At the most it was a matter of a couple of weeks.

'Gosh,' I'd said, 'I suppose I'd better break out my pipe and slippers, then.' I was trying to slide in images of us together in the future and see if she picked up on them.

'You might be better off with walking boots,' was her reply.

I now had a list of things to confront Andrea with, her other men being chief among them. A nagging doubt at the back of my mind hinted that she might have made the whole thing up to make Cat feel better about going all out for the love of her life (file under me). Unfortunately, at the forefront of my mind was the passion with which my fiancée had described her off-white happiness, and how she wished things had been different.

I was determined to have it out anyway. The tape was in my briefcase and I intended to tell her that I'd spied on her. The time for honesty was upon us.

I turned my key in the door. It opened immediately, the deadlocks weren't on, which meant Andrea was home. This was a bit of a shock. I'd thought I'd get in, make a cup of tea, pour myself a brandy and be sitting in my swivel chair stroking a white cat and saying, 'Ahh, we've been expecting you,' by the time she got in.

I don't know why but there was clearly some thought of confrontation on my mind because I was deliberately quiet in my movements. I wanted to surprise her, to take her on the back foot and force honesty from her.

It was then the thought struck me that, if Andrea had been seeing other men, the child might not even be mine. I found myself curiously pleased by the idea as I caught an unexpected and largely undeserved glimpse of the moral high ground.

In the kitchen I could hear her voice, but she was saying something I hadn't expected to hear. I crept nearer the door.

'I love you.' She hadn't said that to me in years, not like that. She'd said 'We do love each other, don't we?' and a number of other things like it, but not 'I love you'.

'I love you too.' It was a man's voice, hoarse with emotion and much less distinct than hers. I thought I recognised it but I couldn't be sure. It sounded, if anything, like Dave the Lesbian. If that was the case I was going to have to go for the 'I'll sue, you limb cracking bitch,' approach, rather than that of threatening black eyes.

'I really do.' Her words were muffled, like she was crying. 'I don't want to lose you.'

The man's voice, its bass muted by the door, said something about 'not losing', followed by, I was sure, 'I won't cause any problems.'

'I don't know how I'm going to tell Dag.'

There was a pause and another muffled response.

I looked down the hall, the church pew, her coat, the umbrella stand her parents had given her and she insisted that we use despite the fact we didn't have umbrellas because we went everywhere by car, that we actually had found useful when I left my job and we got rid of the car, the War on Want poster, my War on Want poster to be precise, from the days when I'd cared about that sort of thing.

War on want, I thought, it just about summed up what I was about to do.

I wished it could have been different. Complex emotions, however, don't suit me. I always find it's the shallow emotions that affect me most deeply – anger, greed, envy. I was called back to my bad mood by Andrea's voice.

Whoever it was she was with, one of the things I felt most jealous about was that she'd obviously taken an afternoon off to be with him. She'd never done that for me, I thought.

'I'll kick Dag out, he won't cause a fuss.'

Perhaps Cat had told her about us. It hadn't occurred to me to ask. Still, I thought I could brush away complication by shouting. It's worked for millions of men down the centuries.

One second I was in the hallway thinking these thoughts, the next I was in the kitchen confronting them. 'Felt a little sick this afternoon, did we?' I said, the slam of the door echoing through my mind. Andrea was kneeling on the floor with her head buried in a man's lap.

Her father turned to face me but her mother hardly looked up from sobbing into her hands at the table opposite.

'Hiya,' I said, as they all started backwards, desperately trying to cover up the 'felt a little sick' line with a breezy approach.

Her mother stopped crying for a second to acknowledge me before crashing back into her handkerchief in floods of misery.

'You said you were ill, I heard as I came in,' I said to her father, hoping that was what the whole thing was about.

'If you keep opening that door like that it's not going to last five minutes,' he said.

'What?'

'You'll bugger the hinges up, I was looking at them this morning, they're banged together out of bits of tin.'

'Dag,' said Andrea. 'Dag!' And she stood and moved towards me, arms outstretched. I took her to me and patted her back uncertainly, like I thought she might be hollow. I looked at her mother, who showed no sign of stopping crying. Bollocks to this, I thought. This is for real. I'm not going to be put off telling her this time.

'There's something the matter?' I said, guessing Mr Ellis had spilled the beans on the fatal illness front. I'd been deterred once, though, and after what I'd heard on that tape I wasn't going to let it stand in my way.

Mrs Ellis looked at me. The last time I had seen that expression on someone's face was when the old woman had been looking at me and Cat after the unfortunate incident in the crypt. It was a look of concern and powerlessness in the face of a world that had refused to respond to instructions.

I was reminded of a motto a bloke I'd worked with at the Biggest Company on Earth had on his desk: 'Nothing that is important can be controlled.' He'd been sacked and I wasn't sure if that proved or undermined his point.

'Dad's got some terrible news.'

'Oh, no,' I said. Because I already knew what he was going to say, I didn't feel this situation was totally real. I was thinking more about Andrea. I'd seen an episode of the *X Files* when a teacher had turned out to be the devil, as they do, and had gone all melty at the end to prove it. It seemed Andrea might do the same. Like in *Alien* when you find out that bloke's the android. Was I going to end up running her through with the clothes prop and watching all her electronics spark?

No one noticed my lack of engagement. Mr Ellis lacked social graces but was instinctively polite and saved me any lengthy pretence. He came straight in to tell me the news I already knew.

'It seems I've got some sort of growth,' he said, 'the chances aren't good. I thought I should tell Andrea and her mother first. But now you know.'

I wondered why he'd told them.

'He tried to hide it from us but I found the referral letter,' sobbed Andrea's mum as if she'd read my thoughts.

'You're having treatment for it?' I wanted to get Andrea on her own, to end this quickly.

'I . . .'

'He is,' said Andrea and her mother simultaneously.

'Gosh,' I said.

'The doctor's told me there's a good chance it will have spread.'

I found myself bouncing on my toes. There is never going to be a good moment to tell her, I thought, you just have to do it.

'I don't know what to say,' I said.

Andrea's mother said through her tears, 'We just want to stay here until Tuesday. That's when he goes in for his treatment.'

'I'm kicking you out of our room. You'll have to sleep on the sofa,' said Andrea to me, 'unless you feel like kicking Henderson and the Lesbian out into a B&B.'

'The sofa's fine,' I said, 'I'll ring up and order a double bed for the spare room.' I meant it. I still liked them a lot even if I was about to say goodbye.

'Oh, I'm all right on a camp bed,' said Andrea's mum, shaking her head violently, as if I'd suggested that we all spend the evening smoking crack with a couple of mean hoes from Ruislip.

'Are you sure?'

'Yes, we don't want to be any trouble.'

The trouble with people who don't want to be any trouble is that invariably they are a lot of trouble. It would have been much easier for me to have called a local shop and got them to deliver a bed rather than having to traipse down to a camping store and find a camp bed, but there you go. There was no point my arguing with her; she'd think that by spending so much money I was just being polite, not trying to avoid inconvenience. Mind you, from the state of my bank account she might have been doing me a favour. The room lapsed into silence, the only time I could remember the four of us being quiet together.

'You'll get through this,' I said. I'd gone into automatic partner-of-Andrea mode, rock in a storm, bulwark against the slings and arrows. I reminded myself that I had betrayed her and she me. Still, there's a time and a place for everything. They let you finish your breakfast before they shoot you. (On this principle, I wonder why no one has ever ordered an all-you-can-eat buffet.)

Andrea looked at her dad and I could see love in her eyes. That's what I had wanted: unconditional, total love. Only I hadn't been worthy of it, had I? I hadn't listened to her, I hadn't helped her. All I'd done was slink off behind her back. It didn't matter that she'd been seeing someone maybe longer than I'd been seeing Cat. Well, it did, and I was still going to finish with her, but in front of her parents? Funny that, your parents spend your childhood saying 'not in front of the children' and you spend your old age saying 'not in front of the parents.'

Sod it, I thought, now or never.

Andrea's dad gave a huge yawn. 'Hmm,' he said, 'actually, can I lie down? I'm feeling a bit tired.'

'You lie down,' said Andrea's mum, 'you need your rest.'

Andrea told her dad to go up and use Henderson's bed.

I showed him to the room, although he knew the way. It seemed a way of proving I cared for him. He entered Henderson's room which was typically tidy and well organised. The tiger mobile was still in place, the travel alarm clock and packet of Alka Seltzer the only indication that he was staying there.

'This bed?' said Andrea's dad, gesturing to the French nineteenth-century iron masterpiece.

'It's the only one in the room.'

He smiled, indulging me despite the darkness that dogged his every step. Do you know what's been going on? I thought. Do you know about these 'men'?

He sat down on the bed and a look of concern shot across his face. He waggled from side to side.

'Who put this bloody thing together? It's wonky.'

'It's how it came.'

'I don't know.' He shook his head and lay down.

'If you want anything, just call,' I said, leaving the room.

Downstairs, Andrea and her mum had gone into the front room and her mother was regaling her with medical details, re-regaling her if Andrea's questions and 'didn't you say'-ing were anything to go by.

I felt unable to do anything other than make the situation worse, completely overtaken by events – more than overtaken, shunted off the motorway, across the hard shoulder and up the grass verge.

I told myself I couldn't let all this cloud my judgment. That Andrea might be miserable now but I would be sentencing her to a more drawn-out misery if I stayed.

'Mum has something to ask you,' she said, emerging from the front room with her mother.

'Yes?'

'Pete and I were thinking that, whatever happens in the coming year, we want to renew our marriage vows and we were wondering if you'd like to be his best man?'

No, have the guts, refuse, o slayer of corporate dragons, iconoclast, fixer man. You would bend the business world to your fiery will or see it burn before you.

I rolled my shoulders, priming the authoritative cuffs. Looking at them, I noticed that they didn't have their normal razor crease. I'd been rather neglecting that recently.

'Yes,' I said, wondering why Andrea's dad wanted me to be best man when he didn't even particularly like or trust me. Rightly, it seemed.

'Good. Thanks, Dag. It means a lot.' You could see the gratitude in her eyes.

I don't know why but I find direct expressions of emotion very embarrassing so I turned away, saying, 'Great.' I wondered when I was going to bring up Andrea's infidelities and what effect that would have on the forthcoming ceremony.

Andrea was looking at me in a very strange way, like someone had lashed her with a wet kipper. Her face seemed incapable of holding any particular expression and had just melted into the fuzzy, gormless mask I'd seen when we tried dope once. I thought she might be ill.

'You're so nice. I love you, Dag.'

I smiled. You don't love me, I thought, and I'm going to someone who does.

'Actually,' I said, 'could I speak to you in the kitchen for a minute?'

'Sure. You'll be OK here, won't you, Mum?'

'Oh, yes, I shall just rest my eyes.' I could see mild concern on Mrs Ellis's face. She was probably thinking that I didn't really want to be best man and was going to complain to Andrea about it. Like most people, she assumed the things that were most important in her life were most important in the lives of those closest to her. Like Andrea and her work, me and having a good time, she was entirely focused on her concerns and thought we would be the same.

In the kitchen Andrea sat in her normal seat, facing the door.

I asked her if she wanted a cup of tea but she said if she had any more her head would fly off.

'Andrea?'

'Yes?'

'This is very hard to say.' In my mind I could hear The Who's 'Who Are You?' which was very annoying as I've always hated that track.

'What?' Her face was neutral. She didn't seem to have any idea what was coming.

'What do you really think of me?' Now I could hear The Who playing 'Substitute'. I hadn't realised my subconscious had such a detailed knowledge of hoary old rockers who used to be mods.

'I've told you, I love you.'

'Totally?'

'Yeah, whatever that means.'

I'd seen Prince Charles interviewed when he was marrying Diana Spencer. I can't recall the exact words but the interviewer had asked something like: 'Do you love her?'

'Whatever that means,' Prince Charles had said.

'The answer's no then,' my mum had said to the telly.

'I don't know, it's just something that's got into my head. Are you seeing anyone else?'

Why couldn't I spit the words out? I am, you are, let's call the whole thing off.

'No.' She said it a little too flatly, like when I'd told Cat I hadn't got a girlfriend or a wife. I sensed a lie of exactitude. If she really hadn't been seeing anyone she'd have been a lot more shocked by the question, I thought. Now Daltrey and Co. were on to 'Won't Get Fooled Again' in my brain, one of my least favourite songs of all time, jostling neck and neck with most of Meatloaf.

'Dag,' she said, 'I'm having your baby. I want to be with you. I've been with you nearly ten years and I'll be with you another ten and beyond. What more do you want from me?' Now the mod masters were banging away on 'I Can't Explain'. I hadn't even known that was one of theirs.

'Wait there,' I said. I went out into the hall to get my briefcase. It was theatrical and it was stupid but I wanted to use the tape to shock the truth out of her. Obviously I wouldn't play it with her mum there but I could hold it up and say, 'Do you know what this is?'

'Who have you been talking to?' said Andrea as I returned.

'The Who,' I said.

'What?' 'Pinball Wizard' came into my head. My subconscious had finally lost it.

She looked hurt and vulnerable and, annoyingly, I felt protective towards her. Sod it, I thought, use that anger, tell her the truth and bugger the consequences. Her mum and dad will find out eventually, better they all do at one go. I looked at my watch: 6 p.m. Six hours until I'd said I'd be with Cat.

'I'm . . .' I don't know what I would have said next. I'm seeing someone else . . . I'm having an affair . . . I'm not very good at DIY.

As it was it didn't matter. All that mattered was the sound of the gunshot that came from Henderson's room.

19

A Loaded Gun
Won't Set You Free

I really didn't see how the whole thing was my fault, although Mrs Ellis seemed to think it was.

We rushed up the stairs to find the room reeking of gunsmoke and spattered with blood.

Henderson's shotgun, half poking out from underneath the bed, was still pointing at an ugly wound in the carpet and a lesser, but messier, wound in Mr Ellis's side.

'Peter,' said Mrs Ellis, 'there was no need for this!'

I whipped out the mobile and hit 999. 'Ambulance,' I said, 'gunshot wound,' and gave our address.

'What do we do?' asked Andrea.

'What do we do?' I asked the person on the emergency line. Make sure he's breathing and then leave him alone was the answer.

A deeper man might have felt his heart melting with the pity of it all. A shallower man might have thought, Sod it, I'm going to tell Andrea anyway. A man like me, however, in fact the man that is me, thought, Damn, I've just repainted this place. I didn't want to think it, I just did. I'm afraid you'll have to make your own judgments.

Mr Ellis was reaching up and trying to say something.

'Yes?' said Mrs Ellis.

'I did it for him,' said Mr Ellis, pointing up at me.

'Me?' I said.

'The bed's all wonky. I was trying to fix it and I caught my hand on the gun. It's his job, he's a bloke, he should have fixed it.'

'So it was an accident?' said Andrea's mum, fixing me with the kind of gaze that might be useful to the quarry industry for shifting particularly hard pieces of rock.

'I didn't do it bastard deliberately,' said Mr Ellis, groaning. I felt my hands form into a strangling shape. When was this old twit going to stop having one calamity after another and let me finish with his daughter without feeling like the bleeding Anti-Christ?

'You've gone too far this time,' said Andrea's mum, pointing at me. There have been other times? I thought.

What I wanted to say was that when I had bought the nineteenth-century French iron bed there had been three unspoken caveats behind my decision to purchase it. One, that it was a handsome piece, ideal for guests. Two, it rattled a bit but since it was only for occasional use that didn't matter. Three, that it wouldn't result in the fatal wounding of my intended father-in-law. Sorry, make that my unintended father-in-law.

In fact what I said was, 'Er, sorry,' which sounded like an admission of guilt. Maybe he was right. I was a bloke and I should have fixed it. Mind you, that was the least of my failings. My problem seemed to be that I had retreated from the normal role models of masculinity – provider, source of truth and authority, etc, but hadn't quite arrived at any others. I read that in the *Guardian*.

Another way of saying it was that I had retreated from the traditional role model of feckless shite who would do anything for an easy life and a skinful of beer, and was being forced into playing an active role in life, something I look on as wholly unnatural for the male. I'd always modelled myself on the lion when growing up: lie around looking great while the women do the work.

Do you know, according to a documentary I saw, the male lion isn't a hunter at all. His mane sticks out of the grass too much so the antelope can see him. He just waits until the lady lion has duffed up a wildebeest and then comes along and tells her to sod off until he's finished eating. Keeps her slim too. Deplorable behaviour but nice work if you can get it. Hats off, Leo. Oh, God, I'm sounding like Henderson.

The ambulance was there in no time. Andrea and her mum went in it while I waited for the police. I explained that it was Henderson's gun and gave the cops his numbers at as many addresses as I could think of, rather shamingly reflecting that it might keep him out of Cat's way for the evening.

I then leaped into the Range Rover and gunned it down to the hospital.

Of course I thought of phoning Cat on the way but anything I said would only sound like an excuse. Andrea's dad shot-gunned sounded like one of those stories people come up with, hoping that they sound so unlikely others will have to believe them, reasoning no one could come up with such a stupid excuse. Cat would never go for that. She was too clever to believe the truth.

I knew my only option was to get the whole thing out of the way before midnight. Otherwise the lecherous spectre of Henderson would be standing by to pick up the pieces.

I made Casualty in no time and was admitted to the ward, disturbing a group of medics who were sitting around having tea and complaining about staff shortages.

Mr Ellis lay on his bed behind curtains. Normally I'm not very sympathetic to illnesses. I need proof that you're not feeling sorry for yourself. However, a full oxygen mask, tubes in the arm, big pad on the chest and two nurses fiddling with things around the bed says, even to me, that you're not laying it on thick.

'Christ,' I said, 'is he going to be OK?'

'No thanks to you and your stupid mate if he is,' said Andrea's mum.

'We've got an Australian doctor, though,' said Andrea. This was important to her, I knew. Our only other experience of the NHS was with English doctors, people with all the humility and common touch of the Eton Upper Sixth from the *Jeunesse Dorée* period of the 1920s. Generally you got the idea that you were lucky to be ill in order to receive the time and attention of such special people.

New World doctors were different, we'd discovered. They found it enough to be well-informed and caring medics, without giving you the added value of condescension as well. Personally, I like the traditional English arrogant toff. You might be ill but at least you get a chance to hob-nob with your betters.

'We're waiting to get his notes faxed up from Ipswich,' said one of the nurses.

Mrs Ellis looked to left and right to make sure no one was listening. 'His "complaint" means there may be complications.'

'Don't feel you have to stay, Dag,' said Andrea, 'there's nothing you can do and I know you've work to do.'

'I'll stay,' I said, almost reflexively. 'I'll stay.'

I could call Henderson, I thought. He'd be able to explain to Cat what had happened, be able to check for her that Mr Ellis had indeed been shot. He'd even be able to show her his magistrates' summons to prove it eventually. He couldn't, wouldn't, be after her. Not when he knew how I cared for her. He was just being nice to her, surely, looking after her. His finer instincts were in play. In case they weren't, however, I decided not to call him after all. It would be better just to turn up at Cat's no matter what happened. I didn't seem to be able to take Henderson seriously as a rival on a deep level, although I knew it was in my best interests to act as though I did.

'We'll get through this,' said Andrea, taking her mother's hand and mine, 'together.'

'You haven't got any spare anaesthetic, have you?' I nearly asked the nurse. I really did feel that things might go better were I fitted up with the machine that goes bing and everything.

'We're ready for theatre now,' said a nurse, poking her head around the curtain.

Andrea and Mrs Ellis kissed him on the forehead. I didn't really know what to do. I went to shake his hand but thought better of it. 'Best of luck, old bean,' I said. Mrs Ellis fixed me with a stare as hard as poverty, something she'd once known all about.

We could have returned home but none of us felt like it. Instead we went for a curry and played with our food, then to a pub where we played with our orange juices. When we returned to the hospital we still had an hour to wait. It must be a great consolation, I thought, to have faith in gods or devils. We had no prayers to send or fetishes to rattle and, even if we had, gods are primitive sorts who can be rather set in their ways. I don't think they'd have quite grasped the kind of complex request I wanted to make. 'Well, do you want me to smite or to bless?' they'd have said. 'You can't have this "save him then get him out of my life" nonsense.'

Left with only the modern religion of self, with no psycho-analyst or counsellor to ask us how we felt, we sent out our modern orisons of worry, hoping the depth of our anxiety would protect him.

By 8 o'clock I'd made up my mind to tell Andrea I was off to Glasgow on some emergency business do. I'd finish with her later in the week.

At 8.05 we were called to the reception desk and taken into a small curtained area.

After a couple of minutes a good-looking man in his mid-thirties poked his head around the curtains.

'Mrs Ellis?' he said. From his Australian accent I guessed he must be the surgeon.

'Yes,' said Andrea's mum.

'He's going to be OK. I'm Mr Everington the surgeon.'

See that? Aussie doctor. A British bloke would have started by telling you how difficult the operation was, how it had been touch and go, only the expertise of the team, etc, and finally, 'He's all right,' like someone announcing a prize-giving in reverse order.

A tall woman in glasses swished in through the curtains. She announced herself as Jane Hancock, the hospital manager.

'Thank God he's well,' said Andrea's mum, rushing up to hug Everington.

'There's one thing, though, a slight irregularity,' he said.

'Yes?' said Mrs Ellis.

'The wound was very deep and, although he didn't sustain any serious damage to the vital bits, a small amount of lead went in as far as the bowel.'

'Yes?'

'It says on the fax of his notes that he's due to start treatment for bowel cancer. I don't know what twat made the diagnosis but I couldn't see any signs of it at all and I had most of his guts out on the table. I've never seen a healthier fudge funnel. I'd get a double check on that if I were you.'

'He's all right?' said Andrea's mum.

'If it was as advanced as they reckon in the notes then I'd see it, no question. I'm not saying he hasn't got an illness, but whatever symptoms he's been suffering aren't caused by cancer. There's no visible sign of it and there'd need to be if it was at that stage.'

'What is it then?' said Mrs Ellis, who looked more shocked than delighted.

'Irritable bowel syndrome? God knows, could be anything. He's not recently started eating curry, has he?'

Mrs Ellis shook her head wordlessly.

'Who did the diagnosis?' said the surgeon.

'Mr Morton.'

Manager and surgeon both whistled through their teeth.

'Rocket Morton,' said the manager.

'The beast from the East. The fastest oncologist in Britain,' said the surgeon.

'I'm sorry?' said Andrea.

'Mr Morton is noted for speed rather than thoroughness,' said Manager Hancock. 'It's best to see him out of the salmon fishing season.'

'Right, as everything's fine,' I said, 'I'll be off then.' It popped out without my thinking, really it did. Luckily no one took any notice of what I was saying.

'I'm here to explain the legal position to you,' said the manager. 'We're not saying Mr Morton made an incorrect diagnosis. We're saying Mr Everington here has made a different one, and that his is most likely correct. He has taken a biopsy and if it confirms what we suspect – Mr Ellis could live to be a hundred.'

'He's going to see the baby grow up!' said Andrea.

'I didn't say he would, I said could. That's not a legally enforceable guarantee,' said Hancock. 'He could drop dead tomorrow, but it won't be from bowel cancer.'

'I'm going to sue until I'm blue!' said Mrs Ellis, who was undergoing very much the sort of trouser-splitting, turning green and muscly transformation mild-mannered Dr Bruce Banner used to if you got him rattled.

'Will we be able to speak to him tonight?' said Andrea.

'He'll be round in about half an hour. You can say a few words but you don't want to tire him out.'

'We'll wait,' said Mrs Ellis.

'Actually,' I said, 'this sounds terribly selfish but I've a course in Glasgow tomorrow. I was going to take the sleeper before all this came up – is there any way I can get off? We need the money.'

'No, you go,' said Mrs Ellis, who was a great respecter of money, largely through never having had much, 'you've been very good.'

She kissed me on the cheek.

'We'll get through this,' said Andrea, 'we'll get through it.'

'Sure,' I said, 'I'm leaving you then.' At least I'd said it to her technically anyway, allowing me scope for a lie of exactitude.

Andrea didn't like driving when pregnant so I shot back to the house in the car to grab a few essentials. I phoned Cat to tell her I might be a bit late but the phone was engaged – calling Henderson a sherbet dab, no doubt. I have this weird thing when I get stressed – I sometimes break out into rhyming slang. I think it makes me feel a bit more of a wheeler-dealer, rough-and-ready sort, able to ride the knocks.

I tried again as I parked the Range Rover in the drive.

Her mobile was switched off, as was Henderson's. I stepped from the car. Lee Junior – who liked to sleep at night in the shed – snuffled up to me.

I breathed in the sweet air of the garden. Whatever happened, good or bad, I knew I was finally being true to myself. Andrea not wanting me was the icing on the cake really. In a year she'd be glad we'd parted – maybe in a day if the video was anything to go by. She wasn't even really in love with me. She was just acting, for the sake of the baby, crossing her fingers and hoping that by performing the rituals of love, the tea towel flicking, the professions of desire, she'd begin to feel the content. And she'd betrayed me too, I couldn't forget that. We hypocrites are very strong on outrage. I looked down at Lee Junior, wondering when I'd ever see him again. I gave him a little ruffle of the ears. 'How are you, my baby?' I said. 'Oooooh, he's only a puppy.' The dog rolled over and I tickled his tum.

If I'd never met Cat, I'd never have found out that Andrea only had a so-so love for me, and could have gone on for years not knowing.

I had an image of my dad at home, watching the racing on the telly. Racing without betting, food without taste, life without love. That's what I had risked and what I was about to walk away from. I'm not a brave man or a clear sighted one. Even knowing what I knew I might never have finished with Andrea had I not met Cat. If she had disappeared there and then I'd still have gone back to Andrea. Half a love is better than none at all.

With Cat, though, if I could just persuade her how serious I was, I could have the real deal. Love like it's meant to be, in the stories, in the songs.

I felt ridiculously calm and happy despite the upset I was about to cause and despite the fact that it was only 80 per cent certain Cat would have me. Sod that, my heart knew otherwise. 100 per cent.

I patted the car. 'You've been a helpful Range Rover today,' I said affectionately. What can I tell you? It's how I felt.

I mentally went over what I'd need to take with me. Liberatingly I realised that, apart from my suits and credit cards, the answer was probably nothing. I didn't even want my records. Cat had lots of music and it was time for a new start.

'I wonder if Dave the Lesbian's in,' I said, bending over the dog. I had a weird feeling he'd approve of what I was doing. 'Loyalty' it said on the tag. For the first time in ages I felt like I was being loyal to my true feelings.

So Andrea and I had wasted eight years? Her parents would probably be sorrier to see me go than she would. It might be sad but at least it was simple. If I could only convince Cat to take me back, and I was sure I could, then my life was going somewhere at last and I was going to be truly loved, by her and my kids.

'Excellent,' I said, standing up with a self-satisfied rub of the hands as the baseball bat exploded into my kneecap.

20

Lame Excuse

'Could you pass me my mobile phone? There's been a change of plan,' I remarked lightly as I awoke from my coma.

Silence greeted my request. I was in a hospital bed with nothing for company but a bowl of fruit and the kind of headache I'd last felt the morning after my first works do with free drink when we'd gone on to a club and played the world-famous bait-the-bouncer game.

I could remember that I'd been in the hospital very recently and something about a shotgun. I couldn't recall being shot, however.

The grapes had been half eaten so either I had been awake or someone had been in to see me. I felt incredibly indignant that someone had been at my fruit, though something at the back of the scrambled egg platter that was functioning as my brain at that moment told me I had more to worry about than that. I started to piece things together and realised I had been rather running ahead of myself on my list of worries by addressing my attention to the grapes. Number one, I was in hospital. Now that was never right.

Number two my leg was in traction. Even I could see there

must have been a story behind that. I tried to recall how I'd got there. A blank. My bowels, I remembered, had been part of it. No, that was Mr Ellis's bowels and, though he had been noted to cause a bit of an olfactory riot when sleeping off his dinner, he had never done anyone any actual physical harm.

I felt my face. There were a few cuts there but nothing to write home about. Car accident? I thought. I could remember patting the Range Rover.

Next to the bowl of fruit was my mobile phone. I picked it up. It was fully charged. There was a text message up on the screen. 'Call me when you wake up – very busy, A.' So much for the softly weeping partner waiting at the bedside, the lambent light of hope in her eyes, I thought.

It was a lovely sunny day and I felt curiously relaxed as the light came through the blinds. I looked hard at my mobile. I definitely wanted to use it but I couldn't for the life of me think why.

I accessed my voice mail. The first message was timed at 9 a.m. that morning. The clock on the wall showed 2.

I listened to the message hoping it would shed some light on why I was there.

'Hope you enjoy Glasgow,' said Cat. I could tell she was crying. 'You'll hear from me again through my solicitor. I can't believe you set out to hurt me in this way. I'd bought champagne and everything. Don't try to contact me, don't try to come near me with some lame excuse. I hate you, you bastard! And yes, I do fully intend to go out with your friend.'

This did not improve my headache.

What was all this stuff about Glasgow? The firm didn't have any business in Glasgow. My Slush Puppied mind shoved forward the rather relieving idea that I may have forgotten some major deal north of the border.

Get a grip, Dagman, I told myself, something big has happened here.

I scrolled through the phone book and dialled Cat's number. 'The number you have called has not been recognised.' She'd had it disconnected, or not paid the bill, or whatever. Things were not looking good. My senses were returning and I could definitely recall something about me promising to be round at Cat's. In fact, preparing to go round to Cat's.

Grimly, like a fat chap going back just once more to the food cupboard to confirm that, yes, he had had the last Penguin, I called her flat and her work number. Zeros on both fronts.

I looked down at my leg, attached by lines to weights and pulleys. No hope of sprinting round to the Stoke Newington pad, then.

My thoughts were ordering themselves and I recalled with a lurch that I was meant to be finishing with Andrea. Cat's voice came back to me. 'If you're not round by midnight, Rapunzel, you shall never see me again.' I later found out she'd never said this, but it was the general gist.

I also recalled that she was going to move into her mother's, although I hadn't had the presence of mind to discover the address. The last time I remembered feeling this bleak was watching my auntie doing 'The Birdie Song' at the pub Christmas party while Permed Darren who runs the over-40s disco at the rugby club tried to get off with her.

Well, that's it, son, I said to myself, game over. Though it hadn't quite sunk in why.

I pressed message two. It was my mum, all I needed.

'Dag, I really must speak to you. There's some very bad aspects in your cards, very bad. I don't want to say too much on the phone except be very, very careful in places of great danger. And Andrea . . . she's not the girl for you. I've been trying to understand this reading for years. You're not meant to be with her. Oh, and Henderson – it's not entirely clear but he's out to steal her. That's what the cards say – unless you've got another girlfriend we don't know about, of course! And you must buy a pet. Expect money soon. Take an umbrella if you're going out, too. That's the weather forecast, not the stars. It's Mum, by the way.'

I looked up at the cloudless blue of the sky.

I have to confess to more than a mild curiosity about what had happened to me. All I could recall was a thumping white light in my head and a voice whispering in what appeared to be an American accent, 'Julie says hello.'

I went back over events. I had phoned Cat, stepped out of Henderson's Range Rover, patted Henderson's dog, wondered aloud where Henderson's minder was and then heard the 'Julie says hello,' in an American accent. No, I still couldn't work it out. I went over it again.

I had tried to call Cat, stepped from Henderson's Range Rover, patted Henderson's dog, calling him 'my baby', wondered where Henderson's minder was, started towards the house where Henderson was living and then been belted unconscious by someone who had thought it right and proper to mention Henderson's wife's name – a woman whose dad had what might be termed a 'robust' approach to problem-solving and who had once, I had heard, demanded 'revenge' for an inappropriately targeted mailshot he'd received.

I remembered having a conversation with Julie at a fund-raising event she'd held.

'Of course,' she'd said, 'in one way or another Dad gives a lot to the hospitals.'

'He donates money?' I'd said.

'Well, patients, really.' She'd smiled tightly, miming shooting at my kneecap. 'He's a huge fan of the NHS.'

'I thought you all went private?'

'Oh, we do, but as Dad always says, without the Health Service's wonderful doctors and nurses he'd have been looking at a full murder charge rather than GBH on more occasions than he can remember. Vol-au-vent?'

It became all too plain. The Iron Julie, or her dad, had finally decided to give Henderson the kind of beating he so richly deserved. The only problem was that their aim had been a little off. I still couldn't quite understand the American accent but, from what I know of gangsters, they're all into *The Godfather* and I was sure there was something about someone saying hello in a manner other than a firm but friendly handshake in that.

I had a thumping headache so I decided to rest a little more, not a difficult decision when your leg's supported by a working model of the Severn suspension bridge. The next thing I knew Andrea was standing over me.

'Hello,' I said.

'Oh, Dag, you're round, we were so worried about you.'

So worried you weren't here, I thought. 'What happened to me?' I said.

'The police think you disturbed burglars.'

'Have they any idea who it was?'

'They're getting the CCTV images.'

'I told you that'd come in useful,' I said. Andrea had said I was being paranoid when I'd had it installed.

'This is hardly the moment for point scoring,' she said. Now this is wrong, technically. In the world of the oppressed and downtrodden management consultant it is always the moment for point scoring. Always.

'I'm sorry we weren't here when you woke up, but with Dad and everything it's been so tiring.' I hadn't looked at her for ages. My obsession with Cat had seen to that. She looked beautiful, if almost unfeasibly pregnant, as if the laws of physics alone might step in at any minute and say, 'Hey, that'll never do, down comes that baby.'

'How long was I in my coma for?' I asked.

'You weren't in a coma.'

'Yes, I was, I just woke from it now.'

'Oh, don't dramatise, Dag. You came in, you had your leg set, you went to sleep and you woke up.'

'Felt like a coma to me,' I said under my breath. 'Has Henderson surfaced yet?'

'No, he's nowhere to be seen, even his mobile's turned off. You've had a few calls but I've told everyone you're in Glasgow.' I wasn't really listening. My mind was on Henderson.

I bet it is, I thought. I could just see him with Cat: 'Oh, never mind, dear. Yes, he's a bastard, care for a life together?' his game eye glinting over her breasts. What would become of the business? I thought. There was no way I could go on working with him.

'We were worried, Dag,' said Andrea, patting my hand. For

someone who didn't love me she did a very good impression of the real thing.

'I know, I know,' I said.

My phone rang and I leaped. My mum's number. I nearly didn't answer.

'Did you get my message?'

'Yes, Mum.'

'What did you think?'

'What about?'

'My readings.'

Even though I was battered, separated from the love of my life, facing possible financial ruin and life with a woman who would only try to love me, the top thought in my mind was not to upset my mum.

'Very good. Very apt.'

'I thought so. I was very worried about the Andrea thing. I've been trying it again and again. I don't think you're going to finish up with her at all. There's no point resisting it, the cards have marked you down for someone else.'

This is precisely the kind of bullshit I can't stand. When she'd last asked me how I was getting on with Andrea I'd said, 'OK, you know,' which she had translated as 'terribly', and she was now wrapping that up as some mystical insight.

'Is there another point to your call, Mother?'

'Yes, there is actually, if you can take that tone out of your voice.'

'What tone?'

'That tone of irritation with a poor old woman.' Oh, Christ, I thought, she's going to cry.

'Sorry, sorry.'

'The point of my call, Mr Nasty, other than advising you which route you need to take to happiness, however hard that route may be, is to tell you that your Uncle Tim died of a heart attack at eleven o'clock this morning. I know for a fact you're the only person in the will.'

'What else, exactly, did the cards say?'

'You're going to be spending about a week in hospital,' said my mum, 'nasty complications with a broken leg. Oh, and I've seen the sort of pet you'll be having when Andrea leaves you.'

'A cat?' I said, hopefully.

'Yes,' said my mum, 'or a terrapin. The cards really aren't too clear.'

We said our goodbyes and I looked up at my fiancée.

'I've brought some magazines so you can choose a suit for the wedding,' she said, softly.

'Thanks,' I said. 'I'll look at them later.'

21

When A Child Is Born

'Move, limb of Satan!'

For a moment I thought Mrs Batt was talking to me, exhorting my bad leg to faster action. I'd had my eyes fairly glued to the pavement in an attempt to get away with just a 'Morning, Mrs Batt', without having to be oppressed by sympathy for my limping condition.

However, as I looked up, I noticed that the limb of Satan in question was not my leg but a youth in a bad boy rapper's reversed baseball cap. Mrs Batt must have viewed him as a particular enemy of the tribes of righteousness because she was propelling him across the road with the sharp end of the lollipop, the method reserved for her most bitter foes.

'Good morning, Mr Dag!'

Oh, no, I thought, now he knows she knows me. I was already sure I'd heard 'Good morning, Mr Fag!' from some pit-fleshed youth on my way to the bank the previous day. It was OK when she was there to protect me, but what if I met a gang of these thugs on my own, particularly with my bad leg?

Mrs Batt started to make her way towards me but I quickly averted my eyes to the gravel and scuttled up the drive, as much as one can scuttle when two days out of hospital with a broken leg.

The Batt situation was getting ridiculous. I hadn't been out of hospital forty-eight hours, after nearly two weeks inside, and I'd nearly run into her about six times.

I wouldn't have been up and about by choice but, lying around the house, the twin motivators of the doctor telling me I needed to walk on the leg and a boredom-fuelled biscuit lust had propelled me to the shops time and again.

I regained the house with an effort and opened the packet of Derrida Crumbles in the hall. My leg felt weird, I realised, not so much because of the plaster, but because of the absence of Lee Junior. Since Henderson had gone missing and Andrea was so heavily pregnant, the Ellises had taken him home with them.

'Where do you think Henderson is?' Andrea had asked. 'I'm quite worried about him.'

'That's nice to know,' I'd said, 'I'll just hobble along here and try not to leak any stroke-causing bone marrow into my blood stream, shall I?'

Andrea had appeared to be somewhere else.

'Since the Lesbian's missing too I doubt any harm's come to him,' she said. 'Perhaps he thinks Julie's on to him and he's decided to lay low for a bit.'

This fitted in one way. We were quite lucky in that we'd been asked to prepare a report on the management systems of the Endless Delay train company with a view to running seminars in the autumn. We, or rather I as Henderson never did any analysis, had a good couple of months of site visits – just possible with the broken leg – and wading through details of reporting structures, signing off procedures, etc, which I could do from home.

Henderson had a good two months during which he should have been looking for business but could in fact get away with doing nothing. I knew he'd have to be at Gatwick by 7 March, though, as that was when the ski-trip was set for.

In the end I'd decided that giving the police too much information was more trouble than it was worth. The CCTV we had installed had picked up two figures belting the living daylights out of me and the police had circulated the pictures but beyond that I'd heard nothing.

They had contacted me about Henderson. They wanted to do him for keeping a shotgun with no licence and no secure cupboard but were drawing blanks at every address I had for him.

'Do you know,' I said, 'I'd forgotten one – why don't you try him at his girlfriend's?'

With aching heart I read Cat's address down the phone.

I did take a wander, or as we know it in management consultant circles a cab, up to Stoke Newington myself. All there was was a 'to let' sign outside the flat and a feeling of a good thing gone.

I let myself in using my keys and hobbled up to Cat's room. Tidy for once, with nothing in it but the Blu-tack marks on the walls and a single tube of hair thickener, proud as a cock, on what my mum would call the vanity unit. Poignancy in spades, I think you'll agree.

I picked up the hair restorer and flipped it in my hand. It is better to have loved and lost than never to have loved at all, I thought. No. Not when it means the rest of your life is lived in the half light, thinking you see them on buses or tubes, catching a glimpse of hair like hers or a coat she used to wear.

In a way me and Andrea were good company, I thought. Both crushed by dreams, a vision of the beautiful rendering everything else ugly. As I stood tossing the Gift of Youth conditioner up and down I knew she'd be in the living room back home at our house, for the fourth time checking her maternity kit, warm socks, toothbrush, tennis ball.

It was driving her mad that she couldn't find where in La Stoppard's pregnancy book it explained what the tennis ball was for, though she knew she had to take it.

She'd also had some considerable difficulty squaring the above Stoppard's advice not to buy too much new baby stuff with her equally sage observations on the perils of buying too little.

'How about buying just the right amount?' I'd suggested, but this was obviously too easy an option.

I'd been buying baby clothes too, despite Henderson's efforts to leave me nothing to do. I couldn't believe the amount of stuff he'd bought us: clothes, nappies, a pram, a baby bouncer. He reminded me of a rabbit I'd had when I was a kid that had got a phantom pregnancy. It tried to suckle an old toilet roll tube.

In the end I contented myself with buying a small romper suit with 'Daddy's Boy' written on it. I was hoping to force the Almighty's hand in the direction of the sex of the child. I knew that if he saw I'd been presumptuous enough to pay £25 (I kid you not) for a male garment then he'd give me a girl. Obviously I hid it from the Almighty that I intended to let the child wear it, whatever its sex.

Andrea's mum hadn't liked this, as she'd made clear to me and my parents on a hospital visit. 'You shouldn't confuse the genders. If you put a girl in a boy's suit you never know what might happen,' she'd warned, 'she might turn out "sporty".'

'A career in professional tennis can be very lucrative,' my mum had said, flipping a Tarot.

My dad looked like he was going to speak but, since he hadn't said anything worthwhile since 1976 when he'd predicted Olga Korbut's relatively poor showing in the Olympic Games, decided not to break his run and just rolled another cigarette. He'd rolled four while he'd been in the hospital and was revving up to go outside and smoke one. It wasn't the embarrassment of leaving us that was stopping him, it was just, as he'd said when he came back, that it was a bloody long way to the exit.

Normally of course it would have made my blood run cold to allow both sets of parents in together but, stuck in hospital, almost anything counts for amusement. The only time people such as Andrea's parents come into contact with people such as mine is when the likes of my mother come selling heather at the door.

It seemed that the impending baby had brought a measure of rapprochement. Andrea's parents didn't really connect with mine, though they bowled along well enough. Our fathers talked about time in the services – both having been caught by the last year of National Service. Andrea's dad hadn't enjoyed it, as he'd seen it as time wasted; my dad hadn't enjoyed it because it was very difficult to skive off in the Navy, but there had at least been something in common. Andrea's mum and mine talked about their own experience of childbirth and Audrey let my mum read her cards.

'A discovery brings great anger,' she'd said, holding up a card, 'see, the lightning-struck Tower! And here, the Fool exposed!'

Awaking from my memory I read the label on the hair thickener. 'May stain cloth. Keep away from clothing.' Difficult, I thought, considering you put it on your head. I laughed, though I noticed I was crying. If I get nothing else out of this, I thought, at least I'll be in line for the self-pity team at the next Olympics.

'What am I going to do?' I wondered. Then God, or whatever privatised company is running the universe at the moment, gave me an answer. My mobile rang. It was Andrea.

'Dag, where are you?'

'Out and about.'

'Well, come in and here,' she said, 'I'm going into labour.'

'Are you OK?'

'No, I'm in labour, which is why I want you round here now.'

'I'm on my way.'

I limped furiously down Church Street and got a minicab. As we sped home I sat wistfully looking at the road whizz by through the hole underneath my feet. Something weird had taken over me. I felt my emotional turmoil lifting and a strange feeling of elation descending. Here we go, I thought, here comes the best time of my life. That's the great thing about feelings. Sometimes they bear no relation to the facts.

It took about an hour and a half to get home. I paid the mini cab a northerner's mortgage (Henderson's expression, not mine, I only come out with such stuff under stress) and dragged myself through the door and into the lounge.

'Hello,' said Andrea, smiling up at me from the sofa. 'Just packing. Again.'

She was loading nappies into a bag. As environmentally concerned whining tosspots we'd obviously gone for the cloth variety to protect the world from the evils of disposables. I'd give it about a week before we were on Pampers.

'How are you?' I said. 'I thought you'd be rolling around the floor in agony.'

'Only during the contractions, I'm fine apart from that,' she said, zipping up the bag. 'Do you know I've packed that thing about eight times now, just for something to do?'

'Have you called the hospital?'

'I have to come in when the contractions are every five to twenty minutes and last for between thirty seconds and a minute.'

'How often are they now?'

'About once every half an hour.'

'Well, I'll make a cup of tea and you let me know when the next arrives and we'll get timing,' I said.

'Thanks, Dag.'

'For what?'

'For being here. I know we've had our problems but I really think we're going to be all right.'

'Of course we are.'

I was halfway through making the tea when I heard Andrea shout 'Surf's up!' from the other room. 'I'm timing now,' I shouted. Then I had a thought. I'd never seen a contraction before.

I went into the room to see her leaning forward, grasping her tummy and panting.

'Are you all right?' I said.

She held her hand in the air.

'Can I get you anything?'

She shook her hand.

'What is it – what are you trying to say?'

The contraction ended and she got back her breath. 'I was trying to say, don't ask me any questions,' she said. 'It's like when you stub your toe and someone's going "what happened" at you. It's incredibly irritating.'

'Sorry,' I said and went back to making the tea. I'd enjoyed the timing, though. For the first time in the pregnancy I felt I was actually involved. I'd had rooms to decorate, clothes to buy, classes to attend, but now here I was actually doing something at the child/world interface. It felt very good.

I brought the tea in with a packet of Derrida Crumbles, slogan, 'Taste *La Différence*!'

'So,' I said, 'what do we do until the next one?'

'Scrabble?'

And that's what we did for a couple of hours, Andrea managing to get down 'improbity' while halfway through a contraction.

You know me by now, I am not a cynic. But it struck me that the heftiest and most powerful contraction, the one that convinced Andrea she had to go into hospital, came in our third game, just as I was placing the word 'zymogenic' down, after I'd very kindly allowed her 'Moge', which was the name of a wizard cat in a kids' book she's bought (Andrea likes to plan early). I was grinning smugly and edging the 'ic' towards the triple word when she clasped her belly.

'How long was that since the last one?' she said.

'About fifteen minutes,' I said, suspiciously.

'And how long was it?' she gasped.

'Forty-five seconds,' I said with narrow eye, 'exactly in the middle of the range specified in the book.'

'That's it! I need to go in. Get the stuff out to the car.'

'Are you sure?'

'Totally.' She clasped her belly.

'How much longer have we got at this?'

'I, not we, could have anything from a couple of hours to a couple of days,' she said.

She looked to be in such bad pain I couldn't imagine her taking it for another two days.

I put my arm around her. 'We're going to be all right, don't worry,' I said. 'We'll be fine.'

'What's this we?' said Andrea, panting out of the contraction.

'I meant you.'

'It's me who's suffering the pain, and it's your go. Finish the word.'

'Quite,' I said. 'I can't go, I thought I had zymogenic but it's not spelled like that.' If I can do nothing to help her, I thought, I can at least lose at Scrabble.

'Great,' said Andrea, putting down 'xylophone' on to the triple letter. My triple letter. All that left me with was 'zo', which I knew from playing with the Lesbian was a Tibetan breed of cattle derived from crossing the yak with the common cow.

Andrea inspected her tiles.

'Are we going to be all right, Dag?'

'I hope so,' I said.

She looked very flushed.

'Is there anything you need to tell me?'

I supposed the hormonal storm was bringing this up in her but it seemed a good idea to go into the birth with a clear conscience. My mother's uncannily accurate predictions had been weighing on me and a large part of me was inclined to get it out in the open, to live the rest of our lives on the basis of honesty.

'You mean, about other women?'

'No, about relaxation techniques. You're meant to remind me of them.'

Luckily she was seized by a contraction at that point.

'I was only joking,' I said.

'You didn't look like you were joking.'

'That's what makes it more of a joke.'

'It's in poor taste, I think. Have there been other women?'

'No,' I said, 'believe me, there haven't. Have there been other men?' I knew the answer to that one, of course, but I thought that if she came clean first it would pave the way for an airing of laundry on my part. I needed that. There were great areas of our lives that had been concealed from each other. If she knew and I knew everything then we could begin again.

'Oh, God,' said Andrea, 'I think my waters have burst!'

From the mess on the sofa it seemed that they had.

'I'll call the hospital,' I said, 'and your mum and dad.'

'No,' she said, 'wait until it's over. I don't want them worrying.'

This wasn't as selfless as it sounds. If I told her parents they would worry, which would mean that, in addition to the pain and worry of birth, Andrea would have to contend with the anxieties of a couple of excitable pensioners. They were best left in Ipswich.

There was no point calling my own parents. My mum would probably have foreseen it and my dad would only show an interest when it came to wetting the baby's head.

As I waited for the hospital to answer I started to talk to myself.

'This is it, son,' I heard myself say. 'Here we go.' I felt exactly like I had when sky diving with Henderson, but this time it was like stepping through the plane door unsure if you had a parachute, unsure of even where the ground was.

The hospital asked me a few questions, the details of which I can't remember, and told me to bring Andrea in. Luckily we still had Henderson's Range Rover. I picked up all the essentials, Andrea's maternity kit, the Scrabble, a camera, and was making for the car when I remembered something else. I went to the pew in the hall and picked up the large badge I'd made just for this eventuality out of the back of a cornflake packet. It read 'Stewart Dagman' in large letters. I wasn't taking any further chances with mistaken identity.

Luckily the Range Rover was automatic, so not too much trouble to drive with the bad leg.

We had a bit of a problem getting into the car because Andrea couldn't carry anything and I couldn't really balance with all the stuff. So I loaded everything on to me and then hopped to the car using her shoulder as a support. We looked like something from a war report about displaced persons.

We drove to the end of the drive and I hobbled out and opened the gate. Then I was back in the car. I looked left and right to check for traffic and then turned ahead. Something was obstructing my vision. I recognised the Day-Glo orange of the 'Stop,

Children!' sign, held across my windscreen like one of those lollipops they use in Formula One pit stops to tell the driver to engage first gear.

'Yes, Mrs Batt?' I said, winding down the window. 'We are in a bit of a hurry.'

'I've been trying to talk to you for days, Mr Dag, you're always zooming off. Why are you always so busy?'

'Various reasons, Mrs Batt. On this occasion because Andrea here is about to give birth.'

Andrea wasn't contracting at that moment and gave a little wave from the passenger seat.

'Then I shall try to be brief,' said Mrs Batt.

'Oh, do,' I said.

'I have deduced who is behind the attack on you.'

'We know that already, Mrs Batt,' I said, going to wind up the window.

'Has he been imprisoned? Is that why you've got his car?' said Mrs Batt.

'I'm sorry?'

She produced a piece of paper from somewhere within her luminosity.

It was the CCTV image the police had handed out with the rather indistinct faces of my assailants on it. In the background you could just about see my hand clasping my mobile phone, like the Lady of the Lake's with Excalibur.

'I saw your friend talking to those men who set on you, a week before you were bashed.'

'What?'

'The one who looks like a vampire and dresses like a teenager. He was talking to them here.'

'Is your trouble returning, Mrs Batt?' I recalled the loony bin.

She looked embarrassed and I felt sorry for being so sharp with her. But I was in a hurry.

'No. I feel bad saying it because I like your friend, he's very polite, but he was showing those two men in the police photo around your house only a week before you chewed gravel.'

I found this a bit difficult to take in.

'Did you mention this to the police?'

'No.'

'Why?'

'I don't like to cause a fuss.' She was going red. 'And anyway my evidence would be useless. Between you and me, I'm still nutty as fudge.'

'Fudge doesn't always have nuts, Mrs Batt.'

'Exactly,' she said, tapping her nose. 'That's the wonder of modern drugs. But you try convincing a court of that.'

Andrea began to contract again in the passenger seat. 'Thank you, Mrs Batt,' I said, 'I'll act on this later.'

'And give the bastard one for me!' she cried, shaking her fist in a jaunty manner. I wondered if she'd ever considered joining the Lesbian in the protection game.

We sped off to the hospital, me with my head in a spin. Why had Henderson been showing those men around?

Andrea was recovering from the contraction.

'You don't suppose she could be mistaken about that, do you?' I said.

'I don't suppose she could be anything else.'

'Why would Henderson want me beaten up?'

'I don't know,' said Andrea. 'Can we cut the speculation and concentrate on this massively life-changing event?'

'Sorry,' I said.

We arrived at the hospital carpark and got out. There was no way I was going to be able to make it the distance to the hospital and carry all the things, so Andrea waddled off and fetched me a wheelchair.

I did feel mildly guilty being pushed up to the entrance by a heavily pregnant woman, and it was a great inconvenience having to wait for each contraction to finish as she literally laboured up the slope, but the hospital were short-staffed on porters and couldn't find anyone to help.

We made it to the security desk but there wasn't anyone there apart from an adolescent girl graffiti-ing something in Tippex on to the top. I had a flash forward fifteen years and saw my own daughter doing the same. How do you prevent that sort of behaviour? I thought.

'Do you know where maternity admissions is?' asked Andrea.

'Down there, unless they've moved it since I had mine,' said the girl with a sweet smile.

Christ, I thought, how do you prevent *that* sort of behaviour?

I was having second thoughts about having a daughter. I suppose I'd be comfortable with the idea of her having sex once she reached, say, her mid-forties, but before that, never.

We followed a long corridor out to the right and eventually came to a reception desk where a reassuringly efficient receptionist met us. I began to wish that there had been some more obvious sign that my leg was broken. The swelling was well hidden by my tracksuit trousers and, though I was wearing slippers, that's the sort of clothing my dad used to attend job interviews in. Where was the cuff of authority now? Even my crop had been allowed to grow out and instead of being sharkskin smooth to the touch one way, sharkskin rough the other, it was more teddy bear shaggy in both directions.

I'm going to pot, I thought as I stood out of the wheelchair to sign the forms the receptionist put in front of me.

'Not too worn out from getting your partner here, sir?' she said

'I've got a broken leg,' I replied.

'Only the one?' said the receptionist archly.

We gave our details and were asked to sit down: 'Although I see in your case you've already done that.'

After a few minutes the hospital midwife arrived, a Linda Biggs, and took us into a delivery room where we were introduced to a Dr Hobbs. I looked at his face. He was about thirty-three, with vaguely long hair and side burns, like you imagine a doctor in the 1970s would have looked. I knew that, weirdly, I would remember him for the rest of my life and he would forget me within a day. What was it my dad used to say: 'Every day is dull for someone'? He'd meant it as a comfort, that when you were bored you should remember the good times and be thankful for them, or something like that. It hadn't quite come over that way, though.

'How are we doing?' said Dr Hobbs.

'Fine, I think,' said Andrea.

'Have you brought a maternity bag?'

'Here,' I said.

'Do you mind if I look inside?'

'Go ahead.'

He opened it up. 'Yes!' he said, turning to midwife Biggs, who put her hand over her eyes.

'What is it?' said Andrea.

'Oh, nothing, I just had a bet that we'd get at least five tennis balls today.'

'What are they for?' said Andrea.

'Don't know,' said Dr Hobbs, 'no one does, but everyone brings them so they must be useful.'

He left to get some equipment, telling Andrea to get changed into a gown, which she did.

'Anything I can do?' I asked.

'I'd like a drink of water,' said Andrea.

'There's a vending machine in the entrance,' said Hobbs.

When I returned Andrea was having the fetal heart monitor attached, which I hadn't realised actually had to go on to the child, to whom there is only one means of access. Normally I'd have felt quite queasy seeing this, but I actually felt excited as I saw the heartbeat come up. All that time it had been inside Andrea, she could feel it move and kick. All I could do was put my hand on her belly to have any contact with it. Like when I'd had my Kawasaki KRIS dyno-tested and seen the peak of the horsepower registering on the read out. Somehow it felt more real than when I was riding down the road, seeing it represented on a top bit of kit.

'Is there anything else I can do?' I said.

'Just try comforting your partner,' said Hobbs.

'How long will it be now?'

'I'd guess no more than seven hours.'

Seven hours of comfort was considerably longer than I had given anyone in my life. Normally I limit myself to the occasional 'chin up, old girl', not wanting to encourage people to be self-indulgent. Seven hours of solid sympathy. Still, looking at her, sweating and dishevelled in a hospital gown, I felt I could give it. In fact, I felt I could give seventy hours or seven hundred.

Time began to melt. Hobbs came and went, as did the midwife. Andrea got in and out of the bath, had hot water bottles, shoulder massages, and made one very important call to the Sudan which she said really could not wait.

There's a great drama to the birth which I hadn't realised existed. Take the cervical dilation. It has to be 9cm before the baby can be born. The midwife checks it every hour and it's a bit like the countdown for the moonshot.

'Dilation 7cm, 11 p.m.,' says Midwife Biggs.

'Dilation 7cm, 11 p.m.,' notes Dr Hobbs.

'Dilation 7cm, 11 p.m., Baby ETA 2 a.m.,' I say in my best NASA radio voice.

Funnily enough Hobbs and Biggs seemed to like this and relayed further information as if through crackly radios. It seemed to break the monotony for them. Amazing that even birth can get boring eventually. Andrea didn't mind except it made her laugh, which hurt slightly.

What can I say about the rest of it? Procedures, movements, offers of epidurals, incredibly brave refusals. They came and went. I comforted and worried, fretted and reassured. There was no world outside, no Cat, no nothing, just Andrea condensing the pain of twenty-one years into a few hours in return for twenty-one years of child-given pleasure, a bargain with God. I'm sorry if that sounds hopelessly soppy but that really is the sort of thing you think.

At 2 a.m., and to the sound of Oasis's 'Hello', which Andrea had bizarrely decided on, little Zane was born. I'm only kidding about the Zane. Little Jim, a suggestion that had appalled Andrea's mum, popped out into the world.

'How are you?' I asked Andrea shortly after I'd done something I never thought I'd do in my life and cut the umbilical cord.

'Knackered,' she said, cradling the child and beaming at me. Amazingly he had settled down shortly after he had emerged and was now quite quiet.

'Do you realise that's the first word he ever heard his mum say?'

'He had his head out when she said, "Shitting hell, I wish I'd had the epidural," ' said Hobbs.

I kissed them both, mother and baby. It was then that I noticed the colour of the baby's eyes.

A deep, beautiful blue, bright with the light of his soul's journey across the galaxies. Sorry, there I go again. In short, they were rather like my own.

'I love you,' I said.

'I need to sleep, Stew,' said Andrea.

I felt tired but elated, immersed in the present and not worried about the future.

'We'll be taking her up to the ward as soon as the placenta's come through. You should go home,' said the doctor. 'You can visit tomorrow.'

'Can't I stay?' I said. 'I'd like to.'

'Fathers have to go home.'

'Go home,' said Andrea. 'And don't forget to call my mum tomorrow morning.'

'How could I forget that?' I said, soppily. I was beginning to see why people go 'ahh' when they see the sweet little kids on the adverts and don't instinctively retch, as I had always done before.

I hobbled out into the carpark, feeling worn out and in need of a shower. The night was clear and, despite the strong lights of the city, I could see a star, or maybe a planet, far on the horizon winking down.

I had never known weariness like I felt then. I had been concentrating completely, physically and mentally, for the best part of ten hours. I know that's getting off lightly compared to what happens to some people, but it was enough for me. Still, I don't know what it was, some rush of endorphins in the blood or just an old-fashioned feeling of contentment, but I couldn't stop smiling. It could just have been the tiredness. I felt I would hardly have the energy to lie down, and that perhaps it would be easier to sleep standing where I was. Coming up the road was an ambulance. I was in the mood for trite thoughts so I allowed myself a couple.

One life beginning, another ending, I thought. So the world turns. The last thought was particularly trite and, even in my baby-tenderised mind, I flinched a bit at that one.

Weirdly I wanted to call Henderson. I phoned his number. It wasn't switched off, for the first time in a couple of weeks, but it was on answerphone.

'It's a boy, you bastard, and his tadger's a credit to his father,' I said. Indeed, the child's rock python had been of frightening dimensions. 'I've been beaten up but I feel marvellous. Phone me, we need to talk. We'll work something out.' The kid had given me a tremendous bond to Andrea, everything else seemed irrelevant. If I never came into contact with Cat's kids then maybe I could live the rest of my life happy with Andrea, drawn together by our child. Far above me the star winked.

Wish on it, I thought, make a wish. 'I wish the rest of my life, of everyone's life, could be this fulfilled,' I said.

The ambulance slowly made its way up the ramp to where I was standing. I felt strangely ennobled by the birth, like I was possessed of rare gifts, perhaps of healing or creation. I thought that whoever was in the ambulance would only have to stand near me to benefit from my life-giving properties, to get up from their stretcher and walk. I made the sign of the cross towards the ambulance, which in retrospect was awfully arrogant and absolutely asking for it from the Almighty.

It's going to be all right, I said to myself, it's going to be all right. I didn't know how or why, but something inside me told me that it was. The star winked down in confirmation. It seemed to have grown bigger, though that, I thought, must have been my imagination.

The ambulanceman moved to the back of the vehicle and opened the doors. He helped a hunched figure down.

'Lean on me, love,' said the man as the figure descended the steps.

I couldn't see them clearly but I could see that in one of the hands that was resting on the ambulanceman's shoulder was a tennis ball. He stepped away.

'What in the name of God are you doing here?' said Cat.

I looked to the heavens in disbelief. It was then that I noticed the star had grown bigger still and seemed to be making a fair bit of noise as it descended in the direction of Heathrow.

22

When Another Two Children Are Born

I was sitting in another delivery room watching Hobbs taking Cat's blood pressure.

He seemed to be having some difficulty concentrating on the job in hand and kept shooting me anxious glances.

'Is there a problem, doctor?'

'No, no, it's . . .' He appeared to have difficulty framing the words. 'It's just these long shifts, I'm sure.' He brushed his arm across his face. 'All blends into one after a while.'

He looked at his clipboard again.

'You're the father?'

'Yes.'

'Of these twins?' Hobbs had picked up a cup of coffee and was staring into it like a sibyl trying to make out a vision in the liquid.

'Yes.'

He shook his head. 'Best get on with it then,' he said.

Another midwife was in attendance, Midwife Biggs having ended her shift. Hobbs, as a junior doctor, had no such relief. He was, he told me, on for another forty-eight hours.

'I'm just nipping out for some, er, stuff,' he said. He beckoned to the midwife and they both left.

'Henderson hasn't come with you?' I said to Cat, seizing the moment of privacy.

'Why should he?'

'Haven't you two been with each other the past few weeks?'

'No,' she said, looking genuinely puzzled.

'I thought you were going to start seeing him?'

'I only said that to get at you,' said Cat, 'he's not my type. And besides . . .' a great ball of tears welled up from within her '. . . I only ever wanted you. But you weren't there.'

'I was attacked,' I said, tapping my leg. 'I was on my way over and was beaten unconscious. I woke up and I thought you'd gone off with Henderson.'

'Why are you fixated on that?' she said. 'I've only seen him a few times.'

'So where's he been while he's been missing from our house?' I said.

'I don't know,' said Cat, still crying. 'Now can we please get on with this once-in-a-lifetime event and stop talking about your mates?' Christ, I thought, just like Andrea.

'Sorry,' I said. 'I'm here now and I'm not going away.'

I explained to Cat, in between contractions, how I'd been set upon on my way round to see her, and how the going to Scotland story had been evolved to avoid looking unprofessional in front of our clients – there being nothing more unprofessional than being mugged. When she'd called Andrea pretending to be a client, that's what she'd been told.

She seemed unable to take it in. 'Just hold me,' she'd said. 'I've missed you so much.'

'And I've missed you,' I said, pulling her to me.

'How did you know I was here?'

'I'll explain later.'

The wonderful thing about birth is that it concentrates one's mind on the immediate. She'd been too busy contracting and controlling her breath to take it any further, I'd been too concerned for her to wonder how I was going to explain everything, or what might happen following the birth.

'Where have you been?' I asked.

'At my mum's in Kew.'

'She didn't come with you?'

'She's got my sister's kids for the weekend.'

'That was well organised,' I said.

'They're premature,' said Cat, holding on to my shoulder. 'I feel very weak.'

'Would you like anything?' I asked.

'Just some water.'

'It's out in the reception area,' said Hobbs, re-emerging with a gas and air canister.

'I know,' I said, without thinking.

I walked back out into reception and got the water. I had the same feeling of elation I'd had at Jimmy's birth, the same nervousness and apprehension.

'This is too confusing,' I said to the water cooler.

'Just flick the little switch,' said a bloke in a dressing gown from behind me. 'You haven't got a light have you?'

'It's a no-smoking hospital,' I said.

'Reception's not really the hospital, is it?' he replied, greyly.

Back in the delivery room Hobbs had finished taking Cat's blood pressure and was flicking the tennis ball off his bicep and catching it in his hand.

'Note that down,' he said to the midwife.

'What?' said Cat. 'Is my blood pressure too high?'

'No, it's just the fourth tennis ball of the day. I've got a bet going that I'll get five on my shift.'

'What are they for?' said Cat.

'Don't know,' said Hobbs. 'I did think it might have been very pushy fathers trying to train hand-eye co-ordination from an early age, but apparently it's not. Why did you bring it?'

'It's recommended in a book I read. Miriam Stoppard says they relax you.'

'Never seemed to do John McEnroe any good.' Hobbs smiled.

The fetal heart monitors were attached and all was well, though Hobbs was still giving me funny looks.

He left the room with a form we'd filled in at reception and, after about five minutes, returned.

'Might I have a word, Mr Dagman?' he said, beckoning me outside.

'Sure.'

We stood in the corridor. I was knackered myself but I could almost smell Hobbs's tiredness coming off him.

'OK, what's the game?'

'What do you mean.'

'You were here with that last woman, now you're here with this one?'

'Yes.'

He looked me up and down, strangely dwelling over my midriff as if trying to assess whether my wedding tackle was up to fathering three children. Perhaps doctors can tell this sort of thing, though if they can't tell cancer from irritable bowel syndrome then I doubt if determining the way a man dresses would yield them much information about his fertility.

'Munchausen's,' said Hobbs.

'What?'

'It's a disease where the person seeks medical attention, despite being well.'

'So?'

'No one's ever suggested that to you?'

'No.'

He wagged his finger excitedly. 'Munchausen's by proxy – where someone seeks medical attention by faking illness in someone else. Faking illness in the normal presentation but pregnancy in this one. You're faking pregnancies in women in order to draw attention to yourself. This could be an extraordinary case.'

'Except these fake pregnancies have already yielded one baby and are about to yield two more.'

'Hmm,' said Hobbs, 'bang goes my Nobel Prize for medicine. What's going on then?' He said it like a schoolmaster demanding a confession from a pupil, certain of guilt but aware that without a cough proof is impossible.

'I made them both pregnant. Not deliberately, but there it is.

That's my girlfriend in there. The one you saw earlier was my fiancée.'

'No!'

'Yes!'

'Do they know about each other?'

'No. Well, my fiancée doesn't know about my girlfriend. They just went into labour very close to each other, which is a bit of a pain to say the least.'

'Oh, dear, that is bloody marvellous,' said Hobbs. 'Wait till I tell this one in the canteen.'

'You can't, you've got a duty of confidentiality.'

'Not when something's this funny!' said Hobbs, cackling into his clipboard. 'Two labours back to back – it's going to kill you, man!'

I pursed my lips. 'You're doing it.'

He straightened himself up. 'True, but I'm used to it and I lack the emotional involvement.'

A thoughtful look came into his eye. 'I suppose it's going to be a bit difficult for you visiting the both of them in here, especially when they start swapping pictures of the doting dad.'

Clearly not everyone who went into medicine did so because they didn't have the nous to make it in business, I thought. Hobbs had put his finger on my problem almost exactly. I took a De Sade Chile Bake from my pocket and bit in. Exquisite Agony: that was the advertising line.

I wasn't going to bore him by telling him that Cat knew about Andrea, I thought he'd already deduced enough.

'So, in an ideal world, you would like the mothers kept apart?'

'Yes.'

'Five hundred quid and it's done.'

'Is this blackmail?'

'I find that insulting,' said Hobbs. 'This is a demonstration of your gratitude for a service rendered. It's private medicine. Credit me with a certain amount of decency and intelligence. If I was blackmailing you I'd be setting my fees considerably higher.'

'How do you want paying?'

'There's a cash machine near the foyer. Any time before we roll her up to the ward will do.'

Some people would have been angry about this. I, however, was quite pleased. I'd have paid a lot more than £500 to keep the two women apart.

'Shall we go back in?' I said.

'Babies, eh?' said Hobbs. 'You wait all your life for one and then three come along at once.'

'If you could try to minimise the jokes at my expense, at least until I'm out of here.'

'Certainly I will minimise the jokes, but I'm afraid it will have to be very much at your expense.'

We re-entered the room. Again, something weird happened to the time. The nearest I can say is that it passed like light entertainment. While I was in there it seemed to go on forever, but now I'm out of it I can remember almost no details at all.

The next thing I recall, Hobbs was looking inside Cat and saying, 'Mission Control confirms astronauts in loading area!' with a knowing wink to me.

She by this stage was screaming the house down.

'You've written on your birth plan that you don't want an epidural,' said the midwife.

'Actually, I've changed my mind,' said Cat, before being seized by another mighty wave of pain.

'We'll try the gas and air,' said the midwife, unhooking a line from the canister.

Cat breathed deeply, and seemed to relax a little.

'Don't I get an epidural?' she asked.

'Not if we can get away with it.'

'If I really ham up the pain?' She didn't look like she was hamming it up.

The midwife had bent to look inside Cat. Strangely I felt more curious than repelled and bent myself. I thought we might as well all have a look.

'See anything coming out?' said Cat, gritting her teeth.

'I don't think you'll need to ham anything up in a while,' said the midwife, 'your cervix is nearly at full dilation. I'd say you'll see your babies within an hour.'

'Brilliant!' I said. I couldn't believe how excited I was getting. I was missing the fact that these kids might never look at me and call me 'Dad'.

'I think I need an epidural,' said Cat, who was now on her hands and knees on the bed, roughly the position she'd been in when she conceived.

'You're through the worst of it, there isn't time,' said the midwife.

I noticed the back of Cat's hospital gown was soaked in sweat and felt a wave of sympathy come over me. I went to comfort her. I hadn't felt a wave of sympathy like that, well, ever really apart from with Andrea. But as I watched Cat shaken by the contractions it was as if I too was giving birth to something – a better set of feelings inside me. I knew I wanted Cat, more than I wanted Andrea but, there again, only because I knew Andrea was compromising with me. If I'd not known that I would have found the choice much harder. As it was I was resolved to tell Andrea as soon as possible, if Cat would have me, which I felt sure she would. Now I know I had been sneaking goes on the gas and air, but I prefer to think it was the positive attitude caused by the birth that was making me think that way.

The doctor entered the room and there was more inspecting of machines and charts. The midwife bent again to measure the cervix. 'Nine centimetres.'

'Ready to rock and roll,' said the doctor. He propped Cat up on some pillows so that she was sitting almost upright. For some reason he looked at his watch, holding his hand in the air as if he was going to start a race. 'In your own time, Cat, squat and squeeze!'

She appeared to be in a trance, although one that involved screaming at the top of her voice quite a lot. 'Push, push!' I shouted, like they do on the films.

'I have a right to a fucking epidural! Give me an epidural, you bastards!'

'It's too late, you're going to be fine.'

The medics bent over her and I felt incredibly nervous, fully aware at that moment of how fragile life was. I took another hoot on the gas and air and had some more profound thoughts I won't burden you with here.

I don't know how long it lasted, it could have been forty-five minutes, it could have been two hours, but I will never forget seeing little Carlotta's head for the first time. It was unbelievable. It poked out, the midwife wiped the mucus away and immediately the baby started screaming, even louder than her mother was. I was transfixed – me who didn't think he could possibly look, who hadn't thought he would ever be able to have sex with the mother again if he did. The reverse happened. I felt waves of love coming over me. No matter that the head looked like a Chinese dragon's or something you shoot on a video game, something inside me told me to protect and look after her and her mother forever. Bit by bit she emerged, shoulders, trunk, legs. Finally she was out in the world, howling madly at the injustice of being taken from such a warm place. She was bigger than I thought she'd be: 6 lbs said the midwife. As I watched her being weighed, taking her first steps into the social order of humanity, I knew that there was no way I was going to let her go without a struggle.

I can hardly remember what happened next, the clamping of the umbilicus I think, but then the midwife was offering her to me to hold.

'Shouldn't she go to the mother?'

'There's another to come yet.'

I took Carlotta in my arms and just sat there, grinning at her like I've never grinned before. I will say now that I had nothing, *nothing* to do with the naming. I honestly believe names in Britain should only be selected from an approved list, or that children called John or Mary should get preferential access to top schools, tax breaks, something. I don't want to have to treat someone who's called Kai like a human being, for God's sake. Whenever I say this Andrea always reminds me to allow for their ethnic equivalents, which I do – even though I don't know what many of them are. I don't mind your Mohameds or Sunils either, providing the child belongs to the appropriate ethnic group and isn't the progeny of some mind-fogged hippy.

Anyway, I have to say that I have never felt such warmth towards something as intensely ugly as Carlotta. She was wrinkled, tiny and red but I couldn't quite cope with the feelings she was stirring in me. I noticed that tears were coming down my face.

'Look, look,' I said to Cat, 'it's a girl!'

She just grinned at me and put up her thumb, a gesture most unlike her, before falling once more into a fit of wailing as Darius (not my choice, again, clearly) began his descent.

This time the head didn't slowly emerge, as it had with Carlotta, it simply popped out and turned sharply to the left like that of a tank commander surveying the landscape on the western front. The midwife wiped him and he seemed to give a little nod, as if to say, 'Ah, the world, much as I expected.' The rest of him was born quickly in one mighty shove from Cat.

The midwife took him, slapped his feet and, like someone reminded of an onerous and largely symbolic duty, he began to cry. 6½ lbs with a tadger to do his father proud.

Cat was breathless and exhausted, but she smiled, beamed really, as I passed her Carlotta. The midwife gave her Darius. 'That,' I said looking proudly into the doctor's eye, 'is my son.'

'And a fine boy he is,' said Dr Hobbs, who despite my prejudice against medics I was beginning to think was a great bloke. 'They're a fine pair. Massive considering they're quite early.'

The midwife came over to Cat and said something about delivering a placenta, I said I could drop it off on the way home and the room went quiet. 'Sorry,' I said. Quickly recovering from the weakness of the joke, the midwife began to examine the babies, noting their colour, breathing and crying, and even gently pulling back their eyelids to check for jaundice.

'You'll have to go now, we'll take her up to the ward,' said Hobbs.

I kissed Cat on the forehead. 'We've had a wonderful couple of kids together,' I said. 'This might sound presumptuous, but can I see you again?'

'Come in tomorrow,' she said, 'we'll talk about it then.'

For the first time in hours I looked at my watch: 12 noon. I hadn't slept and I hadn't eaten and in three hours Andrea would expect me at visiting time.

23

The Uncomic Dog

I returned to find a note on the table. It was from Henderson.

'Sorry to hear about beating,' it said, 'must have been painful. Gone to see Andrea.'

I should have guessed he wouldn't have bothered with visiting times and just given them some story about how he had to be in Manchester or something. I could have done that but I really needed some sleep so I took the opportunity to get my head down for a couple of hours.

Even though I was tired I didn't really sleep that well, a combination of fear and excitement plaguing my dreams.

I knew that I wanted Cat, that much was certain, but I still didn't know if she really wanted me. She'd been quite welcoming when giving birth, as you are, but I wasn't sure she'd feel that way once she'd recovered.

If she didn't want me then I reasoned I should stay with Andrea, for the sake of the baby and, to be honest, for the sake of myself. It would be too much of a psychological readjustment to be on the cusp of happy-families-ville then be cast out into the dark bachelor wilderness again. Besides, as I've said before, I loved Andrea. The main impediment to our relationship was just that she didn't love me. People live with worse.

I suppose the honourable thing to have done would have been to finish with her anyway, no matter what happened with Cat. But, you know, I still enjoyed being with Andrea. If she wasn't entirely happy with me maybe I could make her that way. If anyone in the world knew her well enough to find what it would take to make her forget bender Mike then it was me. Ironically with my first best in Cat gone and her first best in Mike gone we were even in a way. We were each other's best shots at happiness. Maybe that was why she'd stayed with me, the feeling she wasn't going to do any better. And if she'd bonked a couple of other blokes, so what?

I wasn't going to forgive her but part of me was relieved that she'd so conveniently shagged my guilt over Cat away. I'd only been with one girl, she'd been with at least two men she'd said, which gave me one more crack at the whip before I had to feel guilty again. I realised that wasn't a very good way to think and that I was forgetting the child in all this. It would be different betraying him. Whatever happened, I hoped to God Andrea and Jim were going to be all right. Waking, I gave her a quick call to see how they were.

'They're keeping me in for a bit,' she said, 'because I've lost a bit of blood. Nothing serious, though, and the baby's beautiful.' We had conversations about her blood loss – she said she felt well – and when the baby had woken up, how she was trying to feed him, how great the staff had been – Dr Hobbs even moving her to a private room with the whole en suite stuff. Good old Hobbs, I thought, worth his £500.

She then gave me a list of about four hundred things to do, including preparing for her parents' visit that evening. Despite the fact they knew Andrea was ready to give birth and that they'd been expecting for the best part of a month to come down they still needed a morning to 'lock the house up'.

'I'll be round right away,' I said.

'Don't, actually,' said Andrea, 'the baby's sleeping and I don't want you to wake him.'

'Isn't Henderson there?' I said.

'He's just leaving,' said Andrea.

'Where's he been?'

'He says "here and there".'

I said I'd come in to see her at 8, which would allow me to sneak in to see Cat just before. Despite my feelings towards Andrea it was still my intention to try to make it work with Cat. I had come too far and felt too strongly to do otherwise.

It was then time to call my own mother.

'Brilliant news,' she said, 'but I have clarified the reading. The pet you end up with is definitely a terrapin. There's no cat in the picture.'

'Great,' I said.

At 6 I arrived at the hospital. It turned out I needn't have worried too much about the women bumping into each other, as Cat was packing to go home. Her mum had been and gone and there was a large box of chocolates on her bedside table.

'Isn't that a bit early?' I said, peering into the cot. The kids were beautiful, exactly like babies only beautiful. I'd never seen that in them before. Well, apart from Jimmy, of course.

'No, it's the domino system. Providing everything's fine they get you out as soon as they can,' she said.

'Will you stay with your mother?' I was still convinced she was going to tell me to go.

'Yes, until . . .'

'Until what?'

'Until whatever.'

'I've never lied to you, Cat.'

'Apart from basing our entire early relationship on total deceit,' she said.

'There was that,' I conceded.

'So when you said you never lied, you were in fact lying,' she said. She was keeping a straight face, the way she always does when she's joking, but for all I knew she could have looked like that when she was deadly serious too. The only emotions we'd done together were the first flush of love and desperate misery.

'Although my heart was true,' I said, striking a pose like you see in those Spanish photographers' windows, where the groom stares lovingly into the bride's eyes. 'Will that be enough?'

She smiled. 'Unfortunately, yes.'

She came up to me and put her arms around me. Although the words were what I wanted to hear, there was a part of me that was expecting a headbutt at any moment.

'I do love you. I realised that a long time before the birth but it really came home to me when I was having the babies.' She smiled softly. 'But if you fuck up once more I really will wreck your life.'

'And if I don't fuck up?'

'Then I'll make it the best life anyone has ever lived.'

I kissed her forehead. 'That's the most nauseatingly sickly-sweet thing I've ever heard,' I said. 'I feel honoured that you think so much of me that you're willing to sacrifice all self-respect in such a way.'

'Women do it all the time,' she said, gracious as a courtier. 'So will you tell her?'

'Not quite sacrificed *all* self-respect then?'

'No,' she said, 'I'll expect you to have severed the ties by this evening.'

I think I preferred the nauseating love talk.

'I will,' I said. I still couldn't get my head around walking in there and telling Andrea she was now a single parent, but there you go. I knew I had to.

Walking Cat down to get a cab I was incredibly self-conscious, looking up at the hospital and imagining Andrea staring out of the window. I told the cab we'd meet it out on the road. I didn't want to risk bumping into Henderson, the Ellises or anyone.

The babies were incredibly light and I carried them easily through the carpark barrier and out on to the road, past the entrance to a place where I thought we'd be safe from prying eyes.

'I swear to God, I'll be over by nine tonight,' I said.

'And I swear to God that if you're not, I'll be over at your house tomorrow.'

That clarified things a little bit.

'I love you,' I said.

'And despite everything, I do love you,' said Cat.

We kissed, deeply, without closing our eyes, until we heard the cab pulling up.

Cat asked him to wait and we kissed again. I could hear someone shouting in the carpark.

'Say goodbye to Daddy,' said Cat. 'Kiss them both, Dag.' I took Darius and kissed him, then I picked up Carlotta and held her up, happy and gurgling. 'I can't believe it,' I said, 'I'm a dad, I'm a dad.'

I kissed Cat one more time. We stood locked in a deep embrace. I was taken by the smell of her. It was different, strange.

'I'd forgotten just how you smell,' she said, as if reading my thoughts.

'Bad, eh?' I said.

'No, it's lovely, I missed it at night.' We kissed again. It was then that I felt the familiar stirring of my trousers. There are two facts that I still find surprising, looking back on that moment. One, that a bloodhound can pick up a niff over the whole length of a carpark. Two, that a woman of Mrs Ellis's age can summon enough adrenalin when faced with the sight of an escaping puppy to pursue it at speed across two hundred yards and over a high embankment. Apparently the hound had been forced to quarter the ground for a while to pick up my scent. Still with Carlotta in my arms and my lips on Cat's, I looked down to see Lee Junior attaching himself to my leg.

'I'm sorry,' said a voice from the top of the embankment.

'Not as sorry as I am, Mrs Ellis,' I said, reaching down to remove the dog from the source of his addiction.

24

Eye To Eye Contact

The journey up in the lift was not entirely comfortable. Small talk is difficult in these situations. Luckily ample distraction was provided by an ambulanceman.

'You don't recognise me, do you?' He beamed. He must have been a man of an unusually caring disposition, because he clearly recognised us. Most medics wouldn't remember the patients they treat only briefly, it would be surprising if they did.

'So what's today's calamity?'

None of us answered.

'It's me, Derek, the ambulanceman.' He waved his face from side to side and pointed his fingers at his head, while pulling a stupid face. 'From the beating and the shooting.'

'Hello,' I said. I didn't recognise him. Hardly surprising, really, given the levels of stress I'd been under at the shooting, and the fact that I'd been unconscious after I got beaten up.

'So what's up? Everyone recovered?'

'As a health professional seeing people look miserable, do you ever think that some calamity might have befallen them which they might prefer not to discuss?' I said. He looked hurt. I expect the average ambulanceman thinks that though he doesn't get paid that much in money, he is well compensated in terms of thanks. Derek took on the look of the vastly short-changed.

'We're here to visit our daughter who has given birth. Unfortunately her fiancé here has another family he hasn't told us about, we've just discovered,' said Andrea's dad.

'Apart from that everything's fine,' I said.

The temperature seemed to rise in the lift. 'Ah,' said the ambulanceman, pressing three on the console to stop the lift at the next floor.

'Mine, I think.'

The doors opened and he was gone. When they closed again the silence was hermetic.

Fuck it, I thought, I should have told them ages ago.

We were at the fourth and stepped out. I turned to the Ellises. 'I'll tell her.'

'You should tell us first,' said Mrs Ellis, 'what exactly has been going on?'

'There's not a lot to it. It was like you saw. I've been having an affair, they're my kids. The truth is I was going to finish it with Andrea until she became pregnant. Then I thought I'd stay with her, then the girl you saw told me *she* was pregnant. I'm sorry.'

'Why were you going to leave Andrea?' said her mum.

'We were going to leave each other.'

'She never said,' said Andrea's mum, like I was lying.

'I never trusted you,' said Mr Ellis.

'Why, Dag? Why?' said Mrs Ellis.

'I never meant any of it.'

'No, but you did it,' said Mr Ellis.

'I'll tell her,' I said.

I went down the corridor to Andrea's room while the Ellises waited in the day room.

I entered to find Andrea in bed reading a book: *Raising Übermensch.* (Hothousing is for slackers!) Jimmy was asleep in his cot.

'Hi, how are you?' Her face lit up to see me. She looked

almost back to her state of health before the pregnancy.

'Well, how are you?'

'OK. They say I can go home tomorrow.'

'Good.'

There was a short silence and I felt the guilt dripping off me.

'I need to tell you something that's going to change everything between us.'

'You've been having an affair with a transvestite weightlifter called Vladimir?'

'Not far off – I have been having an affair, seriously.'

'Seriously? You aren't joking?'

'No. With the journalist you met – Cat. I've been having an affair with her.'

'Why are you saying this, Dag?' I could see Andrea still thought it was an attempt at humour.

'Because it's true. When she met you it was just because she wanted a look at you. I asked her not to but she did.'

'Are you serious?'

'Tell her about the babies!' shouted Mrs Ellis, angrily. She'd been listening through a gap in the door and, true to form, had decided I wasn't coming to the point quickly enough.

'Let them do it in their own time, Audrey!' hissed Mr Ellis.

'What? Mum? What?' said Andrea.

'He's been keeping another woman in this hospital and they have babies together,' said Mrs Ellis, baring a fang. 'She gave birth to twins on the same night you did.

'He was kissing her in the car park,' said Mrs Ellis, her husband holding her as if pulling her away but not really getting anywhere.

While I couldn't argue with the facts of the case I didn't like the way Mrs Ellis was presenting them; disjointed, unsupported, they sounded all the more unpleasant.

'What? Is this true?' Andrea's voice was high and shocked-sounding.

'Old blue eye is back! Left me mobile,' said Henderson, popping his head around the door in what, in other circumstances, might have been a funny way. 'Whoops, bad time, I shall withdraw. Back in ten minutes.'

If a situation's tense enough for Henderson to feel uncomfortable then it's tense indeed.

'It's true. I love her and I want to be with her.'

'You bastard,' said Andrea's mum. 'Well, what are you going to do about your son?'

Andrea had started to repeatedly flex her hand into a fist.

'Let us discuss this alone,' she said with the air of a no-nonsense policeman who isn't going to wait all day for a confession.

'That's what he'd like,' said her mum. I'd never seen her look so angry.

'You'll wake the baby,' warned Andrea.

This appeal to consider the child was the only thing that seemed to get through.

'We'll wait outside,' said Mrs Ellis. Then, in a whisper to me, 'You're the lowest of the low, you with your fancy job. You think we were impressed? Well, we weren't. You're nothing.'

I said nothing and watched them go.

'So where did you meet this woman?' I couldn't stand the look of desperation on Andrea's face, I couldn't stand to see her cry, although I wasn't sure I could stand it if she didn't. Even then, as I rejected her, I wanted proof that she loved me. A selfish feeling and I'm not proud of it, but unfortunately it's true.

I spilled the whole can of beans, reminding her that we'd been hardly seeing anything of each other and that the conception had been the first time we'd gone to bed together in ages, pointing out that I'd been about to finish with Cat when she'd told me she was pregnant, reassuring Andrea that I had genuinely loved her.

She still hadn't started crying. She was looking at me with white-faced rancour.

'I trusted you. I tried to save this relationship and all the time you were going behind my back.'

'You said you didn't love me! What about Mike, wonderful

gay Mike, he of the electric sex rather than the electrical? What about these other men?'

This was typical of my rowing style. Equate one tiny misdemeanour – the fact she'd loved someone else – with one large misdemeanour – the fact I had fucked someone else. I know it shouldn't be that way around, but that's the way it is.

She looked shocked. 'I've never told you about him or anyone else.'

'No, but I know about them.'

'How? Did that bitch tell you?'

'No.'

'Then how?'

'I hired a private detective to record you when you met her at the Hilton. I wanted to know what was said.'

'I bet you fucking did!' Andrea shook her head. 'Just get out. Go now before I lay you out.'

Miraculously Jimmy hadn't made a noise throughout our row. Now he stirred, not to cry but just to gurgle from the crib.

'You've woken the baby,' she said.

'Sorry. I suppose that's the least of my crimes.' Then I was crying. 'I'll call you later when you've had time to think about it.' I still couldn't tell her that I wanted to leave her.

'Don't bother,' said Andrea, a single tear on her cheek. 'I was loyal to you but I've cheated myself. I should have left you years ago.'

'I thought we needed to stay together for the kid,' I said. I couldn't believe it. I wanted to finish with her and I was talking like I wanted us to stay together.

'Even when you've betrayed him?' said Andrea. Strangely I hadn't really thought I'd been betraying the kid before, just Andrea.

'Well, I half loved you,' she said, 'and that seemed enough. I was willing to stay with you and make it work, for him and for you.'

'I'll come back later,' I said.

'Just go!'

I went to the bottom of the bed and looked into Jimmy's crib.

Mark Barrowcliffe

I stared into his eyes which looked back at me – aging, faithless git of a father – one blue and the other a distinct shade of hazel.

25

Old Blue Eye Is Back

In the day room Henderson and Hobbs were sitting in front of the television watching a chat show that involved several very fat people who, remarkably, had not only persuaded one person to marry them but two.

'Everything all right?' said Henderson as he saw me coming in, mighty in my clouds of thunder.

'No,' I said, 'not really.'

'Whatever it is it'll pass,' he said, 'post-natal blues most likely.'

'I can't see this one passing in a hurry,' I said. 'Would you like to follow me?' I had a feeling of cold rage, the kind of hyper-calm that documentaries assure us many psychopaths feel shortly before getting busy in the shower with the breadknife.

Henderson shrugged and followed me back out of the day room, down the corridor and past the Ellises – who were fizzing like a couple of Alka Seltzers – into Andrea's room, where she stood cradling Jimmy in her arms.

She dropped her head in shame or exhaustion or something as Henderson entered.

'Would you care to explain this?' I said, pointing to the child's eyes.

Henderson peered down while I tried to remember exactly how my father had performed his famous chop with which he'd felled a platoon of men. Henderson obviously didn't see what I was on about immediately.

'Well, a gentleman and a lady get together,' he said, 'and ask Jesus very nicely if he'll send them a baby.'

I felt my hand stiffen into the chop.

'Look at the eyes, Henderson,' I said.

'He's ours, Lee, he's ours,' said Andrea.

Henderson peered into the child's face and then his hand rose to his left eye.

'This is my child?' he said, mismatched eyes wide like a fried egg and a tomato above that sausage of a smile.

'Yes,' I said, having finally remembered how to do the chop, 'would you care to proffer an explanation or would you like your beating now?'

'It's over?' said Henderson, talking largely to himself. 'The gym, the clubs, the going out? I'm free? Can it be true?'

'Get your face ready,' I said, testing chopping movements against the palm of my other hand. 'How did this happen?'

'I had sex with her,' said Henderson. He looked upset but defiant, like a 1950s schoolmaster caught kissing the postman and trembling out, 'I love him, and damn the consequences!'

'So that's it,' I said. 'At least it rules out the midnight insemination by cake baster theory. When did this happen?'

'About nine months ago.' Henderson wasn't giving me much here that I couldn't have worked out myself after a period of cool reflection. Cool reflection, however, was in short supply at that second.

'You've given my son your genes, you bastard,' I said. 'How did you get his eyes to change colour?' When I'd first seen Jim both eyes were blue. I was fixated on Henderson's eyes. It was the right that was hazel and the left blue – exactly like Jim's now. There couldn't be any doubt.

'Most babies' eyes are blue when they're born,' said the sleepless spectre of Hobbs, who had wandered in sucking one of those plastic fags they give you when you're trying to stop smoking. 'They get their eye colour any time from birth to six months. Remarkable really,' he yawned.

'So if Henderson wasn't a freak I might never have known?' I said.

'It is a wise father that knows his own child,' said Henderson, staring down at Jim. He appeared to be in some sort of reverie.

'I'm a dad,' said Henderson, 'a dad! Now it's you who has to find someone to go ski-ing with, it's you who has to go to raves! I'm all right, Jack, I'm bound for the playground with a song in my heart. I knew I was right to enrol him in soccer school. I had a trial for Arsenal, you know.'

'Yes,' I said, 'failed, didn't you? OK on the burgers, but kept burning the pies.' This was true. Henderson had gone for a job on the hot dog stand at the North London club during his college holidays but they'd rejected him for being too clumsy.

'I could have played at the highest level if I'd got the breaks,' he insisted.

'Like being someone else, that sort of break,' I mocked. Henderson could hardly kick a ball no matter what he said.

'Can we confine this conversation to the matter in hand?' said Andrea, somewhat wearily.

'Sorry,' we both said.

'What were we talking about? Oh, I remember, you giving my fiancée one,' I said.

'He didn't stop at one,' said Andrea.

'Well, I don't stop at one when I'm with Cat either,' I said.

'I don't get to one when I'm with you,' Andrea growled.

'There's no need for bitterness, dear,' I said. How could I have missed all this? I thought.

I'd assumed Henderson was after Cat when he wasn't at all. Had it all been a diversion, to take my mind off what he was doing with my fiancée? I put this to him.

'Why did you try to get off with Cat then?' I wondered if Andrea was aware of that little manoeuvre.

He sniffed, pulling out an eye-refreshing pad from his pocket.

'I didn't, but I was disgusted by your behaviour and thought you needed teaching a lesson. Somebody needed to look after the girl. You were so wrapped up in yourself you didn't seem able to.'

It was the one explanation I'd overlooked – that Henderson was a nice bloke.

'She said she got near to sleeping with you?'

'Did she?' said Henderson, looking like he might have missed a trick. I reminded myself why it had been so easy to overlook that 'nice bloke' theory.

'How about your behaviour in sleeping with my fiancée? Weren't you disgusted by that too?'

'I don't know about you,' said Henderson, looking at the eye pad in disbelief and lobbing it into a bin, 'but I find it so much easier to be moral when judging other people's lives than I do my own.'

'So you didn't fancy Cat,' I said, 'you were just getting at me?'

'I thought the more you thought someone else was after her, the more you'd go after her,' he said, back in front of Jimmy's crib. 'You are ridiculously competitive. Hello, little Lee, hello.'

'He's not called Lee,' I said. 'And naturally you wouldn't have bothered picking up any collateral shag that came your way.'

'Absolutely not,' said Henderson, 'Andrea's the one for me. And now we are linked forever by this little bastard! Sorry, mate. I am sorry,' he said, doing me the favour of looking sheepish.

'Well, before you drag her off into the sunset, let's hear what she has to say. Aren't you forgetting that she has a tiny role in this?' I was going, I knew, for a fairly unlikely conversion to feminism but my brain was throwing in anything it could.

'You mean, getting pissed and shagging your best mate?' she said with a shrug. 'I don't think anyone's forgotten that.'

'You don't know she wants you,' I said to Henderson, trying to ignore her.

Andrea tried to speak but Henderson raised his hand to stop her. 'Do you realise,' he said, taking out what looked like a tiny tube of tooth whitener from his pocket and putting it into the bin, 'that you're arguing against the very outcome you want the most.'

He was right in a way but there was something inside me that couldn't just let Andrea go like that. Did I want her? No. Did I want her to be alone? No. What did I want for her then?

Don't know.

'What's been going on, Andrea?' said her mum, who had just entered the room.

'Oh, come on in, join the merry throng,' I said. 'You haven't got any spare genes that have landed anywhere we should know about, have you?'

'Stop being so sanctimonious, Dag,' said Andrea, 'you're hardly blameless in this yourself.'

Out of the corner of my eye I could see Hobbs getting up and making for the door – to fetch security, I supposed.

'Well, go on, o Faithful One,' I said, 'enlighten us on what you intend to do.'

'I'm going to . . .'

'I thought you were sterile,' I said to Henderson.

'I'm going to . . .' said Andrea again.

'Low sperm count. Very nearly but not quite,' said Henderson, and unconsciously made the same move with his fist as when he'd clinched the Most Fluky Putt award. 'It's just Julie would never do the IVF thing. Fear of needles.'

'So why did you say you were infertile?'

'I'm going to . . .'

'Sexier,' said Henderson, 'more decisive.' He made a thumping motion.

'You've been betraying me,' I said, 'my best friend and my fiancée, I don't believe it.'

'You've *both* been betraying us,' said Mrs Ellis, 'and all the family, and everyone you know. You've let us all down with your philandering, not least of all the child or children in all this. It's them I feel sorry for.'

Whenever you feel down you can always trust a parent to put one arm around your shoulder and show you that things are truly desperate.

'Oh, bollocks,' said Andrea, 'no one care's what I'm going to do. I'm going to go to bed.'

'I should have thought you've been in enough trouble in there already,' said her mum. Andrea stayed where she was.

'I think we should stop making a fuss over this,' she said.

'Yes,' I said, 'fuss over nothing really. Perhaps you'd like to come round for tea this evening, Lee, if you're not too busy impregnating anyone else's sexual partner,' I said, metaphorically casting the first stone.

'Well, you're hardly without sin yourself, are you? You've been porking that Cat for the best part of a year.'

Hobbs had reappeared in the doorway, bringing with him a couple of nurses. Far from intervening they seemed to regard the whole thing as a right old hoot. Behind them I could see the figure of the Lesbian quietly looming. He had a bunch of the carnations I'd seen in the hospital shop.

'You knew he was seeing someone else? Why didn't you tell me?' said Andrea.

Henderson shrugged. 'He's a mate. There are certain lines you do not cross.' It occurred to me then to ask if he had any ear wax remover on him. I clearly wasn't hearing too well.

'Oh, thanks for the loyalty,' I said. 'It's nice to know that the limit of your indulgence is attempting to shag my girlfriend and banging my fiancée up.'

'Well, I'm not a complete bastard,' said Henderson with a shrug.

'But you tried to persuade me to stay with Andrea.'

'When I thought that was what she wanted, that it would make her happy. You know, I love her and I love you. I didn't want to hurt either of you.'

The nurses gave a little sigh and Hobbs let out a low whistle. For a moment I felt touched, I don't know why.

'Though not literally,' said the Lesbian from outside the room.

'Dave, please keep out of this,' I said.

'As you wish,' said the Lesbian, raising his eyebrows in what, in retrospect, I recognise to have been a 'you'll regret not hearing this' way.

'And you were so keen to avoid hurting me that you shagged my fiancée?'

'Anyone would have, even if they didn't love her,' said Henderson. 'I mean, she's an attractive woman. You clearly think so or you wouldn't have been with her. You find her attractive, that's OK. I do, that's not OK. You are such a hypocrite,' he said, discarding dental floss.

'That's not proper reasoning,' I said.

'I didn't do anything you haven't,' said Henderson. 'If you hadn't got in there first I'd be going out with her now. I've always been mad about her, I just wasn't with her at college and you got in there before I could. I had first call on her and you jumped in.'

Andrea and family all tried to speak again.

'What makes you think that?' I said.

'When I came up to see you after college I told you I fancied her, and then four years later you started going out with her.' Henderson made a nervous turning motion with his leg. To the outsider he would have looked like someone doing an impression of an arthritic Alsatian. To me, however, he looked very much as if he was climbing up on to a high horse, a high horse that was rightfully mine to ride.

'So because you once thought you fancied her at college, and did nothing about it for four years, that invalidated eight years of my going out with her?'

'I feel I had first dibs, yes,' said Henderson.

It was lucky that the nearest thing to hand happened to be Cat's tennis ball which had unaccountably ended up in my pocket. In a fit of rage I threw it at Henderson, catching him in the eye. In subsequent years it has been a source of some worry that my overriding emotion at that point was one of self-congratulation for the accuracy of my shot. In my defence, I'd say I've never been very good at games and it was quite pleasing to see that I could deliver when the chips were down.

As the ball ricocheted off Henderson and over towards the television I heard Hobbs comment, 'Oh, so that's what they're for.' At least we were providing him with some amusement.

'No one has dibs on me!' shouted Andrea.

'Don't I?' I said. 'After the best part of ten years, not even a single dib?'

'Actually,' it was Andrea's father who spoke, 'can I introduce a practical point here?'

'Yes,' said just about everyone, hoping, I think, for the voice of calm reason.

'Am I to take it that this is a threat to the wedding?'

'I'll say,' said Andrea.

'Yes,' I confirmed.

'Well, in that case, you should be thinking about cancelling the caterers because if you leave it any later you're going to get banged with a hell of a charge.' He shook his head at the very thought of it.

'He's got a point,' said Andrea's mum. 'You'll have to do the car and flowers and everything, too.' Both Ellises assumed expressions of deep anxiety.

'Dad, I don't care about the money,' said Andrea.

'You say that now . . .' said her father.

'You can't throw money away, love, especially if you're going to be a single parent,' said her mum.

Andrea had been quite calm and mildly sarcastic up until that point. At the words 'single parent', however, she let out a protracted howl. The only time I'd ever seen wailing like that before was when I'd been persuaded to go to an am-dram production of one of the girls from work. The wailing in question had been performed by an adolescent Lady Macduff whom the local paper had picked out for the 'gusto' she brought to the role, and which followed the words 'what, all my babies dead?'

Henderson and I stepped forward to comfort her. He got there first. Something inside me didn't feel up to grappling with him over the offering of comfort, especially since I had caused most of the distress.

I watched as he took her in his arms. 'Come on,' he said, 'everything's going to be all right.'

I was still having a great deal of difficulty seeing Henderson in the role of *pater familias* – *pater* of my *familias* anyway. More than anything, though, I felt angry that he hadn't just blown the lid off the whole thing earlier. He could have saved us all a great deal of trouble.

'So why didn't you tell her I was seeing Cat?'

Henderson had one arm around Andrea. With the other he reached into his pocket and pulled out a tube of moisturiser.

'Andrea said she owed it to you to stay together. It was what she wanted. I love her so I wanted what would make her happy.' He lobbed the tube into the bin.

'And realistically, getting off with your best mate wasn't going to be exactly fantastic for the business, was it?' said Andrea. Now she was giggling through her tears.

I was puzzled. 'All this presupposes you're basically a nice bloke. You're not a nice bloke, though. You're a laugh and you're bright but you're not nice. You've never done a nice thing in your life.'

'He has for me,' said Andrea, 'beyond the baby. He's got a lot more clue about what a woman wants than you have.' Henderson had released her and was now rooting through his briefcase. A bottle of Oil of Olay joined the other stuff in the bin.

'Him?' I said. '*Him*? *He* has a better understanding of women than me? He's all sodomy and stupid jokes.'

Andrea looked puzzled. 'I'm sure I would have remembered at least one of those and I really can't.'

'Wait until he tells you he loves you. Everything has its price,' I said. Henderson had removed a couple of sheets of paper and was now emptying out his briefcase properly. Sanotogen, cod liver oil, starflower oil, a funny electronicky looking thing ... they were all going into the bin.

'He's already told me he loves me,' said Andrea, 'haven't you been listening? I think you're confusing him with the bloke you've hung around with for twenty odd years. He's only that person when he's with you or a bunch of other perpetual adolescents. With me he's more mature.'

Henderson attempted to rip up his gym membership card but couldn't quite manage it. In fairness I don't think there's a Nautilus machine that exercises those muscles.

'Here, Doc, you have this,' he said, flicking it towards the doctor. Hobbs picked it up off the floor and smiled, obviously fondly remembering the days when he had a life outside a hospital.

'So he puts on a mask when he's with you,' I said. 'Give it a couple of months and it'll slip.'

'I doubt it,' said Henderson, taking out a packet of Wind-eze and electing to keep it, 'because it's not a mask. Neither is it when I'm with you. It's just you're different people in different situations, aren't you?'

I looked about me. No, I wasn't in a student coffee bar so there must have been some other explanation for Henderson coming out with this drivel.

'I'm true to myself,' he said, 'there are just different selves. And I happen to have seen enough of the one I am with you. For the moment. Wind-eze?'

'No, thanks.'

'Oh, go on, have one.'

You haven't got any Pro Plus in there, have you?' said Hobbs.

'Q10 energy release?' said Henderson.

'I'll give it a bang,' said Hobbs. Henderson reached into his briefcase and flipped a packet over to him.

I wanted so much for some better pill, not to settle the stomach but to settle the soul. They don't do those in our chemists, though I'm sure there'd be a market for them.

'Do you love him?' I asked Andrea.

She walked to the crib and looked down at the baby.

'I haven't let myself think about it,' she said, 'but it looks as though I'd better make up my mind.'

'Regaine?' said Henderson to Hobbs, proffering the baldness cure.

'I'm fine,' said Hobbs, with a glance at one of the nurses. He ran his hand through his hair and I was sure I could see a band of mortal pink beneath it.

'Sure?' said Henderson.

'Oh, go on, one of my flatmates might want it,' laughed Hobbs nervously.

Henderson held the briefcase open upside down. It was empty.

'Do you love her?' said Andrea.

'Yes,' I said.

'More than you do me?'

'Yes,' I said, meaning, I think so.

'Then let's call it quits,' said Andrea, opening her arms to me. Sod it, I thought, everything I've been trying to protect has fallen to bits. There's no point trying to preserve it any more. Andrea's gone and to whom she goes is none of my business. (Can I note that it is of some considerable comfort to me that I am capable of using words such as 'whom' in a crisis. I'd always thought you needed a top education for that but here I am, a comprehensive kid whoming with the best of them. If I can just crack 'notwithstanding' I'll be home and dry.)

If I truly want Cat nothing else matters, I thought. I was suddenly overwhelmed by a feeling – that my love for Andrea had finally clicked into place and that the place was distant from me. A love of the heart not of the loins, more pure in some ways but not nearly so diverting.

'Oh darling!' I said, rushing forward to meet her. I imagined the wind in my hair, the waves rippling across the corn, like in a romantic novel, the corn rippling through the pages.

'I don't love you,' she said as she hugged me.

'I've been waiting so long to hear you say that,' I said, holding her tight and though the thought was new in my mind it was as if I'd always had it. 'This could be the beginning of something so beautiful.'

She kissed me. 'Shall we be separate always, excepting the occasional dinner party and weekend away with partners and kids?'

'I promise we'll never spend another moment alone together,' I said.

'We've got the whole of our lives apart,' she said, her eyes sparkling with the promise of the future. 'Oh Dag, I'm so happy.'

'Me too, I think,' I said.

'I'm free!' said Henderson. He put his hands out like an

aeroplane and did a quick loop of the room to the tune of 'The Great Escape'.

'Well let's hope this bugger's more use with a spanner,' said Mr Ellis shaking his head.

I looked at my watch. All I had to do was be at Cat's mother's house for nine o'clock. So it was with some surprise that I caught a cab easily, experienced light traffic and was knocking on the door by 8.30.

26
Faithful In Small Things

I'm here, where for nearly eight years I expected to be, in the little Suffolk church where Andrea's mum and dad got married, waiting for Andrea to come in.

I watch as she comes up the aisle. She looks beautiful, but there again, she always did to me. The wedding dress suits her so well. I really do love her. I always will.

And just because she never fully wanted me, and she's had a kid with another man and now I'm with someone else, won't mean that I'll stop. I know I'll die wondering what would have happened if I'd never gone to that works party. Oh, that's right, Andrea would have shagged Henderson anyway and I'd probably be alone, broken-hearted and childless now. Just as well I did then. Anyway, when I said I'd die wondering what might have happened it was only because of the wedding. They do tend to bring out the blarter in a fellow.

Henderson's next to me, nervous, almost floating above the floor ready to go. His right ear is a little cauliflowered. It turned out that he had paid for the beating I received and tried to disguise it as Julie's work, even going to the lengths of leaving a letter in his room. It seems he knows my nosiness a bit too well.

It all came out after the Lesbian strongly suggested that Henderson marry Andrea instead of me. He pointed out that marriage is as much a property deal and a foundation for children as it is something about love.

'You may as well get married now that a lot of it's been paid for. It's the most cost-effective way,' he said.

'We don't need to worry about the cost.' Henderson had flicked out his dismissive wrist.

'You're skint,' I reminded him.

'I have a little tucked away out of the clutches of Julie's lawyers.'

'That would be £200,000 in the Biggest Company on Earth shares, £40,000 in Baal Properties, and miscellaneous funds in the Pineways Habitat Decimation trust in Scotland,' said the Lesbian, reading from a notepad.

'How do you know about those?' said Henderson, retracting the dismissive wrist and placing it on his chest.

'Well, you didn't really think I was working for you for free, did you? No, Julie's been paying me to keep an eye on you and find out exactly how much you're worth.'

'You betrayed me?' Henderson said, with a look on his face like a Medici pope hearing Galileo say he was quite sure the earth went round the sun.

'I'm sorry if that offends your moral code,' said the Lesbian. 'If it's any consolation I was meant to pull your ears off after I'd found everything out, but I'll spare you that because I like Andrea.'

Henderson had a small smirk on his face.

'I can also see from that small smirk that you are thinking of transferring the money to where the lawyers will never find it,' said the Lesbian, 'which is why, if you do, I shall be forced to inform the police who exactly ordered the attack on Dag here. After I've ripped your ears off, of course.'

'What?' I said, looking for something a bit heavier than a tennis ball to throw at Henderson.

'This is pure supposition,' said Henderson. The dismissive wrist was back.

'No, it's not,' said the Lesbian. 'The lollipop lady saw us with the heavies, and you told her we were planning to have a conservatory installed as a surprise and not to tell anyone.'

It suddenly clicked: move your possessions out before the trouble starts, Mrs Batt had told me. She'd meant building work. Henderson had told her to keep it quiet but she'd thought it was only Andrea who was in for a surprise. She naturally thought I'd have been consulted, as man of the house.

'It was for your own good,' Henderson assured me, like I was being unreasonable. He appeared to have been taking lessons from my mother.

'In what way?'

'I wanted Andrea to myself for a while, to try to get her to change her mind about me.'

'Technically that's more for your good than mine.'

'If you'll let me finish?'

'Pardon my manners, I'm sure. Sorry if I've caused offence. Would you consider it more polite if I communicated via baseball bat?'

Henderson tried to look dignified, a bit like his dog. 'You were drinking too much. I thought a spell of enforced abstinence would do you good. And count yourself lucky – I wanted you out of action for a month but they didn't do a proper job. Besides, you've always deserved a good beating, you know that, it was long overdue.'

'That's your idea of doing me good?'

'You were embarrassing in front of the clients, and it worked, didn't it? Don't think of it as a beating, more as fracture therapy.'

'You could have just suggested a course at AA.'

Henderson sniffed. 'The problem with traditional cures for alcoholism is that you have to want to change. Fracture therapy, you don't. It instantly changes your patterns of behaviour.'

'How?'

'Well, it makes it more difficult for you to walk to the pub.' He actually laughed.

'What about the "Julie says hello"?'

'To throw you off the scent,' said Henderson. When he said

'scent' he shook his jowls, rather like the bloodhound.

This, it turned out, is why he'd disappeared. When the police had called about the shotgun he'd heard 'this is the police' and assumed that the beating had gone wrong and the thugs had blabbed about his and the Lesbian's involvement. He'd decided to lay low until he at least thought of a decent excuse – or the Lesbian leveraged his contacts within the Crown Prosecution Service and police to get someone to 'lose' their file. As soon as he'd found out they only wanted him for an unlicensed weapon he'd hopped back on to the scene.

'Did you have Pete shot too?' said Andrea's mum, eyes wide in incomprehension.

'Er, no, that was straightforward incompetence, I'm afraid,' said Henderson. 'I did genuinely think Julie might have it in for me until I realised she was just going to go for a savage divorce settlement. I'm willing to do anything to make things up, naturally.'

I couldn't think how I could ever forgive him, until he told me he was off ski-ing. So I made him pay the Lesbian the £800 spending money earmarked for ski passes, hire and general après-ski drollery to give him a similar hammering to the one I'd received – all funds to charity, of course. In this case the Manor House Lesbian Boys' Social Fund. No hard feelings.

Afterwards the Lesbian had even done Henderson the favour of saying, 'It was only business, H, I always liked you,' like they do in *The Godfather*. So in a way Henderson felt good about it – he'd taken one of the scary rides in the gangster theme park. All the lads would respect him now and the Iron Julie would at least feel he'd tasted some of her wrath, after she'd seen the photos. It was quite amusing, waiting for the ambulance, with the Lesbian standing over Henderson in our – sorry, Henderson and Andrea's – garden, saying 'Say cheese' as Henderson lay clutching his broken ribs on the floor.

Considering this, it was remarkably good of him to hire the Lesbian's relatives in the Wood Lane Lesbian Band to play for us. I've heard that they're not all actually from Lesbos but – like a lot of things in life – they'll pass if you don't ask too many questions. Most of them are at least Greek, I think.

The church is nice, though they couldn't afford to go big on the flowers. Julie, after all, did sink her fangs into a good portion of Henderson's money, and though the business is improving it'll be a while before we're back up to a decent living. Mrs Batt with her lollipop won't make much of a triumphal arch when they leave the church, but I suppose it's the thought that counts.

Not everyone's got their mind on the ceremony, though. There's Dr Hobbs, who got the day off specially to come, sleeping like a baby in the aisle – unlike the babies who are sleeping like junior doctors and causing a fair bit of noise.

My kids are at the back of the church, irritating everyone by crying and generally wrecking things, the way kids always do at weddings. Lee Junior's with Mrs Ellis in the front. That's Lee Junior who used to be called Jim, Lee Junior the human, not the dog. He's been renamed Niffer.

Henderson looks like shit, but then that was always his ambition. The gym-toned belly has gone and is sagging, the baldness is exposed not hidden – he's even got a bit of a tan. He's got the green light to middle age and his foot's down heavy on the accelerator.

Does Andrea love Henderson? I don't know. She's marrying him, so I suppose she might.

'He has a certain maturity to him,' she told me.

'Oh, yeah?' I'd said. 'A man who once chained himself to South Africa House singing "Jail Winnie Mandela", for a bet?'

'That was years ago,' said Andrea. 'He's changed, haven't you noticed?'

I've been trying not to, I suppose.

I take a glance over my shoulder at Cat, who's trying to control C and D, as I've called them since I can't bear their real names – but, like Cat said, if I had wanted to be involved in the naming I should have been around when it was being discussed. At least we've moved into Camden now, so the kids will avoid the hell of a rural or suburban upbringing. I've already got my eye on a miniature electric guitar for Darius and a stage school for Carlotta. With the right kind of influences they'll be in night clubs by the time they're fourteen, leaving me and Cat free to enjoy each other.

Do I love her? So far. Will I always love her, the way I know I'll always love Andrea? I don't know but I do hope so. We've a long way to go but it looks good so far. I'm no longer doing admin for the football or the badminton, so that's a good sign. I love the kids, too, so that's a bond.

Andrea and I used to find very little time to be together. Cat and I don't really get time apart. We still do the walks on the Heath but now, instead of listening to the wind and the call of the trees, instead of stealing clandestine heterosexual kisses in the gay dominion, we watch the kids, comment on their development and almost forget how much our lives have changed. It's a different kind of fun, I suppose.

It's something I've never known, developing our relationship through and round the kids, loving three people instead of just one. Well, I've loved two before, but this time it doesn't seem like too many.

Could I have made it with Andrea if we'd had kids earlier? Could she have loved me if she'd never met Mike? Might I have woken up one morning, looked at Cat and thought, You need someone your own age, instead of noticing that, since the children, she has become much more like someone of mine? I do wonder if things might have been different. But the difference is that I only wonder; I don't want. Actually I didn't want to meet someone else before, I just did. As Henderson said in that poem he wrote for that creative writing class – between the intention and the act falls a shadow. I was sure I'd heard that somewhere before – Andrea claims she made it up, though I think I did.

As we step out into the afternoon sun, throwing the confetti at £5 a bag and thinking how much more sensible Americans are to use rice, I can see no shadows and I have no intentions towards anyone but Cat and the kids. And, as Henderson has pointed out, when a man attends a wedding and the thought of copping off with one of the flower girls doesn't even occur to him, he has achieved a rare equilibrium. Though obviously I fancy a couple of them. I mean, you can't have everything.

I can really see myself properly for the first time in years, not in dreams of children with hoops but in realistic images of watching Darius play football for the school, taking the half-time oranges along with Carlotta, getting into the traditional brawls with the parents of the opposing team. Perhaps I'll take the Lesbian to help crack a few heads, though that would perhaps be introducing an unacceptable note of professionalism into a proudly amateur sport.

'You look far away,' says Cat, taking my hand.

'Just worrying about the terrapins,' I say. My mum had bought us two as a wedding gift. I'd pointed out we weren't the ones getting married. She'd just tapped the side of her nose and picked up the Queen of Cups.

'If that's all that's bothering you, I'd say you were a lucky man,' says Cat.

'I am,' I say, 'I can't believe it's all worked out so well.'

'Apart from the cards,' says Cat. 'According to your mum the kids are going to give us hell.'